Latent Hazard is Piers Venmore-Rowlar   ...ιy
years, his desire to write crime fiction   ...uowed by the
demands of his work. Time out convalescing gave Piers the opportunity to put pen to paper and *Latent Hazard* was born.

Piers was brought up and went to school in Hertfordshire. After
graduating from Reading University with a BSc in Estate Management
and an MA in Contemporary European Studies, he worked in the
West End of London where he qualified as a chartered surveyor. His
interest in the investment markets prompted him to study at City
University Business School where he gained his MSc in Finance. He
became a member of the Society of Investment Analysts in 1983 and
worked in the City of London as a real estate and financials analyst.

In a career change, Piers moved to City University where he was a
professor, a head of Department, a member of the business school's
executive committee and a member of the University Senate. He took a
leading role in setting up the university's real estate and investment
management postgraduate programmes and as a visiting professor at
Kingston University he developed a web-enhanced Masters degree.
Over 1,000 undergraduates and 5,000 full- and part-time postgraduate students have been taught by him, and he has been a frequent
speaker at national and international conferences.

Piers is widely published; his works include: UK and US journal
articles, jointly authored academic textbooks and professional pub-
lications on property, pension funds and indirect investment. He
served on two HEFCE University Research Assessment Exercise
Panels.

As an academic, investment analyst and consultant he has worked
with leading UK and international companies, and his employment
has taken him to over twenty countries around the world.

Piers is now a full-time writer. He is married, with three daughters,
and lives in Suffolk by the River Deben.

PIERS VENMORE-ROWLAND

Latent Hazard

Galleons
Green

This paperback edition published in 2008 by Galleons Green.
1

Galleons Green Ltd
PO Box 278, Woodbridge,
Suffolk, England IP12 9BS
www.galleonsgreen.com

A CIP catalogue record for this book
is available from the British Library.

ISBN-13 978-1-906960-00-1

Typeset in Linotype Sabon by Hewer Text UK Ltd
Maps illustrator: John Plumer – www.jpmapgraphics.co.uk.
Printed and bound in England by CPI Antony Rowe Ltd.

To the memory of my father, Owain Venmore-Rowland.
His love, encouragement and all the happy
times he bestowed upon me will long
be remembered and cherished.

Acknowledgements

I would like to thank Lorna for all her encouragement and assistance without which I would not have had the courage to pursue my interest in writing.

My love and thanks go to my family: Lorna, Nina, Robyn and Sasha for their understanding, patience and ability to laugh; to Beryl who despite everything has unfalteringly continued to be there for her children and grandchildren, and to Mark for his constructive comments.

My gratitude goes to Daniela Nava for her attention to detail and for her input in making my text accurate and readable.

LONDON

Enfield
Woodford
M11
M1
Hampstead
Heath
Stoke
Newington
Stratford
West Ham
Willesden
Junction
CITY OF
LONDON
Liverpool
Street
Paddington
Green
Canary
Wharf
London City
Airport
Heathrow
Thames
miles 5

0   25   miles 100

N
W   E
S

Shetland
Islands

NORTH
SEA

Orkney
Islands

Pentland Firth
John O'Groats   Duncansby Head

Butt of Lewis

St Fergus
Peterhead
Cruden Bay

NORTH
ATLANTIC
OCEAN

Stanton
Banks

Scotland

Outer Hebrides

Glasgow   Edinburgh
Prestwick
Hunterston
Troon

Malin Head

Mull of
Kintyre

Newcastle upon Tyne
Hartlepool

Northern
Ireland

Sellafield

UNITED

Heysham

Kingston upon Hull
Easington

Irish Sea

KINGDOM

REPUBLIC
OF
IRELAND

DUBLIN

Manchester   Sheffield
Liverpool

North
Walsham   Bacton

Wales

England

Great
Yarmouth

Birmingham

Sizewell
Ipswich

Colchester

Great Amwell

LONDON
Heathrow
Stratford
Grays

Cardiff   Bristol

Aldermaston

NORTH
ATLANTIC
OCEAN

Southampton

Thorney Island

Newquay   Plymouth
Devonport

English Channel

Scilly Isles

Cherbourg   Le Havre   FRANCE

⚓ Port
✕ Airport

Part 1

The splintering crash of the front door hitting the floor woke Rafi Khan with a jolt. Terrified, he sat bolt upright, but was too slow; before he could get out of bed, a harsh voice barked, 'Don't move, or we shoot.' There was no escaping the bright red dots which danced on his chest.

'Move your hands to where we can see them.' Rafi slowly lifted up his arms, but at that second the wind was knocked out of him. Under the weight of his assailant, he fought for breath. His hands were pulled behind his back in a vice-like grip, and in a matter of seconds he was expertly trussed up, blindfolded, gagged, dragged off the bed with a bump and left lying on the floor.

'Suspect apprehended and in our custody. Flat secure. You can come up,' a harsh voice called out.

Rafi's heart pounded. His chest ached. He was bewildered and scared. He couldn't move and the blindfold across his eyes was painfully tight. It took a full minute for his mind to catch up and start functioning again. What on earth was happening?

'He didn't give any trouble,' said the curt voice. 'His front door was a piece of cake; when will people learn?'

'Thank you, sergeant,' said the man in charge. 'What have we got here? Cases packed; ready to leave. It's lucky we got here when we did.'

The tone of his voice changed. 'Rafi Khan, I'm arresting you under the powers conferred under section 41 of the Terrorism Act. You will be held in detention and informed of the charges against you within the prescribed period.'

The man paused. Rafi sensed he was standing very close to him. 'Put those guns away and take him down to the van, then search this flat from top to bottom. Let's see what's hidden here.'

'Yes, sir.'

A pair of strong hands grabbed Rafi and forcefully dragged him across the floor like a sack of potatoes.

1

What the hell was going on? Things had happened so fast. Three flights of stairs later, Rafi felt like damaged goods. He was man-handled into the cold February air. From his blindfolded world, he could make out the sound of a diesel engine.

The man pulling him shouted, 'Constable, help me lift him into the back.'

Rafi landed on the metal floor. His expletives were muffled by the gag and came out as little more than irate grunts. The tape across his mouth held firm. He was dragged on to the side bench. The door slammed shut. A bang on the side of the van signalled it was time to go and it lurched forward. In his dark world he heard the police sirens blaring. The van was travelling fast through the deserted streets of London. Just as he was becoming accustomed to his environment, it came to a sudden halt. Rafi was untied and hauled out. Fresh air washed across his face.

He was now sandwiched between two men.

'Start walking.'

Rafi moved forward. His shin bumped into a solid object. Pain shot up his leg. He stopped.

'Oi! Keep moving!' bellowed one of the men next to him. 'Keep moving!' he repeated.

Rafi tried to proceed in a straight line, but his sense of balance had deserted him. He staggered along in an ungainly manner.

'Stop! Stand still!' came the stern order.

To the best of his ability he tried to obey. There was no warning of the ripping sound that came next. Pain seared across his eyes as the sticky tape removed chunks of his eyebrows and eyelashes. He'd hardly drawn breath when the gag was ripped from his mouth.

'Bloody hell!' he yelped. He screwed up his eyes in the bright fluorescent light. Either side of him were two burly policemen in full protective clothing. In front of him, behind a tall wooden desk, was the duty officer, with a pen in his hand.

'Name?' he inquired in a no-nonsense manner.

'Rafi Khan.'

A series of quick-fire questions followed: 'Address? Date of birth? Nationality? Personal effects: pyjamas, watch . . . Yes, sign for them 'ere. Stand 'ere, height – 175 centimetres,' the duty sergeant read off the measure on the wall. Turn to face me.' The flash of the camera surprised him. 'Turn sideways.' Another flash. 'Hands out.'

In a whisk he was fingerprinted. The whole process was like a production line.

'Come over 'ere! Remove your pyjamas! Bend over!' Unceremoniously, he was strip-searched. His dark-skinned legs showed a selection of new purple bruises. The one on his left shin looked particularly spectacular.

'Been clumsy, 'ave we?' enquired the duty sergeant. No reply was sought. 'Get dressed in these.'

Rafi awkwardly put on the drab clothing. It swamped his slight frame. 'Take 'im away.'

He was led to a basement cell. It was claustrophobic and depressing. A desolate overhead light shone starkly. The door closed behind him with a thud. He hardly had time to take in his surroundings before the heavy metal door swung open.

'Follow me,' said a guard. 'Don't get any ideas! This way!'

He was led down a bare corridor to an interrogation room. One wall was obscure glass; like everything else in the police station, the room was devoid of character, bleak and utilitarian. Two interrogators sat on the other side of a narrow desk in a steely silence. The guard pointed to the chair opposite them. Rafi sat down; his stomach knotted with apprehension. Their manner made him uncomfortable: one smirked, the other scowled.

The smirking interrogator, Andy, looked at him carefully. His bright blue eyes were framed by slightly over-length blonde wavy hair. 'Let's get started,' he said, switching on the tape recorder next to him.

'Am I not entitled to a solicitor?' asked Rafi. 'I've done nothing wrong!'

'Flaming hell!' said Mike, the scowling interrogator. 'You are a terrorist suspect. You don't get a telephone call and no one gets to see you.'

'But what about my human rights?' asked Rafi anxiously.

'The rules are different. You've absolutely no rights. No calls, no visits, nothing,' replied Andy.

'A terrorist suspect? How have I broken the law?' asked Rafi bewildered.

'All in good time,' said Andy.

'Surely I should at least be told why I have been locked up?'

'No!' replied Mike. In contrast to his colleague, he had black crew cut hair and a scar running across his left temple into his hairline.

'The law makes it very clear. Terrorist suspects can be detained without charge,' said Andy, 'for rather a long while, as it happens. So don't get your hopes up. You're going to be cooped up here for weeks or until such time as you tell us what we want!'

'Mr Khan,' said Mike, with menace. 'You can either make this relatively trouble-free and help us, or be difficult, which would be very unwise.' His scowl deepened. 'Being difficult or uncooperative isn't your best option. We have evidence that puts you in the middle of a major terrorist conspiracy.'

Rafi couldn't believe his ears. He opened his mouth to say, 'You what?' but nothing came out.

Their questions rained down and they became increasingly intrusive. Rafi tried his best to answer Andy and Mike as they interrogated him on his religion, contacts, reading habits and favourite websites, but they were dismissive of his answers. Their fierce questioning was frightening him and he was reeling from the onslaught.

'I'm a law-abiding British citizen. I'm innocent! Tell me what you think I have done and I will prove my innocence,' said Rafi in desperation.

'That's not the way it works. Sod off back to your cell and think about the dangers of not cooperating fully,' said Mike.

Back in his cell, Rafi sat on the corner of his bed, shaking. He was cold and his nose was running, but he had nothing with which to blow it. His mind was in turmoil – he'd been accused of being a terrorist. It was all incomprehensible. He was scared. What the hell did they think he had done?

A ndy and Mike stayed in the interview room. They were frustrated. They agreed that they had got nothing out of their suspect. It was as if he had been expertly tutored in the art of interrogation. He gave answers, but they revealed nothing relevant to his crime. The evidence they had against him was substantial.

'He's a slimy bugger,' said Andy, 'and a first class actor.'

'Gives the impression that he ain't got a clue why he's here,' replied Mike. 'Obviously he's been well trained.'

'He is going to be a hard nut to crack,' said Andy. 'When do you reckon we move on to the Bishopsgate police station bombing?'

'As I see it he knows damn well why he's here, so I reckon we don't need to tell him,' replied Mike. 'Anyway, we've got weeks before we have to charge him – my inclination is to use the time to break him.'

'But time isn't on our side,' said Andy. 'Our intelligence indicates there could be a follow-up bombing. We have got to get information out of him, or more lives could be lost.'

'If he ain't going to crack soon, what's the hurry? Shouldn't we go for a confession, add it to all the evidence we have and secure a conviction?' said Mike.

'But we need information, now,' replied Andy.

'He'll break given time. Who wouldn't in these surroundings? Hell's teeth, just think of the praise we'd get,' said Mike.

'So you let another bomb go off just to prove a point and suck up to our political masters?' said Andy uncertainly.

'It's an option, but – Bugger it you're right! We've got to bring things to a close as quickly as possible,' said Mike.

'OK let's see if we can tie this up in record time,' said Andy.

Rafi was sitting in his cell. He'd asked for a blanket, but did not get one. He was reflecting on his helpless predicament and his utter lack of rights when his cell door swung open.

'You're wanted. Now! Get a shift on!' bellowed the guard.

Rafi sat down opposite his two interrogators. He sensed they were raring to get started again.

'We've evidence that puts you in the frame for the Bishopsgate police station bombing. We've got you on CCTV talking to the bomber next to the cashpoints in South Place, on Thursday lunchtime, the day before the bomb blast,' said Andy.

Rafi was dumbfounded. He couldn't recall speaking to anyone. He'd been in a hurry.

'Watch the tape,' said Andy.

A grainy but unmistakable picture appeared on the wall-mounted screen opposite the one-way glass window.

'The City of London has cameras everywhere now. The camera on the corner of Moorgate and South Place picked you up.'

The screen showed the row of five cashpoint machines on the return frontage of the nearby Barclays bank. Moments later, there he was joining the back of a queue in a smart suit with his neatly cut black hair. His turn came; he withdrew his money and turned. Behind him, to one side, was a man dressed in nondescript clothes with a hoodie largely obscuring his face. They talked for a minute and then the man gave him a hug. His hoodie slipped back off his head, revealing a tanned, ordinary-looking face. The CCTV footage stopped, framing the man standing right in front of him. Rafi was passing something to him, but it was largely obscured from view by the other man's body.

Rafi's mind raced. He tried to recall what he had handed over. Slowly it came back to him. The man had passed him an A to Z map book, and asked if he could show him which underground station he should use to get to Finsbury Park. Rafi had not needed the map, and explained that Moorgate station was just round the corner, where he could catch a train straight to Finsbury Park. It had been an utter surprise to Rafi when the stranger had hugged him to show his gratitude.

Rafi looked at the picture on the screen, bewildered.

'Caught red-handed!' said Andy. 'Tell us how you know Imaad Wafeeq.'

Rafi thought for a moment. The CCTV footage painted a very misleading picture. It made an innocent conversation look very incriminating.

'I didn't know that was his name and that was the first time I met him,' Rafi replied. 'I was just getting some cash for my boss, Jameel Furud.'

'Cobblers!' burst out Mike. 'You can do better than that. Do you think we're dead from the neck up?'

Rafi saw malice in his dark eyes and sensed that the table between them would give him little protection.

'That was the first time I'd ever seen him,' he repeated.

'Bullshit! We know that you know Imaad Wafeeq, the Bishopsgate bomber. Lying to us is pointless. Why else did he embrace you as a friend? Look at his body language.'

Rafi was dumbstruck.

The two interrogators fired questions at him.

'Who else was involved?'

'What's the next target?'

They kept on at him for what seemed like hours.

Rafi kept pleading his innocence. There was little else he could do, but it only infuriated his interrogators. Eventually their patience ran dry. Bland answers were not what they wanted.

Mike looked straight at Rafi; his eyes were like those of a cold-blooded snake. 'Let's get this straight: with the evidence we have against you and the new laws, you've next to no human rights. We can send you to Belmarsh Prison, throw the key away and leave you to rot. No one will give a toss! Foxtrot Oscar back to your cell and do some very careful thinking. When you come back, we'll expect answers, or else . . .' Mike raised his hand in the direction of the one-way glass wall. The door to the interrogation room swung open and a guard walked in.

'Take him back to his cell,' commanded Andy.

'Yes, sir,' replied the guard, under his breath. He was ugly, seriously ugly. His face was pockmarked, his nose was bulbous and bent, and he made the dour interrogator look like a softy. He escorted Rafi to his cell in double quick time and slammed the door shut behind him.

Rafi tried to come to terms with what he'd seen. It was absurd. He had never met that man before; he had just wanted directions. The implications shook him. Thoughts flooded through his head. The horrific bombing had taken place on Friday morning. It was now Saturday. There must be hundreds if not thousands of CCTV cameras in the City of London. How did they pinpoint the terrorist meeting him so quickly? OK, the camera was only a couple of blocks away from where the bomb had gone off, but still Rafi couldn't help wondering whether the police had managed to retrace the bomber's movements, simply been lucky or been tipped off. It all seemed far-fetched.

As his circumstances and plight struck home, his brain moved into panic mode. He realised that he was staring at the back of his dark brown hands. He was a secular Muslim, not a fanatical extremist. He surmised that his skin colour, religion and the misinterpreted CCTV evidence put him squarely in the frame.

Slowly, Rafi regained control of his thoughts. He was in serious trouble. With the new draconian laws, it would be easy for them to hold him in this hellhole with no charges for weeks on end. He looked around at his surroundings: the bed was solid, the floor and walls were bare and there was a slops bucket in the corner. Superficially, the cell looked fairly clean, but there was an all-pervading smell of stale urine and the feel of grime everywhere. It was deeply depressing.

The stark overhead light gave no warmth and just provided glare. It was getting to him. Its rays penetrated remorselessly into his eyes. He closed them. The light was still there. It was as if the bulb had been doctored to give maximum discomfort. He was tired, but he had to keep his brain working. He had to think, and think carefully. The only logical conclusion he could reach was that somebody had set him up. But what might he have done to make someone go to all that trouble? Nothing in his life, both private and professional, sprang to mind as unusual. At work things had been pretty normal, except for the research Callum and he had been pursuing. So by process of elimination that had to be at the top of the list . . .

The thud of the cell door caught him by surprise.

'You're wanted again,' growled the guard.

'Jump to it you little oik! Time to be on parade!' he shouted when he noticed that Rafi wasn't in a hurry to follow him.

He wore irritability in his craggy face and didn't try to hide his hatred for Rafi.

'Get up you little sod. I bet they want your balls for dinner.'

Rafi winced as he was pulled forcefully to his feet and pushed down the corridor to the interrogation room. He was stuck in a nightmare.

'You said that you didn't know the Bishopsgate bomber, Imaad Wafeeq. So why did he have one of your £20 notes in his pocket when he died? Let's see you wriggle your way out of that!' barked Mike.

'Yes, go on!' said Andy. 'The £20 note was from the sequence you took from the cashpoint. Three policemen so far have lost their lives and several others are gravely ill. Don't give me any bullshit! You knew the bomber, didn't you?'

Rafi remained silent.

'Playing the innocent, are we?' interjected Mike.

'Do you think that we are stupid or something?' said Andy. 'I am waiting for a reply.'

'Can I have a lawyer?'

'No you bloody well can't!' came the retort from Mike. 'The likes of you forfeit all their rights. You don't get a lawyer until you've been charged, and that could be weeks away.'

The questions rained down on Rafi – 'Who else?' 'Why?' and 'What are they planning next?'

His lack of helpful answers was seriously annoying them.

'We haven't got all bloody day. Start talking or we will get *real* mean.' Mike's dark eyes narrowed and stared threateningly, just inches away from Rafi.

Rafi's brain was in turmoil.

'Talk!' ordered Mike threateningly.

'We have two cast-iron pieces of evidence against you. The CCTV footage and the £20 note. Case closed! We keep you here for weeks, break you, get your confession, have the courts lock you up and then throw away the keys,' said Andy.

'With the evidence we've got on you, you've become invisible and the system doesn't give a bloody monkeys!' added Mike.

'But I'm innocent, I tell you. All I can think of is I stumbled on something at work which upset some people,' said Rafi.

'Like what?' snapped Mike.

'Breaking the City rules on takeovers,' replied Rafi.

'What?' burst out Andy.

'Bullshit!' Mike's manner was becoming increasingly intolerant.

'We want to know about the bomber and what his colleagues are planning next. Not about some poncey City insider dealing,' said Andy.

'Be very clear there'll be no respite. We'll hound you night and day. We *will* win and you *will* lose,' said Mike.

Rafi felt sick with fear. His stomach churned. What was he caught up in? The evidence against him was impressive and the only explanation he could find was that someone had gone to a lot of trouble to implicate him. All he could think of was the research that Callum and he had been working on, but what the hell was the link?

'Are you going to talk?' asked Andy.

'Or do we let you rot forever?' demanded Mike.

How long would it be before they started getting really rough? Soon, thought Rafi. He sensed their physical aggression bubbling just below the surface.

'Make a start and tell us how you were financing the bomber, Imaad Wafeed,' said Andy.

'I wasn't,' replied Rafi.

'Get real!' shouted Mike.

'I think I've been set up,' said Rafi. 'At least hear me out.'

There was a momentary silence. 'OK,' said Andy, 'but it had better be good.'

'I stumbled upon some information that suggested my employers, Prima Terra, and a group of Luxembourg fund managers were in serious breach of the City takeover code,' said Rafi.

'Go on,' said Andy, looking nonplussed.

'Thursday before last, I received a phone call from Callum Burns, a friend who worked as a financials analyst at Landin Young. He is fantastically good at his job and I've been one of his best clients. He wanted to talk about Renshaw Smithers, a niche finance business in which my company, Prima Terra, is a major investor, but he didn't want to have the discussion over the phone, so we met for a drink at a local bar that evening.'

'And?' asked Mike.

'How much do you know about fund managers?' asked Rafi.

'They look after other peoples' money,' replied Andy.

'At Prima Terra we have £30 billion of funds under management, of which I manage £4 billion of equities. It was quite a bit more, but we too got caught by the stock market crash. Have you heard of the Stock Exchange Blue Book?' asked Rafi.

Andy and Mike shook their heads.

'It's the rule book governing company shareholdings and takeovers, by which as fund managers we have to abide.'

'Obviously,' said Mike, 'but how the hell does this relate to the bomber?'

'Callum thought Prima Terra had possibly broken the rules. He said he'd found something very dubious that was being hushed up,' said Rafi.

'I still don't see how this relates to the bombing,' commented Mike, thrusting his jaw forward at Rafi. 'If you're taking us for a ride, remember we can make life seriously uncomfortable for you.'

'Callum suspected that Renshaw Smithers was being controlled by unknown offshore investors and wondered if there might be a connection to Prima Terra – the largest investor in the company.'

Mike raised his arms and was about to cut Rafi off.

'Before you throw the keys away, what's the harm in hearing me out?' pleaded Rafi. 'I spent last weekend trying to substantiate Callum's theory. To start with it was like looking for a needle in a haystack. Then it hit me; all I had to do was look at the companies in which Prima Terra had large shareholdings – there are just fourteen companies where they have more than 7.5% of the shares. So I checked their shareholders' registers for the dubious nominee names Callum had identified.' Rafi paused then went on, 'There were no matches!'

'What the bloody hell! Why are you pissing around wasting our time?' Mike thumped his fist on the table centimetres away from Rafi.

Rafi flinched. 'Then I speculated that they'd be smart and cover their tracks. So I went through each shareholder's register with a fine-tooth comb.'

'So?' asked Mike aggressively.

'I found three more companies that had a large number of untraceable nominee names on their shareholders' register.'

'And . . .' prompted Mike, whose short temper was getting the better of him.

'Last Monday morning I gave them to Callum to investigate,' replied Rafi.

'And . . .'

'I met Callum in a nondescript pub just off Moorgate on Monday evening. He was concerned. He had passed the three shareholder lists to his colleagues. My suspicions were confirmed. Callum's colleagues had spoken to the companies' registrars who said that it was all to do with a switch to a new nominee name management business, and they were having a few teething problems. They promised that the lack of information on the owners of these shareholdings would be rectified shortly.'

'So this is a red herring,' interrupted Andy.

'No, I don't think so. These shareholdings, when added to Prima Terra's big shareholding, give them control of these companies and break all the rules. *And* there has to be a reason why I was set up.'

'Tell us more about these four companies you singled out,' said Andy.

'Renshaw Smithers and Unicorn Sceptre Finance are niche finance businesses. ESSA is an executive recruitment agency and Dewoodson is a property consultancy business.'

'So what is special about them?' asked Andy.

'Callum and I couldn't come up with any reasons why these companies might be worth controlling. They are unexciting and hardly takeover candidates,' replied Rafi. 'But there *has* to be something, otherwise why incriminate me?' mused Rafi.

'You're taking the piss,' said Mike. 'Sounds to me as if you're just trying to distract us from your links to the bomber. Bullshit isn't what we need.'

Rafi looked at Mike's frustrated eyes. 'Whatever I say you're not going to believe me, are you?'

'Sod off back to your cell. We'll deal with you shortly,' said Mike irritably. 'Your time is running out. We'll break you and you will want to talk to us very soon.'

Their lack of interest in his story and Mike glowering centimetres away from him made the knots in Rafi's guts clench even tighter.

Fifteen or so minutes later, the door of Rafi's cell opened. A man in catering uniform entered. 'I've got you some food. Where do you want it?'

To Rafi's surprise, the tray fell to the floor. He bent down to pick it up. With the speed and strength of a black belt, the man let fly a kick. It struck home just below Rafi's left shoulder blade. It was followed by a punch to the kidneys. Doubled up, Rafi slumped to the floor.

'You effing murderer! Prison's too good for your sort!' He stepped towards Rafi, who tried to shout. He had to get the attention of the guard but only managed to let out a strangled noise. To his relief the guard stuck his head around the door.

'The nobhead seems to have slipped on 'is food! 'E should be all right soon, when 'e gets 'is wind back. Shame 'e didn't get to eat it. Still, no doubt it'll do 'im good to go hungry.' With that the man left.

The guard looked at the crumpled body on the floor. 'You silly ijut! What a waste!' He turned and pulled the door closed.

Rafi remained where he was: an untidy heap amongst the food. He was too sore to get up.

His thoughts went back to his phone call with Callum on the previous Tuesday morning. Callum had been excited, as he had managed to arrange a trip to Luxembourg.

'A couple of meetings have cropped up. I thought it was too good an opportunity to miss! I fly out early tomorrow from City airport and fly back from Amsterdam on Thursday evening. I'm seeing a local REIT. But it gets better: they've lent me a car for the drive from Luxembourg to Amsterdam. One of their directors works in Luxembourg, but has a home in Amsterdam and he's lending me his Porsche. Isn't that great?' Callum had said.

'So a bit of a detour via Germany?' Rafi asked.

'You got it in one. I've always wanted to take a Porsche through its paces on an Autobahn without the fear of speed cameras, or blue flashing lights in the rear view mirror.'

Rafi went cold. How the hell had he managed to forget to tell his interrogators that Callum was dead? In the interrogation room he was acting like a rabbit caught in the headlights. He had to think carefully. When was he going to tell them that Callum had given him a USB memory stick, with details of the shareholder lists and the work that they had done on the companies?

Rafi was suddenly jolted back to reality. There, standing in the door frame, was the ugly guard, staring at Rafi slumped against the cell wall, surrounded by a sea of cold, inedible food.

'I see you've been having fun, you silly little wazzock,' he said, almost smiling. 'You're wanted again.'

Waiting for him were the two familiar faces.

'You look worse every time we see you,' said Andy.

'At this rate we'll need to get a move on,' added Mike, 'or you'll be in no fit state to talk at all.'

'You're a slimy little bugger,' said Andy. 'Explain why you didn't tell us Callum was dead?'

'Bloody good ploy, if you ask me,' commented Mike. 'Stops us checking your story!'

'He was murdered.'

'Bullshit!' said Mike. 'The local police say that he was driving a Mercedes hire car and hit black ice. Are you going to tell us what's really going on?'

'But, he should have been driving a Porsche . . .' Rafi hesitated. 'Can I explain what Callum was doing in Luxembourg?' asked Rafi.

Andy considered this, then nodded.

'According to a colleague of his at Landin Young, Callum had five meetings in Luxembourg: one with a REIT – real estate investment trust – then a couple of tax advisers, an FCP investment fund and another meeting in the afternoon. The REIT was picking up the tab for the trip. Callum was due to fly back from Amsterdam on Thursday evening.' Rafi paused. 'The MD at the REIT had agreed to lend Callum his Porsche. Callum had planned a detour via the German Autobahns.'

'Bloody bollocks!' burst out Mike. 'The local police have spoken to the REIT director. Callum phoned him to cancel the offer of the Porsche, as he'd be running late.'

'Good try,' added Andy, 'but your story doesn't fool us!'

'There's more,' said Rafi with a touch of desperation in his voice. 'The afternoon Callum died, he phoned me. He was excited. He said he'd found some proof. He was about to tell me what it was when he was cut off. I tried calling him back but his phone went straight to voicemail.'

'That proves sod all!' said Andy.

'One of the people he saw was in on the shareholdings' cover up. I'm sure of it,' said Rafi. 'He got too close—'

'If you refuse to cooperate and continue to mess us around, we do have other options,' said Mike, in a steely voice. 'We've an, er . . . understanding with the Americans. We suggest to them that you're holding back information that they might find helpful and, magically, through the rendition process you're whisked away to some god-forsaken place.'

'I hear Guantánamo Bay will shortly get its first star,' interrupted Andy disparagingly, 'though its rooms are minimalist!'

The knots in Rafi's stomach tightened another notch.

'It's got great sea views,' jeered Andy.

Rafi started to speak. His voice was hoarse from the tension and lack of fluids. 'If Callum had found out who was running the clandestine nominee names and could prove that Prima Terra was involved, wouldn't this give them a motive for his murder?' Rafi was aware that this seemed to have nothing to do with the bombing on the surface, but he had to keep talking about it as he could find no other reason for finding himself in this nightmare.

'Bloody hell! Not that old story again,' said Mike. 'Tell us about the Bishopsgate bombing first. We can get back to Callum later.'

Rafi slumped in his chair and looked away from his interrogators.

'Get real, you uncooperative little sod! You've told us the square root of nothing. If you continue to take the piss, remember that no one, I repeat, no one has the ability to come and find you. You have disappeared off the radar screen. There is absolutely nothing anyone can do to help you,' said Andy.

'You're deluding yourself,' spat out Mike. 'You're trying to convince yourself that you're innocent, but in reality you're guilty – as guilty as hell!' He looked like a pug that had licked a nettle.

'Look at the bloody evidence,' said Andy forcefully. 'The CCTV footage of you conspiring with the bomber and the proof that you gave him money is more than enough. Take this bastard back to his cell while we consider whether Belmarsh is too good for him.'

Rafi started to panic but did his best to fight back his feelings of helplessness.

T he scene looked more like Gaza than the City of London. In the foreground was the burnt-out shell of the building in which the police garage had been located. The offices above had also been devastated. On the other side of the narrow street, the windows of the 1950s office building had been blown out and venetian blinds flapped in the wind.

The stage-managed news conference had all the hallmarks of a major media event. The top political reporters and their cameramen were hemmed into the narrow space behind Bishopsgate police station.

In pole position, with his entourage behind him, strode the Home Office minister towards the prearranged spot in front of the gutted garage. He was a man with a mission. He looked determinedly at the destruction, conscious no doubt that the TV cameras were trained on him. One of the burnt-out police cars had been pulled out of the garage and now would conveniently provide the backdrop for the minister's meeting with the commissioner of City of London police. On the ground next to the car lay a police helmet in a pool of dark liquid. It gave those watching a stark reminder of the tragic loss of life.

The commissioner was looking agitated. He had been expecting the Home Secretary, with whom he very much wanted to talk. But at the last moment he had been advised that his number two would be coming. He had been standing in the cold February air, waiting for over thirty minutes, whilst the minister's PR team got the location ready for the press and the arrival of the minister. Their attention to detail when it came to dealing with TV shoots was legendary.

As the minister turned the corner, the commissioner walked across to the agreed rendezvous point close to the burnt-out car and the forlorn police helmet. The senior political reporters were nearby, ready to ask their questions. The minister, dressed in shirt sleeves and a Metropolitan police flak jacket, shook the commissioner's hand and turned towards the TV cameras.

'You see before you the latest carnage wrought on our society by fundamentalists who seek to challenge our freedoms. I can assure you that the appalling loss of life here will spur us on in our quest to bring to justice all those who assisted the suicide bomber, Imaad Wafeeq, in this heinous act. As I speak I can reveal that we are already making good progress in our investigations. We have in custody at Paddington Green police station a man, who we believe to be the financier of the terrorist cell responsible for this outrage.'

The minister turned to the commissioner, who unlike him had not had the opportunity for a makeover before facing the cameras. 'I understand that the investigations are progressing well.'

The commissioner paused before making his reply. He had his concerns. The modus operandi of the attack troubled him. The bomber was *not* a suicide bomber and had *not* intended to be a victim of the bombing. It looked as if the timer had set off the bomb sooner than expected. Then there was the rucksack of explosives. It had produced far more damage than would have been expected from home-made C4 explosives, the telltale trademark of bomb attacks orchestrated by the ITS – Islamic Terror Syndicate – to which MI5 seemed convinced Rafi belonged. And how the terrorist had managed to get into the garage unchallenged worried him. He had personally reviewed the security of all his police stations only weeks earlier. The garage should *not* have been unguarded. At least he had been able to secure a copy of the CCTV footage showing the suspect's meeting with the bomber.

'We have a number of ongoing enquiries, which look promising,' replied the commissioner.

'Excellent. Please let me know if you require any additional re-sources. I shall be available 24/7. My Government has every confidence in your ability to track down and bring to justice these barbaric criminals.'

Had the cameras not been trained on the minister, they would have spotted a fleeting frown on the commissioner's face. He had asked to interview the suspect, but had been thwarted. 'It is a matter for MI5, given the gravity of the situation,' the commissioner had been told by his political masters. He had lost three of his police officers and had several more on the critical list. He did not like being out of the loop and had gone to the top. A meeting was being scheduled for Monday with his longstanding friend, the head of MI5. He wished it could have been sooner. The commissioner stood there while the minister took questions from the press, anxious to get on with his work.

Suddenly a signal was given and the interview was over. The press officer spoke to the reporters. 'The minister will now be visiting the injured at the Royal London Hospital, in Whitechapel Road, and will be available for further questions there. Those of you with red press passes have been allocated seats in the hospital's press room.'

The commissioner watched as the flak jacket was tossed to an aide. 'Nice touch, that helmet,' said the minister. 'What did you use for the puddle?'

'Coca Cola,' came the aide's reply.

The minister smiled and strode off towards his chauffeur-driven car without so much as a goodbye to the commissioner, who turned and headed back to work.

B ack in his cell, Rafi sat on the bed trying to sort out what was going on. His thoughts went back to the previous Thursday. The early morning meeting had been an upbeat affair. His boss, Jameel, announced that he'd arranged an impromptu lunch to mark the upturn in the stock market.

During the morning Rafi had tried ringing Callum a couple of times, but his mobile was still on voicemail.

Just before lunch Jameel walked over to Rafi's desk. 'I think we should be prepared for some serious celebrations,' he said. 'I need to go across to *The Bishop of Norwich*, the restaurant, to line up a few things. Could you do me a favour and drop by the cashpoint and draw out, say, £500 in case I don't have enough cash for the bar bills and tips?'

'Fine,' replied Rafi, thinking nothing of it. There was a row of cashpoints between the office and the restaurant, in Moorgate. By the sounds of things, it was definitely going to be a session and a half for his drinking colleagues. Lunch was booked to start at 12.30 p.m. The whole fund management team was invited.

The restaurant welcomed the unexpected request for lunch for twenty-eight and arranged an area for just Prima Terra. No expense was spared; the food was first-class and, judging by his colleagues' remarks, the champagne and wine were excellent. Before, during and after lunch the drinks flowed freely. Rafi's colleagues became increasingly well lubricated and were on great form. Rafi, for his part, did not drink.

Ben, a burly East End lad who looked as if he'd missed the opportunity of being a second row forward, was revving up for a long session. He and a group of his colleagues decided that it was the perfect night to visit a nightclub. They'd recently returned from a stag night in Warsaw and had coined a new expression: zloty for totty. This was their war cry, which the dealer next to Rafi was chanting. It was going to be a very long and lively celebration. Ben and his friends decided that they'd have a few more drinks and move on to a cocktail bar in the West End, before some visual entertainment.

Rafi looked at his watch; it was approaching six o'clock. Half an hour earlier, Jameel had given his apologies and left to catch his flight to Paris. Rafi still hadn't spoken to Callum. He rang his mobile without success, then decided to ring his office and leave a voicemail message, but to his surprise his call was diverted. A kindly-sounding woman from Landin Young's HR team answered the phone. 'Mr Khan, I'm sorry,' she said and then, after a short pause, added, 'Callum Burns has been killed in a car accident. His Mercedes hit black ice, crashed and caught fire in Luxembourg on his way to Belgium. Can I get one of his colleagues to phone you tomorrow morning?'

Rafi could not reply straight away. He was nearly sick on the spot. Disbelief was his immediate reaction. Then the shock struck home and tiredness swept through him. His hands shook. 'Thank you, that would be helpful,' he said weakly and hung up.

He tried to put on a brave face. He wanted to leave and go home there and then. But he did not want to draw attention to his premature departure. He bought a couple of bottles of Champagne for his colleagues and then quietly slipped outside and headed for home.

Sitting on his hard cell bed, his thoughts remained on what had happened to Callum and whether his death might be linked to the bombing. Too many things just didn't make sense: why was Callum driving a Mercedes and not a Porsche? Why had he been driving straight to Amsterdam and not via Germany? What had Callum gleaned in Luxembourg? How many people were involved? Was he in the frame too? What should he do? Or could it all just be a coincidence? Rafi's thoughts went round in circles. Eventually he came to the realisation that he didn't have enough information to understand what was going on.

His thoughts were suddenly interrupted by the cell door swinging open. The ugly guard stood a few feet away, scowling.

Moments later Rafi was back in the austere interview room, facing his two interrogators.

Andy started the ball rolling. 'We are concerned that there will be further bombings. We need to know how to stop further carnage and bloodshed. Our patience only goes so far. If you don't cooperate, we have a good mind to lend you to the Yanks.'

'I'm not sure that I've any information that will help you,' replied Rafi.

Andy erupted like a Roman candle. 'What the bloody hell do you think you're playing at? You drag things out, waste our time and refuse to talk. Lives are at stake!'

The grilling went on for what seemed like ages. Rafi answered the very few questions he could.

The interrogators knew they were getting nowhere and their behaviour had become even more intimidating. Rafi had repeatedly been in and out of the interview room like a yo-yo, but he was never allowed to settle in his cell. If he tried to sleep he was hauled back in front of his two interrogators. He had lost sense of time – he guessed he had been interrogated for all Saturday and it was now probably Sunday. He was mentally drained and his recently acquired bruises ached like hell, as did his eyes. His head throbbed from the lack of sleep and the relentless stress. It then dawned on him that he would not be able to withstand the verbal assault for much longer.

'You're close to your sister, aren't you?' asked Mike.

'What?'

'We think that she can help us. We've been looking into her research work at the University of Birmingham. She is, we're informed, very bright. We think that she could be involved,' said Mike.

'How about we pull her in?' said Andy

Rafi felt the fury building up inside him. His little sister was the one person in the world he would protect with everything he possessed, even with his life. He felt shocked and angry.

'My sister is 100% innocent. She has nothing to do with this,' he pleaded.

'As we are not getting very far here, I think it's time for a two-pronged attack,' said Mike. 'We send him for a stint of solitary at Belmarsh. Meanwhile we can put pressure on his sister.'

'I agree,' said Andy. 'She is bound to crack like an egg under pressure.'

Rafi was visibly shaking. 'I'm not telling porkies. Can't you bloody well see I've been set up? Stuff you! I can't frigging well help – I know sod all about the bomber.'

Mike lent forward. 'Don't worry; your sister will tell us what we need to know!'

Rafi weakly tried to swing a punch at Mike who, despite being inches away, caught his fist and smiled.

'Last chance to come clean or Saara gets the full treatment!' said Andy.

Rafi said nothing.

'Bog off back to your cell and think of the fun we'll have with your sister.' Mike stood up to emphasise his height over him. 'You'll talk, you *know* you *will*.'

Back in his cell, Rafi thought long and hard. Time had run out; the case against him viewed from the interrogators' standpoint was overwhelming. They didn't give a shit about what he and Callum had found on the four listed companies. They'd played their trump card: his sister. He sat, shoulders hunched. The knowledge that he'd involved her in this frightening world scared him.

His thoughts drifted back to happier times, living at home with her and their parents. He treasured the time he had spent with her. She was eighteen months younger than him, but at times she had treated him like a younger brother. He was an able student; in contrast Saara was exceptionally bright. He watched with admiration as she excelled in everything academic: she had been top at school, achieved the highest mark in her undergraduate year and her PhD dissertation had been deemed exceptional by her professor.

Saara's successes had spurred him on. With a BSc in Business Studies and Accounting and a couple of years' experience working in the treasury department of a bank under his belt, he'd set his sights on working in the equities markets. He completed a full-time MBA and found a good corporate finance job. Eighteen months later his and Saara's happy lives had been shattered by their parents' untimely death in a car crash.

The money from his parents' estate and his savings had enabled him to muster the deposit needed to purchase his flat. He'd worked on an old adage: 'There are three important things to consider when purchasing property, namely: location, location, location.' So, he'd spent the summer evenings four years ago visiting smart residential areas in London. He'd added a fourth element: access to open space. He'd zeroed in on Hampstead and purchased a two-bedroom flat in the attic space of a large red-brick house in Well Walk, close to the Heath and an eight-minute walk from the tube station. The entrance to the flat was off a narrow path – Well Passage.

Rafi put his hands over his eyes and forced his brain to think. They were convinced that he knew the bomber. Why the hell wouldn't they listen to him? It was as if his bloody interrogators weren't interested in the potential wrongdoing Callum and he had uncovered. The more he thought about it the more certain he became that there *had* to be a connection between his finding out about the dubious shareholdings in the four companies and his being set up. He had to find a way to get them to look at things from his perspective. But how?

Rafi turned his thoughts back to the one piece of evidence he had that they might want: the USB memory stick Callum had given him.

The devastating news of Callum's death had shaken him to the core. Once back home after the office party on Thursday evening, he had slumped in an armchair and done nothing for several hours. It had slowly dawned on him that he was wasting valuable time. He had to plan for the worst – and assume someone had killed Callum. And it might not be long before the Financial Services Authority and the fraud squad spotted what Prima Terra were up to. Callum's USB stick might just be his insurance policy or even a valuable bargaining chip if he was confronted by the authorities.

He needed to hide the USB stick away from prying eyes. His mind was in disarray. He recalled wondering whether he was being paranoid – *no*; after Callum's suspicious death he could not afford to take chances.

He recalled looking at his watch; it was 3 a.m. and inky dark outside. Where could he hide it? He considered places in the building and its small garden, but ruled them out as being too obvious or too close to home. So where then? It needed to be within walking distance of his flat and easy to find but, perversely, somewhere people wouldn't look.

An idea came to him. He had changed into warm, dark-coloured clothes and wrapped a black cashmere scarf around his neck. He looked at himself in the mirror: with his dark skin he would be practically invisible in the shadows – or so he hoped. He picked up his gloves, put them with a number of things into his pockets and slipped quietly out of his front door on to the landing. Slowly, in the pitch black, he went down the three flights of stairs towards the communal front door leading out into the alleyway.

He was about to open the front door, when the seriousness of his predicament properly sank in. What *were* the chances he was being watched? Could someone be outside waiting for him to make a move? He felt a cold shiver run down his back. It was preposterous, but he needed to be careful. His friend Callum was dead.

He checked in his left pocket: keys, torch, gloves – all there. And in his other pocket: USB stick and chewing gum – excellent. Tentatively he opened the front door. The catch clicked back like the bolt of a gun being cocked. He jumped, imagining that everyone could hear him. He recovered his composure. His heart raced, but everything around him remained hushed. He pulled the door ajar, stopping for a moment to test his night vision. Quietly, he slipped outside, closing the door behind him. The passage was sheathed in darkness. He turned right and, hugging the wall, walked slowly up the murky passage towards the next street.

Near the top of the alley, before turning right towards the Heath, he stopped and looked back. At the bottom of the alley, across the other side of the road, was the silhouette of a Mercedes car parked sideways-on. Large Mercedes cars were popular around where he lived.

Rafi stood still. Then his heart missed a beat. Was he seeing things? Inside the car there was a small orange glow. The glow of a cigarette tip brightening as someone inhaled. He was petrified, his feet glued to the spot. The small blob of light moved. Oh sod it! There was someone there, watching. He wished the path would swallow him up. If the person had seen him slip out of the front door, surely he would have followed him? Or perhaps he was waiting to see which way he went? Whether they were on to him or not, Rafi needed to keep moving.

He headed towards the Heath, and to The Pryors – an upmarket, Edwardian-style apartment block. He turned left off the side of the road and made his way carefully down the path alongside the tall wall of The Pryors. The trees on the edge of the Heath appeared ghostlike, just visible, towering over him. He was feeling utterly terrified. The hairs on the back of his neck stood up. There was stillness – a cloak of silence around him. A rustling in the undergrowth startled him. His senses were on their peak setting. He stood still. The noise faded and he moved on again, his heart racing.

He put his hand into his pocket, pulled out the packet of chewing gum, quietly unwrapped four pieces and put them into his mouth. Sod it, his mouth was parched. Fear had turned off his saliva glands. 'Think lemons, think lemons,' he said to himself.

Rafi turned right and followed the garden wall around a corner for a short distance. In summer, the deep verge between the wall and the path was overgrown with nettles and brambles. In winter long grass, dead brambles and weeds remained. There, against the wall was a small, dark object, barely visible in the gloom. He had first spotted it a couple of summers earlier, when he had gone to retrieve a ball for a child; it had intrigued him and he had carefully inspected it. He approached it tentatively, stopped and turned around to check that there was no one was behind him. He breathed a sigh of relief; everything was still. He stepped forward, took off his glove and placed his hand on top of the frost-covered metal, slid his fingers over the curved front and felt for the protruding letters. Yes, this was the marker post. The raised lettering on its front clearly stated: 'London County Council Boundary'. There was a small gap between it and the wall. Unlike the other boundary posts Rafi had subsequently looked at next to the wall, the flat metal back of this one had been broken, leaving a small but hidden hole near its top.

He put his hand back into his pocket and pulled out the USB stick; he raised his hand to his mouth, spat out the blob of chewing gum and pressed it to the side of the USB stick. He put his hand around the back of the cold iron post and with his fingertips felt for the irregular hole. He reached inside and pushed the USB stick firmly up into the top section of the post. He smiled as the chewing gum stuck. The main part of his job was done.

Rafi retraced his tracks to the road. He'd been gone probably no more than twenty minutes. His eyes had become accustomed to darkness and he could clearly pick out the outline of the houses fronting on to Heath Road. He looked up into the sky. The cloud cover, thankfully, remained impenetrable. He glanced across at a small bedroom light in the distance. Early birds, he thought. On a normal working day like this, he would only be in bed for another couple of hours and therefore he needed to get back home as quickly as possible.

Although it was still dark, he was aware that just one light switched on near his front door would scupper his return, making him clearly visible to the person in the Mercedes car. Rafi slipped across the road and retraced his steps back to the passage. At the corner he stopped; in front of him was the last straight leading to his front door.

Gingerly, he peeped round the corner. Was the Mercedes car still there? Oh hell, it was. On the way out he'd initially been oblivious to it. Now the black silhouette was straight in front of him. It looked menacing. He studied the car carefully. There was no sign of a lit cigarette. Either the person had stopped smoking, or he had got out to follow him. Oh shit, he thought, what if he was in the shadows waiting for him? Rafi hesitated and then forced himself to move, lest the light of an early-rising neighbour gave him away.

He moved carefully down the passageway, hugging the wall on his left. He reached his front door. Everything around him was dark. He slipped his key into the lock and turned it. At that precise moment the light from a nearby flat came on. It was as if he had been caught in the arc of a spotlight. He pushed open the door, slipped inside and closed the door behind him. Had he been spotted? Only time would tell. He was relieved to be back on home territory. Quickly, with a bounce in his step, he climbed the stairs in the dark. As he reached the landing, he froze. Could he smell cigarette smoke? Could the person from the car be waiting for him in the shadows? He peered up the last flight of stairs into the darkness, but could make nothing out. He stood still, listening for anything.

Not eight feet away his neighbour's front door opened, lighting up the landing.

'Oh bejesus!' exclaimed the neighbour. 'What the bleeding hell are you doing here? You scared the holy shit out of me.'

If he knew what he'd done to Rafi's nerves, he'd have apologised. Rafi stuttered, 'Sorry mate, just got back from a night away with the girlfriend. I was creeping in trying not to make any noise.'

'You lucky so and so,' he commented, smiling at Rafi.

The neighbour turned on the stairwell light, closed his front door, muttered, 'Must get going, I've got the early shift at work today. See you around,' and went on his way in a cloud of cigarette smoke.

Rafi climbed the last flight of stairs, went into his flat and stood there, shaking. He felt as if he'd aged years.

Was the Mercedes still on guard duty out front? He needed to check so he climbed the narrow staircase to the top floor bedroom. It was in darkness. He stopped before the window, dropped to his knees and shuffled forward, resting his elbows on the windowsill in order to peer down towards the road. The Mercedes was still there, its dark shape hauntingly visible, but he couldn't make out if the person was still inside the car. He stayed on his knees, surveying the dark shape parked across the road. Who could it be? Did he really want to find out? His mind was full of questions and precious few answers. He dozed off, leaning on the windowsill.

The distant buzz of his alarm clock woke him. Rafi raised his weary head and looked outside; it was still dark. He came back to reality with a bump. The Mercedes was still there. He shuffled backwards, stood up and hurried downstairs to turn off the alarm.

He was sure he was being watched, but by whom? He decided that he had no option but to continue as normal. He slipped into his early-morning routine. Twenty minutes later, he was sitting at the small kitchen table, staring at a bowl of cereal and milk. Normally he ate breakfast quickly. This morning, his appetite had vanished and the coffee tasted bitter. He gathered up his things and left for work.

Rafi carefully opened the entrance hall door. Would the Mercedes still be there? If so, would he have the courage to walk by it on his way to the underground station? He stepped out into the shadows of the narrow alleyway and looked left towards the road.

The Mercedes was nowhere to be seen; Rafi breathed a sigh of relief.

On the tube, Rafi hid behind his Friday's *Financial Times*, taking in little of its news. His head was in turmoil. Act normally, he kept telling himself. His mind was trying to stay rational, but his body was under a different set of controls. He felt his hands shaking and steadied them.

At last, Moorgate tube station arrived. He got out and made his way to his office round the corner in South Place.

Rafi greeted the security guard with a wave and headed for the coffee machine. He felt like death warmed up. The office was like a morgue. You idiot, he thought to himself, as he recalled the celebratory lunch and the previous evening's festivities. His spirits rose a little as he realised that at least he would look a whole lot better than most of his colleagues.

The office started to fill up. The open plan floor on which he worked was the quietest he could remember; the telephones were being answered in hushed tones and no one was really in the mood to work. By all accounts, the previous night had been an unreserved success; the bar bills would have been huge and the accounts team would no doubt have to do some creative juggling with the expenses claims!

By 9 a.m. the office was regaining some of its momentum and the noise level had moved up a notch from deadly quiet to hush. The coffee machines were in demand, but unlike normal days there was little gossiping going on around them. At one of them Rafi bumped into Jameel's secretary.

'Did he make his flight last night?' he enquired.

''Fraid not! He missed it by a mile,' she smiled. 'It was a good session yesterday, though, wasn't it?'

Rafi recalled seeing her perched on the edge of a table, enjoying the adulation of a group of dealers.

To his surprise, she said, 'Didn't you see Jameel first thing this morning? He told me he had a couple of things to sort out before he rushed off to London City airport to catch a flight to Paris. Luckily, I managed to rearrange all his meetings.'

'Is he still due back next Tuesday?' Rafi asked.

'As far as I know.'

Why had Jameel missed his evening flight? He'd left the party early and had plenty of time. Rafi wondered what he had been up to.

Minutes later, Seb Warren, a colleague of Callum's, phoned. 'Judy Ballantyne of HR asked me to give you a call.'

Rafi could vaguely put a face to the young individual. He was of a similar age to Callum, but not in Callum's class.

'Is there any further news?' asked Rafi.

'Sorry, nothing. All we can glean is that he'd finished his work and was on his way to Amsterdam. The local Luxembourg police aren't saying much. His body should be flown home early next week. I understand that his family is arranging the funeral for next Thursday somewhere near Bristol, I think.'

'Callum was seeing some people for me,' Rafi said, hoping Seb wouldn't pick up his white lie. 'Could you run through who he saw?'

Seb hesitated briefly, but then went on. 'Yes, OK. He had a meeting with a REIT, followed by a couple of meetings with tax lawyers. He had lunch with a local investment fund manager and then went to see a contact in the same building for an afternoon meeting. Rafi, I spoke to Callum as he was leaving the afternoon meeting. He was very upbeat, saying, "I've done some useful research for Rafi, he will be very interested." I don't know what he meant – sorry – do you?'

'Not really,' said Rafi disingenuously.

Seb paused and carried on. 'He was in a hurry, said he was late for his rendezvous with the REIT director.'

'I tried ringing him at around 6.30 p.m. but got put through to his voicemail,' said Rafi.

'So did I,' replied the youngster.

'Before you ring off, could you tell me who he had lunch with?'

'I'm not certain if I should, but I know Callum was a good friend of yours so I'll tell you off the record. He met Hubert Vynckt of CPR Investment Funds.'

'Thank you Seb, you've been a great help, and I'm so sorry about Callum.'

Rafi made a mental note of the name and had just stood up to go to the library when the whole building was rocked by a dull thump.

'What the hell was that?' asked Gavin, a director who sat near to Rafi.

'Oscar has self-imploded,' quipped Dominic, to Gavin's left.

A voice from across the room said, 'That was a bomb blast.'

'Are you sure?' asked Gavin.

All eyes in the open plan office focused on the office junior. He was seen but usually never heard. 'Not close, but definitely in the Square Mile. I reckon it went off somewhere to the east of us.' He paused before adding, going rather pink, 'I'm in the TA so I am used to these sorts of bangs.'

'So now what?' asked Gavin.

'There could be a follow-up bomb. People should move away from the windows.'

'OK,' said Gavin, 'do as the man says and get away from the windows. We'll wait for some news; it'll be all over the screens very soon and then we'll decide what to do.'

Rafi looked at the newsflash on his trading screen. 'Bombed – Police garage at the rear of Bishopsgate police station, opposite Liverpool Street Station.' The newsflash continued. 'City of London police are unable to confirm whether there will be any further attacks. The London Stock Exchange and Euronext.liffe have closed.' This was followed by, 'London underground and all mainline stations are shut.'

Gavin stood up. 'The office is closed for business. You are free to stay put or leave for home whenever you wish.'

Rafi knew that news of the bomb blast would be plastered across the media, so he picked up the phone and dialled his sister's number at her university department.

A colleague of hers answered.

'Is Saara there? It's her brother speaking.'

'Sorry, she's nipped out. I'll tell her you rang.'

'Thanks,' he said, 'could you put a note on her desk to say that I'm fine.'

'Will do,' she reassured him and the line went dead.

Rafi decided it was time to leave. 'See you Monday. Have a good weekend,' he called across to Gavin.

Outside, it was bright February sunshine. The streets had an unreal feel. There was the sound of sirens in the distance. It was the expressions on people's faces that were different. They had a sense of anxious determination. The buses and taxis were still working but the queues at the bus stops and cab ranks were very long. Rafi considered his options. He wanted to get home. There was nothing for it but to walk and hope he came across an empty taxi on the way. With a coffee break in the middle, the six-mile walk was not too bad.

The walk gave him the opportunity to think things over. He would take a holiday. If he went abroad and Prima Terra were investigated by the authorities, they might think he was escaping from them so he decided to find a comfortable hotel in Cornwall. He would leave first thing the following morning; being a Saturday it would be a good time to travel.

Just under three hours later Rafi was opening the front door to his flat. It was a relief to be home. He stripped, showered and, with a bath towel around his waist, headed for the dining room table, opened up his laptop and went surfing for hotels in Cornwall. Into the search engine he entered: Cornwall +hotel +sea and scanned through the very long list of possibilities. He changed sea to "good food" and looked at the new list. Near the top, Headland Hotel, Fistral Bay, Newquay caught his eye. He clicked on the link. Its location looked great. Its restaurant had two rosettes and they were doing special deals on stays of over five days – perfect. He opened up another window, pulled up the search engine again and found National Rail Enquiries. London to Newquay was a five-hour journey from Paddington and there was a 10.05 a.m. train.

He picked up the phone and dialled the Headland Hotel. In the space of a couple of minutes he'd booked himself a small suite with ocean view for ten days, extendable to fourteen, starting the following night.

He decided he would travel light and packed some clothes into his computer rucksack and briefcase. He would look businesslike in the hope of concealing his escape plans. Tired, he turned in for an early night.

A few hours later his living nightmare started, as he was dragged from his bed and taken to the godforsaken police station.

Rafi lurched back to the present. From the memories he had managed to piece together, he concluded that Jameel, his boss, with some persons unknown in Luxembourg were involved in something highly illegal and could even be linked to the terrorist attack. Callum *must* have unearthed proof of what was going on.

But why did they want him out of circulation? If Jameel *was* involved and something sinister *was* going on with the four companies, what were they up to? Why was he a danger to them and why hadn't they killed him, as they'd done with Callum? Perhaps two deaths close to home would raise too many questions, and setting him up as the bad guy achieved the desired effect?

Rafi's head ached from the lack of sleep. The absence of edible food and the small intake of fluids were also taking their toll. The physical side was unpleasant but didn't overly concern him. It was the mental fatigue that worried him. Without a brain he wouldn't get out of there, he told himself.

His thoughts changed tack. How long would it have taken for the evidence to be fabricated against him and the bombing to be planned and carried out? And how many people might be involved? His conclusion was that the bombing had already been scheduled and it had simply been a convenience to link him to it.

So how was Jameel, a finance heavyweight, involved? Jameel was a big picture man: fine print and micromanagement weren't his biggest strengths. Therefore, he had to be working with or for someone.

Next question, mused Rafi: what was Jameel's and Prima Terra's part in the plot? It had to be something to do with the City of London – one of the three great financial capitals of the world. His thoughts drifted back to the research that Callum and he had been working on: the clandestine nominee names and the four companies in which Prima Terra was a large investor. Might they have thought he was on to them and close to unravelling what they were planning?

In simple terms, he had two sets of obstacles to get over. The first was to show that the evidence against him – the CCTV footage and the £20 note – was contrived. The second was to get his interrogators to believe that he was on their side and potentially was the key to unlocking a larger terrorist plot.

'I've got it!' It came to him, out of the blue. What he needed was someone they trusted to do the persuading for him. Someone who would wish to look carefully at the four companies and work on what Prima Terra were up to. In the eyes of his interrogators he was guilty and he knew they wouldn't be prepared to listen to a word he said as long as he insisted on protesting his innocence. Corporate finance was a blank in their book. Who might they listen to? His mind ached.

It needed to be one of them! Yes, of course that might work. He needed a police officer who could put his case to them. Furthermore, he needed someone who was familiar with the workings of the City and understood corporate finance. His mind raced. Ideally it would need to be someone from the Corporate or Economic Fraud Squad at the City of London police force. Would they be prepared to help him? Bloody hell, it was going to be a tall order. The bomber he was accused of being linked to had killed three – or was it four? – City policemen. He would be seriously unpopular with them. But it was on their turf and they might be interested in his story if they thought it would hasten the arrest of those who masterminded the bombing. He thought through the practicalities: he needed to get someone from the City Police to visit him. He could give them the location of the memory stick, but he was aware that it wouldn't be wise to tell MI5 as they might then not let the police be involved.

There was a problem, though. He probably only had twelve hours left before it all became too much for him to handle coherently. In particular, the lack of sleep and water were taking their toll. As he wondered how best to get things moving, the cell door swung open.

In the interrogation room, he faced his two least favourite people. He was desperately tired and had lost track of time, but felt as if he had missed a night's sleep.

Before Rafi could speak, Andy started talking. 'We passed your laptop to our boffins. They've found nothing to do with the four companies.'

Thank goodness he hadn't copied across the files from Callum's USB memory stick, thought Rafi.

'Very suspicious if you ask me,' said Mike. 'So where is the information Callum and you put together on the four companies?'

Rafi's stomach tensed up; he had to play things very carefully. The information on Callum's USB stick might just be his passport out of there.

'It's rather complicated,' said Rafi.

29

'Proceed. Do we look thick?' added Andy.

Rafi allowed himself an inward grin. He hesitated; time for a bit of financial gobbledygook.

'Oi! Wake up and get your arse in gear!' shouted Mike as if every second was urgent. 'You're here to talk to us not to daydream.'

Rafi drew breath and started: 'Do you understand what I mean by butterfly positions in the forward financial futures markets, when a leveraged investor is speculating on a break out of a trading range, precipitated by new knowledge coming into the market?' He stopped. The two interrogators looked at each other, dumbfounded.

It was bullshit, but not total bullshit. 'OK, I'll go through it slowly. In the futures market you have two positions: calls when you're a buyer and puts when you're a seller of the market. With a call position, you make a profit if the market rises more than is anticipated and in a put contract you make a profit if the market falls by more than anticipated. OK so far?' Rafi carried on before they had had the opportunity to respond. 'Leveraged derivatives are when you've borrowed money to finance your positions in the market, thereby making your profits bigger. Do you follow me?'

'Er . . . Could you perhaps speak English?' said Andy.

'Where do these butterflies come in?' asked Mike in a bemused manner.

'They're a type of trade where you mix call and put contracts together. It's the information flows that make the derivatives market appealing in highly volatile times.'

The two interrogators obviously didn't have a clue what Rafi was talking about. Their faces showed that as much as they wished to follow his line of thought, it wasn't their area of expertise.

'Perhaps we should have a break whilst you check out what I've said?'

Mike scowled. They chatted between themselves for a couple of minutes. Apparently they'd had enough trouble understanding what an equity was, let alone a futures product.

'By the way, I have a USB memory stick with the data on it, which will back up my assertions.'

'You what?' exploded Mike. 'Why the hell didn't you tell us earlier? Where is it?'

Rafi remained silent.

'You devious little sod,' said Andy. 'Back to your cell while we decide what to do with you.'

R afi was bundled back to his cell. He lay on his bed and hoped that they'd make a decision relatively quickly.

The bolts on the cell door clunked loudly and the door swung open. There, standing in the doorway was his *bête noir*.

'They want you back, now!' the guard said ominously. 'Come with me,' he barked.

Rafi struggled to sit up; his back had seized up as a result of the blows he'd received from the man who had brought his food. He rolled on to his side, slid off the bed and on to his knees. Yes, he could stand up now, he thought as he straightened his knees.

He was too slow. Suddenly he felt the vice-like grip of a pair of hands locked around his neck and was forcibly hauled upright. He couldn't breathe and started to struggle, which had no impact other than to increase the pressure on his neck. Rafi felt himself starting to black out.

The guard was strong, very strong, and with ease he pulled Rafi up. Then in one movement sent him flying towards the corner of the cell.

Instinctively, Rafi tried to cushion the impact by stretching out his right arm in front of him – it hit the inside rim of the slops bucket taking much of the brunt and was unceremoniously lying in the contents. Then his shoulder hit the wall with a sickening thud. Rafi felt sick as pain shot up his arm from his wrist.

'You messy little git,' said the guard. 'Can't take you anywhere without you making an effing mess of yourself. Phwaaw! You smell like a sewer rat. Better not keep 'em waiting.' With that he hauled Rafi to his feet and frogmarched him down the corridor.

His wrist was already swelling up and going a deep purple-blue colour. Rafi tried to move his fingers; they hurt like hell, but he found he could still partially move them – at least nothing seemed broken.

As he pushed Rafi towards his chair, the guard hissed under his breath, 'You won't be so lucky next time!' His distinctive company's badge – the BlueKnite emblem – was inches away from Rafi's eyes and impressed itself in his memory.

'Silly idjut tried to get here in too much of an 'urry, slipped and put his hand down the karzi. A right plonker, in't 'e?' said the guard.

Rafi laid his swollen wrist and reeking wet sleeve on the table. He looked at his two interrogators and tried to give them his best grin.

'Phew, you stink! Before we go any further we need to get you cleaned up.' Andy beckoned to those behind the one-way glass window.

31

A couple of minutes later there was a knock at the door and a new face appeared. The man was carrying a clean shirt and a plastic first aid box.

'Meet Sergeant Chris Archery. We thought you should be checked over before we continue.'

Rafi slowly unbuttoned his shirt and then got stuck.

'Could you help me pull it off?' Rafi sat there, leaning slightly forward in his chair, and, as his shirt came off there was an involuntary intake of breath.

'Bloody hell, mate!' said the sergeant. 'You're looking a bit rough aren't you?'

Rafi's wrist had swelled up to nearly three times its normal size and had turned a deep shade of dark blue and purple. He couldn't see the bruises on his back, but they ached like hell.

'I can't do much about your back, but I can strap your wrist,' the sergeant turned to the two interrogators. 'Can I give him a couple of painkillers, or are they off the menu?'

'Don't see why not. Don't want him accusing us of treating him badly,' said Mike sarcastically.

The sergeant carefully lifted Rafi's arm up. 'Looks painful; let's get it washed and strapped.' He opened his first aid box and pulled out a couple of sterilised cleaning towels. He cleaned his forearm, wrist and hand.

'Hold still; this may be a little uncomfortable' – an understatement if ever there was one. The sergeant quickly and efficiently strapped his wrist from the base of his thumb to his elbow and helped Rafi put on the clean shirt.

The sergeant rummaged again in his box and took out a plastic bottle of a yellow-looking liquid. He opened it, poured some of the contents on to a piece of cotton wool and wiped Rafi's swollen hand. 'Nothing to do with the treatment – I thought it might cover up the smell; it's the best I can do on the deodorant front,' he said grinning at the two interrogators. 'If that's all gentlemen, I'll go now.'

As soon as the door closed, Mike recommenced the inquisition. 'Tell us where you have put the USB memory stick – and why the files are important. If you don't, we'll send you on holiday to the Americans.'

Though the threat was probably hollow, the idea of what they *might* do scared Rafi. He remained silent for a moment.

'I suppose a phone call is out of the question?' Rafi asked hopefully.

'Bloody well right!' said Mike.

'What was on the files? Tell me! Then you get a phone call,' added Andy.

At last he had something to go on. Up to then he'd been hitting a brick wall. 'I've a proposal,' Rafi said quietly.

'Yes, what is it?' said Mike.

'I'd like to speak to someone, but I'll need your help.'

'You must be bloody joking!' interjected Mike.

'Please hear me out,' said Rafi.

'Make it quick,' replied Andy.

'Find me a detective who's an expert in corporate fraud or economic fraud. The City of London police force has a specialist economic fraud team. I know they're bloody livid with me as a prime suspect, but if you can get one of them to interrogate me, they'll understand what I have to say.'

There was silence; it was definitely not what the two MI5 officers had expected to hear.

'One of our specialists should be able to understand,' said Andy, who looked as if he'd just eaten a lemon.

'Should be, I'm afraid, isn't enough. I need to speak with someone who really knows their stuff. The people at City Police are experts and won't suffer fools gladly. If I'm seen to be pissing them around, they'll no doubt tell you,' countered Rafi.

'I don't think your suggestion is viable. They're not MI5, or anti-terrorism, so they are outside the group of people we work with,' said Mike.

'Even though they've got a vested interest in the Bishopsgate bombing?' insisted Rafi.

'Oh hell, you're a little shit, aren't you? We've got enough to bang you up for decades. Your bargaining position is crap and yet you're asking to be interrogated by a plod from the City of London.' Mike looked far from pleased.

'Bloody nutmegs, if you ask me,' cut in Andy.

'Yes, I agree,' said Mike. 'I think he's just trying to give us the runaround.'

'We'll ask the boss, but I reckon the answer will be a categorical no,' said Andy.

They left the room, leaving Rafi to wait anxiously. A couple of minutes later they reappeared.

'We've a proposal. You tell us the information and we then pass the tapes to City of London police.'

'Are you sure there's time?' Rafi asked. 'All I'm asking is to meet a detective from City police; you can record the conversation and hear everything we talk about.'

'I still don't think it's a good idea,' mumbled Andy under his breath.

'Time for you to go back to your cell,' said Mike.

Rafi was ushered to his cell by another guard who had obviously been to the same training school as his ugly colleague.

Back in his cell Rafi waited nervously. He rehearsed in his mind what he was going to say. He waited and waited. Finally they came for him – the walk to the interrogation room felt like the longest of his life.

As Rafi entered the now familiar place, his heart sank. There were just two people in the room: Andy and Mike. His request had fallen on deaf ears. There was no one from the City of London police to interrogate him. Rafi felt despondent and broken. His hope of having someone to help fight his corner evaporated.

Mike started the conversation. He was looking very pleased with himself. 'Let us recap why you're under arrest. We've got CCTV footage of your meeting with the Bishopsgate bomber; one of the £20 notes you took from the cashpoint was found in the dead bomber's wallet; you've hidden a USB memory stick with crucial data on it *and* you've consistently refused to cooperate.'

'What the hell is your defence?' added Andy.

Rafi's mind was close to calling it a day. He hesitated. A phrase a former hostage had once used in a TV interview came to mind: 'It's your belief in there being a future that pulls you through the ordeal'. Sod it, he thought; even if the City Police weren't there, he still had to give it a try.

'Could I have a whiteboard or a flip chart?'

The two interrogators looked at each other. 'No you bloody well can't,' snapped Mike.

'It would speed things up and make things clearer,' Rafi countered weakly.

'The answer's still no,' said Andy.

'How about some paper and a pen?'

Andy pushed his pad and a pen over to Rafi, who picked up the biro in his left hand and transferred it across to his swollen right hand and winced as he started writing on the paper sheet. The pain wasn't too bad if he supported his swollen wrist with his left hand. In the middle of the sheet, he wrote:

£20 note
CCTV footage

Packed to leave
Callum's car crash
Prima Terra / Jameel
USB Memory Stick.

The handwriting was awful, but it was legible. Rafi smiled; he had a framework from which to operate. All he had to do now was to get his exhausted brain to remember everything he had to say and to put it across clearly.

The pain in his right hand had reached a point where he wondered if he could deal with it. He tried to ignore it and continued shakily. His throat was dry and his voice scratchy. 'Any chance of a cup of coffee, white with sugar and no salt, please?'

Andy nodded and, as if by magic, a cup of hot coffee was brought into the room a few moments later. It gave Rafi a much needed boost.

'You have me here as your prime suspect. Let me explain why I'm innocent.'

'This better be good,' Mike interjected under his breath.

'I'm an innocent bystander, but at the same time I *am* linked to those involved,' said Rafi. He looked at the two of them. He'd got their attention. 'The CCTV footage showed me taking £500 in £20 notes from the cashpoint, one of which ended up in the dead terrorist's pocket. How did this happen? Your records will confirm that, after taking the money out, I went straight to the *Bishop of Norwich* where my firm was holding a celebratory lunch. Jameel Furud asked if I could sub him £360 towards the restaurant tip. The total tip was £500. If you check with the restaurant, you'll find that the denominations of the notes that they received were fifteen of my brand new £20s and four £50s.' Rafi knew this was just a calculated guess, but was prepared to bet he was right. Jameel was a big tipper, liked round numbers and £50 notes. 'Jameel pocketed three of my £20 notes, and it was one of these notes you found on the dead body.'

Rafi wondered whether he was talking sense. He had a splitting headache. 'Let's turn to the CCTV footage. My office in South Place isn't that near to Bishopsgate. I reckon that there must be thousands of CCTV cameras in the Square Mile. Let's assume that there are 4,000 cameras – that's something like 100,000 hours of recordings. Finding the bit showing me handing the money over to the bomber would have been like looking for a needle in a haystack and yet it was found in a matter of hours. I'd make an educated guess that it was found thanks to an anonymous tip-off and not by tracing the movements of the bomber. Where did the tip-off come from? It was the person who arranged for me to bump into the bomber; the person who had asked me to go to the cashpoint before going to the restaurant to get cash for the tip. The same person who knew that there was only one set of cashpoints between my office and the restaurant. All the evidence points to me being set up by Jameel Furud, who has conveniently left the country.'

Andy and Mike looked straight at Rafi. Their blank faces gave nothing away.

'I would now like to explain the items at the bottom of the sheet of paper.' Rafi dropped his head for a few seconds, partly for effect and partly because he felt like death warmed up. His body was crying out for some rest.

'The Stock Exchange takeover code, the Blue Book, sets out strict rules on the disclosure of shareholdings in companies listed in London. Callum and I had found four instances where Prima Terra's large disclosable shareholdings were mirrored by large clandestine nominee shareholdings. These nominee holdings are run out of Luxembourg. Before Callum was killed he'd meetings with specialists in this field. He'd called his colleague, Seb Warren, and implied that he'd found proof that would verify the data on the USB memory stick and substantiate that Prima Terra was linked to the clandestine nominee names. This would be a major breach of the rules.'

Rafi paused. 'To reinforce my allegation that Callum was murdered, please consider the following. He'd arranged to borrow a Porsche and drive it to Amsterdam via the German Autobahns. He was really excited about the Porsche and wouldn't have given up the opportunity of driving it. So why was he found in a rented Mercedes, driving east towards Belgium and not west to Germany? My answer is: his assassins put him there and set fire to the car to cover up any evidence.'

Mike and Andy looked at Rafi as if he was as mad as a box of frogs.

'My premise to you is that there's more to this than meets the eye,' continued Rafi. 'You've quizzed me about impending attacks on police stations, railway stations, airports and other public places. You've got this wrong. Jameel is one of a team plotting something far larger. I believe they wanted me out of the way as they thought I'd stumbled on to something that could uncover what they're planning.'

Rafi raised his aching head and looked at the interrogators. 'The data on the USB memory stick holds the key to this conspiracy. That's why I want an interview with someone from the City of London police. They're uniquely placed to understand the data and to put it into the context of the workings and intricacies of the financial markets. I implore you to let me be interrogated by one of them. What have you got to lose?'

'So where is the memory stick?' asked Andy.

'Safe,' Rafi replied.

'Do continue,' said Andy.

'Why was I packed to leave? And why was I not going abroad? Quite simply, I feared for my life and wanted to go somewhere safe to mull things over. I booked ten days' holiday in Cornwall. If I'd been involved with the terrorists, surely I'd have gone to a safe haven overseas?'

Rafi looked at his two interrogators. He reckoned he had at best a 50:50 chance as to whether they believed anything he'd said. They remained silent, their faces unfathomable. He sensed he'd lost. He wasn't going to get out of jail – ever.

Just then the door opened. A smartly dressed police officer stood in the doorway, pausing momentarily to take in the scene in front of him, then strode in, head up high. He introduced himself as Commissioner Giles Meynell of the City of London police. He came and sat opposite Rafi, next to the two interrogators.

He had a calm yet forceful voice, packed with authority, no doubt gleaned over many years of high ranking service.

Rafi was gobsmacked. Oh hell, why did the commissioner have to arrive late? He'd have to do the whole presentation again and realised he physically couldn't – he was just too tired.

The commissioner studied the prisoner. 'Mr Khan, I've listened to what you've had to say. It's too early to determine whether there's any truth to your story.'

Rafi's hopes rose and then fell.

'However, even if there's an outside chance that your theory has substance, I'm duty-bound to investigate.'

Rafi could have leant across and hugged him. He felt he had been given a new lease of life.

The commissioner looked at Rafi gravely. 'You're no doubt aware that the Bishopsgate bombing has robbed my force of four excellent police officers. A further three are still in intensive care. My first instinct would be to leave you with these professionals and let them break you. However, my police training and experience tell me that I need more information. I have one question.' He carefully studied Rafi. 'Where exactly is the USB memory stick?'

'Could I use your notebook, please?' replied Rafi.

The commissioner unbuttoned his outside breast pocket and passed a small notebook across to Rafi, open at a blank page. A biro was attached to the side.

Rafi gestured 'thank you' and carefully put the biro in his swollen right hand, hunched over the pad so that the CCTV cameras couldn't see it and with a feat of great willpower started writing. He looked down at his scrawl, closed the pad and handed it back.

The commissioner opened it and glanced at the page as if keeping his cards close to his chest whilst playing bridge, and replaced it into his pocket.

Their eyes met. 'When your analyst has the memory stick, I'd be happy to explain the contents to him,' said Rafi.

The scribbling in the commissioner's notebook had caused a significant amount of consternation amongst the two MI5 officers. Andy and Mike both started to protest.

'Sir,' said Andy, 'may we please see what Mr Khan wrote? As you know it falls under our jurisdiction.'

The commissioner drew himself up to his full height and studied the two MI5 men carefully. 'All in due course, gentlemen. I am conducting a murder enquiry and it is my duty to determine the validity of what Mr Kahn has written. I can assure you that the information is in safe hands. We shall discuss whatever we find as soon as it is appropriate.'

Rafi moved his gaze from Mike's shifty eyes, betraying a character as hard as nails, to the commissioner, who gave a totally different impression: middle-aged, smartly dressed and with a thatch of neatly combed white hair. His blue eyes didn't have Mike's ruthlessness; nevertheless Rafi hoped that he never crossed him.

'Mr Khan. Provided you have not sent me on a wild goose chase, you can expect to see one of my team here later today. They will pick your brains, in particular on the contents of the USB stick. And be in no doubt, if they believe you're telling lies or half-truths, Andy and Mike will be more than welcome to do whatever they like to you and then throw away the key. Whilst those who helped the Bishopsgate bomber are still at large I shall leave no stone unturned.' With that, the commissioner stood up and left.

The faces of the two MI5 interrogators were as black as thunder. They turned to look at one another and spoke in hushed tones.

R afi was escorted to his cell, a little less roughly this time. He sat down, mentally and physically exhausted. If the interviewers guessed he'd reached the end of his tether, the game was over; they could easily wangle any confession they wanted out of him. He was almost past caring. He sat on the edge of his bed and waited. Time passed slowly. Two hours later Rafi had started to worry that the commissioner had changed his mind.

The cell door swung open.

'Someone's 'ere to see you,' said the guard.

Rafi was bundled into the interview room. 'Sit! They'll be 'ere shortly.'

There was a knock at the door. Rafi looked up and saw the slightly nervous face of a female police inspector. She rapidly regained her composure and closed the door behind her.

'Good afternoon,' she said. 'I'm Detective Inspector Kate Adams of the City of London police.'

She sat down, as if waiting for someone or something.

Rafi looked carefully at the policewoman opposite him. Her wavy hair was tied back severely. It was a warm rusty colour. She had pale skin which was covered with splashes of freckles and her eyes were a deep hazel brown.

Kate meanwhile had been trying to size up the dark, dishevelled, grubby-looking man hunched in front of her. His straight black hair was greasy and bedraggled. He looked in bad shape.

Their thoughts were interrupted by the guard. 'Someone else 'ere to see you.'

A tall serious man, with strong angular features, walked into the interview room.

'Mr Khan, I'm Chief Superintendent David Pryke, Detective Inspector Adams's boss.'

He sat next to DI Adams and nodded for her to start.

'I've looked at the Excel files on the memory stick. Your analysis is detailed. How many companies did you start with?' asked Kate.

'Seventy-six, which I whittled down to fourteen.'

'These were?'

'The companies in which Prima Terra had large stakes,' replied Rafi.

'How many companies did you find with a link between Prima Terra and unknown nominee shareholders?'

'Four,' he replied.

'What were the typical combined shareholding percentages?'

'Between 38% and 47%'

'Did you find other companies which had similar untraceable nominee shareholdings?'

'No.'

'As a fund manager, what would happen to your business if you were found to have breached the Blue Book, not once but four times?'

'A big corporate P45 served on us by the FSA and yourselves,' replied Rafi.

'Your analysis may lead to a dead end. It seems to us that the only explanation of why anyone would want you out of the way is if you were on to something,' observed DI Adams.

'If it's a dead end, we'll have no compunction to let MI5 loose on you again,' added CS Pryke, beckoning for one of those behind the one-way glass to join him.

Andy and Mike appeared at the door.

'I have a message from the commissioner. Could you ring his mobile? Here's his number,' said CS Pryke.

Andy took the piece of paper and they left.

CS Pryke said in a quiet voice, 'We're moving you to Wood Street police station to see if you can help us unravel this terrorist plot.'

Rafi could not believe what he'd heard. He suddenly felt light-headed.

Minutes later, Andy and Mike returned; they looked less than happy.

'I have made the call,' said Andy. 'Bugger me if I didn't find myself talking directly to the head of MI5.'

'Can you repeat what he had to say?' asked CS Pryke.

'We are to let you have Mr Khan and are to arrange for a van to be waiting in the rear car park.'

'You lucky little sod,' scowled Mike.

'Suppose you will want a blanket to cover Mr Khan's head?' said Andy as he left the room with Mike.

The chief superintendent turned to Kate. 'Time isn't on our side. Transporting Mr Khan in a police car or van would attract too much attention. Mr Khan, you'll be doing a switch with my driver. He'll be making the journey to MI5 headquarters. You will in reality be travelling to our police station, handcuffed in the boot of my car. Any complaints?'

Rafi shook his head, by now dumbfounded by the rapid change of events.

The chief superintendant turned to DI Adams. 'I'll leave with lights and sirens blaring, and go to MI5. I'll stay there for fifteen minutes and meet you back at Wood Street. A bit of a charade, but we can't let anyone guess what we're up to. Slip out quietly after I've left. I suggest you look like you're going off duty. Right, let's go.'

CS Pryke then hesitated but soon continued, 'Oh, sorry, I forgot to tell you part of the deal is that we get Jeremy Welby, an MI5 operative. He'll be responsible for making sure that the interrogations – sorry – interviews are done properly. Don't be fooled by his boyish looks. His CV is very impressive. If he isn't waiting for you in the car park, he'll no doubt turn up at Wood Street. Remember, we must keep Mr Khan off the radar screens. The fact that he's not at MI5 must remain our secret. Understood?'

'Yes, sir,' replied DI Adams.

Rafi was handcuffed and a blanket draped over his head. DI Adams led him to the rear car park. She opened the boot of CS Pryke's unmarked car. 'Climb in.'

Rafi did as he was told. He hated confined spaces, but this one he welcomed.

Away from prying eyes the blanket was put over CS Pryke's driver and the switch was made.

Part 2

Rafi was glad that he was only 5' 9" as it was a tight squeeze. His initial panic of being huddled into a small space had soon disappeared. The claustrophobic boot was definitely better than facing Mike and Andy.

Their arrival at the City of London police headquarters in Wood Street was low-key. Kate parked in the covered rear car park. Rafi was sound asleep when she opened the boot.

The rocking motion of the car had lulled him into a deep sleep. He heard a woman's voice saying, 'Wake up,' and felt his body being shaken and prodded.

'Christ, I thought you were unconscious and for a horrible moment that you'd been asphyxiated. Roll over and let me take your handcuffs off,' said Kate. 'In case you have any ideas let me point out that this is a secure compound. You are going to cooperate, aren't you?'

Rafi nodded. 'Sorry to have scared you,' he mumbled. 'I haven't had any sleep for a couple of days. I could have slept in a dustbin and not given it a second thought.'

With the blanket draped over his head, Rafi was hurried though the back door by Kate. They made their way up the back stairs to a modestly sized office on the fourth floor.

'This is where I work. Let me introduce you to Detective Constable Emma Jessop – my ever-helpful sidekick,' said Kate.

Rafi looked across the room and saw a beautiful woman sitting behind a computer screen. She had a mop of curly fair hair, light brown eyes and a disarming smile.

Kate surveyed Rafi carefully. 'First we need to get some ground rules sorted out. You are to remain with us until this is all over. You *will* keep a low profile. As far as everyone else is concerned, you're being held by MI5. In the meantime Emma and I will try and make your stay here as comfortable as possible.'

'Thank you,' Rafi replied.

'I think we need to get you cleaned up. A shower and a shave wouldn't go amiss,' said Kate.

Rafi stroked his left hand over the beginnings of a beard.

'Would you like a coffee and something to eat?' Emma asked.

'Yes please,' Rafi replied in a hoarse voice. 'And some water, please?'

Emma smiled, 'Thirsty, are we?'

Rafi nodded. He was badly dehydrated; he hadn't peed for probably twenty-four hours.

Emma left the room and returned a couple of minutes later with a bottle of chilled water and a can of cold Coke. 'I thought that this might keep you going.'

He was going to like working with Emma.

'What do I call you two?' Rafi asked.

The two women looked at each other and smiled.

'Kate and Emma would be fine, Mr Khan,' replied Kate.

'Rafi, please.'

'Done!'

The phone rang. Kate picked it up and listened intently.

'That was the commissioner. It seems Special Branch downstairs have found an eyewitness who was standing behind you in the queue at the cashpoint. She confirmed that you put your cash straight into your wallet. It seems she was amazed to see so much money coming out of the machine and didn't believe it would fit! Also, she overheard your conversation with the terrorist, during which you simply gave him directions and handed him his A to Z back. This substantiates your claim that you were an innocent bystander and therefore we are going to give you the benefit of the doubt and treat you as a colleague. MI5 have arranged for Jameel Furud to be put under surveillance.' Kate paused, then went on, 'Mr Kahn – sorry – Rafi, please use *only* those parts of the police station we tell you to. Be aware, if you are uncooperative we reserve the right to hand you back to MI5. Understood?'

Rafi nodded.

'That's settled then.' Kate left the room, leaving Rafi to enjoy his drink. He looked around his new surroundings and found them to be typical of an old style office building: plain and functional.

Kate returned clutching a pair of dark blue tracksuit trousers, some white jogging shorts, a pair of white socks and a Harlequins rugby shirt with the number 14 on the back.

'Best I could find but at least they're clean. I hope that they fit.' In her other hand was a large white towel and a bottle of shampoo. 'Sorry I couldn't lay my hands on a razor,' she added.

'Don't worry,' replied Rafi, 'my wrist isn't up to shaving.'

'Follow me,' said Kate.

Rafi was taken off to a utilitarian washroom with an adjoining shower cubicle. 'I'll come back and get you in fifteen minutes,' said Kate.

Rafi beckoned her to stay. 'Actually could I possibly have some help, please? I'm having problems getting my shirt off!'

'That's one of the worst chat-up lines I've ever heard,' Kate said with a smile.

Rafi hesitantly unbuttoned his shirt with his left hand and she helped him slide it off.

There was silence. She stood there, looking at his back. 'I'm sorry . . . I didn't realise. How the hell did you cope in the boot of the car? The bottom of your back looks as if it stopped a runaway train, and your shoulder is a hideous mixture of black and blue. Bloody hell, your arm looks awful too.'

'You should see my legs.'

'Don't tempt me!' Kate turned to leave. 'Please lock the door when I've gone.'

Rafi stepped slowly into the shower and stood under the flowing water, still holding the cold water bottle in his left hand. The warmth of the shower and the ice cold of the drinking water were pure bliss.

He had no idea how long he'd been there when there was a knock at the door. It was Kate. 'Can I come in?'

'Yes. Give me a moment.' At the third attempt he managed to wrap the towel around his waist with his left hand. He unlocked the door and stepped aside to let Kate in; she was clutching a first aid box.

'I thought this might come in handy. Your bruises look horrific, but I'm afraid there's not much I can do for them. She started to work on the grubby wet Elastoplast support. There was gauze underneath the sticky plaster bandage on his wrist, which made removing it an uncomplicated task. She cleaned his arm.

Kate considered the swelling; his wrist was at least twice its normal size. The angry colours of the bruise spread up his arm to his elbow and down to his fingertips. They matched the bruises on his shoulder, lower back and calf. She glanced at his wet hirsute chest. His physique, for a lightly built man, was very good, but – my God – he had taken a battering.

45

'Do you have any water left?'

He nodded.

'You might like to take a couple of these. They'll ease the pain.'

She carefully restrapped his wrist. There was no gauze in the first aid kit. She hoped she wouldn't be the one to take the sticky plaster off. 'Would you like a sling?'

Rafi shook his head. 'Thanks, but no thanks; I have some writing to do.'

Kate raised her eyebrows. 'Forgive me for asking, but how precisely do you propose to hold a pen?'

'With difficulty,' came the modest reply. 'Could I ask you a favour, please?' said Rafi.

Kate noticed he'd started to blush.

'I'm not very good at bending down at the moment and my right hand doesn't like gripping things. If I move over to a dry bit of the floor could you help me with my shorts and tracksuit trousers up to my knees?'

Kate pointed to a spot not two metres away.

Trousers and shorts in hand, Rafi walked slowly to the spot and dropped the two items of clothing on to the floor. It was a close-run thing between his towel unknotting and slipping down, and the shorts and trousers being pulled up.

Kate had to smile to herself. She liked what she saw, despite the bruises.

Minutes later Rafi was fully dressed, hair combed and looking and smelling like a normal human being. He ached all over and felt desperately tired, but was much better equipped to meet the world again.

Back in Kate and Emma's office he was shown to his desk. 'This part of the fourth floor is your home for the foreseeable future,' explained Kate. The Gents across the corridor is for now off bounds to the rest of the force here. That's as far as you can go, understood? If you need to go elsewhere, please ask.'

Rafi nodded.

Kate looked carefully at him. 'Giles, the commissioner, thinks it's best if your presence here remains our secret. Please bear in mind that Emma and I lost a good friend in the Bishopsgate bombing and our colleagues may not be as welcoming.' She hesitated, 'We look forward to your earnest cooperation.'

Rafi looked at Kate. 'I am so sorry about your colleague. Believe me, I want these bastards caught as much as you do.' He paused then continued, 'I need another favour, please.'

She looked a little nonplussed.

'On the basis of me being innocent, could you check that MI5 hasn't arrested my sister, and if they have arrange for her release.

'I'll ask Jeremy Welby to sort something out as soon as he gets here,' replied Kate.

'Thank you.'

Rafi was given a desk opposite Kate's. Across the room, to his left, was Emma and to his right there were a large whiteboard and a pair of empty desks positioned back-to-back. Scattered around the room were a number of filing cabinets and a networked printer next to Emma's desk. The room had a lived-in feel. Paperwork was every-where.

Kate looked across at Emma. 'I think we need to tidy up. Any empty filing cabinet drawers?'

Emma nodded. 'OK, let's collect all the paperwork that doesn't relate to this case and for the time being put it in the empty drawers.'

Fifteen minutes later the room had taken on a minimalist look.

'Nice work,' said Rafi to them both.

'Yep; now we can make a start by looking properly at your USB memory stick. But first let me tell you more about the team you'll be working with. This is Emma, who you have already met. She got a first in something or other highly numerical from Imperial College and is great at finding things out. Point her in the right direction and wait to see what she uncovers. She's our little Exocet missile. Before she joined us, she qualified as an accountant, so knows her way around things financial. Then we have Jeremy Welby who is being seconded here from MI5 to keep an eye on you and, no doubt, us and to help where he can, but otherwise I know very little about his previous experience.'

'It depends what you mean by experience,' said a masculine voice from the doorway. 'Mine's OK but I've recently spent far too much time undercover. My section commander Neil Gunton thought I might like a change of scene.' He paused, then continued, 'It seems that your commissioner pulled an impressive flanker on us to get our friend here sprung from Paddington Green.' Jeremy grinned and went on, 'A good move, no doubt. My instructions are simple: "Help them get whoever is behind the Bishopsgate bombing. Find out what they're up to next and please make certain that Mr Khan doesn't go missing." Neil has offered us whatever support we require because, in his words, "This is a joint venture." Basically, I'm here to help get to the bottom of what's going on.'

Kate looked at Jeremy. He was in his early thirties and in great shape; his handsome tanned face and his boyish good looks were emphasised by a strong jawline. She introduced Emma and herself. 'We're part of a specialist team that looks into major corporate and financial fraud. We tend to do the research side of things and from time to time are allowed out. We report to Detective Chief Superintendent David Pryke who's on his way back from MI5 headquarters, having given the press and anyone else interested in Mr Khan the runaround.'

'Sorry not to have been here sooner,' Jeremy hesitated as he decided how much to tell his new colleagues. 'I had a couple of matters to deal with after this morning's Joint Counter-Terrorism meeting. Mr Khan, you have split the group. The majority still think that you are part of an ITS and that you are still locked up at Paddington Green.'

'What do you mean by ITS?' enquired Rafi.

'Islamic Terrorist Syndicate – it's our catch-all phrase for Islamic groups hell-bent on terrorist activities in the pursuance of their fundamentalist ideals.'

Rafi nodded, 'Thank you.'

'As I was saying,' continued Jeremy, 'my boss Neil and I have been told by the head of MI5 to run with Rafi's line of thinking. The head of Five reckons there are inconsistencies that need investigating – quietly – off other people's radar screens. Neil's section and I have stuck our necks out on this one, so Mr Khan I look forward to you proving your doubters wrong!'

Jeremy stopped talking and looked around the room. 'How many people know that Mr Khan is here?'

'The three of us plus David, our boss, and Commissioner Giles Meynell,' replied Kate.

'Good. Let's keep it that way. My section is briefed and will be able to provide you with back-up.' Jeremy turned to Rafi. 'I look forward to hearing what you suspect is going on. By the way, you pissed off the two of my colleagues who interviewed you. It seems that you managed to evade their questioning for over sixty hours without any sleep and practically no food or water. I dropped by to see them before I got here and they looked absolutely knackered. They thought that they'd got you hook, line and sinker, and are – how can I put it? – in the doghouse. They'd never seen so much evidence stacked against a terrorist suspect and have the bugger slip through their fingers. I'm sorry for the harsh treatment the guards gave you.' Jeremy paused, 'It seems that you were set up good and proper.'

Jeremy looked at Rafi. 'Mr Khan I hope we can forget Paddington Green and focus on unravelling what the hell is going on.'

'Fine by me, but do call me Rafi – please.'

'Good; thank you,' said Jeremy. 'Kate what have you got planned first?'

'David should be back shortly. I suggest we then have a council of war to sort out our strategy. In the meantime I've asked Greg Thompson, our IT specialist, to pay us a visit to set up some more PCs. He should be with us any time now.'

As if on cue, Greg, a bespectacled thin man of indeterminate age, walked into the room. 'How can I help? I have arranged for extra networked desktops to be set up. Do you need anything else?'

'When you have a spare minute could you ring Ray Isles, our IT gatekeeper?' said Jeremy. 'And Kate, who would you like to have in the loop with my section at MI5?'

'Emma and me, please.'

'Greg, please chat to Ray and sort out the necessary encryption software so that they can read copies of my emails. Also, can you give him Kate's and Emma's mobile numbers?' Jeremy turned to Kate. 'I will run you through the text message codes which will alert you when an important email has been sent.' He turned to Greg. 'Ray is a bit sensitive when it comes to his security software. If he stalls you, tell him you have clearance from the top.' Jeremy smiled. 'You know how it is?'

Greg nodded. 'If that's all, I'll be off.'

As he was leaving the room, Kate turned to her team. 'Let's get started. I propose we get Rafi to give a short presentation on what he has found and believes is going on. How long will you need to pull your thoughts together?'

'Ten, maybe fifteen minutes should do,' came Rafi's hesitant reply.

'Excellent,' said Jeremy. 'It's rather nice working somewhere new. Oh, by the way, in the taxi I passed *Luigi's*, a small restaurant round the corner; it looked family run. Is it any good?'

'Yes, but we tend to use the canteen downstairs,' replied Kate.

'I've been living off cruddy food for the past eight weeks,' explained Jeremy, 'I could do with something to perk me up; if it's all right with you lot I'll nip out to see what they do. How about I put the first lot on my card and after that someone else can have a go?'

Everyone looked sheepish.

Rafi suspected that expenses for food weren't reclaimable. 'Does anyone know where my personal effects and wallet ended up?' he asked.

Kate looked at Rafi. 'We got you out of Paddington Green in a bit of a hurry. Sorry, I've no idea.'

'I've a suggestion,' Rafi continued. 'Could you get *Luigi's* to run a tab and as soon as I'm in the clear I'll pay the bill?'

'Great plan Rafi. I'm going to enjoy working here.' Jeremy looked delighted and was off out the door.

Kate and Emma were looking a little surprised and uncomfortable.

'I'm uncertain how to say this Rafi, but it doesn't seem fair,' said Kate.

'I could do with some good quality food, and I owe you for getting me out of that hellhole. Don't worry; I'm good for the money regardless. We're in the City, remember? "My word is my bond" and all that.'

Emma smiled. 'Most unusual, but thank you.'

The door swung open and Jeremy entered, acting like a conjuror who was about to pull a rabbit out of a hat. He was clutching three bags with *Luigi's* restaurant logo.

'Here we are! Sorry for the delay. Luigi is a great chap. We've lined up a tab with him and have put it in your name, Kate. I hope that's in order. Seems the guys downstairs were helpful when someone tried to break into his restaurant several months back. He's very pleased to help in any way, any time of day. Who's for coffee? I got cappuccinos and some pizza . . . Help yourselves!'

The two women looked at the pizza and hesitated, thinking of the calories, then grinned at each other.

'I should tuck in, you don't know when we'll next have time for a break,' said Jeremy. He looked at his watch with a smile, 'Or even time for a meal!'

Rafi sat savouring the food and drink.

'Now that Jeremy's back and Rafi has done his thinking, let's get started,' said Kate. 'First question: how does the Bishopsgate bombing fit in with your theory of what is going on?'

'I'm not entirely certain,' replied Rafi, 'but my gut feeling is that it was meant to be part of a bigger plan. My other thought is that it was in the heart of the City so perhaps it was designed to heighten tension.'

'So you believe that the bombing will be followed up by another?' asked Emma.

Rafi nodded and looked at Emma wishing he'd more understanding of what was really going on. 'Yes, my hunch is that they'll be targeting the weakened financial markets, but at this point in time I too am working in the dark as to what exactly they might be planning.'

'OK,' said Kate, 'let's come back to how Bishopsgate fits in in due course. What else do we have?'

'The spreadsheets,' said Emma.

'I am sure that Callum Burns was on to something in Luxembourg and his crash was no accident. Why go to such trouble if all you're up to is price fixing. I reckon that this is just the tip of the iceberg. I suggest we need to work out why they were using the clandestine nominee names in just the four companies, and see where that leads us.' Rafi told them about Callum's concerns, then shuffled off to the whiteboard and gingerly picked up a felt-tip pen. 'What we could do, first of all, is look at the exact role that the four companies might play.'

He wrote on the board the names and a short description of each of them. It was slow progress, though, because his hand ached like hell.

The first company he wrote down was very familiar to him. The others weren't, as his funds weren't invested in them.

Renshaw Smithers: a small financial intermediary – a deal maker focusing on public sector projects and outsourcing companies.

Unicorn Sceptre Finance: poor quality credit providers; focuses on students.

Dewoodson: property services company; includes a chartered surveying arm.

ESSA: executive search and selection agency; with executive placement and corporate PR divisions.

Rafi's hand ached.

Emma looked at him. 'How about I do the writing for you from now on?'

Rafi smiled and nodded.

'If one adds together Prima Terra's and the unknown nominee holdings, how large are the combined shareholdings?' asked Emma.

'Between 38% and 47%' replied Rafi.

Emma scratched her head. 'The Stock Exchange Blue Book states that shareholders acting in concert with more than 30% of a company must bid for the whole company.'

'Precisely, which is presumably why they've gone to the trouble of concealing their stakes through clandestine offshore nominee names,' said Rafi.

'Surely someone would blow the whistle?' said Kate.

'Let's say that the company and its registrars were sold a good story about changes to the nominee names management businesses and were happy that nothing untoward was going on – I don't see why it should come up on the radar screen. If you look at the long list of shareholders and the vast array of nominee names, only a very diligent analyst like Callum Burns might spot something odd going on. The story is that the ultimate investors are major European fund management groups who changed their nominee name management business when they moved their funds to Luxembourg,' said Rafi.

'Perhaps the executive directors were happy with these shareholders?' suggested Kate.

'Surely,' said Emma, 'the question is why do they only have huge shareholdings in these four companies and why don't the dubious nominee names show up in any of the other listed companies Rafi looked at?'

'Perhaps they're after making money on a takeover,' suggested Kate.

'I've thought of that one. The rewards don't seem to justify the risks,' said Rafi.

'And surely they'd get caught when the payouts were made and the FSA cast its eye over things.'

'Good point Kate,' said Emma. 'How's about they want to influence the board of directors and use the company for something?'

'Oh hell! Why didn't I think of that? But what use might these companies have?' added Rafi.

'That's precisely what we hope you'll help us find out,' said Kate. 'Emma could you research what each company does? Basic stuff at this point I suggest.'

'I know Renshaw Smithers and its activities very well, but next to nothing about the other three companies,' said Rafi, 'perhaps you could concentrate on them and I'll do a short summary of the bank's activities.'

'Will do,' said Emma.

'Next on our list we can add the people and businesses Callum visited in Luxembourg. According to his office he visited CPR Investment Funds run by Hubert Vynckt, a couple of tax lawyers, a REIT and had a fifth meeting in the afternoon with a tax specialist, I think. The REIT is a friend, I think, but I reckon one or more of the others may be dodgy,' said Rafi.

'Anything else?' asked Emma.

Rafi thought for a moment. 'I've one other thought, purely on a hunch and totally off the wall, but it's about the way I was treated at Paddington Green.'

Jeremy raised his eyebrows, but didn't interrupt.

'Well, whereas my two interrogators were,' Rafi paused, 'belligerent and aggressive, they were professionals. It's just that the BlueKnite guards and caterers seemed to have it in for me – the way they went about things seemed over the top – it's probably nothing, though.'

'We'll bear that in mind,' said Jackie. 'You look dead on your feet. Perhaps after a short nap, you'll be able to get your mind into gear?'

Rafi nodded.

'OK, follow me.'

She led him down to the basement cells, with the blanket over his head. She picked up a second blanket and a pillow and ushered him into a cell.

'Not five-star accommodation, but at least it's quiet. I'll come and get you in a couple of hours. I'm sorry but I need to lock you in, otherwise the duty policeman might investigate.' The door swung shut behind her.

Rafi smiled. And a few seconds after his head hit the pillow, he was out. The next thing he knew, Kate was standing over him.

'Come on sleepyhead, time to get going.'

He followed her back to the office. A cup of black coffee was waiting there for him.

'How goes it?' Rafi asked Emma.

'Give me a few minutes and I'll show you where I've got to. We're running through our strategy in a meeting with David, Jeremy and Kate in fifteen minutes' time.'

'OK here's what I've done so far,' continued Emma. 'I've been looking for links. Renshaw Smithers: their new private finance initiative and public private partnerships projects teams were head-hunted by ESSA. It says so on their website. As far as Unicorn Sceptre Finance and Dewoodson are concerned, I'm still working on them. I'm afraid it's been slow progress.'

'Keep going,' said Rafi, 'I'm sure something will start to gel.'

'I've been considering the nominee names,' said Kate. 'Why are you so sure that they're run out of Luxembourg?'

'That's what Callum said the company registrars told him,' said Rafi.

Emma thought for a moment, 'Why don't we pick up the phone and speak to the registrars of the four companies?'

'Yes, but,' said Rafi, 'how can we be sure that someone won't report our enquiries to their terrorist masters? Look what happened to Callum. At the moment, the terrorists don't know we're on to them.

And I'm not keen for them to find out.' After a short pause he continued, 'Would it be possible for me to be kept up to date with the movements of a person?'

Jeremy put his head up. 'Who do you want to know about?'

'Jameel Furud,' Rafi replied. 'He left for Paris last Friday morning and is staying at a smart hotel until tomorrow. I'd love to know whether he's coming back into the UK or whether he is going to prolong his holiday. I'd put good money on him moving to a country where the extradition treaties are less than easy to enforce. And can you see if he's by himself? If you take me out of the picture as the prime suspect, I reckon Jameel steps in to fill the gap.'

'Leave it with me,' said Jeremy. 'I'll find out the latest. Last I heard he was being put under surveillance.'

Just then David arrived and Kate called the group to order. 'OK, where have we got to?'

Emma ran through what they'd been discussing.

'Rafi, do you have anything to add?'

'Only that my sixth sense tells me that time is running out.'

'Thank you for that,' said David. 'We know that there's a large jigsaw puzzle and we're missing a lot of pieces. I'd encourage you to embrace lateral thinking. And, Rafi, you should think carefully if anything else could have been a catalyst for Jameel and his associates wanting you out of the way. Could you be back here for a 7 a.m. start, please? I've got to go now. I'll see you tomorrow.'

Rafi smiled to himself. David had such a nice way of giving orders.

Kate received a phone call from reception. 'Anyone expecting a delivery?' she called out. 'It's in reception and I'm told you'll need a helper.'

'Oh, good,' said Jeremy. 'It's for us – a spot more food from *Luigi's*.'

'A spot more food' turned out to be an understatement. When Rafi saw the spread, he turned to Jeremy. 'This is more like it.' Since he had started working in the City, such events had ceased to surprise Rafi. To him it seemed that everything was on tap to help lubricate the wheels of finance and commerce twenty-four hours a day. Emma and Kate, on the other hand, looked a little taken aback.

They ate as they worked. Rafi and Emma focused on the four companies. They made some progress but couldn't piece anything together which might help point the investigation in the right direction. They looked at the board of directors, downloaded the company accounts and supporting documents and trawled through their websites.

By 12.30 a.m. Rafi's head had had enough. He needed to stop and was discretely shown to a cell by Kate. 'See you tomorrow morning. I'll bring you a toothbrush.'

'Thanks.'

Tuesday had been a gruelling day, but at least he was away from Paddington Green. Sleep came easily for Rafi.

He awoke to find Kate standing beside him. 'Good morning. I hope you had a good sleep?'

'Fantastic. I still ache all over, but I'm feeling a hundred times better than yesterday. I can't wait to say goodbye to this hard bed, though!'

It was 7.05 a.m. when Rafi entered the fourth floor office. Emma and Jeremy were hard at work. At 7.15 a.m. coffee and bacon croissants arrived from *Luigi's* together with fresh orange juice.

Emma looked at Jeremy and asked, 'Is the food always like this at MI5?'

'It would be if I had anything to do with it,' said Jeremy. 'I was starved of an edible diet for eight weeks working undercover. I thought Rafi and I should catch up.'

The whiteboard had been wiped clean. Rafi's scribbles from the previous evening had been removed.

'I hope you don't mind, Rafi. We decided on a colour-coding system: red for – important, blue for – it could be relevant and black for – background information thought to be of minor significance. A green circle means it needs following up,' said Emma with a smile.

On the whiteboard, written in red, were the names of the four companies which Prima Terra and unknown others effectively controlled. The activity of each was abbreviated to a couple of words as an aide-memoir.

Kate looked across at Rafi and asked, 'Why do you think that time is against us and that worse is still to come?'

'In part it's just a gut feeling and in part it's to do with the nature of the markets Jameel and I work in. I've £4 billion of funds under my discretionary control and Jameel has almost twice that. To Jameel, dealing with very large sums of money is second nature. Prima Terra, under the stewardship of Jameel, has invested in four companies with market capitalisations from £10 to £400 million. These aren't vast sums in terms of takeover plays. In my professional view these companies aren't the sort that others would pursue or wish to buy. Therefore, it *has* to be something that the companies do, or something they have that Jameel and his colleagues need as part of their game plan.'

Jeremy, who had been very quiet, sitting at his desk finishing off his second croissant, put his hand up and said, 'Excuse me? These moneys you have – they're not yours, are they?'

'No,' Rafi replied.

'What's to stop you flushing the lot down the pan? If you're a terrorist, you don't go around making things better, you do the opposite; particularly if you're playing with someone else's money!'

Rafi looked at him. He'd stated the bloody obvious. He wished he'd thought of it first. 'Thanks, I reckon you've got something there.'

'Let's look at the four listed companies from that perspective,' said Kate.

Emma stood, pen in hand, by the whiteboard.

Rafi started the ball rolling. 'Renshaw Smithers are specialists in finding financial backers for Government-backed projects like new hospitals, prisons and schools, and they are a big lender to businesses that provide the outsourcing services to these Government-funded schemes.'

'If this company suddenly became insolvent, what would happen?' asked Kate.

'I'm not certain,' Rafi replied. 'It depends on how much impact it would have on the PFI and PPP sectors. If it caused some of those providing outsourcing services to go under, then a large number of hospitals, prisons and schools could stop functioning.'

Jeremy whistled.

Kate looked across at Rafi. 'That sounds ominous. So, how does Unicorn Sceptre Finance fit in?'

'It's a small business,' said Emma. 'They lend money to students and people with poor quality credit ratings. If it went bust, surely it wouldn't be much of a problem in the scale of things?'

'Could it be a front for lending money cheaply to a select group of students, for example, to the bomber Imaad Wafeeq and others like him?' asked Jeremy.

'Possibly,' nodded Kate.

'Dewoodson are property consultants; heaven only knows why they want property expertise?' said Kate.

'If you look at ESSA, they're a leading executive search company; they've an excellent list of blue chip clients,' said Emma.

'Being cynical, could they be used to get bent ringers into key positions in companies they need for some specific purpose?' asked Jeremy.

'If they used a dodgy international bank to sort out the bungs,' said Rafi, 'it would be an ideal way to pay the people put in place by ESSA to do the terrorists' dirty work!'

Jeremy's phone rang. He listened intently, put the phone down, got up and with a red pen added Marrakech next to Jameel's name. 'If I wanted to go somewhere safe as a Muslim, Morocco would be an excellent choice. Jameel has booked a ten-day stay at a luxury five-star golf hotel on the edge of the city where he is scheduled to arrive later this morning. We've sent a colleague to keep an eye on him and to report back should he meet anyone.'

'I thought he'd do a runner,' said Rafi smiling.

'One question,' said Emma. 'How long do we think that the share stake-building exercise has been going on?'

'I remember the Dewoodson's IPO,' said Rafi.

'What?' asked Jeremy.

'Sorry, initial public offering; when a company raises money from the market. It was eighteen months ago. Prima Terra picked up its stake in the company at the flotation.'

Jeremy grimaced.

'What's wrong?' asked Kate.

'That's bad news. In my book any bad guy who plans something for a couple of years is definitely up to no good. We're up against a very well-planned plot, whatever it might be.'

Rafi sat there, thinking about what Jeremy had just said. Then, as if from nowhere, an associated thought flashed through his mind. He was gobsmacked.

'Are you feeling ill?' asked Emma.

'Er . . . No, I just remembered an IPO launch I attended a few weeks ago and an incident that completely slipped my mind. Please bear with me for a moment,' Rafi began hesitantly. 'Let me try and recall it. It may seem like a shaggy-dog story, but it's relevant, I'm sure.'

Rafi closed his bloodshot eyes and took his mind back to the bright January morning a few weeks earlier. 'It was a Wednesday, three weeks ago. I'd had a hectic morning. The market was buoyant. I had lunch scheduled with a bank and some brokers who were launching an IPO. It was a normal sell-side promote. I was running late and took a taxi. It dropped me a couple of minutes' walk away from their smart new office building on the South Bank; a stunning development scheme. Great attention to detail: black granite walkways, fountains for children to play in and even a small "Pooh sticks" stream which flows down the middle of the walkway to Tooley Street, almost 400 yards away. Sorry; I digress.'

Rafi paused to collect his thoughts. 'After the short presentations, the cheeky beggars pushed through lunch at a cracking pace, as they were running two sittings. At 1.15 p.m. I was politely offered my coat and a couple of minutes later I was standing in front of the building feeling rather pissed off. My nice lunch had turned into a fast food experience. I stood there, taking in the view across the Thames. It was a lovely afternoon; the winter sun was out and London looked great, so as I wasn't expected back in the office before 2.30, I decided to stretch my legs and walk back to the office rather than take a taxi.'

Rafi smiled. 'I set off towards Tower Bridge, along the river walkway past the London Assembly Building.'

'Is that the one with the unfortunate nickname relating to a part of the male anatomy?' enquired Jeremy.

'Yes,' Rafi replied, 'a singularly imposing building,' he paused. 'I then made my way up the distinct granite steps of Tower Bridge. By the time I reached the far side, the cold wind had got to me. I considered wimping out and take a taxi back to the office, but eventually opted for the exercise and turned down the steps that cut under the bridge, went past Dead Man's Gate and headed out into the sunshine past the Tower of London. Whoops, sorry I'm rambling again.'

'Don't worry. As long as you remember something useful we don't mind if you ramble on a bit,' said Kate reassuringly.

'I continued my stroll and headed along Lower Thames Street. I crossed the road and walked up St Mary at Hill then turned into a narrow cobbled street – St Dunstan's Lane. What prompted me to go that way, I don't know. Perhaps it was because I was enjoying my amble and the lane, with its cobbled surface, looked quaint. It was an impulse. On the corner where St Dunstan's Lane turns into Idol Lane there was a delivery van blocking the single carriageway.' Rafi paused again. 'Behind it, fifty metres up Idol Lane, was a chauffeur-driven Mercedes facing me, with its door open waiting for someone to come out of a building.'

Rafi stopped; time seemed to stand still. He stared towards the printer to the right of Emma's desk. It all came flooding back as if it were an action replay. He continued with his story. 'I walked around the corner behind the parked lorry and reappeared just in time to see someone getting into the car facing me. The person looked familiar. At that precise moment the lorry driver leant out of his window and called to me. I turned and walked back towards him. He wanted to know where the nearest McDonald's was. I apologised, saying that I didn't know, but thought that there was one in Cannon Street and pointed to the end of the road. He thanked me and drove off.'

Rafi's eyes widened. 'As the lorry left, it was followed by the Mercedes; no wonder the person in the car had looked familiar: it was Jameel! I smiled at him and our eyes met fleetingly but he didn't acknowledge me. At the time I assumed that he was engrossed in his work. What must it have looked like to my boss? One moment I was there, the next I had hidden behind the lorry. He couldn't have known I was speaking to the driver.'

'It would have looked suspicious,' said Emma, 'like you didn't want to be seen.'

'So what did you do next?' asked Kate.

'I walked to the top of the Lane and passed by the building Jameel had come out of. It was nondescript, with the numbers 2-4 on a plain dark blue front door. There was nothing to give away who or what was based there. At the time I wondered who Jameel had been seeing but, as I didn't think it was important, I dismissed the thought and carried on back to the office,' said Rafi.

'Anything else?' asked Kate.

'That's it,' said Rafi, looking up at his audience. 'Sorry it took a while to get to the punchline. Could my spotting Jameel doing something he wanted to keep secret have triggered his interest in me, particularly if he thought I was spying on him? What do you think?'

Emma looked up. 'Rafi, did he look sheepish when he left the building in Idol Lane?'

'No, just businesslike.'

'I think I should get a list of all the occupiers,' said Emma. 'You can then see if any ring a bell. I'll nip downstairs and raid our database.'

'Good idea,' said Kate.

A short while later Emma returned looking rather pleased with herself; she walked confidently up to Rafi's desk and handed him three sheets of paper.

'Here is the list of occupiers for Idol Lane. Bit of a rabbit warren down there. In case your boss was visiting someone nearby, I took the liberty of checking the adjoining streets as well,' said Emma.

'Thanks.' Rafi was impressed. He liked the way Emma worked. He scanned the list at speed, a skill he developed at work, honed by going through piles of brokers' reports, newspapers and journals every day.

The knack was to skim through the material looking for something out of the ordinary. Most of the material that passed over his desk was either a regurgitation of known facts, or a relatively standard analysis thereof. What he looked for was new information, something different, something that stood out. On finding such an item he would take the trouble of thoroughly reading it and carefully assimilating its contents.

Rafi continued his scanning. He was two thirds down the second sheet when he came across a company name he recognised but couldn't immediately place: AGVC Ltd. The initials look very familiar. He highlighted it, paused and carried on to the end of the third and last page.

He went back to the beginning of the first sheet and started reading the names of the occupiers again. Nothing untoward stood out on page one; there were some well-known names, but none he could link to his boss. Rafi moved on to page two and to AGVC Ltd. He looked at the initials and wondered why they were familiar, particularly in the context of his boss – where had he come across them before?

His memory was working overtime. From the dim and distant past he recalled meeting the managing director of AGVC at a company function. It must have been about three years ago. Rafi racked his brain, trying to remember where it was and who had invited him from Prima Terra.

'Emma!' he called across to her with more than a little anticipation in his voice. 'I've a company I could do with you researching, please.'

'Thank God,' muttered Kate. 'I was beginning to wonder whether we were chasing shadows.'

'Emma, could you find out what AGVC does, please? And could you get me a large-scale map which shows exactly where their offices are?'

Only a few minutes later she had the information up on her screen. 'Right, here goes. AGVC – business type: venture capital company and financiers. Any good?'

'Bingo,' said Rafi. 'That's what I was hoping for.'

'They're located halfway down on the left-hand side of St Mary at Hill.'

'Hold on a moment,' said Kate, 'I thought you said you saw Jameel in Idol Lane?'

Rafi looked at her slightly crestfallen. 'Good memory,' he said looking at Kate approvingly. 'Yes, you're right.'

Emma smiled. 'No problem, the two properties back on to each other.'

'Excellent! Who are the occupiers of 2–4 Idol Lane?'

'Rainer Spencer and Mitchell,' answered Emma. 'Says here that they're chartered accountants and company secretaries.'

'What's the link?' said Kate.

At that moment someone on high must have been smiling on Emma. Breakthroughs come about in mysterious ways and her answer to Kate's question, unbeknown to the team, would propel them forward.

'Link?' said Emma. 'If the buildings were physically linked or interconnected this would allow Jameel to keep his visits to AGVC's offices secret. Shall we see if the two buildings are in the same ownership?' Emma's fingers worked quickly over her keyboard. 'Right, I'm into the Land Registry website; let's take a look at AGVC's offices first. The address and postcode?' Before anyone could answer, Emma had cut and pasted the information into the Land Registry boxes. 'Oh dear, not much help: the freehold is owned by British & Scottish Property Company.'

'A major London listed property company,' Rafi chipped in.

'Hold on a minute,' said Emma. 'I shouldn't have been too hasty. There seems to be a long leasehold interest in the property owned by a company called PREH.'

'OK, what about the building next to it in Idol Lane,' said Kate.

'Would you believe it; it's owned by PREH as well.'

'That's fantastic, so they *are* connected.' Kate was standing behind Emma, and gave her a friendly pat on the back and then did the same to Rafi.

He almost jumped out of his skin. 'Ooouch!' he exclaimed.

'Whoops, sorry,' said Kate. 'I forgot your bumps and bruises.'

It was now 2.05.p.m. on the Wednesday afternoon. Kate had a smile on her face. 'At last we've got something concrete to go on and three more businesses to research: AGVC, a venture capital company; Rainer Spencer & Mitchell, a firm of chartered accountants and company secretaries, and the property company PREH. Let's see what we can find on these organisations and their directors and partners. Emma and Rafi, can you trawl the web and do detailed Companies House searches on their accounts, shareholders, etc.? See how quickly you can get a picture of these businesses. Jeremy and I'll look into the individuals involved and get as much as we can from the tax people.'

'I've a suggestion,' said Rafi. 'How's about we find out as much as possible on the private companies AGVC is financing. I reckon it'll be one or more of these that will be of interest and not the company itself.'

'Got that,' said Kate.

'Bloody hell,' Rafi blurted out. 'Sorry,' he said, looking around.

'Never mind me,' said Kate.

'I've just remembered where I know AGVC from. The boss there, Basil Tatall – no – Dr Basel Talal,' Rafi corrected himself, 'did his PhD at the London College of Finance with my boss. I met Dr Talal several years ago, when Jameel invited me to a finance talk at the college. I was introduced briefly. But it was only when one of their contemporaries turned up that I found out they'd been fellow students.'

'That's interesting,' mused Kate.

'It could be that they were two university friends meeting for a chat and nothing more than that,' said Rafi.

'Or equally that he was visiting the occupiers of 2-4 Idol Lane on an unrelated matter to what we are investigating,' said Emma.

'But something triggered Jameel's distrust of Rafi and this is the best we've got, so let's run with it and see where it takes us,' suggested Kate.

Jeremy strode back into the room. 'Sorry to have deserted you. I've been liaising with my MI5 colleagues. They're expecting another series of bombings. The consensus of opinion is that the target will be a transport hub. Security levels have been increased and leave has been cancelled. Rafi, they still think you're a bit of a red herring. Talking of food,' said Jeremy, 'would you like a cake?' The food had arrived fifteen minutes earlier and been put on the top of a couple of filing cabinets next to Kate where it had been forgotten.

Jeremy tucked in. 'Yum, I must give Luigi a ring and thank him.' Emma looked across at Kate and smiled. She was about to add something when Jeremy caught her look. 'If you'd spent two months living off Pot Noodles and black coffee . . .'

'Sorry, I forgot,' apologised Emma.

'Jeremy, I'd like you and one of my colleagues to visit the London College of Finance and ask about two doctors: Jameel Furud and Basel Talal,' said Kate.

'You mean, what are a couple of medics doing at a finance college?' joked Jeremy with a schoolboy grin.

'Ha, ha. No. They were former students. That's where they got their PhDs, their doctorates,' replied Kate. 'It would be helpful to know when they were there, the names of their close friends, the titles of their PhD theses, etc. See if there's anyone who studied with them still living in London. I'll ask the commissioner to smooth your path,' said Kate.

Emma, on the ball as ever, found the vice chancellor's address and that of the administration department. She walked over to the printer, collected the sheet and passed it to Jeremy.

'Who's coming with me and which car can I borrow, please?' he asked Kate.

'Oops, I forgot to chat to John from the Special Branch,' replied Kate. She picked up the phone. 'Hi John,' she said in a friendly tone, 'would you have a spare moment? I need some help, please. We've unearthed something that has a direct bearing on the Bishopsgate bombing. I could do with a seasoned brain to give Jeremy Welby, our MI5 friend, a hand. Yes . . . Yes, I know you're very busy and dislike spooks.'

She paused and listened. 'Yes, I appreciate everyone thinks it's going to hit the fan. We've come up with an angle which may open up a whole new dimension. I need *your* input and not that of a sidekick, please. Fantastic, thanks. Jeremy's on his way down to the car park. Is your car there? Excellent. He knows where you're going and will brief you on the way. I owe you.'

Kate looked across to Jeremy. 'Your chauffeur awaits downstairs. Detective Chief Inspector John Dowsing has volunteered to drive you and to work with you. He can be a bit of a gruff bugger, but he's got a great nose for information and has a good sense of humour once you get to know him.' She smiled. 'One other thing, Jeremy. Rafi reckons that time is of the essence. Please keep in touch. Don't take no for an answer and if possible be back asap.'

Jeremy nodded and left.

'Let's see what we can dig up and reconvene at, say, 5 p.m.,' said Kate. 'I'll book a slot with David and the commissioner for later this evening. They're keen to be kept up to date and we need their goodwill.'

'This Rainer Spencer & Mitchell lot keeps a low profile for a firm of chartered accountants,' observed Emma. 'It's only got eighteen mentions on Google, the sum total of which is next to nothing. It makes me think that they're either very secretive or look after a very select client base.'

'That could fit in nicely with the activities of AGVC,' commented Rafi.

Emma got into the Companies House online database.

Rafi wondered what their searches would reveal – for all British companies, there are pieces of information that have to be put into the public domain: the name and address of each director, each shareholder and the company secretary; its accounts and a register of all properties with a legal charge over them, all of which have to be filed at Companies House.

It transpired that PREH and AGVC were the acronyms for Prime Real Estate Holdings, and Acorn Growth Venture Capital. Emma downloaded the .pdf files for their accounts, annual returns and mortgage register, and printed them out.

None of names of the directors except for Dr Basel Talal looked familiar to Rafi, though he noted that Talal was a director of both companies. The company secretary wasn't a person but a company – CGF Company Secretaries Ltd.

Rafi called across to Emma. 'We've got another company to look at: a specialist company secretarial business.' In less than ten minutes Emma had downloaded the documents, printed them and passed them to Rafi.

'What are you looking for?' she enquired.

'Anything would do!' he replied cheerfully. 'First of all, let's see whether CGF Company Secretaries Ltd is involved with the property company PREH. Look at this! It is!'

'Who are the directors of CGF Company Secretaries?' asked Kate.

'Christopher Rainer, George Spencer, and Frank Mitchell.' Emma beamed. 'Well I'd be damned; we have Messrs Rainer Spencer & Mitchell operating in another guise.'

'Emma,' said Rafi. 'I've found next to nothing on the venture capital company – AGVC. It seems as if they and the companies they have invested in are *very* low profile. I've had a thought – what if *all* the companies that AGVC has funded use the same company secretary to look after their corporate paperwork? It's a long shot, but it would enable them to keep an eye on their investments, and they *are* next door.'

'Yep. It's worth a try,' said Emma.

'Could you use your influence and get Companies House to give us a list of all the companies for whom CGF is the company secretary?' Rafi asked.

'And we could include any other companies that Basel Talal and his fellow directors are involved in,' said Emma.

She was on to Companies House straight away.

It was just after 3 p.m. Rafi wondered why he kept looking at the clock. It was as if his subconscious sensed they were working to a strict deadline.

Emma was speaking to a helpful data manager at Companies House.

'I'm glad there shouldn't be any problems.' She switched on the speakerphone. 'How long will it take?'

'Usually seventy-two hours to process such a request.'

'What? Seventy-two hours?'

'Yes and could you please put your request in writing?'

'Couldn't you do it quicker? Time is of the essence at this end – we need the information as of now!' asked Emma.

Silence.

'As I said, please put it in writing and I'll ring you to discuss how quickly we could get this done.'

'Your fax number, please?'

Emma put a hand over the phone and called across to Kate, 'Could you put some headed paper in the printer tray, please?' Meanwhile Emma's fingers were flying over her keyboard. Typing, cutting and pasting the information into a letter.

'Could I have your name and address, please?'

'Arnold Owen, Manager, Data Handling, Companies House, Crown Way, Cardiff.'

'Yes . . . Excellent.' Seconds later the printer whirred. 'Kate, be a darling,' said Emma. 'Sign the letter and fax it off.'

'OK, Mr Owen, I'd be grateful if you'd go over to your fax machine and collect the fax that's coming out. Thank you,' said Emma.

Less than a minute later Mr Owen was back on the phone. 'Thank you; I have your wish list in my hand.'

'Mr Owen, I've got a favour to ask: my boss is leaning on me and I'm against a deadline of er . . . this evening. I'm sorry, were you about to go home?' asked Emma. 'We could do with your help.'

'Could I let you have the information first thing tomorrow morning?'

'I'm afraid that may be too late. We could do with your help now. Please, don't hang up.'

The phone went dead.

'Oh bugger I lost him. I bet the little sod has just gone home early.' Emma was furious.

'I'll need to pull rank,' she continued. 'Is the boss in?'

'No. He'll be back at 4-ish – in twenty minutes – I think,' said Kate.

Emma got up to vent her frustration on someone or something. As she was going out of the door, her phone rang. She scampered back to her desk. It was the Welsh tones of Mr Owen on the other end. Emma sat down, visibly relieved.

'How nice to hear from you, Mr Owen.'

'Please call me Arnold. Sorry to have hung up; I needed to make a call. I was meant to be taking my granddaughter out for a birthday treat. I've arranged to be at her party later. Now, about that information you need . . .'

'You'd make a good policeman,' said Emma.

'Funny you should say that; three years ago I took early retirement after twenty-five years of service.'

'In strictest confidence, could you please do a search for companies which use CGF Company Secretaries?' requested Emma. 'And then pull off copies of the accounts, annual returns and mortgage registers for the companies that show up on this list. And lastly, could you do the same for Basel Talal and his co-directors in AGVC?'

She thought she heard a muffled 'Oh hell, why today?' at the other end.

'If you let me have your email address, I'll start pushing things through the system at my end. Probably best if I send the files through in batches as and when I have them. It'll give you something to work on sooner rather than later,' said Arnold.

'By the way,' said Emma, 'when you're next in London do drop in to say hello. I owe you a drink, or make that a lunch with your granddaughter.'

Kate came off the phone and walked over to the printer to gather up the paper that had been billowing out of it for the past few minutes. The tax office had emailed through most of the requested information on the venture capital company, PREH, and the partnership of Rainer Spencer & Mitchell, and were now working on CGF Company Secretaries. The material contained a summary of their business activities, their accounts and such bank account details as they had. MI5 had also been busy and had sent through what they had on Basel Talal and his co-directors, and had placed the partners of Rainer Spencer & Mitchell under surveillance.

At 4.13 p.m. the first email came through from Arnold. It comprised a list of twenty-seven companies that used CGF Company Secretaries. 'Oh flaming heck!' said Emma. 'We're suckers for punishment. When we said we wanted information to get our teeth into we didn't bargain on this amount. This is bloody unreal.'

This was followed a few minutes later by the name of one further company where Dr Talal was a director.

Arnold came on the phone to Emma. The speakerphone was switched on. 'Were you expecting so many companies?'

'Unfortunately, no!'

'Well I've some good news for you. If one whittles out the dormant companies and those which have as yet to trade, it reduces the numbers to ten for CGF Company Secretaries and one for the directors. Oh, and could I ask a favour?' said Arnold.

'What is it?' said Emma.

'I'd hoped to get home at some stage. You see, like I mentioned before, it's my granddaughter's eighth birthday party this afternoon. If I could let you have the files for these eleven companies and then disappear off for a while, it would be most appreciated. I'll come back to work after I've given her her present. I can then check that there's nothing out of the ordinary with the other companies.'

'No problem,' said Emma, 'you're giving us lots to work on. Thanks for your assistance.'

'I'd normally say no problem,' said Arnold, 'but today your timing is terrible. You might like to take down my private mobile number, just in case.'

Emma scribbled down the number and thanked him again for his help.

'I've brought forward the meeting with David and the commissioner to 5.30 p.m.' said Kate. 'Let's see what we can deliver that's concrete. What we need is an overview of the companies that the venture capital company is supporting and hopefully Jeremy and John will have something to report from their meeting at the college.'

Rafi made a list of the companies that used CGF Company Secretaries Ltd; his wrist still ached like hell, but the painkillers made it bearable. He wondered how many were funded by AGVC Ltd – the venture capital company. If their hunch proved right, it would be one hell of a breakthrough. He frowned as he looked at the eclectic list on the whiteboard:

SPAD Ltd	Security Protection & Defence Company
UKSOIL Ltd	UK Students Overseas Initiative Live
HFFF Ltd	Hotel Frozen Fish Foods
PSSAF Ltd	Public Sector Services and Facilities
AEIEA Ltd	African Estonian Import / Export Agency

PREH plc	Prime Real Estate Holdings
CCVH Ltd	Central City View Hotels
SJFR Ltd	Small Joe's Fish Restaurants
CDAFO Ltd	Commercial Development & Fit Out
AGVCFoF	Acorn Growth Venture Capital Fund of Funds*

Rafi was working on AGVC when Kate called across. 'Have you had a chance to look at the mortgage registers?'

'Sorry, not yet; I'll get on to them now.'

Emma meanwhile had gathered together several piles of paper and stacked them neatly along Jeremy's and the adjoining desk, and was sorting through the pile of faxes Kate had received.

Kate's phone rang. It was the commissioner's personal assistant, Beverley. 'Thought you might like to know that Giles and David are back in the building; you can expect them in the next couple of minutes.'

'Thanks, Beverley.'

In the few moments before the bosses arrived, Rafi was frantically trying to get up to speed with the mortgage registers. AGVC, according to its accounts, owned no property. PREH – the property company – was a different matter. The list of addresses on its mortgage register ran to three pages. Rafi was starting to enjoy himself. He liked working under pressure, especially when he felt he was making progress. The room had a familiar buzz to it and felt like his office in the middle of a takeover battle.

Rafi looked at the addresses; they were a mix in terms of locations. He spotted the Idol Lane and St Mary at Hill, London EC3 properties. There were a couple of shopping centres, High Street shops and central city office buildings in major towns and cities; after that there seemed to be a rather odd mix. There was a property in North Walsham, another in Prestwick, one in Hartlepool and one in Peterhead. Not the first places that would normally spring to mind when dealing with prime locations, he mused. Rafi was about to look at where the properties were precisely, when Commissioner Giles Meynell and Chief Superintendent David Pryke walked in. Both looked very serious.

Giles turned to his colleague. 'What do you reckon, David? We leave them alone for one day and they take it upon themselves to see if they can fell half the trees in the Amazon rain forest.' He turned to

---

* A list of the companies is also set out in Appendix 'A' on page 425

Kate and smiled, 'I'm pleased to see you haven't been hanging around – where would you like us to sit?'

Emma got up and moved the two chairs next to Jeremy's desk forward. She looked a little nervous; she rarely came into such close contact with her ultimate bosses.

Kate approached the whiteboard. 'Since we last spoke we've made significant progress. We believe we've uncovered what Rafi did to make Jameel suspicious of him. His subsequent unmasking of the four companies with Callum appears to have made him a real threat. We've exposed an impressive and wide-ranging network of companies over which we believe the terrorists have control. There are four London listed companies summarised here.' She pointed to their names and activities on the whiteboard. 'We've also found that our suspect Jameel Furud has a connection with AGVC, a venture capital business, which has ten corporate investments, one of which is a large property investment company, PREH – Prime Real Estate Holdings.'

She paused to let her bosses take in what she'd said. 'Our investigations have only started snowballing in the past three hours since we managed to find the oblique connections between Jameel Furud and Basel Talal – the MD of the venture capital company. They studied together for their PhDs. John and Jeremy are currently talking to the vice chancellor of the university where they studied.'

Kate glanced at Rafi. 'Can you explain your concerns to Giles and David?'

Rafi looked across at the two men to whom he owed his freedom and started, 'I have been trying to piece together why the suspects should want me out of the way; what do I know that most other people don't? Companies and the markets are my area of expertise. What do Jameel and Basel have in common? University, a love of money and an in-depth knowledge of companies and the markets. My hypothesis is still woolly . . . I am wondering whether their ultimate aim is to target the financial markets.'

Rafi suddenly hesitated. A cold chill went down his back. His hands went cold and his mouth bone dry. Oh Christ, he thought, it couldn't be, could it? He was still immersed in his own thoughts, when he heard Kate saying, 'Are you OK, Rafi?'

'Sorry, the potential magnitude of what the terrorists might be planning has just struck me. If at the same time as their attacks, they speculated on the derivatives market and there was another sudden fall in the stock market, they'd reap *huge* profits. And this would compound the problems faced by bruised banks, to the point where the Government would have to throw more money at the financial sector.'

'Could it be the straw that breaks the camel's back?' asked Emma.

Rafi cleared his throat and spoke in a croaky voice. 'Might be – things are still precarious in the City and the Government's finances are pretty dire.' He fell silent.

You could have heard a pin drop while the people in the room digested this latest piece of news.

The commissioner studied Rafi, deep in thought. 'Could there not be a simpler or more straightforward explanation of what the terrorists are planning?'

'What did you have in mind, sir?' replied Rafi.

'I am not sure. The problem is that neither Special Branch, nor MI5 or the Met has turned up any tangible leads relating to the Bishopsgate bombing, so we are still very much in the dark. This leaves us with your theories as the best we have so far.' The commissioner glanced across at Kate, prompting her to take up the running.

'Sir, if we follow Rafi's thoughts, then there are two things we should think of: firstly, timing – I believe we should assume that they are close to their endgame. And, secondly, secrecy – we should be extremely careful not to let them know that we are on to them.'

'How long will you need in order to put some flesh on this gruesome skeleton?' asked the commissioner.

'We'll be working through the night. By breakfast we should have a clearer picture.'

The commissioner looked at David, Kate's boss. 'Any observations?'

'If Jameel believed Rafi was on to them, then linking Rafi to the Bishopsgate bombing was a shrewd move.' He paused. 'I worry, Kate, that you've too much circumstantial evidence. Until such time as we can confirm what the terrorists are planning, we should keep our minds open to other alternatives.'

'Good point, David,' said the commissioner, who was looking perturbed. 'I agree with what Kate says about secrecy. However, if things blow up before we release this information, our heads and other extremities will be lopped off in a very public fashion. How long do you think we can sit on this, David?'

'We could delay that decision until we reconvene first thing tomorrow morning. By then we should have a clearer picture.'

'Agreed? We'll see you all tomorrow at 7.45.a.m. And, as Kate says, we keep this strictly under wraps.'

'Yes sir,' came the replies in unison.

'If you need anything from either of us, just ask, whatever time of day it is. You've got our mobile numbers, haven't you?'

'Yes, sir,' replied Kate.

'David and I are guests at a charity dinner at the Goldsmiths livery company this evening. In the circumstances we wondered whether we should attend. But as it's for a good cause we thought we should. We will be nearby – must dash now; it doesn't look good to be late.

John and Jeremy had an uneventful drive to the London College of Finance. John's frostiness thawed as Jeremy brought him up to speed on Rafi and the leads that Kate's team had uncovered.

Jeremy had decided that it was best to take the bull by the horns. 'What in particular do you dislike about spooks?' he enquired.

'Basically too bloody secretive by half and treat the rest of us as if we couldn't run a frigging whelk stall.'

'Fair point,' said Jeremy. 'Do me a favour; if you think I'm freezing you out then tell me . . . No excuses, but from time to time we have to watch our backs. Cock-ups put people like me in danger, so we can get a bit obsessive.'

They drew up in front of a smart, white, Georgian terrace and made for the vice chancellor's office. The reception hall could have graced any palace. No expense had been spared – the crystal chandeliers, ornate ceiling cornices, the large, period, gilt-framed mirror, the old grandfather clock and an array of oil paintings gave an air of refinement.

John walked over to the reception desk. 'The vice chancellor, please. He is expecting us.'

'And you are?'

'Detective Chief Inspector John Dowsing, Special Branch, City of London police.'

The smartly dressed, forty-something receptionist looked uncomfortably at John and imperceptibly squirmed on her seat. 'Sir Gerald Staniland is rather busy at the moment. If you could please wait, I'll find out when he can see you. Would you like a cup of tea while you wait?'

'He *is* expecting us. How long do you think he might be?' John looked displeased. He didn't like to be given the runaround.

'I really can't say. Unfortunately, he's left strict instructions not to be disturbed and his meeting could go on for quite some time.'

'Tell the vice chancellor we're here and it's not in his best interests to mess us around.'

The receptionist picked up the phone. 'Margery, I've two policemen to see the VC. They don't want to be kept waiting. Can you help? Thank you. Gentlemen, if you could go upstairs Sir Gerald's PA will look after you.'

Margery looked a formidable gatekeeper. Her anteroom dripped with antiques. John guessed that few students made it this far. He approached the ample, well-manicured PA.

'Sir Gerald is expecting us,' he announced waiving his warrant card under Margery's nose.

'There maybe a bit of a problem . . .' she started.

'Too bloody right! If he doesn't see us here and now, he'll spend the rest of the sodding afternoon in an interview room and he won't be offered flaming tea and biscuits!' said John.

Jeremy had moved in front of a pair of tall double doors. 'This his office?'

'You can't go in.'

'Thank you,' said Jeremy as he opened the doors and beckoned John to follow him.

The vice chancellor's office was huge. He was sitting behind an antique desk at one end of the room; in between him and the door was a set of comfortable-looking armchairs in front of an ornate fireplace to one side and, on the other side, a boardroom table which wouldn't have looked out of place in the dining room of a stately home.

The VC looked up from his paperwork. 'I'm busy, go away.'

Undeterred, John and Jeremy entered, closed the door and walked towards him.

'The commissioner phoned you to ask you to see us, so here we are. If you cooperate it won't take long, or would you perhaps like to see where we work?' said John.

Jeremy took up the running. 'We're here to get information on two of your former PhD students: Jameel Furud and Basel Talal. What can you tell us about them?'

The VC stalled. 'When did they study here?'

'About ten to fifteen years ago.'

'Ah! We've a problem there: we archive most of our old student records; data protection and all that, you know. It doesn't pay to get on the wrong side of the law,' he replied looking at John over his half-moon glasses as if he were a student who had just had an appeal turned down.

72

'We'll come back to your former students in a moment. Tell us about the college's PhD programme,' said John.

'We offer one of the largest PhD programmes in the field of Finance. The college takes on between fifteen and twenty-five new applicants each year and we have over 100 PhD students coming from more than fifteen countries.'

'How many non-EU students are there at the college?' asked John.

'Nearly 500 out of almost 850,' came the reply.

'So, roughly speaking, I guess your college earns, say, £10 million a year from its overseas students . . . and without them would it be fair to say that you wouldn't have a business?' enquired John.

'Er, yes, I suppose so, but that's not relevant,' snapped the VC.

Jeremy stepped forward. 'It is, as I can arrange for the visas of all your non-EU students to be rescinded. It would take just one phone call.'

'Who the ruddy hell do you think you are barging in here, threatening me with something outside your powers? The City Police can't take away visas.'

'Correct,' said Jeremy, 'but MI5 can! Here's my identification,' he said flashing his warrant card under the VC's nose.

'Now let's start again,' said John.

'What do you know about Drs Furud and Talal?'

'Nothing! Why do you ask me this banal question?'

'OK time's up,' John said. 'Gerald Staniland, I'm arresting you in connection with knowingly hindering police investigations into a terrorist activity. I must advise you that under the new anti-terrorism laws, you do not have the right to legal representation.'

A deep scowl came over the VC's face. 'It is Sir Gerald to you. You have no right to accuse me of some trumped up charge. Get out of my office and don't forget to close the doors behind you.'

'You just don't get it, do you? You're implicated and in the proverbial shit.'

'You can't talk to me like that! Get out of here or I'll call security and have you thrown out.'

'Gerald Staniland, I have reason to believe your college is being used as a recruiting ground for terrorists and, should you be convicted, you will formally and publicly be stripped of your title by the Palace,' said Jeremy. 'John, pass me your handcuffs. If the bastard wants to play hardball, so be it; read him his rights and take him away.'

The VC's confidence crumpled. His face turned ashen grey.

'Alright, alright, I'll help. The files are in the registry building – the building next door. Margery knows where to find them.' He picked up the phone.

Moments later Margery appeared at the door. 'Vice chancellor?'

'Please show these two gentlemen to the registry where the student files are kept.'

I t was 7.20 p.m. on the Wednesday evening. It was all hands to the paperwork at Wood Street. Emma was busy printing out and collating all the documents coming in from Companies House, while Rafi was sifting through them.

Arnold had been busy.

'Emma,' said Rafi, 'all we need to do at this stage is to prove that the venture capital company is linked with the private companies which use the services of CGF Company Secretaries Ltd. After that we can focus on what they're up to.'

The door swung open. 'My goodness, you've been busy,' said Jeremy as he entered the room. 'Where on earth did all this paperwork come from?'

He was followed by John, who looked equally surprised and impressed.

'Had a useful time?' asked Emma, trying to sound upbeat.

'Too right,' said Jeremy beaming from ear to ear. 'I reckon that the vice chancellor just aged a year or so, don't you John?'

'Well, he was being rather obstructive.'

'OK, the suspense is killing us,' said Emma, 'what did you find out?'

'We have three more names for you,' replied John. 'Jeremy has his colleagues at MI5 digging up as much as they can on them. Before we start briefing you, we've got a few things in our notes to sort out.' John shot a momentary look at Jeremy, who nodded.

'Perhaps we could chat over a bite to eat in a few minutes, while I tidy up a few loose ends with John?'

'Pardon?' said Kate.

'Oh, we stopped off at *Luigi's* and ordered a selection of things to keep us going – a sort of buffet supper. It should be here shortly. In the meantime John and I will tidy up our notes,' said Jeremy with a grin.

M inutes later the food arrived in reception and the two Js, deep in conversation, went off to collect it.

'I've no idea what we've got here,' said Jeremy as he came back in. 'I hope you find something you like. Help yourselves. We've organised our notes. Shall we bring you up to speed whilst we eat? John, do you want to start or shall I?'

'OK, I'll go first. The vice chancellor we visited is living the life of Riley. He's on a different planet,' said John.

'Lord Muck was well out of order. He tried to take the piss. Didn't take John seriously, refused to help. We sort of leant on him, didn't we John?' interjected Jeremy with a cheeky grin.

John quickly finished his mouthful. 'Jameel Furud and Basel Talal were part of a clique of PhD students. There were two others: Sheikh Akram Tufayl and Miti Lakhani, an Asian–African. They were thick as thieves for the three years they studied together. There was another member of the clique: Maryam Vynckt, Talal's younger sister, who was studying for a Masters in Law around the corner.'

'Bloody hell! I think she must be related to the Luxembourg financier that Callum visited just before he died,' said Rafi. 'Sorry; do go on.'

'We tracked down one of their contemporaries, Dr Mario Lutchins, a senior lecturer at a business school in London. We dropped in to see him on our way back,' said Jeremy, reaching over to help himself to more food, whilst John took up the running.

'To cut a long story short, it transpired that the VC is caught between a rock and a hard place. His problem is that Sheikh Tufayl agreed to make a hefty donation of half a million pounds a year, but he is most worried, as the sheikh has a signed and witnessed letter requiring the donation to remain secret or else the money becomes repayable. Without the money the VC's lifestyle would go down the pan.'

It was now Jeremy's turn. 'The four individuals certainly made an impression on Dr Mario Lutchins. He was going out with a secretary in the Faculty Office. Jameel turned on the charm, had his way with her and then dumped her. It was part of a bet, I believe. Mario has never forgiven him. He has subsequently followed Jameel's and his colleagues' activities with a sinister interest. And has been most helpful in filling in the gaps.'

Jeremy looked down at his notes. 'Tufayl, Furud, Miti, Talal and his sister frequented the same mosque. Sheikh Akram Tufayl was the man with the money. He had a lovely duplex flat in NW8 overlooking Regent's Park, close to the Central London mosque. He led the high life.' Jeremy took a mouthful of food and John continued.

'Sheikh Tufayl was outwardly religious, a driven man, always on the go. He was seriously wealthy, with money seemingly of no object and enjoyed a Western lifestyle. He thought that studying for a PhD was a great way to live, particularly as it kept his father off his back. He liked to hypothesise and seemed to be more interested in the big picture side of things.'

John looked down at his notebook. 'To quote Mario, "The sheikh despised us for Iraq, couldn't stand our meddling and aggressive foreign policies. And he thought the UK had become too soft and trusting and forgotten one of the key rules of economic and personal survival – when the chips are down, the oil-rich countries look after themselves. Or put another way: if a country runs out of energy, it's stuffed.' John paused and took another mouthful.

'The sheikh completed the last eighteen months of his PhD from home in the Gulf, following his father's death in a freak skiing accident. My MI5 source tells me,' continued Jeremy, 'that he fell into a small ravine. The fall didn't kill him, but he was injured sufficiently badly that he wasn't able to climb out. He died from hypothermia. Sadly for him, his mobile phone's battery was knackered. Sheikh Tufayl, who was on holiday with his father, moved shortly afterwards from London back home to take over the running of the family business, or should I say, the oil wells that were now his. Two years after, the sheikh received his PhD; the VC hosted a reception to acknowledge Sheikh Tufayl's support for a high profile annual finance lecture. The great and the good were invited; the sheikh turned up and mixed with them. The sumptuous dinner afterwards was at one of the oldest livery companies. The vice chancellor planned it personally with military precision and it has subsequently turned into an annual event.'

'Now let's turn to the number two in the clique: Basel Talal,' continued John. 'According to Mario he was moderately wealthy by Arab standards – bloody rich by yours or mine. He lived within walking distance of the sheikh in a smart apartment block. He had an incisive and practical brain, and paid great attention to detail. He was an excellent manager and manipulator. He's been successful in the venture capital business, but he's kept a surprisingly low profile. Mario believes that Basel has a wealthy offshore backer. His guess is that the money comes from the sheikh.'

'Oh, did we mention that Basel was the sheikh's cousin?' interjected Jeremy.

'And now on to number three in the clique: your erstwhile boss Jameel Furud,' continued John. 'He was a close friend of the sheikh and his cousin, but lacked their money. He shared their interests in discussing economic strategies and how markets worked, and whether they could be manipulated. He loved the high life and his particular talent was his ability to charm the ladies. This talent went down especially well with the sheikh, who loved to party and to have a beautiful woman on his arm. After his PhD, Jameel spent time setting up and running a fund management business in the Gulf. He was very successful. He looked after the sheikh's newfound wealth and over time the business grew to include the money of the sheikh's friends. The business moved from the Gulf to Zurich for a short while, before moving to London where it was rebranded as Prima Terra. Mario found it strange that since his return to the UK, Jameel never promoted the fact that he had a PhD.'

'I suppose he likes his wheeler-dealer image,' said Rafi.

'According to Mario the fourth member of the group was Maryam Talal, now Mrs Maryam Vynckt. She's the younger sister of Basel and of course cousin to the sheikh. She was educated at top private schools in the UK,' said John. 'This was followed by a gap year in the Gulf and then she read Law at Cambridge, followed by a two-year Masters in Law in London. Her dissertation was on "Cross border investment vehicles and cross border taxation." According to Mario, she possesses a grace and Eastern beauty that makes her very attractive. She's a fantastic linguist – speaks most of the main European languages as if they were her native tongue.'

John read his notes. 'Maryam's first job was with the international legal firm Tollemarsh Ruddock and Leveritt in the City where she specialised in corporate acquisitions. There she met Mr Hubert Vynckt; he'd read Business Studies at the Judge Institute and had been in the same Cambridge college as her. Hubert's family investment business, CPR Investment Funds, was a big client of her employers.'

'John, you're losing out on the food,' commented Jeremy. 'Let me do the next bit. Maryam, as a specialist on structuring funds and minimising taxes, visited Hubert frequently and he became a valuable client of hers. Then Hubert made Maryam an offer she couldn't refuse: head up his private clients division *and* a wedding ring. They married and she moved to Luxembourg. Then, out of the blue, her division was bought by the Gulf Trade Bank. Maryam, as CEO, merged the private clients side of CPR with that of the Bank. She now works from the Bank's headquarters in the Gulf and from its offices in Luxembourg, which are in the same building as Hubert's CPR Investment Funds.'

Rafi sat bolt upright. 'Bloody hell! I bet Callum met her before he died.'

'Good point, I'll get that checked out,' said Jeremy.

'According to Mario,' said John, 'gossip has it that she was very close to her cousin the sheikh, and they were more than just good friends. Whether her relationship with the sheikh continued after university is anyone's guess. Mario reckons that Gulf Trade Bank is part of the sheikh's business empire and that the bank's acquisition of Hubert's private clients division was the sheikh's way of ensuring that Maryam was nearby. Ah yes, I nearly forgot. Mario says Maryam is the most driven of the clique.'

'That leaves us with the last member: Miti Lakhani,' said Jeremy. 'He struggled to make ends meet whilst in London. It seems that the money was there but his father wanted his son to work and not play and so kept Miti on a tight financial rein. Unfortunately, after five years he went home to Mogadishu with an MPhil and not the expected PhD. He drew the short straw. His supervisor, it seems, was more interested in his consultancy work than tending to his academic flock. Miti's family owns thriving import/export businesses in Sudan and Somalia. Mario reckons they also own a lot of land there.'

'Now for the scary bit,' said John looking at his notes. 'To quote Mario, "In a crazier world, the PhD dissertations of Tufayl, Talal and Furud when put together could be viewed as an instruction kit for building a financial bomb . . ."'

Kate, who had been listening quietly and intently, suddenly sat up and took notice. 'Explain, please.'

'Rafi knows more about these things than I do,' said Jeremy. 'If I read out the titles, perhaps Rafi can explain? Sheikh Tufayl started his on: "Sovereign credit ratings and public sector debt", but amended it after his mid-stage viva to: "The impact of energy shortages on the financial markets". Basel Talal's thesis was on "The identification of business failure and contagion in finance, insurance and banking sectors using multifactor models". He looked mainly at the reasons why these businesses got into financial trouble and the ripple effects that this could cause.' John looked at Rafi. 'Does that make sense?'

Rafi nodded.

'Jameel Furud's thesis,' John continued hesitantly, reading carefully from his notes, 'was on "The risks of derivative products in destabilised financial markets". It wasn't an analytical piece of work, but looked at the limitations of the regulatory framework and the shortcomings of the value-at-risk models used by financial institutions.' John paused and looked at Rafi to check that what he was saying made sense.

Rafi nodded again.

'Jameel's thesis considered whether it was possible for a significant number of small items to go below their risk management radar screen, with the consequence that if the markets took a plunge one or more might become insolvent. It considered the associated problem of contagion.'

'I agree with Mario,' said Rafi, 'that if one puts the three theses together – energy shortages, with business failure and large losses in the derivative markets – it makes for a very volatile and potentially dangerous cocktail.'

Emma and Kate looked concerned.

'Do have something to eat,' said Jeremy to John. 'I'll do Miti.'

John smiled and tucked into his food.

'Miti Lakhani's thesis was on "Identifying drivers of economic prosperity in developing countries".'

Wisps of ideas were swirling around inside Rafi's head. They didn't paint a reassuring picture. The Bishopsgate bombing *was* only a distraction. Jameel and his associates were after a far larger target.

Sensing Rafi was deep in thought, Kate stepped in. 'Thank you both. That was an extremely useful synopsis! You did well to find Mario. We're fortunate that he took such a keen interest in the group.'

'All thanks to Jameel's fling with his girlfriend,' said Emma.

Kate looked re-energised. 'I reckon you've found us our ringleaders. I'm uncertain where Miti fits in, though. Thank you both. Any questions?'

'I have one,' said Emma. 'Where's the vice chancellor now?'

'I've arranged for him to spend a few days enjoying the hospitality of MI5, as we couldn't trust him to keep his mouth shut,' said Jeremy. 'His PA overheard John and I talking. We let her think that we have charged him for molesting one of his daughter's underage friends. You should have seen his face when the squad car arrived to take him away. Serves him right!'

'I have one big problem,' said Kate. 'I worry that this is all too circumstantial. Are we going in the right direction, given the starting point of the Bishopsgate bombing? Shouldn't we be looking at other scenarios? Though I'll be damned if I know what they might be.'

John looked at her in a reassuring way. 'Kate, by all means keep an open mind and if another scenario comes along, use my team downstairs to work on it. But for now, you must run with what you've got.'

'Emma and Rafi, keep researching the companies,' instructed Kate. 'John, Jeremy and I will focus on the individuals involved. Let's touch base in an hour's time.'

Emma pushed her chair across to Rafi's desk. 'Can we go back a step? Could you remind me who the owners of Prima Terra are?'

'The directors and senior staff own around 10% of the shares,' replied Rafi. 'Then there are three shareholdings of 7.5% each held by private Swiss banks who passed some of their funds under management to Prima Terra, leaving a stake of 67.5% held via another large Swiss bank. Until now I hadn't given much thought as to who controlled this majority shareholding. I would now put good money on Mario being right and it being owned by the sheikh!'

'Is Prima Terra valuable?'

'Yep,' replied Rafi. 'I'd estimate it has a market value of £1.5 billion.'

'If the sheikh is willing to jeopardise Prima Terra and lose an investment worth over £1 billion, I see what you meant when you said the stakes must be high. He must be confident of making an awful lot of money from whatever he is planning to do.'

'As I see it,' said Rafi, 'the four companies in which Prima Terra and the unknown nominee name have holdings *and* the ten companies financed by the venture capital business are all too small to make the sort of returns they'll need.'

'I agree with Jeremy's theory: terrorists like destroying things – they don't build them up.' Emma frowned for a moment.

Rafi could almost see the cogs going round.

She carried on with her appraisal. 'I agree with your hypothesis: they make the market crash and make a fortune in the derivatives market. There must be enough dishonest international bankers out there who for a fee would provide a front for dodgy derivatives trading. And it would be practically impossible for the authorities to track down the profits,' continued Emma, 'let alone get them back again!' She paused. 'Talking about getting back, if we don't want to upset my boss, we should get stuck into the accounts of the venture capital companies.' She smiled. 'Actually, she's a bit of a softy, but don't tell her I told you so.'

Rafi looked at Emma; she was on cracking form. Working with her – or was it for her? – was fun.

Collating the papers from Companies House took Emma and Rafi longer than expected. Finally the information on each of the ten companies was set out on the tables.

'First, we need to prove that there's a link between AGVC, Talal's venture capital company, and the companies where Rainer Spencer and Mitchell are the company secretary. Let's start with the shareholdings. We've got the accounts and annual returns – it should be straightforward,' said Emma optimistically.

Ten minutes later they compared notes.

'Of the five companies I've looked at, three have the directors as the shareholders, and the other two – the property company, PREH, and AGVCFoF, the venture capital fund of funds – have pages of shareholders, including Prima Terra,' said Emma.

'My five companies just have the directors as the shareholders,' commented Rafi.

'So there's no link,' said Emma dejectedly.

Rafi grinned. 'Did you spot anything strange in the notes to the accounts?'

She looked at him with a 'What did I miss?' expression.

'Maybe my companies are different, but each has tucked away in the fine print a CULS.'

'A Convertible Unsecured Loan Stock?' said Emma. 'Hold on, let me look again at my three where the directors are the main shareholders. She flicked back through the accounts. 'You're right, they've all got one. How did I miss it and you find it?'

'Perhaps I'm a little more cynical than you. I have this theory; the smaller the font size in the notes to the accounts, the more important it is!' said Rafi.

'Remind me exactly what a convertible unsecured loan stock is,' enquired Kate, who had overheard the conversation.

Rafi smiled at her. 'It's debt which at some point in the future can be converted into new shares, or the investors can get their money back.'

Kate nodded. 'Thanks.'

'However,' continued Rafi, 'while an investor holds a CULS their investment is in effect invisible, as they own debt and not equity, and can thus hide their ownership away from prying eyes. In the case of venture capital companies it's a trick of the trade. It enables the loan stock investors to sit in the background, but with those running the company knowing that their venture capital funders can take control of the company at practically any time they wish.'

Rafi got up, walked slowly over to Kate's desk and picked up the printouts she'd received from the tax inspector for the companies with the convertibles. He scanned down the sheets listing the companies' bank details. Three banked with the Royal Provident Bank, one of the large clearing banks. Excellent, he thought and made a note of the bank account details.

'Emma, what are the redemption dates for your loan stocks?' asked Rafi.

'One is 31 December 2016, the next is 31 December 2018 and the last is 31 December 2015,' she replied.

'Excellent,' said Rafi. 'Just like mine – 31 December dates.'

'Why is that good?' asked Emma.

'Well, it gives us a likely date when the loan stocks make an interest payment. *And* most companies don't have much going through their books at the end of December. If we can get access to the bank accounts, these interest payments should be easy to spot and we can then see who they were paid to.'

'The venture capital company, AGVC, I bet,' said Emma excitedly.

'You've got it in one!'

'Not having *too* much fun are we?' enquired Kate. Rafi looked at her for a moment longer than he ought perhaps to have done. There was something in the way she looked back at him that he couldn't place. It was as if she felt left out and was a little jealous of his enjoying working with Emma. He dismissed the thought.

'Kate, you know your boss said he was there to help? Could he arrange access to the three bank accounts with Royal Provident Bank? Tomorrow seems too long a wait. If we can prove the link now, it'll mean we can focus on what the companies do,' asked Rafi.

You're saying if we prove that those three are linked to the venture capital company, then in all probability all of them are?'

'Yes.'

'It seems a bit remote,' said Kate.

Rafi shrugged his shoulders.

'It'll save time and . . .'

'OK,' cut in Kate. 'You've the account details, etc.?'

'Yes.'

Kate, phoned the commissioner on his mobile. He had to call her back. She switched on the speakerphone as she picked up the returned call.

'We've found a way of tying in three of the private companies with the venture capital company run by Jameel's friend, Basel Talal. We could do with accessing their bank accounts at Royal Provident Bank to confirm their involvement – so we can see where the interest payments on the convertible unsecured loan stocks go.'

'Your timing is something,' said the commissioner. Kate waited for a rebuke. Her boss carried on, 'As luck would have it, I just spotted the chairman of Royal Provident Bank sitting a couple of tables away from me. I'll ask him to get one of his people to phone you asap.'

Rafi looked at the clock on the wall – it was 9.05.p.m. He wished he could have his watch back. Kate left the room as if she was going on a mission. She returned with a young constable in tow.

'Let me introduce Constable Peter Ashby to you. He recently joined our traffic division after having transferred from Essex because he wanted to see more of the action. You have a degree in business studies and were interviewed for Emma's job, weren't you?'

'Yes, Ma'am.'

'Unfortunately for him, he came up against a qualified accountant with a 1st from Imperial College,' said Kate looking at Emma approvingly before she continued. 'Peter, I was wondering if you might help us.'

'I'd be glad to, Ma'am.'

'Before we start I have to make something very clear: everything you see and do for us goes no further than these four walls. Understood?' He nodded his head. 'Do you have a mobile on you?'

'Yes.'

'Please give the number to Emma. She and Rafi will brief you. Yes, you thought Mr Khan was locked up. We are treating him as friendly – he is helping us with our enquiries. If you breathe a word to anyone that he's here, your career in the force will be terminated prematurely and permanently, understood?'

'Yes Ma'am.'

Constable Ashby listened attentively as Emma and Rafi explained what he should look for at the bank. Emma gave him a sheet of paper with the three company names and their account details.

'You could have a long evening. Can I get you a coffee while you're waiting?' asked Emma.

'Yes, please,' said Peter. 'White, two sugars.'

As Emma came back into the room, Kate's phone rang. It was a manager from the head office of Royal Provident Bank.

'Geoff Hasslet speaking, how might I be of assistance?' he asked.

Kate explained that she was using the powers under the new Terrorism Act to access information needed in connection with the Bishopsgate bombing. The manager replied that he had the chairman's authority and would be happy to help any way he could.

'I'm sending over Constable Peter Ashby. Thank you for your help at this late hour.' Kate turned to Peter. 'Off you go. If you get this right you won't regret it.'

He beamed.

'Get yourself a driver – your partner would be fine. Any problems, let me know. Remember, not a word about Rafi to anyone!' said Emma.

'Kate! Emma!' Rafi called across. 'Come and see what I've got!'

Rafi had moved on to look at the Security Protection and Defence Company – SPAD – and was reading through the notes at the back of the accounts.

'You know what the cheeky buggers have done?'

'No, but I feel sure you're going to tell us,' said Kate.

'Well, tucked away in the fine print of the accounts is a sentence stating that an exchange rate of £1 to EEK24.1 was used. The EEK is the Estonian currency: the Kroon. The company therefore has some kind of business activity in Estonia. I think we should ask the Estonian security services whether they can tell us what this company does over there,' suggested Rafi.

'Good idea,' said Kate. 'We've had one favour from Giles this evening; time to level the score and get one from David. Jot down what you've got on the company and check to see if any of the directors has an Estonian-looking name.'

Emma piped up. 'There was an Estonian on the board of directors, but he resigned nearly two years ago, so he isn't in the current annual returns and accounts. He gives a Tallinn address. His name is Pinja Koit.'

'Thanks, Emma,' said Kate.

Something was nagging Rafi. He'd seen a reference to Estonia somewhere else. But where? He flicked through his papers and there it was: AEIEA – the African Estonian Import/Export Agency.

Kate added the company to her list, picked up the phone and rang David at the charity dinner.

'Can you speak?'

'Sort of. What can I do to help?'

'How do I find a police or security services contact that we can trust in Tallinn, Estonia? There's some digging around that we need done and quickly,' said Kate.

'That's a good one,' came the reply. The speakerphone went quiet for a moment.

'If you go to my office . . . You know where the keys to my filing cabinet are, don't you?'

'Yes.'

'Go to the second drawer down; near the back is a folder marked EU Money Laundering and Illegal Trade Conference, Amsterdam. If

84

you pull out the folder you'll find a business card stapled to a sheet of paper – Colonel Hendrik Matlik. Give him a ring and say that you're working with me and that you could do with some help. On first impressions he comes across as very severe, but underneath he's a huge teddy bear. He's a real five-star compatriot, very proud of his country joining the EU and determined to keep organised crime out. The colonel is one of their top dogs in their Security Police. Oh yes, and remember to send my love to his daughter, Kristina. She must be at university now. Also ask him to ring you back on a secure line – he'll appreciate that! Good luck.'

A couple of minutes later, Kate had in front of her a conference folder. She opened it and found the business card – Colonel Hendrik Matlik, Kaitsepolitseiamet. On the reverse was the English transla-tion: Estonian Security Police. There was a direct line number. Excellent!

It was 9.40 p.m. in the UK and 10.40 p.m. in Tallinn. As Kate dialled the number, she wondered whether there would be anyone in the office this late in the evening.

'Halloo, tere õhtust.' Kate raised her eyebrows.

'Do you speak English?'

'Of course.' Kate breathed a sigh of relief.

'Could I please speak to Colonel Hendrik Matlik?'

'Do you know what time it is?' came the reply.

'Yes, I'm sorry, but it's important that I speak to him.'

'Can I say who is calling?'

'Detective Inspector Kate Adams, a colleague of Chief Superinten-dent David Pryke, City of London Police.'

'Thank you.'

The phone went silent. The wait seemed to go on for ages. Then a deep voice came on the line.

'Hello, Matlik here.'

'Good evening,' said Kate, 'my boss, David Pryke, suggested I called you as he believes you might be able to help us. Oh, and he sends his kind regards to Kristina.'

'Is it essential that I should help . . . Now?'

'Yes, please,' replied Kate. 'We're investigating the Bishopsgate police station bombing and a follow-up terrorist attack.'

'I read of that atrocity; please pass my condolences to David,' said the colonel.

'If you'd ring me back on a secure line I'd appreciate it,' requested Kate.

85

There was a loud chuckle from the other end of the phone, which turned into a laugh. 'I'm going to like working with you.'

Kate looked blankly at the phone and wondered how David knew her comment would tickle the colonel's sense of humour.

'No need to worry about the phone line. As one of the bosses of the KAPO my line is secure and before you were put through my office traced your call back to Wood Street police station. Isn't technology wonderful? How can I be of assistance?'

Kate told the colonel of her pressing need for information on two UK companies with operations in Tallinn and gave him the name and Tallinn address of the former director, Pinja Koit. 'We sense time is against us. At the moment we've identified a network of companies that seem to be involved.'

'I'll see what I can do to help and get back to you first thing in the morning. If you want to reach me, I'll be on the number you phoned.'

'Thank you,' said Kate, hanging up.

'Well that's another line of enquiry up and running,' said Emma. 'Who knows how helpful it'll be.'

Whilst Kate had been on the phone to Colonel Matlik, Rafi had been working his way through the notes at the back of the accounts of all the companies potentially linked to the venture capital company, AGVC. It was a slow progress. Many of the copies of the accounts were indistinct and it wasn't always easy to read the notes.

Rafi was reading the fine print in the accounts for HFFF – the Hotel Frozen Fish Foods company – when he spotted that vessels were being depreciated. He turned to the back of the accounts and saw that the company owned no properties but were depreciating over £13 m of fixed assets. So in all probability they owned fishing trawlers. He got up slowly and wrote in red on the whiteboard against HFFF: *Trawlers = What?*

Back at his desk Rafi carried on reading through the small print in HFFF's accounts. He was beginning to think there was nothing else of interest, when tucked at the end of an obscure note was the sentence stating that an exchange rate of £1 to EEK23.89 had been used.

'Yes!' he exclaimed and called across to Kate. 'I've got another company for your contact in Tallinn to look into. Emma, could you look and see if HFFF has had any Estonian directors in the past five years?'

Five minutes later Emma walked over to the printer and then placed a piece of paper on Rafi's desk.

'Here you are, Pinja Koit again, but this time at another address in Estonia. Shall I give it to Kate?'

He nodded.

Kate phoned through to Colonel Matlik.

'Good evening, colonel. Kate here from London. We've come across another UK company with Estonian interests: HFFF – Hotel Frozen Fish Foods. Their accounts show that they've a number of vessels – fishing trawlers, we reckon – which operate out of Estonia and we have another address for Pinja Koit.'

'Thank you, I'll add it to our investigations. We'll talk again soon,' said the colonel.

'I have a meeting with David scheduled for 7.30 a.m. UK time,' said Kate.

'Excellent,' came the basso profundo voice. 'I shall phone then.' The phone line went dead.

'I've got Constable Peter Ashby on the phone for you, Rafi,' said Emma.

'Hello? I was wondering whether you could help me. I don't want to sound dim in front of DI Adams,' said Peter.

'No problem.'

'Once I've found the items on the bank statements, then what? For example, I've found a £132,791.60 payment on 31 December last year; it was paid electronically to the venture capital company's bank account. I've the account number, the bank name, its address and its sort code. And I can confirm payments to the venture capital company for all three companies. Is there anything else?'

'No, that's brilliant. See if you can get a printout showing what you've told me,' replied Rafi. There was a brief silence. 'Are you OK?'

'Yes,' said Peter. 'Sorry, Geoff, the manager, is showing me a neat trick on how to get the information printed out.'

'Thanks. I'll tell Kate that you're doing a great job.'

'Oh, that would be kind,' he said.

'If you keep up the good work I'm sure Kate will have more of these errands for you.' With that Rafi hung up.

'What did Peter want?' asked Kate.

'He was checking that he had everything we needed. It seems he's still a little in awe of you and didn't want to bother you. He's doing a good job. He's found proof that the three companies *are* linked to the venture capital company.'

'That's fantastic news,' said Kate. 'We can check out the other bank accounts tomorrow, but for the time being let's assume that all ten companies are linked to the venture capital company and are part of whatever the terrorists' scheme is.'

Emma spoke up. 'The company where Basel is a director but where Rainer Spencer & Mitchell aren't involved is just a service company he is using to stash some money away. It's got £2.7 m in it and that's it. Can we ignore it for now?'

'Yes,' said Kate. 'We need to focus on the venture capital company's activities and the four listed companies in which Prima Terra and the dubious nominee names are investors. Also, let's not forget that ESSA might have been used to place receptive people into influential positions in key companies.'

'Good point,' replied Rafi.

Kate smiled; it seemed she welcomed praise from him. He thought he saw Emma's and Kate's eyes meet for a brief second; he couldn't place the expressions on their faces, but sensed they were knowing ones.

'From what I've gleaned so far I think we should start with: HFFF, SPAD, UKSOIL and ESSA,' said Kate.

'All these initials are a pain,' commented Emma.

'It's intentional; it keeps prying eyes away from the businesses,' observed Rafi, yawning.

'You look shattered – you need some sleep,' suggested Kate.

Rafi nodded.

'Come with me.' She took him down the back stairs to the cells in the basement.

He lay down on the bed – his bruised shoulder and back didn't like its hardness – and pulled the blanket over him. Seconds later he was out; the sleep of the dead tired.

To Rafi it seemed only minutes later that Kate was gently, but painfully, shaking him awake.

'See you upstairs.'

Back upstairs John was perched on the corner of Kate's desk.

'David phoned' said Kate to Rafi. 'John's now on our team. He said we could do with his experience and low cunning.'

John smiled and nodded. 'Pleased to help.'

'And we've also co-opted Peter Ashby from Traffic. He's to be our gofer.'

The phone rang – it was reception for Jeremy. 'OK,' he said, 'I'll be down straight away.'

He returned clutching bags full of steaming cups of coffee and tasty-looking Italian cakes. 'With Luigi's compliments,' he said as he passed the coffee around.

Emma looked across at Jeremy. 'But we only had our supper a few hours ago. When will your obsession with food calm down?'

'This is the afters! Who was it that said "An army marches on its stomach"?'

'Napoleon?' ventured, Peter, pleased to have answered before Emma.

'Precisely; I asked Luigi to prepare us something to keep us going, in case we begin to flag. It's going to be a very long night. And you try living off crap for two months and see if you can keep away from good food.'

'Point taken,' said Kate. 'Now we have Rafi back with us, it would be a good moment to pull together all we've been doing over the past four or five hours, so that we can keep an eye on the big picture and make sure we aren't going off on a wild goose chase. OK, who wants to start?'

'I will,' said John. 'A couple of lads downstairs have been helping me with PSSAF – the public sector services businesses – and are investigating exactly where it is involved. PSSAF is a huge organisation. Arnold Owen at Companies House has been very helpful as limited partnerships have to be registered there. He has been able to give us a detailed list of all the partnerships that PSSAF controls.'

John paused and looked at his notes. 'The scale of its activities is downright impressive or, from our perspective, scary. Their empire comprises numerous operations: security for police cells including – would you believe it? – Paddington Green. They also operate prisons, schools and hospitals. They have a number of "soft" facilities management contracts for the Home Office and the Foreign Office. Through a spider's web of connected limited partnerships they employ over 200,000 people!'

'Wow, that's impressive!' exclaimed Kate. 'What are PSSAF's finances like?'

'They're sailing very close to the wind. They've got a massive overdraft. PSSAF has grown rapidly. They've been very clever in that many of its limited partnership vehicles are joint ventures with leading multinational banks and investment funds. These, we believe, were structured by Renshaw Smithers. What scares us is that PSSAF is the general partner, and the morass of off-balance sheet funding makes it impossible to see what the underlying financial position is. They have management control and carry unlimited liability if things go wrong,' replied John.

'So if you take Jeremy's line that the terrorists will be in destruction mode, PSSAF is a house of cards?' asked Kate.

'Precisely,' said John. 'It wouldn't be difficult to make it collapse.'

'And if it did go bust?' asked Kate.

'It would leave one hell of a mess across the public sector!' John took a slurp of his coffee. 'My team have also come up with another angle. With the help of Arnold Owen we've drawn up a list of all the people who sit on the management boards of these limited liability partnerships. Several of the names are very interesting. There are a couple of politicians and some professional advisers to Government departments! I've given Jeremy's lot the list of names to see what they can make of it.

'Oh, I almost forgot to say,' continued John. 'We had a look at where else PSSAF operate. Would you believe it, one of their businesses provides the guards to the garage at Bishopsgate police station! MI5 has traced their security man who was away from his post at the time of the bombing. He's now on holiday in Spain and rumour has it he has bought a villa out there!'

'I've passed our findings to the commissioner and he's briefing all his opposite numbers that their security may be compromised, and to keep all those involved with PSSAF away from sensitive information. Giles has told them that they *have* to keep this under wraps. So far he hasn't spoken to the Government departments given the number of politicians and special advisers that might be on the terrorists' payroll.'

The atmosphere in the room had perceivably cooled.

Kate finally broke the silence. 'Who would like to go next?'

'Could I run through UKSOIL?' asked Jeremy.

Kate nodded her assent and he continued. 'It promotes itself as a company with charitable aspirations,' continued Jeremy. 'Why a venture capital company is invested in such a company is beyond me. Its profitability is next to nothing. The business has grown into an operation with eight shops-cum-travel agencies,' continued Jeremy. 'On its charitable side it's brought in a number of high profile businesses and FTSE 350 companies which provide valuable sponsorship for the students working for UKSOIL. Their ethos is, "Help them help themselves" and the focus is on Africa.'

'Where are their travel shops and offices?' John enquired.

'Next to universities.'

'Such as?'

'Well in London they have two: one next to the East City Campus University and the other by the London College of Finance. As for the others: four are in the Midlands and two are next to Northern universities,' replied Jeremy.

'Is there anything in particular that might differentiate these universities?' asked Emma.

'They have an above average percentage of foreign or ethnic students and this is mirrored in the make-up of the local population. The one in East London is on the edge of the City, close to the Brick Lane community. UKSOIL comes across as being supported by the great and the good, but we believe it may be a front for recruiting terrorists,' continued Jeremy in a serious tone. 'My colleagues are looking at the CCTV tapes from the cameras outside their two travel shops in London and also into how the airline tickets are booked.'

A pattern is beginning to form, thought Rafi. He glanced around the room. The team were looking worried by what they were uncovering.

'Excellent work,' said Kate. 'Rafi, how are you getting on with the fish restaurants and hotels businesses?'

'Quite well. HFFF is a substantial company and a nicely profitable one at that. It operates a fleet of trawlers out of the UK and Estonia, which gives them a base close to the old Soviet Bloc. Their acquisition of Small Joe's Fish Restaurants and Central City View Hotels gives them ready access to retail outlets for their fish. The increased turnover has enabled them to upgrade their fishing trawlers and grow their business. At this point in time, I suggest we put the fish restaurants and the hotels to one side. Jeremy's colleagues are looking to see if any of them are suspicious. Emma and I are concentrating on their fishing activities.'

Kate looked thoughtfully at Emma. 'Could their fishing fleet provide a way of moving things and people in and out of the country? See if you can locate their trawlers.'

'We're already on to it,' said Rafi with a smile. 'On the Internet there are lists of EU trawlers and their fishing permits. The information includes who the owner is, lots of details on the vessel itself and they're shown by port. However . . .' Rafi looked concerned.

'Are you alright?' asked Kate.

'I'm thinking practicalities. We're talking in terms of trawlers being used to get people in and out of the UK. I agree with their usefulness for getting things in, but I've a problem with using a trawler as the exit vehicle if the terrorists were indeed to launch further attacks. It would be too slow!'

'I agree,' said John. 'Could they use them just to get the terrorists out of UK territorial waters? Thereafter, I personally would want something much faster to whisk me away.'

'That's a good point John; make sure that we pick it up when we discuss the terrorists' exit strategy in more detail,' added Kate.

Rafi got up slowly and shuffled across to the whiteboard, and with his aching right hand wrote in red felt-tip: *Exit – trawlers – Then what?*

'Where have we got to on the property front?' asked Kate, watching Rafi's slow progress back to his desk.

In order to give Rafi a few extra moments to get back, Emma spoke. 'On the property front, I was wondering whether they might use one or more of them to support potential terrorist attacks. Just imagine how much easier it would be to attack something from a secure, nearby property over which you have complete control.'

Rafi by now had sat down and looked up. 'Snap! I've been looking into this. According to PREH's full name – Prime Real Estate Holdings – their portfolio should comprise property investments of institutional quality. Ergo, the properties should be in prime locations. The list of property addresses from the company's mortgage register runs to three pages and among those I've identified four properties which look distinctly out of place.' Rafi studied his scribbled notes. 'They are: a retail park on the outskirts of Peterhead and three industrial estates in Prestwick, North Walsham and Hartlepool. I've given Emma the addresses. She's seeing whether they're near any potential targets.'

'Why do you think that?' enquired John. 'Surely that's a bit over the top. These days a plain van suffices for most purposes, so who needs properties?'

Emma raised her head from the screen of her PC; her face was sombre. 'What if a property overlooked a nuclear power station – would that change your view?'

'Oh bugger, yes!' replied John.

'Well, at a first glance, the Hartlepool property is bang next to the nuclear power station. If you follow the energy theme,' continued Emma, 'the North Walsham property is only a stone's throw away from the huge Bacton Gas Terminal. Peterhead is one of the major Scottish fishing ports and it's close to the vast St Fergus gas facility. The fourth property is next to Prestwick airport and not that far from Hunterston nuclear power station.'

A shocked silence fell over the room. It was broken by Jeremy who spoke to John. 'Remember when we chatted to Mario about the PhD dissertations?'

'Bloody hell! Yes. Energy targets would fit.'

Rafi got up slowly and wrote on the whiteboard in red pen: *Other properties?* and *Top energy targets?*

'How's about we get a large map, plus several sheets of acetate which can be laid over it with the locations of the properties. We can add the other items as we come across them. For example, Emma will soon have the ports that the trawlers are operating out of and the list of key energy installations.'

'We can do better than that,' said Kate. 'Let's borrow the touch screen monitor and the computer with mapping software from downstairs.'

'Great idea,' said Emma with a broad smile. 'I'll sort it.'

'Could I have the last cake?' enquired Peter, who had been sitting quietly to one side.

'Of course, help yourself,' replied Kate.

'Thanks, they're a bit of a treat for us lowly paid constables,' he said with a smile.

His comments jogged something in Rafi's memory: money. He hadn't done any of the financial ratios on the property company. He picked up a calculator and started with the loan-to-value ratio for PREH. It was 51.7%; in itself modest. He moved on to the debt-service-cover ratio and looked at the figure on his calculator. He redid his calculations and they came out the same. The figure looked wrong. It was only 84.9%. He would have expected a ratio of 125% or higher.

Rafi racked his brain. Why was the debt-service-cover ratio so low? Could it be that the bank expected a significant increase in net rental incomes, from new lettings, or perhaps there were properties in course of development? Rafi pondered. So there could be some development properties out there which were not on the mortgage register!

He got up, returned to the whiteboard and wrote in red next to PREH: *Development properties?*

Rafi felt shattered. It was well after midnight. Sleep deprivation was closing in on him. Slumped over his desk, a sixth sense nagged at him; on the one hand, his brain told him it needed to turn off. On the other hand, a thought was niggling at him: he felt sure there was something obvious he'd missed. He would reread the property company's accounts one more time and then get some sleep.

He opened up the accounts for the current and previous years; some sections had scanned badly. He found the note on properties in both sets of accounts. They were not very clear. Rafi took out a blank sheet of paper and started to decipher what was written there. He picked out the word 'external' and a word beginning with 'valu . . .'. It was as if someone had let off a firecracker behind him. He sat bolt upright. His tiredness evaporated. Of course, how bloody stupid of him! The accounting standards required property companies to have annual revaluations.

He called across to Kate. 'There's an external valuer out there with the full details of all the properties in the portfolio. Sorry I've been a right plonker not to have thought of this earlier.' He was annoyed by his elementary slip-up. The nagging had stopped – abject tiredness took over.

'I'm off to get some shut-eye, before I keel over. Kate could you arrange for me to be woken first thing, please?'

'Will do. Sleep well.'

R afi slept soundly. By 5.40 a.m. he was back at his desk with a steaming cup of strong coffee, wondering what Thursday might bring. First, he rechecked the web to see if he had missed anything on PREH. There was little there to help him.

His mind wandered – various pieces of the puzzle swirled around in his head: the bombing of the police station in Bishopsgate in the heart of the City of London just six days earlier; Jameel and his ability to think big; the stake in Renshaw Smithers and PSSAF's massive involvement in public sector services. He glanced at the list of four properties which didn't seem to fit into a prime property portfolio. His eyes alighted on the Hartlepool property. He shivered. Bloody hell! What *if* they really did attack a nuclear power station and put a question mark over nuclear safety and this prompted public opinion to shift away from all things nuclear? And what *if* at the same time PSSAF went belly up? Flaming heck! The Government would get hit with two huge financial whammies at once.

Rafi got up and went to the whiteboard, where he wrote in red: *Renshaw Smithers and PSSAF fallout – say £10 billion* and *Nuclear clean-up / decommissioning – black hole – say £75 billion.*

He knew that the Government's finances were ropey. Their borrowing requirements were already right at the top of what was credible. Oh Hell's teeth! If the terrorists were able to trigger these two financial horrors, the knock-on effect would result in the gilts market falling like a stone, and *then* Jameel and his associates could make monumental profits in the derivatives markets, which would make matters even worse. He pondered the possibility a bit longer. They needed a fixed interest and derivatives expert on board to help unravel exactly what the terrorists were up to. He felt sure that Aidan Gilchrist, the best derivatives man he knew, would be able to work out what was going on.

Rafi looked at the clock on the wall. Property agents would soon be in their offices. The next task was to find the elusive property valuers and quickly. He was pleased that PREH used an external and not an independent valuer. The latter would be difficult to track down quickly as it could have no dealings with the company other than undertaking its valuations. In contrast, an external valuer could undertake other work for the company, and their property lettings, buying or selling work would, with any luck, be recorded on one of the specialist property databases. Rafi realised this was where he had to look. The cynic in him surmised that PREH's external valuers would be rewarded with excellent fees for their non-valuation work.

He shouted across to Kate and Emma. 'As a matter of urgency, we need a contact at a commercial property agent who will do a search of their property databases for us. Do you know anyone? Unfortunately, I now can't trust any of my contacts.'

Kate shook her head.

'Would the commissioner be able to help?' asked Rafi.

'More than likely,' said Kate. 'I'll give him a call.'

A couple of minutes later she had the name and mobile number of a Mr Perryman: a director at a major international property agent. Kate smiled. 'The commissioner hopes that this individual will be more cooperative than the vice chancellor!' she said as she dialled the number and was put through to voicemail. She left a message asking whoever picked it up to return the call as quickly as possible.

Kate hung up, then rang back and spoke to the receptionist. It transpired that there was no one in from Mr Perryman's team. The receptionist promised to get the first one in to phone her.

Ten minutes later Kate received a call from Mr Perryman's personal assistant: Pam Blake. Kate introduced herself.

'Could I speak to Mr Perryman?'

'I'm sorry; he's on his way to a property inspection.'

'I have a problem and was wondering whether you might be able to help. What I am about to tell you is in strictest confidence.'

'I understand.'

'We're investigating a serious crime; my commissioner advises me that your boss is the man to help us access property databases. We could do with his help, now, please!'

'Leave it to me; I'll contact Mr Perryman and ask for his permission to help you.'

Only a few minutes later, Pam was back on the phone to Kate.

'I have confirmation that I may help you, within reasonable bounds, of course.'

'Thank you,' said Kate. 'May I email you a list of property addresses? What I need,' she looked down at Rafi's scribbled note, 'is the printouts from your in-house database and the industry specialist databases – Focus and EGi – giving details of which agents have done deals at these addresses in the past four years. Could you do this as a matter of urgency?'

'Of course! I'll get Mr Perryman's colleague, Justin Smith, to run the searches. As luck would have it he's just walked in the door.'

'Will you please advise Justin that this information isn't to be discussed with any of his colleagues. When he's printed it out, I'd be most grateful if you'd ring me so that I can arrange for it to be picked up. If there's going to be a delay, could you please let me know?'

'Will do.'

'Thank you, Pam.'

'My pleasure.'

Kate turned to Rafi. 'This has all happened so fast. Can you remind me what precisely you are looking for? And what are Focus and EGi?'

'If we can find the external valuer, we can get hold of the property portfolio valuation report. I've a feeling it'll show properties which are *not* on the mortgage register and which *could be* part of the terrorist plans. Focus and EGi are the two huge online databases that property agents use to find information on deals done, amongst other things.'

'If it helps us find more properties, it seems like a good call,' said Kate.

Rafi didn't have the opportunity to answer Kate's comment. She had taken a call from Colonel Matlik.

'Good morning colonel. Your timing is perfect; David has just walked into the room. Let me put you on the speakerphone.'

'Hello David,' said the distinctive voice of Colonel Matlik.

'Good to hear you again,' said David.

'I was so sorry to hear of the deaths of your colleagues; rest assured we are leaving no stone unturned at this end,' said the colonel. 'And we are treating your request on a strictly need-to-know basis, as asked.'

'The import/export business AEIEA looks interesting; they have a number of local mafia contacts, we believe. I have spoken to a tax inspector and asked him to look at their books. He knows nothing of our suspicions. In one hour's time he will be paying their warehouse in the docks a visit. Two of my operatives are tagging along to have a proper look around.' A deep chuckle was heard.

'Regarding SPAD, the security business; initially we were unable to find any link to them, but the name you gave us is very interesting. Mr Koit was well-connected and very wealthy. He had a shadowy past. The FSB – Russian Federal Security Service – had been keeping an eye on him. They tell me that he was killed in a private plane crash several months ago and that he had some very unsavoury connections with people from Chechnya. Through Mr Koit we have traced a local company specialising in executive training in guns and personal security. They are based deep in the countryside, 20 km from Tallinn. Given the similarity with your SPAD, I have sent two of my officers undercover to see what is there.'

'Thank you,' said David.

'We are also looking into HFFF and their connection with one or more fishing trawlers operating out of Tallinn. It seems that your terrorists may have quite a set-up here. What worries me is that they aren't showing the telltale signs of an Al Qaeda cell, but those of a very professional organisation which uses experts rather than recently trained recruits.'

There was a pause. 'My team monitors the activities of Russian investors and mafia. This creates tension from time to time with the Russian FSB, but as there is a Chechen connection they're being most cooperative. Oh, by the way, our laws prohibit us from using phone taps unless we have a Court order from a Judge. A colleague will petition the Judge as soon as the Court opens this morning. I'll let you know if they produce anything useful.'

'Thank you,' said David. 'By the way, how's Kristina – is she enjoying university?'

'Yes, thank you. When all this is over you must come and visit us. We will talk again soon.'

The speakerphone went silent.

David turned to Kate. 'Kristina is his only daughter; his wife was killed by a car bomb meant for the colonel several years ago. It seems that he upset some people in the Russian mafia who were trying to set up business in Tallinn. He's a driven man, determined to right the wrong of his wife's death. Heaven help any terrorist who crosses his path. We couldn't ask for a better ally.'

It was 7.45 a.m. when Giles arrived for his morning briefing. He indicated to Kate that she should make a start.

'Commissioner, we've uncovered a large amount of background material which indicates that the terrorists are thinking big. As the financial markets are involved we believe that the attacks will be sooner rather than later; probably a matter of days, certainly not weeks.'

'Kate, it does no harm to work to a short timescale, but be very, very careful not to overlook critical pieces of information in your quest for speed.' The commissioner glanced up and looked at the others. 'Is that noted?'

'Yes sir,' they chorused.

'What investigations are ongoing?' enquired Giles.

'We have a number of balls up in the air, sir,' replied Kate. 'The Estonian Security Service is investigating the terrorists' activities on a firing range outside Tallinn, an Estonian import/export business and the terrorists' fishing business there. Emma is researching the whereabouts of the terrorists' trawler fleet, as we believe that they may use it as part of their exit strategy.

'Then,' continued Kate, 'Constable Peter Ashby will shortly be doing the rounds with the banks to get confirmation that the private companies we've identified are all linked to the terrorists' venture capital company. Rafi is working on the property angle to see how many of the properties the terrorists own are close to likely targets.'

She paused. 'Jeremy's colleagues are investigating the activities of UKSOIL – UK Student Overseas Initiative Live – and Unicorn Sceptre Finance. They've reason to believe that the former is a recruiting ground for student terrorists and the latter provides them with finance. John and his team are working with MI5 to unravel PSSAF and its public sector businesses. This is proving to be an unexpectedly large project. They're working on the list of its public sector contracts and the senior people on their payroll. The list is long and the names include a couple of Members of Parliament and many very well-connected people. This causes MI5 and us major concerns. Our investigations could be set back if one of these people learned of what we are doing and tipped off the terrorist leaders.'

David and Giles nodded. Kate continued, 'Also, Jeremy has received confirmation that Callum's last meeting was with one of the ring leaders: Maryam Vynckt. She's a director at Gulf Trade Bank and is ideally placed to move money around unseen, offshore.'

Giles turned to David. 'We've got a meeting with the London anti-terrorist committee at 12 o'clock. They're still convinced that the next terrorist attacks will target public places: airports; underground trains, stations, etc. We'll have to break cover soon or else we'll be in deep s h one t, if events conspire against us.'

'Basically, we're caught between a rock and a hard place,' replied David. 'If what we're doing gets out and the terrorists have a plan "B", we're scuppered, with few if any leads to work on as to where they might attack next.'

'Kate, how much longer before we have a clearer picture of what they're targeting?' asked the commissioner.

'Sir, one of our lines of thinking is that they plan to use their property portfolio as the base for attacks on UK energy installations. Rafi believes their aim is also to disrupt further the financial markets and in the process make a fortune in the derivatives markets. They're thinking big, as they seem willing to throw away Prima Terra which is worth around £1.5 billion, *and* we reckon they've invested a couple of years in planning these attacks. Kate paused. We also think that they'll pull the rug from under their public sector company – PSSAF – and all in all give the Government a particularly bloody nose.'

'You're exaggerating the position, aren't you?' asked David.

'Well, no, I'm afraid not; in fact, as things stand I'd be willing to bet a year's salary on this hunch,' said Rafi.

'Do, please, keep me informed. See where you've got to at 2.00 p.m. David and I will make a decision on who to inform at that point.'

'Could I make a request?' ventured Rafi.

'What is it?' enquired David.

'I could do with the help of a top derivatives expert.'

Jeremy, who had been sitting quietly, spoke up. 'Seems straightforward enough – you name him, I get him, problem solved.'

'Agreed,' said the commissioner. 'Please see to it as soon as we finish this meeting.'

The two senior officers stood up to leave. 'We'll be close at hand should you require any, and I repeat, any assistance,' said Giles. 'All this station's resources are at your disposal – just ask.'

'As are all those of my colleagues,' added Jeremy.

The meeting was over.

Part 3

'Jeremy, using your diplomatic skills, could you pick up Aidan Gilchrist from Maine Leadbetter's dealing room? Rafi will give you the address,' said Kate. 'Do it quietly and get him here as soon as possible. Tell him some cock and bull story that you're looking into a money laundering scam for MI5 and if he's not convinced reassure him that you've been given his name as a head honcho and a quiet chat would be much appreciated.'

'Oh, you mean, the could-he-give-James-Bond-a-helping-hand story?' said Jeremy with a grin.

Kate returned the smile and looked across at him. 'You read too many comic books!'

'But it isn't half fun! And what if he's too busy and won't come?' asked Jeremy.

'I suggest you take him somewhere quiet and advise him of the powers of MI5, should they wish to flex their muscles,' suggested Kate. 'I think it would be best if you went alone. It'll raise less suspicion. We don't want Gilchrist's colleagues to know what's going on. I'll arrange for a car to meet you in the rear car park.'

Jeremy picked up his jacket from the back of his chair and was gone.

'Kate, we're going to need a couple more computers and access to some databases,' said Emma. 'Shall I chat to Greg or do you need to clear it with the boss?'

'No problem. I have his delegated authority on this one. Leave it with me,' replied Kate.

'Rafi, could you please explain in laymen's terms why the derivatives market is potentially so dangerous?' John thought for a moment then added, 'And lucrative?'

Rafi looked at John and smiled. 'Put simply, derivatives are a way of betting whether a financial asset will go up or down relative to peoples' expectations. In our case, let's say that the terrorists do something which causes the markets to plunge unexpectedly. If they bought – put – contracts in advance, the more the market goes down the bigger the profit they'd make. If you speculate correctly you can make profits of ten, maybe twenty times your initial outlay. However, derivative markets are a zero-sum-game, thus for every winner there's a loser. They're the rocket science end of things, which is why I could do with Aidan's help.'

'Thanks,' said John. 'So if the sheikh and his associates were to speculate say £1 billion in these markets and they rig things to go their way, they stand to make £10 to £20 billion? Sort of puts all their planning into perspective, doesn't it?'

'I fear so,' replied Rafi.

A concerned look spread across John's face. 'For a payout of £20 billion, heaven only knows what they have planned! Oh, by the way, I've been mulling over something you said about their exit plans. If they're going to use their trawlers, and if they are intending to get *that* rich they won't want to hang around. So I would put looking for a fast motor cruiser at the top of my to do list. Just a thought. Must dash now – I've got a meeting with my team. Let's talk soon.' With that John hurried out of the room.

Jeremy was standing at reception accompanied by a very unhappy individual. 'Give DI Adams a bell and tell her I have Mr Gilchrist with me and that I'm heading for the fourth floor interview room.'

Kate, Emma and Rafi arrived at the interview room moments before Jeremy and a very disgruntled Aidan Gilchrist, who looked as if a thunder cloud was hovering directly over his head.

'What do you want from me?' he enquired in an annoyed tone. 'I thought you were taking me somewhere civilised to talk, not to a bloody police station.' He turned and, on seeing Rafi greeting him with a smile, did a double take.

'What the hell are you doing here?'

Suddenly, it dawned on Rafi that his mugshot must have been all over the papers as the man behind the bombing.

Aidan looked uncertainly at Rafi and, like the first class financial dealer that he was, he quickly regained his composure. He was now acting as if he had known what was going to happen all along.

Kate decided to take charge of the situation and spoke up. 'Let me introduce you to my team: I'm Detective Inspector Kate Adams and this is my assistant, Detective Constable Emma Jessop. We specialise in financial fraud. You already know our infamous friend, Rafi.

We'll shortly be joined by the head of our IT section, Greg Thompson, and you've met Jeremy, from MI5. Please bear in mind that you're here as our guest. I'm sorry that our hospitality doesn't match the standards set by your bank.' Kate smiled with a twinkle in her eyes. 'Rafi has been helping us with our enquiries. He's best placed to explain why we need your help,' she concluded, indicating to Rafi that he could begin.

'Thank you, Kate. Aidan, I'm sorry for the cloak-and-dagger stuff. Basically, I was framed. By accident, I stumbled across pieces of the terrorists' plans. Before we go any further I should explain your position and make it absolutely clear once again that you're here under no coercion. I asked Jeremy to get you as I *need* your help because I believe the terrorists are targeting the derivatives market. Let me explain why.'

'OK, wait a minute. Are you saying that if I think you're talking a load of bullshit I can walk out of here?'

'Yes,' replied Rafi, 'with one proviso: you can't tell anyone you've seen me. Agreed?'

'Agreed,' said Aidan. 'Please start, I'm all ears.'

Rafi sensed that the other members of the team weren't happy with what he had promised Aidan. No doubt the signing of some formal documentation would be the norm. But this was the City of London, where for Rafi and his work colleagues 'one's word was one's bond'.

The phone rang before Rafi could begin. Kate picked it up, listened for a moment and spoke to Jeremy. 'Your delivery from *Luigi's* is downstairs.'

He disappeared out of the room and returned a few minutes later with coffee, croissants and pastries.

Rafi started. 'We've uncovered a network of companies controlled by a terrorist cell. For example, they indirectly run four London listed companies, including a niche finance house, an import/export company and an armaments business. We reckon they've been planning things for over two years. We think that they will attack our energy installations and bankrupt a number of companies. Their aim, I believe, is to trigger a meltdown of the financial markets and profit from their positions in the derivatives market. As a top, if not *the* top derivatives man, could you help us find out what they're up to and help us stop them?'

Aidan had listened intently. 'What help will I have?'

'You'll have Emma to help you,' said Kate.

'That's it? Bloody hell, this isn't going to be easy.' Aidan looked across at Emma. 'Tell me you've got a degree in rocket science!'

'Afraid not,' replied Emma. 'I studied applied mathematics; I've experience as an accountant and . . .'

Aidan cut her off. 'Well, you can't have everything,' he beamed. 'Emma, you'll do fine. What about IT kit?'

'You'll meet Greg, our IT Manager, after this meeting,' said Kate. She looked carefully at Aidan. 'Are you willing to promise that everything you see and do here remains 100% confidential?'

Aidan nodded. 'I have no doubt that you could make life very difficult for me and my employers if I broke my promise.' He took a sip of his coffee. 'My lips are sealed. Shall we get started?'

His demeanour, which to start with had been a mixture of tension and annoyance, was now relaxed and businesslike.

'What we need to know is whether they are trying to short or manipulate the relevant futures or options contracts,' Rafi paused. 'My educated view is that the action will be in the long gilts and interest-rate contracts.'

Aidan looked at Rafi. His face was deadly serious; his light blue eyes, sharp as a sabre, focused on him. 'It's funny – no, let me rephrase that – it's a great coincidence that you should be talking of these two markets. Up to a fortnight ago, they were trading as might be expected in these volatile times and everyone was comfortable with an interest rate scenario where over the next year they move up by a few percent. But now the volume of deals betting on them rising significantly has grown to the point where someone or a group of people out there fervently believe they are heading into double digits. The view amongst the traders is that a few punters have lost their marbles and instead of playing the roulette tables have decided to place some big bets in these derivative contracts. If they're right they'll make huge profits. My informed guess is you could be on to something. I'd be glad to check it out for you. I suggest we initially concentrate on those derivative markets with a central clearing house, as settlement will be simpler for the terrorists who will undoubtedly want to get their money out quickly and surreptitiously.'

'Agreed – thank you – that'd be perfect,' said Rafi.

There was a quiet knock on the door; Greg, not waiting for a reply, walked in.

'Kind of you to join us,' said Kate. 'Let me introduce you to Aidan Gilchrist of Maine Leadbetter, the international bank. He's a derivatives guru and is here to help us. Aidan, Greg is our IT manager. He has an uncanny knack for getting into online databases and making things work. He'll set you up with whatever you need in terms of hardware and software. His budgets are a tiny proportion of yours, so the kit isn't as smart as what you're used to, but it should do the job.'

Greg had found a plate and was enjoying the last croissant.

'Aidan, please tell Greg what you'll need.' Kate shot a brief smile at Greg.

'First of all,' said Aidan, 'I could do with access to my bank's intranet, in such a way that no one can trace it. No – that would raise too many suspicions.' Aidan thought for a moment. 'Would it be possible to arrange access from here via my home IP address?'

'Shouldn't be a problem.'

'Secondly, I need access to the central computers of the clearing house LCH.Clearnet and of the main UK derivatives markets, Euronext.liffe. In due course, it would be useful to have access to the CME – Chicago Mercantile Exchange – and Eurex in Frankfurt. Also, if possible, some names of contacts in their settlement teams would be a real bonus.'

Greg nodded.

'Thirdly, I could do with a desktop PC with a bit of grunt and access to a good printer. And fourthly,' he turned and looked at Emma, 'access to a supply of coffee would be appreciated.'

As if to signal the end of the meeting, Greg slid his empty plate forward and looked up. 'If that's all, I'll get started on your shopping list. If I seem a bit stressed, please bear with me. The commissioner has asked that I give you priority, but why does everything arrive in twos like London buses? We still have a load of unfinished business following the Bishopsgate bombing, which took out their IT servers and means they're using ours. It's all a bit of a bugger's muddle,' Greg added as he left.

'Emma, would you please take Aidan under your wing?' asked Kate, changing the subject.

'Yes, sure. I'd be happy to,' replied Emma.

Kate turned and looked at Rafi. Her eyes twinkled. 'And I'll team up with Rafi.'

She looked pleased, as if she'd got what she wanted. She held Rafi's gaze, gave him a barely perceivable wink and added, 'Which should be interesting.'

105

Rafi got up to leave as if he'd finished a normal business meeting.

Kate looked a little crestfallen by his lack of interest and right at that moment it dawned on Rafi that he had accidentally ignored her gesture.

He looked at her with new eyes. She was attractive in a gamine way, her hazel eyes were radiant . . . He cut short his thoughts – this definitely wasn't the time for distractions.

Aidan stood up. 'Where's my desk?'

'Follow me, I'll show you' said Emma.

'Where do you want it set up?' said one of Greg's team, pulling a trolley with a serious-looking PC on it. Emma pointed to the desk to the left of the whiteboard.

Greg popped his head around the door. 'By the way, do you happen to know your home IP address or would you like me to find it out for you?'

Aidan gave Greg his nine-digit IP address. 'Could you also arrange for my home phone line to be routed through to here?'

'No problem.' He turned and left.

'Will your colleagues notice your absence?' asked Emma 'You might like to tell them you'll be away from the office for some while.'

'Good idea. I'll be able to tell them I'm working from home as soon as Greg has me set up.'

Minutes later he was up and running.

'The printer is where?' Aidan called across to no one in particular.

Emma pointed to a large, outdated HP printer next to her desk.

'Bloody hell! I haven't seen one of those for years. Did you get it from the museum up the road?'

'That's a bit too close to the truth to be funny,' interjected Kate.

Aidan busied himself and in no time the printer was churning out sheets of paper.

Emma glanced at him. 'I didn't know you had your IP address rerouted yet. What are you up to?'

'I thought I'd access some background data from the Web to save some time.'

Fifteen minutes later, the phone on the corner of Aidan's desk rang. He scooped it up without taking his eyes away from his screen, said, 'Thanks' and put it down. He now had access to his bank's intranet.

Rafi went over to Kate. 'I'm sorry I didn't seem enthusiastic about the prospect of working with you earlier. My mind was on other things. Shall we get started?'

Kate looked at him carefully, almost quizzically – she couldn't make him out. 'Where do you suggest we start?'

'Let's work on the property angle. It shouldn't be long before we hear from the property agent,' replied Rafi.

Twenty minutes later Justin telephoned. He sounded rather sheepish. He had put the list of properties through the three databases and had expected reams of information to come out. He apologised that he had only managed to get seventeen pages of information and hoped that this would be satisfactory. The envelope was at their Queen Victoria Street reception desk.

Constable Peter Ashby was waiting nearby in a squad car and made the pickup.

Less than fifteen minutes later he was handing over the envelope to Kate.

It was coming up to 9 a.m. Peter gave his apologies. 'Sorry, must dash. I've my first meeting with a bank manager in half an hour, followed by four more meetings with other banks,' he said with a broad smile. 'I'll keep you posted on how I get on with the interest payments and the companies. Speak later,' and with that he left keenly.

Kate passed the printouts to Rafi to analyse. Six agents showed up. Dewoodson cropped up more than any of the other names. Rafi smiled; so they *were* involved. They would be his starting point. From their website, he located their head office in Manchester, and noted they had offices in London, Edinburgh and Bristol. He passed the contact details to Kate.

She rang their head office – she was slightly nervous as this was going to be a difficult phone conversation and she didn't want to tip them off that she was from the police. 'May I please speak to the person dealing with the property company PREH?'

The receptionist hesitated.

'Oliver Stone, our managing director, looks after their agency deals and William Wesson deals with their valuations.'

'I'd like to speak to Mr Wesson then, please.'

There was a short wait before Kate was put through to his secretary. 'I'm sorry but Mr Wesson is out of the office and isn't expected back until after lunch – I suggest you ring back then,' she informed Kate curtly and then hung up.

Kate rang back and asked to speak to Oliver Stone, the MD. After another wait she was put through to his personal assistant.

'Mr Stone is in a meeting and can't be disturbed.'

'It is important.'

The PA was firm in her reply. 'I'm sorry but Mr Stone has left me strict instructions that he mustn't be disturbed,' she insisted and hung up.

Kate looked across at Rafi, 'I wonder if it was the mention of the name PREH that made them so unhelpful?'

'Quite possibly.'

Kate picked up the phone again and spoke to the switchboard.

'Could you please put me through to Manchester Central?'

Kate spoke to the duty officer. 'DI Adams here. Could you please put me through to one of your senior colleagues in Special Branch – counter-terrorism?'

A Detective Chief Inspector Rick Feldon picked up the phone.

'Good morning, how can I help you?'

Kate introduced herself and explained what she was working on. 'I've good reason to believe that a firm of surveyors, Dewoodson, who are based in Spring Gardens, have information on a property company – PREH – which is linked to our investigations. They're being uncooperative. As a matter of importance and urgency, I'm after a copy of the last valuation report, together with any other information available on PREH.'

'Can you email me details of what you want?'

'Will do.'

'Also, Rick, please bear in mind that this needs to be done with diplomacy and very quietly. They can't know we're on to them. I could do with their MD, Oliver Stone, and their valuer, William Wesson, being interviewed and kept totally incommunicado for at least twenty-four hours.'

'Sounds right up our street!'

There was a short silence before Rick said, 'How's about we pull them in on something else? Leave it with me, I'll come up with something which will enable us to search their premises and confiscate their computers. My colleague, Phil Smith, and I will pick them up as soon as we get your email.'

It was nearly 10 a.m. on Thursday morning. Rafi had his fingers crossed that the valuation report would reveal more properties. If they too were close to energy targets it would confirm his suspicions and fill in valuable missing pieces to their jigsaw puzzle.

Their work was interrupted by a call from Colonel Matlik.

'Good afternoon, Colonel,' said Kate, putting him on speakerphone.

'Sorry for the delay – I had hoped to get back to you sooner. However, your leads have proved most fruitful. Are you sitting down?'

'Er . . . Yes.'

There was an ominous tone to his voice.

'We have checked to see who owns the rifle ranges. They are owned by an unincorporated business that we find is run by your SPAD. Mr Koit owned the surrounding land. I sent a couple of my operatives to visit the executive gun training facility and they tried their hand at shooting on the 1,000-metre range. Behind the firing positions they spotted an area where the winter vegetation was partially scorched – the telltale signs of a missile launcher – and to the side of the targets was what looked like a demolished building. After their session they went to have a discrete look. It was not a building, but a concrete wall over two metres thick. Whatever had been fired at it had punched a hole through the concrete like a knife through butter. It had been hit a couple of times, which explained why it looked such a mess. Beside the rubble, covered by a layer of soil, they found a three-metre by five-metre block of metal. It was made from fifty steel sheets, each two centimetres thick, which had been welded together. It was over one metre thick and it too had two gaping holes in it.'

'Bloody hell!' said Kate under her breath, but she let the Colonel continue.

'I've been doing some research on what could cause such damage. We believe something like the Kornet E Anti-Tank Armour missile was used. It is an impressive piece of equipment and truly destructive if you are on the receiving end. It can blast a hole through one metre of armour; and not just steel armour, but explosive reactive armour. It's the kit that gives the likes of you or me nightmares. In daylight its range is up to 5.5 kilometres and trained users can fire two missiles per minute. To add spice to its capabilities, it can be fitted with either tank busting or high explosive thermobaric warheads. It gets worse: it is very accurate as it has either thermal or optical sights to detect and track the target. And the launcher comes with a tripod – both are transportable.'

'Do you reckon it needs trained operatives to use it?' enquired a horrified Kate.

'One professional would do – though it would be like holding a tiger by its tail. One thing is for sure, though: it should not be fired in a confined space unless the operator wishes to have an early cremation.'

'Can these missiles and the launchers be purchased by any chance on the black market?'

'What can't these days?' replied the deep voice. 'I reckon €50,000 would go a long way in the black market.'

'Very helpful and disturbing. Thank you,' said Kate. 'You have done a fantastic job . . .' she was interrupted.

'There is more. On the AEIEA front, we brought in the manager earlier this morning on the grounds of committing a serious road traffic offence involving the death of a pedestrian. A tax inspector and two of my officers have been searching their warehouse and offices. Amongst the paperwork they found two interesting invoices: one was for five miscellaneous launchers, and another one for twenty miscellaneous missiles. The name of the purchaser was left blank. It was dated eleven days ago. AEIEA's import manifest showed dealings with a private Russian company – Restaya – which is known to the Russian FSB and is believed to be involved in the black market arms trade.'

The colonel paused. 'I have some more bad news, unfortunately. The FSB tell me confidentially that a little while back pro-Chechen rebels captured a consignment of Kornet E Anti-Tank Armour missiles: five launchers with optical sights and twenty missiles, to be precise. They believe that they were sold on by Restaya, a company with which AEIEA has had dealings. This makes it all rather too close to home for comfort!'

Kate was going to speak, but the colonel carried on.

'I have been interviewing the manager. He is pleading ignorance. He insists that he only runs the company and its day to day activities without asking any questions, stating that real decisions are made by the directors whom he doesn't see often. When I interrogated him further, it turned out he did not know to whom the missile launchers and missiles were sold, just that he delivered them to the same rifle range outside Tallinn that my colleagues visited. He described the size of the wooden crates and the lettering on them. Unfortunately I can confirm that they are a match for the missing Kornet missiles and launchers. We are keeping the manager in custody. He is not being allowed to talk to outsiders. His secretary has been told of his driving accident and that he is being held pending a murder charge.'

'How long can you hold him for without him seeing his solicitor?' asked Kate.

'As long as you like,' came the reply, 'now that we know he is involved with a major terrorist plot. Questions will be asked as to why he cannot speak to his solicitor in probably forty-eight hours. My team is currently going through the import/export agency's paperwork with a fine-tooth comb to see whether any other armaments have recently passed through their hands. I will keep you informed of their progress.'

'Thank you,' said Kate.

'That is not all. I have been looking into the other company you mentioned: HFFF. It owns two deep sea trawlers, the Anu Riina and the Anu Maarja; they both operate out of Tallinn docks. Both are at sea – they left five days ago. Before that they spent seven days in port. I would bet that your Kornets are on board. We understand the vessels are somewhere north of the Faeroes. That is all for the moment. I will get in touch as soon as we know anything else.'

Kate looked thoughtful and replied, 'Thank you. You've given us more than enough to get on with. All your help is much appreciated.'

'A pleasure. I must go now. Give me a call if you need anything more. Sorry to have been the bearer of such bad news.'

Kate put the phone down and sat there, thinking.

'Things have just got bloody scary, haven't they?' said Emma. 'When the safety specifications were drawn up for oil and gas depots, or even airports or nuclear power stations, they can't have had any idea that such a monster as the Kornet missile existed?'

'I doubt it,' said Kate, 'or if they did, it was one hell of a cover-up by our political masters.'

'If only we had a better idea of the timescale,' mused Rafi.

'We should work on the basis that the attacks are imminent,' said Kate.

'A thought,' he replied. 'If Aidan and I are right and the financial markets are at the heart of the terrorists' plan, then the attacks won't come today – it's already too late. They'll come first thing in the morning. That way they will get full news coverage and have the whole day to spook the markets. Now whether that's tomorrow or next week, I don't know.'

'We must get information on who the foot soldiers are and what they're targeting. Carry on researching your leads and keep me informed of any developments,' said Kate. 'I need to brief the commissioner.'

John returned with Jeremy right behind him.

'Rafi, I've been thinking a bit more about the terrorists and their possible exit routes,' said John. 'I *really would* put good money on them using a fast motor vessel in addition to the trawlers. Especially as they could easily afford something very fast.'

'Where would you look?' Rafi replied.

'Firstly, I'd look at the ringleaders,' said John, 'and see whether the sheikh, Basel, Jameel or Maryam own a large powerboat.'

'I've a friend at Lloyd's Shipping Register. Let me give her a ring,' said Emma.

It turned out to be a short conversation. 'She says our task will be difficult. There are many large powerboats scattered all around the smart harbours and marinas of Europe. The difficulty is that most are owned through special purpose companies for tax reasons and this makes it hard to trace their owners.'

Emma thought for a moment, then got up and went to see Aidan, who was sitting behind a large volume of paper.

'Aidan, if you wanted to find out if a business contact owned a smart and expensive motor vessel, where would you start?'

He looked at her thoughtfully. 'Anyone who spends several millions on a yacht will no doubt thinks it's the best thing since sliced bread. My bet would be to go and look in their offices, where they're bound to have photos of it.'

'Good idea, but we don't have the time,' said Emma.

Rafi lifted his head up from his paperwork. 'Of the four individuals, I doubt whether Jameel has one stashed away. He's never spoken of boats to me and, to my knowledge, he spends most of his holiday time skiing or playing golf. Basel is a workaholic and I don't see him leaving something valuable tucked away in a marina, unused. That leaves Sheikh Tufayl and Maryam.'

'I'd rule out Maryam,' said Emma. 'She also works long hours and spends too much time between her homes in the Gulf, Luxembourg and London. I don't see a large powerboat and outdoor activities going with her lifestyle.'

'What about her hubby?' asked John. 'He is extremely wealthy.'

'Could be,' said Kate, 'but in my book the sheikh seems to be the most likely.'

'I've got an idea,' said John. 'It's a bit off the wall, but how about we chat to someone working for the tabloid press and see if they've any pictures of Sheikh Tufayl and Maryam's husband, and see if a big boat is in any of them? We must have some good contacts. Should I make a couple of phone calls and get some names?'

Kate nodded. 'But the discussion would have to be in confidence, perhaps in return for a story later.' Ten minutes later, John's phone rang; he scribbled down the information on two contacts: one working for a red top newspaper and the other for a tabloid magazine.

'I could do with a volunteer to pay a journalist a visit,' said Kate.

'Count me in,' replied Jeremy.

'See what you can find,' said Kate.

'Will do.' Jeremy picked up the piece paper with the names and phone numbers on. 'Which do you reckon I should try first?'

'I'd take the first one – he works down at Canary Wharf when he's at home but, like most tabloid journalists, he could be almost any-where.'

'Thank you,' said Jeremy, slightly sarcastically. 'It seems a straight-forward task.' He dialled the first journalist, Pete Lockyer, and smiled when the mobile was answered almost immediately.

'Hello,' said Jeremy, 'I was wondering whether you could help me?'

'Who are you?' said a slightly shrill voice on the other end of the phone.

Jeremy gave a wry smile. 'Someone you don't know. And who probably doesn't exist in any of your files.'

'Are you taking the mickey?' snapped Pete Lockyer.

'No,' said Jeremy. 'I work for a rather special part of the Govern-ment and your name has been put forward as someone who could help us.'

'Sorry mate, I'm rather busy at the moment.'

'OK,' said Jeremy. 'I thought I'd try you first as you come highly recommended, but if you're too busy, not to worry. I've another couple of people to try, including a rather pushy sod at a tabloid magazine.'

There was a pause at the other end of the phone; one could sense Pete considering if he was about to turn down a potentially lucrative story.

'How much of my time would you need?' inquired Pete.

Jeremy tried hard to conceal a large smile and winked at Emma. 'Not long! Perhaps you might have time for a cup of coffee or a glass of wine?'

'It's a bit early for the wine. Let's make it a cup of coffee. There's a decent coffee bar around the corner from where I work.'

Jeremy took down the address. 'Could we meet there in, say, twenty-five minutes?'

'Fine,' said the journalist. 'How do I recognise you?'

'Oh,' said Jeremy, 'I look fairly nondescript. I'm in a grey suit, open-necked shirt, six foot two and I'll be carrying a notepad. My name is Jeremy, by the way.'

'See you in half an hour.'

'Twenty-five minutes would be better,' said Jeremy and hung up. He looked across at Kate. 'Any bright ideas on how I get to Canary Wharf and back?'

'No problem. If you go down to the car park, I'll arrange for you to be looked after.'

'Thanks.' Jeremy picked up his notepad and hurried off on his errand.

The pressure was on. The team had uncovered a number of crucial leads, but the overall picture was still far from clear. There was trepidation in the air.

'Emma, how have you been getting on with your maps?' asked Kate.

'Rather well, actually,' replied Emma. 'Before I show you what I've got, though, I think we should consider how many targets there could be.'

'Good point.' Kate nodded for her to continue.

'They have five missile launchers. Of the twenty missiles they started off with, four were used in Estonia, leaving three or four missiles per launcher. This gives each operative probably one or two targets only. The missile launchers and their tripods are bulky. If the terrorists don't want to be captured and are keen for a quick getaway, I'd go for one target per launcher and use the three or four missiles to knock the living daylights out of it. A well-trained operative could fire four missiles in less than two minutes and then leave the area discretely.'

'What if they fire their first couple of missiles at one target and then take their missile launcher with them to some pre-stashed missiles at a property or a vehicle parked near to their next target?' added Rafi.

'So we could have ten targets!' whistled John. 'Flaming heck! And if they had access to a roof of a suitably located property, they'd have a great launching pad!'

'Or if a vehicle is involved, a nearby property would be useful to keep it out of sight prior to an attack,' added Emma.

'Oh sod it! I suggest we look for ten targets and scale the number down only when we have conclusive proof,' said an agitated Kate.

'I've been making progress on the property front,' said Rafi. 'The mortgage register of PREH gives us an interesting set of addresses. Emma has chatted to John's team who have been helping us rule out the other properties. We're left with our original four properties as possibles: Peterhead, Hartlepool, North Walsham and Prestwick.'

'Now for the clever bit,' said Emma. She was standing next to a large, touch screen monitor which Greg had set up by the whiteboard.

'First, let's put up a map of the UK and add on to it the four suspect properties.' Emma tapped the LCD screen, highlighting the four locations with bold blue crosses. 'We can now add an exit port.' As if by magic a little icon depicting a trawler appeared next to Peterhead.

'Sorry, I'm still working on where the other trawlers are. However, I've done some work on the location of our major energy installations.' She moved back to her PC and, with several clicks of her mouse, a mass of coloured dots appeared on the screen.

Rafi let out an appreciative whistle.

'To make life easier I've colour-coded them,' said Emma. 'The green dots are for major gas and oil plants, red dots for the nuclear powers stations, the large red blob is for the Sellafield reprocessing facility in Cumbria and, lastly, the numerous black dots are the oil, gas and coal fired power stations.'

'Bloody hell!' said John, 'I didn't realise there were so many of them.'

'Absolutely,' said Emma. 'But I reckon we can safely remove the black dots. The fossil fuel power stations, whilst large, aren't in the same league as the others.'

A couple of clicks later and the black dots disappeared from the screen.

'Oh yes!' blurted out Rafi, as green and red dots showed up close to the four PREH properties.

'Precisely what are those dots, Emma?' asked Kate.

Emma pointed at the screen. 'Peterhead is between the vast gas facility at St Fergus and the main North Sea oil pumping station at Cruden Bay. The Hartlepool property – here – is right on top of a nuclear power station. If we go down a bit, the North Walsham property – here – is next to the huge gas terminal at Bacton and just down the coast is Sizewell nuclear power station. *And*, over here, Prestwick is only twenty miles from Hunterston nuclear power station.'

'Phew!' exclaimed Aidan under his breath. 'What percentage of our gas supply comes through St Fergus and Bacton?'

'I guess around 30-40%,' replied Emma.

'The gas market is inelastic,' said Aidan. 'A shortfall of just 10% would cause problems; 30% would be catastrophic – sections of UK industry would have to shut down. There would be electricity blackouts; the financial markets wouldn't like it at all, sentiment would be hit and the falls could be dramatic. On top of this, crippling the North Sea oil pumping station would shut down the oil refineries it serves, causing considerable knock-on effects.' Aidan looked worried.

Bingo, thought Rafi, we've found another trigger for the financial chaos theory.

John looked thoughtfully at the map. 'If we added this little lot up, what would we have?'

'Potentially six substantial energy targets, of which three are nuclear,' said Emma frowning. 'The bad news is, if you look at the screen, there are a number of other possible targets.'

'Oh my God! It's like looking for ten bloody needles in a frigging haystack if you ask me,' said John.

'I've got a question.' Kate was looking worried. 'How does the nuclear fuel travel to and from the power stations and the reprocessing units – and how often?'

'By train,' answered Emma, rummaging around for some paper on her desk. 'Ah, yes, here it is. The trains average one round trip a week.'

'Do any of them by any chance go near London?'

'Yes, the Sizewell train does,' answered Emma. She flipped through her notes. 'It uses the North London line from Stratford round to the marshalling yards at Willesden Junction, before going on to Sellafield.'

'Next question,' said Kate. 'How robust are the canisters that carry the nuclear fuel?'

Emma looked at her paperwork. 'It says here that the design and specification of the canisters have been certified by Government experts.'

'Does this include the ability to withstand state-of-the-art missiles, like the Kornet missile that our terrorists most likely have?' continued Kate.

'Their thickness is . . .' Emma looked for the figure. 'Yes, 900 mm – about three feet.'

'Could a direct hit penetrate a canister?'

116

'Yes, I reckon,' replied Emma, looking at Kate to see if there was yet another question winging her way.

'And a glancing blow would probably ricochet off?' added Kate.

'Probably,' replied Emma, uncertainly. 'However, the experts who determined the safety specifications don't seem to be worried. Somewhere it says that – Ah yes! Here it is – the worst radioactive release following a terrorist attack is calculated to be only 0.0024 of 1% of the nuclear waste escaping as respirable particles. Each canister is reckoned to contain 3.5 tonnes of spent nuclear fuel.'

Emma paused, so by my calculations their figures point to only 0.1 kg of nasties being released, which they think isn't too calamitous. And as I read them, the reports don't consider there to be a remote possibility of a successful missile attack. What scares me,' continued Emma anxiously, 'is I reckon the contents of each spent fuel canister contains about a quarter of the fallout from Chernobyl and it is around a million times more radioactive than the uranium fuel initially sent to the nuclear power stations. I know they say it's as safe as houses, but if a terrorist were to . . .' her voice trailed off.

The uneasy silence was interrupted by John. 'The question that the terrorist leaders would have to ask themselves is: how easy would it be to hit accurately a moving canister? And are the odds ones that they would be prepared to gamble on? Having said that, a successful attack at Willesden would have a major impact – it *is* close to very desirable parts of London.'

'I suggest you put Willesden marshalling yards on your map,' said Kate.

'John's got a good point – nuclear power stations seem more likely targets, don't they?' said Emma sifting through a pile of papers. 'And I've browsed through the reports from the House of Commons and the Mayor of London's office, which have looked at the issue of nuclear waste transport. Neither is best pleased with the nuclear cargo going through London, but they both conclude that the canisters are safe – as advised by their experts.'

'For the time being, let's focus on key oil and gas plants, the nuclear power stations and reprocessing plants,' said Kate. 'Excellent work Emma.'

'I've been thinking,' said Aidan. 'If you go back to what we discussed earlier – the issue Rafi and I have been debating – what would trigger a very sharp rise in interest rates? The Public Sector Net

117

Cash Requirement is currently at record levels – at the top end of what the financial markets will tolerate. Rafi and I agree that a significant increase in the Government's borrowing requirements would be seen as a tipping point and if the Government had to borrow large amounts more, then they would have to offer higher and higher yields to entice investors to buy their gilts. Hypothetically, let's say Hartlepool or Hunterston nuclear power station were to be compromised and shut down following a terrorist attack and radiation leaks. Public opinion could easily swing against all things nuclear. Were nuclear power to become politically unpalatable and phased out sooner rather than later, the Government could get hit with a bill of, say, £75 billion for the radiation clean-up costs and the decommissioning costs of the other power stations. If at the same time a couple of large gas plants were to go out of action causing power cuts *and* at the same time PSSAF went belly up, it would give the UK financial markets a dose of the screaming abdabs.'

Aidan paused. He looked deadly serious. 'The financial markets would drop like a lead balloon, enabling the terrorists to make a fortune from their positions in the derivatives markets.'

'I agree with Aidan,' said Rafi. 'They attack a number of energy installations and at the same time burden the Government with more financial liabilities.'

'So, to put it bluntly, they want to crucify our markets and our economy and *then* walk away with a shedload of money,' observed Emma.

'It looks as if we have two separate issues to deal with,' said Kate. 'The attacks and then what they are doing in the financial markets. Aidan, you focus on the financial markets and the rest of the team will concentrate on the attacks.'

'Will do,' said Aidan.

'Well, who do we think will deploy the missiles?' Emma enquired. 'A student fanatic might be trained to use a semi-automatic gun or explosives, but Kornet missiles are a very sophisticated piece of equipment.'

'I'd go with terrorists with military experience,' said Kate.

'But such people wouldn't be easy to get into the UK, would they? Even on false passports,' Rafi asked.

'Who knows?' replied John. 'As things stand we can't rule anything out.'

'We have to substantiate these suppositions and convince our bosses,' said Kate. 'It won't be an easy task.'

'Oh hell!' The exclamation came from the direction of Emma's desk; she turned to Kate. 'I said that the sides of the steel canisters were 900 mm thick. I was looking at the wrong bloody figures – the ones that are normally used in the UK are only 400 mm, i.e. fifteen inches thick. A thermobaric Kornet missile would literally rip the container apart and spew the contents here, there and bloody everywhere.'

'My God!' said Kate. 'The consequences would be unthinkable.'

'That puts Willesden higher up the list,' added John.

There was a stunned silence in the room.

It was broken by Rafi. 'Aidan, we both believe that part of their plan is to make a financial killing in the derivative markets, don't we?'

'Yes.'

'If ESSA, the head hunting business has placed bent people into the dealing rooms of financial institutions and they are discreetly acting as counter parties to the terrorists' transactions, it would enable the terrorists to build up very big positions, wouldn't it?'

Aidan cursed under his breath before adding, 'The impact of a trader entering into a large number of these derivative contracts at the wrong time could be dire. It would be like walking in front of a Chieftain tank going at 40 mph.'

'It doesn't bear contemplating,' Rafi added. 'And it would make it very expensive for the Government or the Bank of England to stop the financial system going into meltdown.'

'And they would have to react very quickly,' said Aidan.

'Aidan, I know you're busy,' interrupted Kate, 'but could you chat to ESSA using your home phone number and find out what they've been doing in your field?'

'Will do.'

Emma waved a piece of paper. 'Here are their details.' Aidan looked impressed. He was meant to, Rafi thought, spotting Emma's smile.

Aidan made the call to ESSA. The person he needed to speak to was out until mid-afternoon.

A quiet determination filled the office as they concentrated on the work at hand.

Emma stopped what she was doing and sat bolt upright. She was looking frustrated.

'What's up?' asked Kate.

'It's just that I can't place something; I'm looking at the cold store and packaging operations of HFFF. Something is bothering me; I just can't recall what it is that I'm trying to remember!'

Aidan looked up from his desk. 'What makes you think that you're missing something?'

'Well,' said Emma, 'I was reading something which mentioned fishing – and I can't bloody remember what it was!'

Aidan smiled and popped his head back down below his parapet of papers.

'It's a wonder you manage to get any work done, sitting there daydreaming,' he muttered, just loud enough for Emma to hear him.

Emma got up and walked determinedly across to his desk. Aidan sensed that he'd gone too far with his banter. Emma, who was twenty centimetres shorter than Aidan, looked straight at him and hissed, 'Stand up, please.'

Aidan looked a little apprehensive; he stood up and Emma moved closer. Rafi had his fingers crossed that the team wasn't going to come apart at the seams. Emma stood there, milking the anticipation and doubt in Aidan's mind. She leant forward, raised herself up on to her tiptoes and placed a fleeting kiss on Aidan cheek. Emma smiled, wrinkled her nose in a playful manner, turned round and winked at Kate.

'What was *that* for?' asked Aidan.

'Oh it's just that you're brilliant,' Emma said turning round and looking at him. 'It's you and your sense of humour. It gets me thinking in strange ways.'

Aidan blushed slightly.

'No, not that way – it's silly, but you mentioned work and that helped me remember what was niggling me.'

Emma made a beeline for a filing cabinet and rooted through the contents of a drawer.

'What are you looking for?' asked Kate.

'A briefing note on immigration; we got one a little while back setting out the priority employment sectors and how these might be exploited to gain fast track entry into the UK. It highlighted certain industry sectors. Found it! Yes! Fish packers are on that list *and* HFFF employs them. This would give the terrorists a legitimate and easy way of getting undesirables into the UK.'

'It's a long shot. Leave it with me and I'll see what I can find.' Kate phoned the switchboard and got the number for their contact at the Immigration Department.

'Oh blast,' said Kate, 'it looks like they've left their answerphone on.' She left a message asking for her call to be returned with utmost urgency.

A few minutes later the phone rang. It was a man from the Immigration Office. Kate explained what she needed. He gave her a couple of names and mobile phone numbers.

'I must apologise for the delay in replying,' he said. 'I'm here by myself and you caught me talking on another line. I'm sorry. It's these targets – I have to answer all calls in less than two minutes or I get a red mark. Given the complexity of some of the requests, how on earth can I process people in under two minutes? My boss at the department wants me to go part-time; he says he needs to transfer part of my budget across to the growing team of data collectors. He says that way he can show the junior minister he's meeting the targets. If you ask me, it's the doing that matters, not the collating of the performance tables. Sorry for the outburst. If the phone numbers I've given you are busy, please ring me back and I'll see whether I can find you someone else who can help.'

'No problem and thank you for your assistance,' said Kate sympathetically.

The first number Kate tried was switched off. The second was answered with a quiet, 'Hello, Steve Lee here.'

Kate explained her pressing need for information and the importance of confidentiality. 'Can you help?' she asked.

She was greeted with, 'Oh shit! Oh shit not again, why now?'

Kate's face turned very serious; she was about to read the riot act to the person on the other end of the phone when she heard him shout, 'Lucy!' and then louder, 'Lucy, can you rescue me please? The little tyke has done another projectile poo.' There was a brief silence. It seemed that Lucy had arrived in the nick of time and had taken charge of the situation. 'Darling, let me have him; I'll finish off the nappy changing. You can sort out your work.'

Steve was most embarrassed and very apologetic. 'Sorry, it's meant to be my day off. Oh hell, I need to put the phone down again; he got me all down the side of my trousers as well. Lucy is going to love it; I've just backed into the side of the sofa! Look,' he said, 'the sooner I get out of here, the safer for everyone; give me a couple of minutes to change and, say, twenty minutes to get to the office. Ring me on this number in twenty-five minutes and I'll be at my desk where I'll be in a better position to help. I promise that this isn't a brush off.'

'It'd better not be!' said Kate. 'By the way, what's your son's name?'

'Liam,' he said and hung up.

The office returned to a quiet, studious work mode.

Aidan looked up at Emma, who by coincidence had been looking his way; their eyes met for a brief moment but both thought better of saying anything. A couple of smiles later they were heads down, focused on their paperwork.

K ate phoned Steve. 'I'm looking at a company called HFFF – Hotel Frozen Fish Foods. I need to know whether they've employed any non-nationals via fast track visas, working as, say, fish packers or filleters over the past, say, three or four years.'

'Bit of a specific question,' he said. 'Let's see what we can find. Can you give me the company name again and its registration number or address?'

Kate spoke to Emma, who passed her the information Steve requested.

'Thank you,' replied Steve. 'I must apologise since the system is always slow bringing up information. I suspect it's feeling a little overworked at the moment, though please don't quote me on that. Ah yes, HFFF has seen a significant growth in their workforce over the past couple of years. They've put in six – no sorry – seven fast track visa applications for fish packers and filleters. Of these, we were able to process three on the nod as they were for EU citizens from Eastern Europe. The other four were non-EU nationals and all their visa requests have been approved too. All in the past sixteen months! I see from a note on the file from my colleague Roger that they're opening up a large new cold store and packaging facility later this year, hence their recent requests.'

'Would you know where?'

'Sorry, that isn't part of the electronic notes. Roger – the guy who deals with this company – is away on holiday. He'll be back tomorrow morning. By the way, what's your email address?' asked Steve.

There was a brief silence after Kate provided him with the information and then Steve came back on the line. 'I've emailed you the details we have on each of these individuals. I've tried Roger's mobile but it's switched off, as is his voicemail. I'll send him a text message and put a note on his desk letting him know to get in touch as soon as he's back. Wait a minute! I am a berk – of course he's not answering; he's flying back from his holiday in the States. What's your timescale?'

'Yesterday would be ideal. But as soon as possible, please. It's really important,' said Kate. 'Steve, if you or Roger can't get through to me, here is my fax number. Mark any faxes as – *Urgent* – please.'

'Will do,' he said, 'I can't promise that Roger will remember where the new cold store is located. He keeps a number of notebooks, but I've never been able to decipher what he puts into them. One of us will be in touch first thing tomorrow.'

'Oh, by the way, while I've got you on the line,' said Kate, 'what other fast track ways into the UK are available?'

'Off the record, news agency journalism is a good one,' Steve replied. 'Interestingly, representatives of overseas newspapers who are employed and paid in the UK don't need a work permit. All they have to show is evidence that they've been engaged by a news organisation outside the UK and the posting to the UK is a long-term assignment and they have sufficient funds to live here. We don't always have the time to check that the foreign organisation is in business. The process is remarkably straightforward. Like fish processors and filleters, journalists aren't seen as a priority area to scrutinise. The paperwork often gets only a cursory glance. Did you know that after four years they become eligible to apply for residency?'

'Could you look up a few more companies and check if they've made any visa requests that look out of the ordinary?' asked Kate.

When they came to UKSOIL Steve said, 'Bingo! They have an individual who fits your description: an overseas journalist working on their student newspaper. I'll email his details to you.'

They found nothing more.

'Thank you Steve. You've been really helpful,' said Kate. 'Best wishes to Lucy and Liam. Tell them from me that you're a star for coming into the office on your day off.'

Kate printed out the details on the eight individuals and bounced the email on to Jeremy who, as luck would have it, returned a couple of minutes later. 'Jeremy, could you help me track down the eight people I've just emailed you? They're employed by HFFF and UKSOIL and have all taken advantage of the fast track visa application process. It seems that they've been here, acclimatising to the UK way of life, for between four and sixteen months. The likelihood is that they're using false names.'

As an afterthought Kate forwarded the email to Colonel Matlik in Tallinn, with a short covering note: 'These people have come up on our radar screen. Do any of them look familiar to you?'

She then called across to Emma. 'Have you made any progress with the HFFF businesses or their trawlers?'

'Yes; they've got a fleet of eight modern vessels. Four are registered at Peterhead, two at Grimsby and two in Tallinn. I've confirmation that three of the Peterhead trawlers are out in the Atlantic Ocean, somewhere up towards Iceland, and they're due back next week. The fourth, *Northern Rose*, is in port at Peterhead. The two Estonian trawlers are in the Norwegian Sea and are due back in Tallinn late Sunday or Monday. Unfortunately, *Highland Rose* and *Rosemarie* from Grimsby are still unaccounted for.' Emma continued, 'And I've been talking to the coastguard. The talk is that *Northern Rose* in Peterhead is due to sail tomorrow around lunchtime.'

'Good work.'

'And,' added Emma, 'HFFF has a cold store and processing unit in Peterhead, but they're opening fish restaurants and hotels in the south of the country. So why don't they have a cold store in the South of England?'

'The north side of London would be ideal,' commented Kate. 'Somewhere near Willesden, perhaps?'

'Exactly!' said Emma. 'Anyway, I phoned their sales office in Peterhead posing as the manager of a fish restaurant in South London. I enquired whether they operated around London. The reply was that their nearest depot was up North. They do deliveries to London, but there was a large minimum order. The person I spoke to believed there might be plans afoot to open a facility outside London, but she hadn't been formally told as yet. She asked me to give her a ring in six months' time.'

Kate frowned. 'That ties in with the comment from Steve at the Immigration Office about HFFF looking to expand. So they could well have a property somewhere in the South of England.'

Rafi got up and wrote on the whiteboard in red under HFFF: *Property near London? Where?*

The phone rang. John picked it up. It was one of Jeremy's MI5 colleagues. 'Jeremy asked to be kept informed of the whereabouts of Basel Talal. Sorry for the delay; some information has just come through from the Belgian authorities. Your man, Talal, landed in Paris last Tuesday morning almost two hours before Jameel flew out from there to Marrakech. We don't know if they met.' The MI5 man hesitated. 'As Basel had no onward flight we had assumed that he was staying in Paris. The boss, however, wanted us to be more thorough and we gained access to the French, Belgian and Dutch passenger manifests. It transpires that Basel hopped on to the TGV to Brussels, boarded a flight to Copenhagen and then flew on to Reykjavík. He must have antifreeze in his blood to go there at this time of year! We've sent an operative up to Reykjavík to investigate and another is keeping an eye on Jameel.'

'Thanks mate,' said John and hung up. 'Kate, Emma, Rafi, our man Basel has done a runner and – would you believe it? – gone to Iceland.'

Going to Iceland in February seemed a strange move for Basel. What was the draw? thought Rafi. Most likely it wasn't for pleasure. The way in which he had travelled to Iceland was suspicious. Why go to so much trouble unless he'd wanted to keep his destination secret? And why had Jameel chosen Marrakech? He had already taken a skiing holiday at the beginning of the year. Though he was the boss, he never took more than four weeks' holiday in one year. So far, he'd clocked up almost three in the space of seven weeks. It was definitely out of character.

Jeremy's journey across town was straightforward and he arrived at the coffee bar with a couple of minutes to spare, wondering whether he'd whetted Pete Lockyer's appetite, or if he would be wasting his time.

But Pete was on time. Jeremy watched him saunter into the cafe. He was of medium build, slightly paunchy with receding mousey-brown hair. His face told a story of too many late nights. Pete was smiling, which was presumably a good sign.

Jeremy stood up. Pete spotted him, came over and sat down opposite him. Introductions out of the way, the coffees were ordered and they started chatting.

'What have you got that makes it worth my while being here?' asked Pete bluntly.

'I'm doing a bit of undercover work on a rather wealthy individual who has his fingers in some interesting pies and I'm not certain what's in it for you yet.' Jeremy watched Pete. He didn't look overly pleased.

'Have you ever met a real spook before? I thought not. Well at least this can be marked down as part of your professional training.'

Pete had been studying Jeremy, who was athletic in build and had one of those faces that was handsome but did nor stand out. Pete realised he was hooked; he had to find out more.

'Are you really MI5?'

'Yep, have a look at this.'

Pete scrutinised Jeremy's MI5 warrant card, looked up at his smiling face and considered things. He'd just put a good story to bed, had a second almost completed and so didn't really need another one, but he did have a spare hour or so. What the hell! The spook was interesting.

'I might be able to help. It depends on what you're after,' said Pete.

'I could do with tracing a fast motor vessel. I've got two leads as to who the owner might be – both mix with the great and the not-so-good! Can't tell you what it's about as it's highly sensitive, but you'll be the first to know when the story breaks.'

'That's a bit thin,' said Pete.

'My sources tell me you're a man up for a challenge,' replied Jeremy.

'How's about we go back to my office and see if we can turn something up in the library?'

It was a short walk across to the shiny, glass-fronted building. Pete signed Jeremy in and they made for the library via the coffee machine.

Jeremy gave Pete the details of Maryam, her husband and the sheikh, and showed him some photos of the individuals that Emma had sent through on his phone.

'Where do we start looking?'

'First let's look under their names. Let me show you how the manual and electronic cataloguing and indexing work. I suggest you start over here and I start at the other end and we see how we do,' said Pete.

Jeremy looked at the mass of catalogued photos. Bloody hell! If only MI5 had this type of information on people! He was fascinated by the tabloid approach to life. Some of the pictures made the mind boggle and the eyes water. They surely couldn't publish many of them, but he supposed they made for a good bargaining tool!

It soon became apparent that Maryam and her husband were landlubbers; they loved high society, opera and the Arts. There was nothing on boats.

Then Pete struck gold. A colleague had been working on a story about oil magnates and beautiful but hard-up celebs. There were pictures of the sheikh surrounded by beautiful women and there, amongst the pictures, was the sheikh with a movie star draped across the back of a sleek-looking monster of a powerboat.

'Beautiful, isn't she?' said Pete. 'I'd love to get my hands on one of those. It looks like a Sunseeker Predator 75 if I'm not mistaken. Like shit off a shovel. I reckon her top speed would be something like forty-seven knots – over fifty miles per hour.'

Pete looked carefully through the similar pictures. 'Hell's bells, what a bugger! None of the photos show the boat's name. Don't worry.' He picked up the phone and chatted to a colleague, and within moments was talking to a specialist yacht broking agency. He spoke to them for a while and then hung up. 'This is the boring bit of the job – the waiting for someone to phone back with the info. And the coffee's cold!' commented Pete.

They didn't have to wait long. The yacht broker advised Pete that a limited number of these boats were built each year. The manufacturer had given him the names of the boats constructed in the past five years. The broker reckoned that it wouldn't take him long to track down whether any of them were owned by a rich Arab sheikh.

Jeremy smiled. It was great to see a professional at work! Pete didn't give away who he was researching. He reckoned Pete could give a lesson or two to some of his younger colleagues. To pass the time, and not wishing to lose an opportunity, Jeremy pulled together a bit of information on Maryam and her husband.

Less than twenty minutes later Pete's broker contact phoned back. He'd identified three such boats which were owned by Arab sheikhs.

'The first one is owned by a Sheikh Tufayl.'

'Voilà!' said Jeremy

'Her name is *Flying Goddess*,' continued Pete. 'She is usually moored at either Monaco or Cannes and has a full-time captain.'

The information cost Pete €500. On the basis that it would help with a story, he would mark it down to expenses. Pete made a couple more calls and discovered that the boat wasn't in Monaco or Cannes. His contact in Monaco reckoned the boat left late last year for a refit somewhere or other, but not locally.

'Thanks mate,' said Jeremy. 'I can't tell you much at the moment, but odds-on your morning's work will have been your most profitable yet.'

'Exclusive as and when?'

'Of course, but in the meantime our discussion remains just between the two of us,' replied Jeremy. 'Now if you'll excuse me, I must dash.'

On the journey back, Jeremy phoned Emma.

'That's brilliant!' she said. 'You've got the name, the make and the type of boat and even know that she's being refitted.'

Kate called across to Emma, 'Look at Iceland first. If that's where Basel is, I bet that's where *Flying Goddess* is having her makeover. Have a chat to Jeremy's colleagues and get them to pass the information on to their man travelling to Iceland.'

The morning had gone by fast; it was already 12.15 p.m.

Emma called across to Kate. 'You've got a phone call from a DI Rick Feldon in Manchester.'

'Ar'noon, we've pulled in Stone and Wesson,' said a businesslike Mancunian voice. 'The story is that we've linked them with a paedo ring – indecent images, etc. Well, that's what the paperwork says. Could have got it wrong, though,' he said with a chuckle. 'Mr Stone is screaming blue murder. I've put an embargo on either of them seeing any outsiders. His solicitor isn't best pleased – human rights and all that!'

Emma called across, 'Remember to ask him about whether they use outsourcing companies in their police station.'

'Oh shit!' exclaimed Kate under her breath. 'I'd quite forgotten.' She asked Rick.

'Yes, catering,' came his reply.

'Do me a favour. As far as the two from Dewoodson are concerned, treat all your caterers as hostile! I'll explain later.'

'Will do,' said Rick with a hint of surprise in his voice. 'We picked up William Wesson at a property he was valuing. He's like a feral cat – seriously pissed off. I never knew surveyors could be so bloody difficult.'

'Wesson's computer has been set up in the interview room and we asked him to show us all his files relating to PREH. The bugger tried to delete the folder they were in. Thankfully we stopped him. Phil Scott is emailing the valuation report to you as we speak. By the way, if you want any more of the clowns at Dewoodson brought in, please let me know. It would be my pleasure. We've spoken to Mr Stone's number two and explained the sensitivity of the situation. He's agreed to close the office until Monday. Also, a couple of suits from MI5 turned up to give us a hand – said they were friends of yours. They're giving the offices a once-over.'

'Excellent work and thanks,' said Kate.

'Good luck at your end. Cheers!' Rick was about to hang up, when he added, 'Do you have a biro at hand? Here are Phil's and my mobile numbers. If you need anything, day or night, please don't hesitate.'

'Thanks Rick and please make certain that no outsiders speak to either of them.'

The email arrived; Kate opened the attachment and printed it off. Rafi scooped it up from the printer. He went through the valuation, marking off the properties which hadn't shown up on the mortgage register. Two of the new addresses were prime high street shop investments, but two were definitely not prime: some elderly light industrial units in Stalls Lane, Heysham, and a commercial property in

Castle Street, Peterhead. Both were vacant. Result! Two more possible properties, mused Rafi.

He then had a thought and scanned through the tenancy schedule. Windmill Road, Peterhead – vacant; Shawfarm Industrial Estate, Prestwick – one unit vacant; Folgate Road Industrial Estate, North Walsham – two units vacant; and Tees Road Industrial, Hartlepool – vacant.

Rafi typed Castle Street, Peterhead, into the mapping software. It was next to the docks. He did the same for Stalls Lane, Heysham. 'Bloody hell!' he uttered under his breath. It was right next to the nuclear power station.

'Found anything?' enquired Kate.

'We can add another nuclear power station to our list. The Heysham property is bang next to the nuclear power station.'

Rafi was about to continue when Emma piped up. 'Our contact at the coastguard has traced both of the missing trawlers. *Rosemarie* has just finished a refit at the dry dock in Great Yarmouth and *Highland Belle* is at Troon dry dock. Both are poised to set sail.'

'Well done, Emma,' said Kate. 'Are all the other trawlers at sea?'

'Yep. Except *Northern Rose*; she is still in Peterhead harbour. That gives us three exit points,' said Emma, who marked up the location of the two new properties and the two trawlers on the screen.

Rafi smiled. It was as if he was at the centre of the terrorists' web, undetected and slowly but surely identifying the strands of information that might enable them to scupper their plans. There were still too many missing pieces of information, but at last he felt they were getting a clearer idea of their intentions.

Kate stood up and clapped her hands. 'Let's recap on the information we have.' She pointed to the screen. 'We've trawlers poised to leave from three ports. Rafi has located suspicious properties at these five locations, and the terrorists have five missile launchers and sixteen unused missiles.' She scratched her head, as she looked at the screen. 'If we were to assume two targets per missile launcher then how might the properties and targets be paired? Any suggestions?'

'How's about we put the St Fergus gas terminal and Cruden Bay oil pumping station with the properties in Peterhead – as the targets for missile launcher number one?' said Emma

'And then there is the Hartlepool property which overlooks the local nuclear power station,' said John, 'but at the moment the second target in this pair is missing.'

Kate nodded.

'Number three could be Heysham nuclear power station – plus perhaps Hunterston nuclear power station up the coast? And launcher number four could then go with the huge Bacton gas facility and possibly Sizewell nuclear power station,' said Emma.

There was silence.

'Which leaves us with bugger-all for the fifth launcher – could it perhaps be the nuclear train at Willesden Sidings?' enquired John.

'It's all a bit iffy,' said Kate with a note of despondency in her voice.

'But a pattern is emerging,' said John. 'The proximity of the various dots to PREH's properties is too bloody close for comfort for this to be random. If you think back, twenty-four hours ago we had next to nothing!'

The conversation was stopped by Aidan cutting in. 'Can you stop what you're doing for a moment? I need to hear your views on a couple of thoughts.' Aidan looked at them from behind his growing piles of paper.

'I still have more to do, but I've reached the point where I'm convinced that a small group of investors *have* built up sizeable positions in both the long gilt and the interest rate futures and traded options contracts. If the positions I've found at my bank are replicated elsewhere and these speculators turn out to be right and the markets crash – the terrorists will make huge profits and there will be lots of bloody noses.'

Aidan turned to Rafi. 'What *if* we were able to stop the markets from crashing – or more specifically prevent interest rates rising and gilts prices falling – *and* limit the impact of the terrorist attacks.' He grinned, '*If* we could do this *then* we could turn the tables on the terrorists and wipe out their investments in the derivative markets.'

Aidan paused. 'I would be willing to bet that there are also a significant number of murky players with their snouts in the trough, who we could also take to the cleaners.'

'Wooah!' said Kate, 'That wouldn't be feasible, would it?'

'Aidan, it's brilliant!' exclaimed Rafi. '*All* we need to do is pre-empt most of the attacks and make certain that interest rates and gilts remain stable for – how long – a month?'

'No; far less than that. If interest rates remained stable, in a week to ten days the terrorists' positions in the futures markets would become exposed and they would either have to close them and crystallise large losses, or pay large margin calls. However, if interest rates were to fall, 24-48 hours would be enough to crucify them financially. In both cases their investments in the traded options markets would be wiped out.'

'That's all very well and good,' observed Kate, but the *if* is a massively big *if*.'

'Yes, I grant you that,' said Rafi, 'but isn't it nice to know that the terrorists mightn't have everything going their way?'

Kate looked at him with that same look she'd given him when she had asked him to work with her. 'You know what I like about you?' her eyes sparkled as she held his gaze. 'It's your unbridled optimism.'

'Hold on a moment!' said Aidan. 'If we go back to when would be the best time to carry out the attacks in terms of maximum impact on the markets, it would be first thing in the morning as the markets are opening, but not late morning or in the afternoon. The London Stock Exchange opens at 8 a.m. and dawn tomorrow is . . . ?

'7.25 a.m., give or take a bit,' answered Emma.

'What are you getting at?' asked Kate.

'We are led to believe the departure time of the trawler in Peterhead is tomorrow early afternoon, aren't we?' said Aidan.

'Yes.'

'If we are right and the trawlers are to be used as part of the terrorists' exit plan, I reckon that all three will leave at similar times.'

'OK,' said Kate sensing what he was getting at.

'So, thinking about it, I'd be willing to bet that the attacks are planned for tomorrow as that's when the trawlers are leaving, and that they will come between dawn and the markets opening at 8 a.m.,' said Aidan.

'Bloody hell! That gives us less than twenty hours,' said John, quite taken aback.

'We've got too many holes in our hypothesis,' said Kate. 'We've *got* to fill in more of these gaps! To put it bluntly, we *have* to find the missing targets, the missile launchers and the foot soldiers. In the meantime I'll warn the commissioner of our dire line of thinking. And remember, not a word of this to anyone, please.'

Greg popped his head around the door at that moment. 'Did I miss something interesting?'

'Yes,' said Kate, 'have you been there long?'

'No! You buggers are running me ragged. I dropped by to tell Aidan that I've arranged every computer access he should need. Bleeding strange,' said Greg. 'There I was working in my office, drawing up a list of all the databases we would need to get into, when the commissioner walked in and asked me – yes me – what he could do to help. I explained what I needed. He nodded and disappeared as quickly as he'd arrived. Not twenty minutes later he came back saying that he'd pulled a few strings. I've had the head of IT from Euronext.liffe, the CME in Chicago and Eurex in Frankfurt on the phone volunteering their services and wanting to know which secure IP addresses we would be using. They've sent me encrypted user names and passwords and authorised me to access all their databases. Their cooperation is 100%. Bloody marvellous if you ask me!'

He looked at Kate. 'And I walk in here to be asked if I'd been listening at the keyhole!'

Greg chuckled to himself and went on, 'Aidan, if I can use your PC for a moment I'll get it set up to access databases you've only dreamed of getting into.'

Aidan smiled, like a young boy being told he was getting the keys to the local sweet shop. 'Thanks,' he said and got up to let Greg take his seat.

In less than five minutes Greg had Aidan's computer set up.

Aidan's thanked him effusively and called across to Greg as he was leaving the office, 'Any chance of a better printer? There's going to be a lot of paper.' Looking in the direction of Emma and the old printer, he said, 'The old lady over there is getting too slow for me.'

Emma screwed up her face and then smiled at him.

Greg looked at Aidan. 'How big a machine did you have in mind?'

'Anything that prints quickly and has a big memory buffer would be great.'

'I'll see what I can find,' said Greg. Less than fifteen minutes later he was back pushing a printer-photocopier half the size of a desk. 'This little beauty is from accounts downstairs; please look after it.'

John, who had been sitting, contemplating, stirred. 'Why can't we just close down the markets involved and stop the terrorists that way?'

Aidan looked at him. 'In theory yes, but the turnover in these markets every hour of the trading day runs to squillions of pounds. To close the markets for anything other than a short period would be catastrophic for London's reputation. We could close them for a day. The problem is that there are many ways of covering one's tracks and the positions would still be there when the markets reopen. I've identified a number of suspicious contract notes, but it would take ages to look for them all. And this is offshore money via intermediary banks, which electronically can move the money quickly and secretively. It would be nigh on impossible to trace. What makes it really difficult is that we're only focusing on two parts of the market. The terrorists' positions are likely to be spread across a range of products. The two we have highlighted are the most obvious, but Sterling, the FTSE and gold would be good bets as well.'

Kate scratched her head thoughtfully. 'Let us suppose that Sheikh Tufayl is good for £2 billion; his cousins Maryam and Jameel, via their client's moneys, could be good for another £1 billion each and murky third parties put in another £1 billion. If this £5 billion is placed in the futures and traded options markets, and the terrorists get their way, what would their profit roughly be?' She looked at Aidan and Rafi.

Aidan spoke first. 'Conservatively they could make eight times their initial outlay; at the top end maybe fifteen times. Do you agree, Rafi?'

'Yes,' he replied.

'So in round terms the financial markets could be hit with losses of £50 billion,' calculated Kate and after a brief pause continued, 'at which point several banks and insurance companies would get into trouble and the Government would have to step in *again*!'

'Yes, it would be seriously nasty,' added Aidan.

'And the outright winners would be those sitting on key commodities, like oil!' said Rafi

'Thank you – I just wanted to be clear,' said Kate.

Jeremy hurried back into the office and updated the team on MI5's progress. 'Neil Gunton's team is working at full throttle. UKSOIL is at the top of their list. The CCTV footage from outside their shop on the eastern fringe of the City is being looked at. Whizzy new gait assessment software is being used to look at individuals' walking characteristics to identify suspect people. Neil desperately wants to speed up the process and get his hands on some photos to check against the CCTV footage.'

Jeremy smiled. 'On the travel agency front, things are looking promising. The UKSOIL shops collect students' travel requirements and pass them on to an independent private ABTA-approved travel agency – Fly Skywards Travel. I'm off to pay them a visit.'

The buzz of Jeremy's brief visit had gone. Rafi was sitting at his desk. He was tense, his wrist throbbed and his lower back ached. He felt awful. The lack of sleep had suddenly crept up and overwhelmed him.

John finished his phone call, walked over and pulled up a chair next to Rafi. 'Are you alright?'

Rafi gave a small nod.

'I'm sorry to be the bearer of bad news, but I've had a call about Callum's funeral. It's at 2.30 tomorrow in Clifton, outside Bristol. Kate has suggested that we send some flowers via the undertaker. We can't say they're from you. How about a card with something like: "Thank you for your friendship and help." Is that alright with you?'

Rafi sat there feeling desolate and nodded slowly.

'We have his parents' names and address should you wish to write and/or visit them when this is all over.'

He wasn't one for tears, but in his tiredness they welled up. There was nothing he could do to stop them. John briefly placed his arm across Rafi's shoulder as a gesture of comfort.

Rafi looked up to the heavens as if to seek divine inspiration. How on earth can we sort out this horrendous mess? he wondered. A tranquillity came over him. It was as if Callum was in the room alongside him. Rafi's mind was crystal clear – they needed a game plan to stop the adverse effects of the attacks on the financial system. And for that they would need three things: a huge pot of money, a group of people to whom the Treasury and the Bank of England would listen, and a . . . Kate called over interrupting his train of thought.

'If you're doing nothing could you see if you can find another property? We're still a couple of targets adrift.'

As if from nowhere, a possible solution flashed through his mind. His tiredness evaporated. Rafi felt relaxed, collected and strangely on top of things. 'Everyone! Do you have a moment? Can we go some-where quiet to get away from the phones, please? I need to run through an idea,' he called out.

'Let me finish this call and I'm there,' said Emma.

John nodded, indicating he would be there as soon as he, too, had finished his call.

Kate put down her phone. 'We can use the meeting room down the corridor.'

John walked in to the meeting room just as Kate had started to quiz Rafi. 'Why the meeting?'

Rafi started explaining, hesitantly. 'We're piecing together some of the locations of the terrorist attacks and hopefully we'll soon have a good enough picture to stop much of what they're planning. What scares me is their assault on the financial markets. Their two sets of plans are intertwined. So what's been worrying me are the conse-quences of one or two missiles getting through and a nuclear facility being damaged. The loss of life and the radioactive pollution would dent public confidence. The clean-up costs alone could run to billions before one even starts talking of decommissioning costs. Aidan, how big a pot of money do you think that the Government might need to sort out their financial problems if things get nasty? And how much could they take on without spooking the markets?'

'Answering your first question: how long is a piece of string? It could be anywhere between . . .' Aidan hesitated and the room fell totally silent. 'Let's say in excess of £75 billion as a ballpark figure. It could easily be more. Answering the second part of your question, in the present environment, I reckon £15 billion of additional expenditures spread over, say, five years would be containable – a whisker over 1 penny on income tax.'

'What are you getting at?' enquired Kate quietly, as though suspecting Rafi had flipped under the strain. Her eyes still had a sparkle to them and looked at him caringly.

'Well,' said Rafi, 'a few minutes ago you mentioned property – as I was thinking about Callum. He'd been visiting a specialist property investor before he was killed. Who's the biggest owner of property and tangible assets in the UK?'

'The Government, the public sector and its various agencies,' replied Aidan. 'I recall from a recent article in the financial press that it is worth around £500 billion.'

'Precisely!' said Rafi. 'So why couldn't the Government put together a contingency fund, such that it did *not* have to go to the debt markets? Instead it could package up these assets into one or more of the new real estate investment trust vehicles – rather like the Swedish Government has done. Our Government could then issue shares in these REITs to those who require payment, compensation, etc., which is straightforward as they would be listed on the London Stock Exchange. Let's suppose the Government had to pay out and therefore issue a whopping £100 billion in REIT shares over five years. The cost of the dividends would be modest – not far off your 1 penny on income tax.'

'Yes, but I thought that the commercial property market and real estate investment trusts were in the doldrums at the moment.' Aidan paused. 'Sorry, I don't mean to be a wet blanket.'

Rafi looked crestfallen. He thought for a moment. 'OK, how about pepping up the market?'

Aidan looked at Rafi; a broad smile stretched across his tired face. 'What do you have in mind?'

Rafi's mind was racing. 'You could improve the demand for the REIT shares. What if the pension industry and those retiring could use

135

these investments as an alternative to annuities? The REITs would have better yields than Government bonds and would appeal to many pension fund trustees and those with private pensions. Also, property's inflation hedging characteristics would be an attractive feature.' He paused. 'Hold on a moment – *and* property valuations for owner-occupied properties are done on an existing use with vacant possession basis. Whereas the valuations for the REITs' accounts would use the investment valuation method *and* the properties would have a Government lease on them guaranteeing the income flows – the valuations would therefore be a lot higher.'

'Simply brilliant! No, better than that, it's the nuts!' said Aidan. 'Real estate investment trusts would take off. Your sleight of hand would easily produce £125 billion for the Government to use at a manageable cost. Furthermore, if they raised a bit extra they could use it to buy back gilts and keep prices firm. With all their assets they could have a war chest of £400 billion, or more. That would underpin the markets – big time. Bloody magic!'

Aidan paused for a moment. 'Your suggestion would need to be packaged properly and explained to the Treasury in terms that they understood. If it went hand in hand with a modest drop in interest rates and the markets remained stable for a couple of days, then the terrorists' derivative positions would become untenable and they'd be wiped out financially.'

'Hold on a moment,' said John. 'Could you explain what an REIT is?'

'A real estate investment trust is the property investment vehicle of choice for major investors. All it does is group a number of property investments under one umbrella. Investors can buy shares via the stock market, and they receive dividends instead of rents.'

Kate looked at Aidan and asked, 'Is this realistically a possible solution to the impending financial problems?'

'Yes, yes it is!'

'Excellent! In which case let's get back to finding the terrorists with the missile launchers,' said Kate. The meeting had finished. She stepped over and gave Rafi a hug.

He flinched and jumped back.

'Oh sorry,' she said, looking worriedly at him. It was as if he'd repulsed an unwanted invasion of his personal space.

He'd done it again – he'd sent out a contrary signal. Kate turned to go. Rafi reached out and touched her shoulder; she turned and their eyes met.

'I'm sorry,' he said. 'I ran out of painkillers at lunchtime: my shoulder and back are rather painful, not to mention my wrist. Are you OK?'

'Fine,' she replied, 'I'm glad. No, that didn't come out right: I'm not glad you're in pain, but rather—'

'Don't worry,' Rafi cut in.

Part 4

Kate sat at her desk hoping beyond all hope that crucial missing pieces of the jigsaw puzzle would start falling into place. Her instincts as a detective told her that her investigation was perilously poised. Rafi and Aidan's reading of the position could all be a horrendous miscalculation and if their scenario was wrong she would not only look a real idiot, but . . .

Jeremy's phone rang, interrupting Kate's thoughts. John put the call on speakerphone. It was a call from Jeremy's colleague, Gareth, in Iceland. 'How's tricks, Gareth? Jeremy's out at the moment,' said John.

'It's brass monkeys here! And there's no bloody daylight!' came the reply. 'Got a nice hotel, though I'm not certain if I go a bundle on the cod liver oil or the roast puffin. What the heck! At least the locals are hospitable. I've hooked up with the Víkingasveitin, their Viking Squad, who seem to be a cross between our MI5 and the SAS. We've been inspecting all the shipyards and boatyards around Reykjavík – said it was a health and safety check. We have just hit the bullseye at the last boatyard. There was a large yellow-hulled motorboat on the slipway, inside the big boat shed. Didn't look anything like the picture I got of *Flying Goddess*; they'd altered her superstructure and given her a new name to go with her new colour: *Golden Sundancer*. I spotted Talal inspecting the boat with a geezer wearing a captain's hat. We didn't want to tip Talal off, so we left sharpish.'

'Good news that you've found Talal,' said John.

Kate called across, 'Any chance you could find out exactly what work the boatyard has done to her?'

'Whilst Talal is in there, I can't just walk in and chat to the boatyard manager,' replied Gareth. 'It would be too bloody obvious. As we speak, I'm standing outside waiting to see if they leave, which is why I'm so bloody cold.'

'Great work. Keep in touch,' said John replacing the receiver.

'Now we've found Talal and the sheikh's yacht, what we could do with knowing is what they are going to do next,' said Kate.

'I've an idea,' said Emma. 'If I could borrow Aidan for a few minutes and if the people at the Icelandic boatyard speak English, it might work.'

'What do you have in mind?' asked Kate.

'Well, Aidan is the type of guy who might easily be able to afford something like *Golden Sundancer*. Why doesn't he pretend that he's considering buying a second-hand super-yacht which needs a refit? All he needs are the sales particulars of a boat and a contact suggesting the Reykjavík yard. Hopefully, the yard manager will be interested in new business and not consider questions linked to his last four or five fit-outs as suspicious.'

'Good idea,' said Kate, before adding, 'John, see if you can get the contact details of the yacht broker Jeremy's journalist friend, Pete, has been using.'

'No problems.' Several minutes later, after a tortuous phone call, John had the broker's name and phone number. 'My God,' he said, 'that was like drawing teeth. Journalists are too bloody protective of their sources for their own good.'

Emma took the piece of paper from Jeremy and dialled the yacht broker's number. 'Hello, I wonder if you could help me. I'm the personal assistant of Aidan Gilchrist, of international bankers Maine Leadbetter in the City of London. My boss tells me that you're the agents to speak to concerning the purchase of a large powerboat . . . Good, good, thank you. Could you please give me the details of what you have on your books in the €3 million price bracket? If possible located in Scandinavia, which is where his partner is from. I should mention that he's thinking in terms of spending a tidy sum on getting the boat refitted to her taste – lucky lady!' Emma chuckled. 'Yes, I can give you some contact details.' Emma gave her ex-directory phone number and the station's private fax number which came into the station's switchboard.

'Work address? Hold on a moment, sorry the other phone is going.' Emma put her hand over the receiver and shouted across to Aidan. 'What on earth is your work address?'

He scribbled it down for her.

'My boss is a bit impatient. Could you perhaps fax me something at your earliest convenience? Within the next ten minutes would be great. Thank you.'

As good as his word, the yacht broker faxed through the details of three stunning motor yachts, ranging from twenty to thirty metres in length with prices between €2 million and €3.5 million.

Aidan, briefed by Emma, picked up the phone and spoke to the Reykjavík boatyard. One could see very quickly why Aidan was a top financial dealer. He oozed charm, but came quickly to the point. It didn't take long before the boatyard manager was chatting openly and describing the boats they'd worked on.

'So, have you done work on anything seriously fast?' enquired Aidan.

'Yes,' came the reply.

'Excellent.' And before he could ask what, the shipyard manager helpfully proceeded to give a lengthy description of what they'd done to a Sunseeker Predator 75. 'She's had a complete refit; new colour to the hull. We installed long-range fuel tanks, upgraded the engines and the air-conditioning, done work to the bridge and superstructure to make the vessel more comfortable in inclement seas and installed de-icing kit to help her with the local weather. Basically we've enabled the boat to go virtually anywhere at any time of the year,' said the manager proudly.

'Did you do work to the interior?'

'Not much needed – oh we did put in a couple of very large ice boxes, well insulated with polystyrene. They won't run out of beer for ages!' Aidan cut to the chase. 'My brokers and I are looking at . . .' he picked one of the details of the boats in front of him at random, 'a seventy-foot motor vessel, currently moored in Sweden. It'll need its engines reconditioning and my partner doesn't like the colours of the state room or the master bedroom. How soon could you start work on her? I'm thinking of putting a bid in this afternoon – subject to survey, of course.'

Aidan paused and listened to the shipyard manager, and then said, 'Oh that would be excellent. You say that the works to *Golden Sundancer* are completed, yes? So you can start any time from next week, as soon as the boat is delivered.'

Aidan drew breath and continued. 'My partner, Johanna, is rather fussy. Would it possible for her to fly over, say, tomorrow or the next day to see the quality of your work on the Sunseeker 75?'

He paused again. 'Oh that's a shame; she'll be disappointed that *Golden Sundancer* is putting to sea later this evening. Thank you very much for your time though, you've been most helpful. I have your

141

name and contact details so I'll ring again on Monday to discuss the refit works.'

With that Aidan gently replaced the receiver, stood up and bowed to a round of applause from Emma.

'Good work – no – excellent work,' said Emma. 'I knew you could do it. So we now know that the sheikh's boat is leaving within the next twelve hours.'

Emma did some mental arithmetic. 'That would tie in with the possibility of a rendezvous with the trawler from Peterhead, somewhere off the north coast of Scotland tomorrow night.'

'Time is running out,' said Kate. 'We have *got to* find the missing locations and the people who are going to fire the missiles.'

Emma walked casually over to Aidan's desk. 'I didn't realise you had a partner.'

'Ah well, I can be rather deceptive.'

'You can say that again,' said Emma, looking a little crestfallen.

Aidan smiled. 'No you've got it wrong; it's my partner that's the deception.'

Emma brightened visibly.

'Emma, I have a problem,' said Aidan, changing the subject. 'I could do with some more space. I was wondering if you could help. I've printed out the vast majority of the contract notes and I'm swamped with paper!' He flashed one of his most inviting and charming smiles in her direction. 'Any bright ideas where I could go?'

Emma muttered something under her breath which Kate didn't catch.

'Thanks,' said Aidan. 'I need to find a large table or floor: somewhere where I can lay out all this bumph,' he said pointing to the piles of paper stacked on and around his desk. 'I'm almost there but the lack of space is slowing me down.'

Kate stood up. 'You two follow me. Pass me some papers to carry.' They left the room weighed down with printouts.

Kate and Emma returned a couple minutes later to collect the remaining paperwork. 'We've put him in the commissioner's conference room and asked Beverley to keep an eye on him and to top him up with coffee. The commissioner is out, so he should get some peace and quiet,' said Kate.

Half an hour later Aidan called Emma. He sounded pleased. 'Could you, Rafi and Kate come up to look at a few things?'

They walked into the commissioner's conference room and saw it was covered with paper – not just the large oval table but also the chairs, which had been pushed against the walls, and the carpet as well.

'Thanks for coming.' Aidan greeted them with a beaming smile. 'What do you think? Beverley is fantastic; look at all the Post-its she's given me.'

Emma looked around the room; each pile had a Post-it on top of it.

'Is this entire lot colour-coded?' enquired Emma.

'Yep. It hasn't taken nearly as long as I thought it would. I've categorised the contract notes into various different types of deal with colour-coding. Things are falling into place,' he said to Emma. 'Rafi's hunch is right: there's definitely something afoot. Let me summarise where I've got to. I've been focusing on the long gilt contracts. The trades, individually, are modest in size, but when put together it's a different matter. Someone has been position building for several weeks. I started with my book at Maine Leadbetter. I've had six investors writing – selling – put contracts. On the other side, Prima Terra have been buying them via an offshore account. I then looked at deals done by other brokers and I've been able to piece together a relatively complete picture. The other players buying the put positions are using intermediaries, mainly second or third division international banks.'

John stuck his head around the corner of the door. 'I thought that you might be up to something.'

'Come on in,' said Aidan with a smile. 'Let me show you what I've uncovered. I've found the main buyers and sellers of the derivative contracts. Those with blue Post-its are Prima Terra's and the green ones are those which I also reckon are linked to the terrorists.'

'Sorry to interrupt,' said Emma. 'I forgot to ask, how did your call to ESSA go?'

'Oh bloody hell! It quite slipped my mind. What time is it?'

'4.43 p.m.'

'Excuse me, let me make that call,' said Aidan apologetically.

'OK,' said Kate, 'let's rendezvous back here when Aidan has finished his call.'

Ten minutes later Aidan was back in the conference room. 'Where were we? Oh, yes. On the other side to the terrorists' positions, I've identified a number of investors whose exposures could lead to huge losses,' said Aidan pointing to the various piles strewn over the conference room table with pink Post-its. We've two building socie-ties, two insurance companies, one local authority and one metropolitan authority – all have been investing the wrong way around: they should be buyers of these put contracts, not selling them! They have increased their risk exposure exponentially. Bloody strange, bloody silly and bloody dangerous!

'Their risk management systems should have picked this up, unless the contracts were booked in a hidden holding account,' continued Aidan. 'If so, no one other than the dealers would be aware of the positions. The expectation would be that they would be traded on for a profit in a matter of days – this neatly ties in with my fascinating phone conversation with ESSA. Would it surprise you to find that ESSA has placed people at both of the building societies and one of the insurance companies? I only found out about these three. I didn't want them to smell a rat if I rattled off the whole list! My conclusion is that these people have been writing the put contracts that the terrorists have been buying.'

'Very clever,' said Emma.

'Rafi did you read the Bank of England's Financial Stability Report that came out recently?' enquired Aidan.

'Yes.'

'With this scale of potential losses I have uncovered, if things go as the terrorists plan – given the delicate state of the financial sector – contagion would rapidly set in, wouldn't it?' asked Aidan.

Rafi nodded.

'Sorry – I've heard you talk about contagion before, could you explain what you mean by it, please?' asked John.

'If you get measles you're contagious, right? In the financial markets contagion sets in when the troubles of one player are transferred across to another financially healthy player, who, for their part, gets into financial trouble and passes the problem on to more players. We saw it happen in the recent credit crunch when a number of banks that had been financially sound, suddenly found themselves to be in financial difficulty. Basically it's a matter of there being too many forced sellers and too few buyers. Prices of assets fall dramatically, which leaves the financial sector short of capital. In our case, the terrorists have targeted six institutions. And they will very quickly become insolvent. Other banks, insurance companies and financial institutions get sucked into the downward spiral, *unless* the provider of liquidity of last resort, the Bank of England, quickly steps in and provides sufficient cash to help those in trouble,' said Aidan. 'What makes it particularly dangerous is the losses will be heaped on six players and not spread across the market.'

'The Bank would have to act very quickly and decisively or the downward momentum could become unstoppable,' added Rafi.

'I don't think procrastination will be a problem, given their recent experience with the banking crisis,' Aidan scratched his head. 'What concerns me is the UK Government can't keep on borrowing vast sums of money to bail out companies in the financial markets. Very soon they will hit the buffers and find that international investors will not lend to them. Or if they do it will be at massively increased interest rates. Then it will be crunch time.'

'And there could be big costs associated with their missile attacks,' Rafi looked thoughtful, 'so part of our plan must be to put across to the Government the downside hazards in such a way that they can make informed decisions quickly.'

'Good idea,' said John. 'What scares me is that they have resources which rival those of a hostile small to medium sized country. And we should not underestimate the damage they are capable of inflicting.'

Kate's mouth was wide open; she regained her composure. 'Thank you for describing the scale of the bad news. This is seriously frightening. But first things first – we have *a lot* of loose ends to tidy up and time is short. In order of priority: we must stop the terrorists' attacks or at least significantly limit the damage. And then, Rafi and Aidan, we need you to come up with a solution to stop the markets going into meltdown.'

'And third, pigs may fly,' added John.

'No, thirdly we've got to break this appalling news to our bosses – and soon.' Kate stood up, looking pale and tired. 'Aidan thanks for your excellent work.'

Rafi had been thinking quietly about the practicalities of getting the Government and the Bank of England to move quickly. 'One last item, please? Sorting out a strategy to avert the financial mess will take some while and time isn't a commodity we have,' he said, 'I'd like to suggest at our meeting with the chiefs that we get permission to gather together a small team of financial experts who could draw up a briefing document to assist the decision makers at the Treasury and Bank of England.'

'Good idea,' replied Kate.

Jeremy returned, positively bouncing like Tigger. 'Who's a clever boy? I've had a most fruitful time with Dominique, the manager at the travel agent that UKSOIL use. We looked at the typical characteristics of the tickets booked by them. The vast majority were low-cost packages to locations throughout Africa and were generally last minute bookings on to charter and other flights which had unsold seats. The typical duration was between one and three months.'

'Then I got Dominique to see if there were any tickets which were out of the ordinary,' said Jeremy. 'She wasn't impressed as there are thousands of tickets. Specifically, she went searching for business class and full cost tickets, and trips where there were prearranged stop-overs. My logic was that if they were recruiting bombers they'd look after them and want them to go to a training camp as well as do their voluntary work.'

Jeremy smiled. 'We have ten. Yes, *ten* individuals who were given favoured treatment by UKSOIL. And guess what? One of the names that came out of the computer was that of Ima adwafeeq, – or if one puts the space in the right place: Imaad Wafeeq, the Bishopsgate bomber! I've passed all the names to my colleagues, who will send through as much information as they can find on each of them. As we speak all the suspects are being traced and will be put under surveil-lance.'

Jeremy beamed. 'The offer of coffee and doughnuts did the trick. Within half an hour she'd gone back three years and identified all the people who fitted our search criteria. There were literally hundreds of flights that matched. In a tick she had them sorted alphabetically. The number of different names on the list wasn't that great – just below fifty – but only ten had a pre-booked stopover in Somalia. When I pointed out Imaad Wafeeq's name, she went white. She thought I was there to prove she was implicitly involved in the Bishopsgate bombing. It took me five minutes to calm her down and to emphasise the importance of keeping what we had found totally confidential.'

'As a matter of curiosity, where exactly were the stopovers in Somalia?' enquired Emma.

'Mogadishu,' replied Jeremy.

'Hold on a minute – where was it that the other PhD student, Miti someone, came from?'

'What a good memory you've got,' said Jeremy. 'You're spot on. Miti Lakhani's family have a business operation in Mogadishu. I wish I'd remembered that before you did,' he said with a smile in Emma's direction.

Colonel Matlik was punctual. At 5.15 p.m. Kate's phone rang. She was pleased to hear his telltale accent on the line.

'Good evening, I have more news for you,' he said, in his customary succinct manner. 'Thank you for the names and photos you emailed me. You have caused quite a stir. We looked at the mugshots and straight away identified three as being highly undesirable. I hope it's OK – I bounced their details on to the FSB, the Russian Secret Service. The phone lines between here and Moscow have been red-hot. It seems that you have unearthed four individuals who are on their most wanted list! They are using false identities. In reality they are: Rudnik Miromov and Dakka Dudayev, two former Chechen army officers. The Russians lost track of them ten months ago. The other two are: Aslan Popovskaya and Sergy Kowshaya, whose last known occupation was as part of a specialist Chechen hit squad – they also disappeared. Be advised: all four individuals should be treated with extreme caution. They have no scruples and are trained in everything from unarmed combat and heavy machine guns, to missile launchers and high explosives. In the words of my Russian friends these four are "wermin" – the sooner they can be exterminated, the better! Kornet missiles in their hands are a recipe for disaster.'

'Kate, I must tell you, the next person on your list had the Russians rolling with laughter. He's an Arab, from the Gulf originally. Kaleem Shah trained as an officer cadet at your Sandhurst. No doubt your records will confirm this and where he went subsequently. They have him down, until a year ago, as being attached to an international news corps as their minder in the battle zones of the Middle East. We have nothing untoward on the other three names. I have asked a colleague to email you all the details we have on these undesirables. He is sending you copies of both the Russian files and our translation of them. I hope that they help. Sorry to sound like an overprotective father, but if the Russians say they're real shits, tell your SAS to treat them with the utmost caution.'

'Colonel, thank you,' said Kate.

'Unfortunately, I have some further information from the raid on AEIEA's premises. It is not news you will want to hear. Their manifest shows that they made a delivery of four South African 60 mm Vektor mortars and eighty high-explosive shells on the same day as the Kornet missiles were handed over. They're compact and deadly. Their barrel length is only 650 mm, but they have a range of up to 2 km if the firer opts for a ballistic trajectory.'

'Sorry?' said Kate.

'Detonates the explosive round in the air above the target,' explained the colonel. 'The firing rate, in the hands of a professional, is twenty shells a minute. If aimed straight at its target the range drops to half a kilometre and the shells can go through 500 mm of armour or over one metre of reinforced concrete. Basically, they are nasty little weapons – rather useful for attacking soft targets, I would suggest.'

'Such as?'

'In ballistic trajectory mode, their blast radius is thirty metres. They would work a treat against,' the colonel paused, 'fuel tanks – oil and gas storage plants in particular.'

'That fits in with a couple of the targets we've identified,' said Kate. 'Your information is most timely and thanks for all the trouble you've taken.'

'No problem; we Europeans have a duty protect one another,' came the reply. 'Look after yourself.'

'I'll try to,' replied Kate, ending the call.

K ate raised her voice for all to hear. 'Our worst fears have been confirmed by Colonel Matlik. There are four Chechen mercenaries on the terrorists' payroll.' She picked up the phone again and dialled Neil Gunton, Jeremy's boss. Normally she would have waited for Jeremy to liaise with his boss, but time was critical. She got through on the third ring.

'Neil Gunton speaking,' said a gravelly voice.

'Good afternoon, Kate Adams here.' She cut to the chase. 'The names Jeremy sent you earlier from Immigration – how are you getting on?'

'So far we haven't managed to get much on them. Our analysts suggest that three, possibly four, of them are Chechen. However, we do have chapter and verse on Kaleem Shah. We trained him at Sandhurst. He's been working in Lebanon and the Middle East as a journalist with a number of the international networks.'

'At this end we've had a bit of luck,' Kate replied. 'I'm emailing you the information we've just received from David's friend at the Estonian Security Service. Unfortunately, four *are* Chechens and are as bad as they could possibly get. We're advised that in addition to the Kornet missiles, they have four South African 60 mm Vector mortars.'

'Oh, hell!' came the reply.

'We're making progress at this end in identifying likely targets,' said Kate. 'We now believe that the four Chechens will attack two targets each. We're working on identifying or eliminating the number of targets.'

'What do you mean by eliminating?'

'It's just occurred to me that the fifth Kornet missile launcher could be for the terrorists' fast getaway vessel. If confirmed, I believe that there will be eight and not ten targets to find,' said Kate.

'What makes you think a missile launcher is destined for their getaway boat?' asked Neil.

'The terrorists have had a large cool box built into their getaway boat, and the description indicates it is the right size to house the boxes containing the missile launcher and its missiles. We think we now know the location of five of the targets, so I reckon we're now only missing three targets.' Kate paused, then went on, 'An alternative view could be that the fifth Kornet launcher is with the Arab, Kaleem Shah, a professional soldier, and that he has two targets. If so we are five targets short. We have a briefing meeting with the commissioner at 6 p.m. You would be welcome to attend.'

'Thank you,' said Neil. 'Jeremy is keeping me well posted. You've pulled more out of the woodwork in the past twenty-four hours than we've been able to over the past couple of months! I've got a 6 o'clock meeting with my boss too. Shall we talk again after our respective meetings?'

The question was followed by an ominous pause. 'Bloody hell, I see what you mean. I've just decrypted your email attachments,' said Neil. 'These Chechens are mean buggers. I'll speak to the boss immediately and ask that he puts the whole section on standby.'

'Sir,' said Kate in a diplomatic tone. 'The work you and John's team have been doing points to the terrorists having many people in high places. I understand your lengthy list is still growing and includes a special adviser to Number 10, several Members of Parliament and a number of other very well-connected individuals. Should we be worrying about whether any of these people are moles or sleepers?'

'Yes, we should.'

'Well, sir,' said Kate, hesitating briefly, 'our concern is that if the terrorists were to find out through one of these people that we are on to them, they will move to a plan "B" and change their targets, leaving us totally in the dark and up shit creek without a paddle. With the Kornet missile launchers they can have a shot at practically any target they like.'

'You're right, Kate, it's a very tricky situation. The potential damage that one of these missile launchers can do in the hands of a professional is unthinkable. Your reading of the position is very similar to ours,' said Neil. 'MI5 agrees that it would be better to go after the terrorists at known targets rather than let them slip away and blow the ruddy daylights out of a series of other targets when the whim takes them.'

'Thank you, sir,' said Kate.

'What's your latest thinking regarding when the attacks will come?' asked Neil.

'Tomorrow between dawn and the London Stock Market's opening at 8 o'clock. They'll want as much news exposure as possible to undermine the financial markets, so that they can take their huge profits on their derivatives positions. Has Jeremy chatted to you about this?'

'Yes, thank you,' said Neil. 'Sorry, I have to dash, let's talk again soon.'

Rafi looked across at Kate. He sensed that she felt pleased with her team's progress, but was shocked by the horrendous possibilities that were opening up in front of her. He looked across at the clock; it was 5.18 p.m. There was less than an hour to go before the evening meeting with the commissioner and the chief superintendent. They were still missing the extra pieces of property information and he was pinning his hopes on Manchester police unearthing something. However, he was worried that they wouldn't have enough time.

Rafi felt out of sorts and irritable. Something he couldn't put his finger on was missing. He stood up and walked around the office. His tired head ached and he was finding it increasingly difficult to concentrate for anything more than a few minutes at a time. Bloody hell, he needed to get his act together. It was only late afternoon, but it felt like midnight. He walked over and poured himself a cup of black coffee. Back at his desk, he sipped the hot coffee, studied the valuation report again and picked up the last three sets of accounts for PREH.

He turned to the most recent balance sheet and looked at the property assets figure. Oh shit! Why the hell hadn't he noticed this earlier? The figure in the accounts was greater than the total set out in the Dewoodson valuation report. Bloody hell! There was £7.4 million unaccounted for! His mind was like a car without synchromesh. He struggled to think of a reason why it might be different. Of course! Development properties could be held in the accounts at cost – and they wouldn't necessarily be included in the valuation report. Rafi stopped and thought. So somewhere there had to be details of the missing developments – probably a letter from the valuer which simply stated that the developments had a value greater than their book cost. £7.4 million wasn't large, but it could conceal one or more key properties. They had to find this missing piece of information. 'Oh yes!' he exclaimed.

Kate looked at him as if he had a screw loose.

'That devious little bugger Wesson is still hampering our investigations,' Rafi exclaimed.

'What do you mean?'

'We're missing a letter which sets out PREH's development properties. See if Rick can get the valuer to talk and get him to do a word search for "development" on all their computers.'

John called across the room. 'Want an update on MI5 and UK-SOIL?' It was a rhetorical question. 'It seems that the journalist Kaleem Shah is the suicide bombers' quartermaster. The good news is that they've traced and have under surveillance five of the suspects. The question is how the hell do we work out what target, or targets, this little team is going to attack? So far MI5 have drawn a blank!'

'Let's try and narrow it down a bit,' said Kate. 'Do we think that Kaleem Shah is a suicide bomber?'

'No,' said John, 'he's the organiser.'

'Will he stay in the UK or flee with the Chechen terrorists?' asked Kate.

'I reckon he'll hop on board one of the trawlers,' said John.

'I'd put my money on Great Yarmouth,' said Emma, 'and opt for the suicide bombers going for a London-based target, as it would give the highest profile.'

'But where might they strike?' asked Kate.

Aidan, who had returned from the conference room upstairs, volunteered a comment. 'They'll stay well away from the financial exchanges. The last thing they'll want is to have the markets closed because then they won't be able to get their hands on all their profits.'

'Good point,' said Kate.

'Perhaps they intend to use the suicide bombers to scare people?' Rafi ventured.

'What could we put on the list then?' asked Kate.

'Transport hubs,' suggested John.

'Politicians and residential areas where City bankers live,' added Emma, 'and what about top schools, where foreigners working in the City send their children?'

'Anything else?' said Kate.

'The nuclear train?' suggested John.

'I doubt if the suicide bombers' explosives would be powerful enough to do any real damage,' said Emma, 'or at least that's what the reports I've read indicate.'

Rafi wasn't certain where the idea came from, but his thoughts had wandered to other things nuclear. 'Could they target the nuclear arms industry? If an attack resulted in a radioactive leak, others could use it as a way of putting pressure on the Government and the new upgraded Trident missiles programme.'

Everyone turned and looked at him.

'Emma, is there anything in the South-East that might fit the bill?' asked Kate.

'The obvious one is the Atomic Weapons Establishment at Aldermaston, outside Reading.'

'Thank you. Please put it on your screen.'

Emma was frowning. 'Can we go back a step or two, please? Oughtn't we to be thinking of other ways of tracing where the terrorists might be? No doubt MI5 will have gone through the list of possibilities systematically. But, might it be worth checking to see if Unicorn Crescent Finance has issued any of the missing suicide bombers or Kaleem Shah with a credit card which doesn't show up on the usual searches done by MI5?'

'You mean they could be using a credit card, thinking it was safe?' continued Kate.

'Worth a try!' said John. He called across to Peter, 'Did you get that? Can you pass it on to Jeremy's boss, Neil Gunton? Thanks.'

A minute later Peter put down the phone, looking relieved.

'How did Neil take your suggestion?' asked Kate.

'Surprisingly well – all he said was thank you.'

Kate's phone rang; it was Beverley, the commissioner's personal assistant.

'Oh dear, yes of course,' replied Kate. 'Emma could you and Aidan tidy up his papers which are strewn around the commissioner's conference room. He is back and would like to use it!'

Rafi sat there thinking. What else might he have missed? He dozed off.

At 5.55 p.m. Kate lightly shook him but he remained out for the count. She paused wondering which bit was safest to shake a little harder. She softly tapped his leg.

Rafi woke suddenly. 'Ooouch!' he exclaimed.

'Don't tell me you've got a bruise there as well!' said Kate. 'Sorry, but I'm running out of options as to where's safe to touch you.'

'No probs! Was I asleep long?' Rafi sat up to find everyone was looking at him. 'Sorry for the forty winks, but sleep has been a bit scarce.'

'Time to see the boss,' said Kate.

This was going to be make or break, thought Rafi as he followed the team up the back stairs to the commissioner's conference room. He was worried key pieces of the terrorists' plans were still missing. The terrorists had planned the whole affair with great precision. Their plans were multifaceted and this made them very difficult to stop. At least the terrorists didn't know they were on to them. He arrived in the boardroom still wrapped up in his own world.

Rafi was brought back to reality by a gentle touch on his shoulder.

'Are you OK?' enquired Kate. Rafi sensed that a bond of mutual understanding and respect had started to form between them. He turned and looked straight into Kate's warm eyes, not two feet away. He hadn't had the opportunity to look at her face close up – it was her eyes that captivated him.

'Sorry,' Rafi stuttered, 'I was miles away – again. It's just that the terrorists have been very careful to cover their tracks and plan to attack in several places at once. I keep worrying that I've missed something and it turns out to be costly.'

Close up, Kate's smile and her twinkling eyes had a disarming effect. Rafi wasn't accustomed to such closeness; he moved back a pace to give himself a bit of breathing space and stepped straight into the path of the commissioner, who had entered the room at some speed, aware no doubt that he and David were running two minutes late.

'Sorry sir.' Rafi noticed that he'd scuffed the commissioner's pristinely polished shoes.

'No problem,' came the reply, 'let's get started!'

Rafi turned and looked at Kate whose smile was bordering on a chuckle. She looked at him, whispering, 'Whoops.'

At the boardroom table, Kate and Rafi sat opposite each other. The commissioner looked around the table. 'So, how are you progressing? As we agreed at our last meeting, this is crunch time. We will have to inform our political masters sooner rather than later. Kate, please update us.'

Kate looked at the faces around the table. They looked haggard. She just hoped she could do herself justice and convey the gravity of the position to the commissioner. The chips were down and she didn't like what she was going to report.

'Sir, let me summarise the position. Quite a lot has happened since our recent phone conversation. We believe that the missile attacks will come in the first couple of hours of daylight tomorrow morning. Through David's Estonian contact, Colonel Matlik, we have confirmation that the terrorists have five Kornet anti-tank missile launchers and between three and four missiles per launcher. As you know, these missiles are lethal pieces of equipment. In addition, we now find that they also have four South African 60 mm Vektor mortars with eighty high-explosive shells.'

Kate paused. 'We've narrowed down the potential locations of the targets and I'll come back to this in a minute.' The commissioner nodded.

'Following helpful discussions with the Immigration Office, we have identified two fast track and legitimate ways of getting UK visas, which the terrorists have used to get five people into the UK. Colonel Matlik and his contacts in Moscow have identified four as being former Chechen militia. We're advised to treat Messrs Miromov, Dudayev, Popovskaya and Kowshaya with extreme caution. We are told that their training and experience is such that they'll give the SAS a run for their money. The fifth person, a journalist called Kaleem Shah, is ex-Sandhurst and has experience of war zones in the Middle East and urban warfare.'

Kate paused again. 'We believe that each Chechen mercenary has a Kornet missile launcher, a Vektor mortar and two targets. Jeremy has been chatting to a senior contact in the SAS, who advises that they are likely to be operating as individuals. As far as the fifth missile launcher is concerned, we think it is for their high speed getaway vessel, *Golden Sundancer*. She is in the North Atlantic, heading, we believe, for a rendezvous point off the north Scottish coast tomorrow evening.

'Nine UKSOIL-trained suicide bombers have been identified, as has their quartermaster, Kaleem Shah. Jeremy's colleagues at MI5 have traced five of them, but unfortunately Mr Shah and four of the suicide bombers are unaccounted for. Moving on to the ringleaders – MI5 have the four . . . Jameel Furud, Basel Talal, Maryam Vynckt and Sheikh Akram Tufayl – under constant but discrete surveillance. There is a fifth possible ringleader: Miti Lakhani, who runs their terrorist training base in Africa. Unfortunately he has vanished. Maryam and the sheikh are behaving normally. Jameel is enjoying his golf at a luxury hotel in Marrakech and Basel is on board their getaway vessel *Golden Sundancer*.

'Three of the terrorists' deep sea trawlers are in port at Peterhead, Great Yarmouth and Troon and ready to put to sea. All are fully provisioned for a long voyage. Two of the vessels have recently undergone major refits during which new engines and long range fuel tanks were put in. The engines have been fully commissioned over the past couple of weeks. We therefore have three exit points.'

Kate paused and took a sip of water. 'We have either eight or ten targets to identify and protect. Until we have confirmation that the fifth missile launcher is on the getaway vessel we must assume that there are ten targets.' Kate looked across at her two bosses. 'Our current informed guesses are that: terrorist number one will attack Hartlepool Nuclear Power Station, plus one further target currently unknown.' There was an audible drawing in of breath as the word nuclear was uttered. 'They have a vacant industrial property which overlooks the power station,' she explained.

'The second will attack the St Fergus gas terminal and storage tanks and the North Sea oil pumping station at Cruden Bay. Both are close to Peterhead, where the terrorists own two ideally located and vacant industrial properties.

'Number three will attack Heysham nuclear power station on the Lancashire coast where they own a property with a clear line of sight. We think that he will also attack either Sellafield nuclear reprocessing centre or Hunterstone "B" nuclear power station.

'And terrorist number four will attack the Bacton gas terminal. They own a property in North Walsham, a few miles away. His second target is still unknown. This could be Sizewell nuclear power station, or the Grays liquid petroleum gas storage depot on the banks of the Thames near to the Dartford crossing. But our instincts tell us the missing target will be in London. We had the marshalling yards at Willesden at the top of our list, but MI5 report that there are currently no nuclear containers there, so we are still looking. We have an outstanding lead on some development properties and hope they will help fill in some of the gaps.

'As I said earlier, missile launcher number five, we believe, is on board *Golden Sundancer*. Its targets are unknown, but at this point our view is that this missile launcher is for defensive purposes only.'

Kate shifted in her seat. 'Time is *not* on our side. The facts, as we and MI5 read them, point to the attacks coming early tomorrow morning shortly after dawn. In the meantime MI5 has its operatives and anti-terrorist officers en route to these locations. They will remain very low profile.'

'Now for the terrorist game plan, as we see it.' Kate paused, not so much for effect, but rather to collect her thoughts. 'Rafi and Aidan have been looking at the wider picture. This is where things get truly scary. We have reason to believe that the terrorists are trying to engineer the collapse of our already weakened financial system and UK plc. This, we believe, is their primary objective. By so doing, they will reap huge profits in the derivatives market.'

Kate paused again and looked across at the commissioner and the chief superintendent. They were looking shocked and sitting bolt upright, like schoolmasters during the saying of grace. Her face was unsmiling. 'We have confirmation that the terrorists control four public quoted companies and ten private companies. These businesses employ over 250,000 people. Through these companies the terrorists have in their pockets a number of influential individuals who MI5 advise us are being paid exorbitant fees as consultants or non-executive board members. Included within the 300 or so people are: Members of Parliament, special advisers to the Government and people in strategic senior positions. It is MI5's opinion that a number of these people could be the terrorists' eyes and ears and could therefore be invisible sleepers.'

'The terrorists have set up the privately owned company, PSSAF, and six other financial institutions to go bust following their attacks. Aidan estimates that the terrorists stand to make at least £50 billion if all goes to plan, which will add to the financial chaos.'

Kate looked down the table at the stony faces of the two chiefs. 'Now for the better news,' she said, with the beginnings of a smile on her tired face. 'Unbelievably, we – actually, I should say Rafi – have come up with a plan which the Government could use to calm and protect the financial markets. Unfortunately, his and Aidan's cynical view is that our political masters will instinctively move into spin, damage limitation and procrastination mode. This is what the terrorists are expecting. If the politicians procrastinate, all too quickly the downward momentum will be too great for even the Bank of England to stop. However, if – and it's a massive *if* – the Government can keep the markets steady, we can beat the terrorists at their own game. If interest rates and gilt prices can be held stable, the terrorists' derivative positions will become untenable and they and their co-conspirators will rapidly face huge losses. The scale of their losses could set terrorism back several years and even bankrupt many of their financial backers.'

'Rafi's plan is for the Government to put into place a war chest which will enable them to issue shares in Government Real Estate Investment Trusts, instead of tapping the gilts market. These can be used to meet the potentially large increase in their liabilities. It's ingenious, in that they can draw down what they need when it's needed. Aidan reckons that this war chest could have £400 billion in it. This would be more than enough to placate the markets, under all but the very worst outcomes of the terrorist missile attacks.'

Kate paused. Now for the difficult bit, she thought. 'What we need is complete secrecy. MI5's and our worry is that the terrorists' well-placed sleepers include contacts in both COBRA and the Mayor of London's disaster unit. MI5 are still working on the list of names that John has given them. Our concern, and a big one at that, is that if the terrorists were to be tipped off and changed to a plan "B", we would be completely in the dark as to how to stop them. I appreciate the chances are small, but the hazards are enormous.'

The commissioner almost interrupted again, but managed to keep silent.

Kate continued. 'Our advice on what to do in order to contain the damage is that the London Stock Exchange and Euronext.Liffe must, at the last moment, not open tomorrow.' She paused. 'Also, we believe that it's too large a risk to take to expect our political masters to fully and quickly comprehend the scale of what they're up against. Spin, procrastination and aggrandisement have become so ingrained amongst some ministers that we seriously wonder whether they'll move quickly enough. Accordingly, as of now, Rafi would like to bring together a team of four or five senior City gurus, who will be tasked with drawing up an economic plan for the consideration of our political masters, so that they will be able to make decisions based on facts and not on short-term political expediency and spin. Realistically, by this time tomorrow evening Rafi and Aidan will be ready to drop and won't be in a fit state to pitch a financial recovery plan to the Bank of England or the Treasury. Who knows, the City gurus might even come up with a better plan.' At this point Kate shot Rafi and Aidan an unexpectedly mischievous smile.

'Agreed,' said the commissioner, letting Kate carry on.

'Our next proposal is that the SAS and anti-terrorist squads should be brought in to neutralise the terrorists and to search all the properties we have identified as terrorist bases. In addition, the individual terrorists must be stopped from causing damage with their missiles, but if feasible they should be allowed to escape and run to the trawlers. We can then follow them and hopefully pull in all those involved at the top of the hierarchy, who are in charge of this operation.'

'Lastly, we could do with another Nimrod – AWACS. We have one monitoring *Golden Sundancer*. It would be useful to have a second keeping an eye on the trawler in Great Yarmouth.'

The commissioner looked carefully and determinedly at the team around him.

'Thank you, Kate. What you're asking David and me to approve, in terms of our careers, is suicide – if you're wrong! I only have one question for you: have you corroborated the facts as if we were taking these bastards to court?' There were nods all around.

'We've sought supporting evidence to confirm each link in the chain,' said Kate. 'The final proof will be if the terrorists are where we say they are. If they're not, we don't have a clue where else to look.'

'Your suggestion is that the SAS and anti-terrorist squads are put in place to prevent the terrorist attacks?'

Kate nodded.

'It's this statement that I have problems with,' explained the commissioner. 'We're duty-bound to treat this threat with the seriousness it deserves, but with the recognition that if we mess this up, it'll be ranked amongst the biggest police cock-ups on record. The SAS will require full military support at each of the locations, plus field hospital and medical support, in case any of the missiles reaches its target. We don't have the powers to run this scale of operation alone.' Giles turned to David. 'Who do we need to persuade?'

'I reckon we need the say-so of four people: the Home Secretary, the Secretary of State for Defence, the head of MI5 and the chief of staff of the armed services. The Home Secretary is out of the country until tomorrow attending an inter-government conference in Germany. We'll need to get his stand-in. From a practical point of view they'd need to be based here, as this is where all the information is. I agree with MI5: it would be too risky to use COBRA, given the likelihood of there being embedded sleepers.'

The commissioner turned to the chief superintendent and said, 'Are you willing to gamble your career and pension on this?'

'Sir, as I see it, I've no choice. If we don't follow this covert route and MI5 was proved to be right, and the terrorists do have moles within COBRA, it would be a total disaster. They would be alerted and could change their targets.'

'Right, it's agreed: you and I will take full responsibility for this if we've got it wrong.'

'Agreed, sir,' said David gravely. 'I have one other issue, but it can be discussed at a later time. I'm uncertain it would be wise to let terrorists leave the UK mainland.'

'Perhaps one could view it as letting them move to a location where it would be safe to capture them and where the chances of collateral damage would be low,' suggested Kate.

The commissioner tipped his head to one side, taking on board her comment. 'Thank you – your observations and the hard work of your team are noted. However, before our political masters arrive for a briefing, I have two strong requests. First, get confirmation that there are only four missile launchers on the mainland. Second, find the whereabouts of the unknown properties.'

'David, will you please phone the Home Secretary's office and see which minister is covering for him and get their phone number? And get the number for the Secretary of State for Defence. I met with the head of MI5 a couple of days ago concerning Rafi. I promised to keep him in the loop. I'll call him and invite him. I'll also speak to the chief of staff of the armed services who, as luck or good planning would have it, is due to have dinner with me tonight at my West End club. I'll arrange for them to be here for a council of war at 8 p.m. I'll then invite the two ministers. Kate and the rest of you, please find me the missing pieces of the jigsaw puzzle.'

Jeremy turned to John, as Kate's team were leaving the room. 'I think we did rather well there, don't you?'

'Yep, I couldn't have put it better if I'd tried,' said John.

They shot an approving glance at Kate, who had heard their comments.

'Thanks guys, I'm so pleased you kept quiet!'

At that moment the phone next to the commissioner rang. It was Jeremy's boss at MI5. Giles switched the phone to conference mode.

'Evening all. Just a quick call to update you before your meeting ends,' said Neil. Kate and her team moved back into the room and stood by the door. 'We've tracked down and have under surveillance all bar two of the UKSOIL trained bombers. Five minutes ago we didn't have a clue where the man in charge, Kaleem Shah, and the last two suicide bombers were. We took DC Jessop's advice and paid

Unicorn Sceptre Finance's offices an undercover visit. Without too much difficulty we hacked into their system and found the information on their "in-house" credit cards. Thankfully Faakhir – one of the suicide bombers – used his Unicorn Sceptre Credit Card in Tilehurst, on the outskirts of Reading, yesterday evening.'

'We've sent one of our armed response units to the area. I promise that they won't approach the terrorists unless it becomes absolutely necessary. However, we've as yet to track down their exact location.'

Emma looked across at Jeremy and spoke in the direction of the phone. 'Sir, my guess is that they're there to attack the Atomic Weapons Establishment at Aldermaston and/or Burghfield, where nuclear warheads are put together. Both sites hold stocks of plutonium. I was wondering whether the terrorists' logic might be: why should Iran not be allowed to move on to the nuclear ladder, when the UK has decided to climb up several more rungs by designing a more deadly version of the Trident II nuclear missile? I suggest your colleagues look for them around Aldermaston. Kaleem Shah, the cell leader, has many years' experience of living on battlefields. My guess is that he'll want to lie low somewhere near to the targets; somewhere they won't be noticed. In that part of the country, I'd look for a modern horsebox parked in a field somewhere near to the suggested targets, with, say, a 4x4 next to it; something that wouldn't be noticed by the local green-welly-boot brigade.'

'Thank you,' said Neil, 'that definitely sounds plausible. I'll add it to our list.'

'While you're on . . . Do you happen to know where your boss is?' asked the commissioner.

'He's sitting next to me as we speak.'

'Good evening, Giles,' said the head of MI5.

'Hello Ewan. Can you attend a briefing and strategy meeting here at 8 p.m.?'

'My pleasure, see you then.'

The phone line went dead.

'Right, you've got until 8 o'clock to find me the missing information,' said the commissioner.

K ate looked at her team, seated around her in the fourth floor office. They looked very tired. She had to keep their adrenaline flowing. 'We have less than two hours to find a way to get confirmation that the fifth missile launcher is on board *Golden Sundancer, and* we have to find the missing properties – Emma please chase up Rick in

Manchester. In the meantime, Rafi please decide on who you want on the economics team. The commissioner has put his head on the block. Let's tie up some loose ends! We *have* to deliver!'

Emma phoned Rick Feldon in Manchester. After a brief conversation it transpired that the word search of the computers had revealed nothing relating to the missing development properties.

'Mr Wesson is being as uncooperative as ever and suffering from a huge persecution complex. How long have we got?' asked Rick.

'Well, put it this way, by dawn tomorrow it could be too late.'

Rick went quiet for a moment. 'I'm really getting nowhere with Mr Wesson. He's cantankerous and tired; if I push him any more I reckon he'll go into his shell and won't come out again for a long while. Mr Stone has clammed up and is refusing to talk to anyone. I think the only thing I can do is be extra nice to Mr Wesson and see if I can get him chatting about anything – he might let something slip.'

'Good luck,' said Kate, and hung up.

Rafi's thoughts had turned to the economics team when Kate came and sat on the edge of his desk.

'How do you think the briefing went?'

'As well as we could have wished for,' Rafi replied. 'You were outstanding.'

'Thanks. This economics team of yours – I'm looking forward to meeting them, if they're anything like you and Aidan!' she said with a twinkle in her eye.

He nodded. His thoughts were already back on who he needed.

Sensing that his mind was elsewhere, Kate returned to her desk.

Rafi started with the easiest choice: the real estate analyst. It would *have* to be Bob Tieson. He worked for one of the big US banks and Rafi spoke to him on a regular basis at work. His knowledge of European and North American REITs, and the real estate investment trust sector was second to none. Yes, Bob was his first choice.

He called across to Jeremy who was sorting out supper with *Luigi's*. Jeremy sensed that he was needed and gave Luigi carte blanche. 'Supper for, say, ten . . . No make that fifteen, please. Something we can eat whilst working. And orange juice, water and lots of strong coffee, please, delivered in, say, three quarters of an hour? Great – thanks Luigi.'

Jeremy put down the phone and looked across at Rafi. 'What can I do for you?'

161

'I've five people that I need brought in to work with Aidan. Kid gloves approach, but *no* taking "*no*" for an answer. OK?'

'Who did you have in mind?'

'The first person is Bob Tieson.' Rafi gave him the contact details. 'I'll let you have the next four names in a couple minutes.'

'Good,' said Jeremy, 'that'll give me time to track him down.'

Now for the financials analyst, Rafi thought. He wondered who Callum would have picked. His first idea was the sector's star analyst, Steven Moreland, but both Callum and he viewed him as a bit of a prima donna and he was not really a team player. Rafi moved on to the next name: Matthew Wilson who worked for a large European bank. Yes, he was highly regarded, very bright and would work well with others under pressure. And he'd been around for long enough to understand how painful extended bear markets could be.

Rafi passed Matthew's details to Jeremy. He now had two excellent people, but neither had any experience of dealing with the Treasury mandarins or the Bank of England. The economist would have to be someone to whom they'd listen. Rafi had a choice of five or six individuals. Then it came to him: why not get someone from the inside? Yes, Alex Lynton – the relatively new senior economist at the Bank of England. Before joining the Bank he'd held down impressive posts in the private sector and in academia. Was Alex a gamble? What if he'd become institutionalised and unwilling to take painful decisions? The more Rafi considered him, the more sure he became of his choice and passed Alex's details to Jeremy.

Now for the corporate finance specialist – he needed someone who understood real estate investment vehicles. Rafi thought of a name straight away: Donald Hollingsworth. He was a friend of his from his corporate finance days, where he had been Rafi's boss. Donald still ran a very successful corporate finance team. Several years ago he had become a non-executive director of a leading listed property company. He knew his way around the corporate finance market blindfold and had a good working knowledge of the commercial property market. Donald's experience would be a great help and he was undoubtedly very well connected in financial circles.

Jeremy took the fourth name and what Rafi could remember of Donald's contact details.

'How are you getting on?' enquired Rafi.

'We've tracked down Matthew and my colleagues are working on Bob as we speak.'

The fifth member of the team should be able to think out of the box. Rafi thought for a few moments. He needed an individual with a clear and incisive mind, who didn't necessarily come from the financial markets, but understood the need for a clear hypothesis and a distinct solution. His sister fitted the criteria perfectly. He scribbled a note for Jeremy. 'Here's the fifth name.'

Jeremy looked at it. 'Saara Khan of Birmingham University. Ah, your little sister; our background research shows her to be an impressive academic and just as unassuming as you are! She's in Birmingham . . . Do you think that she would prefer a smart squad car or a helicopter?'

'Which do you think would be the faster?'

'Let me make a call.' A few minutes later Jeremy replaced the phone. 'They have arranged a car with a couple of motorbike outriders to keep the road in front clear.'

Jeremy then spoke to his colleagues back at MI5. 'We've traced the other four: Donald Hollingsworth and wife are on their way to Dorset, where they have a cottage. We've sent a helicopter down in the direction of the A303 and have the traffic police between here and Yeovil looking out for their car. John has left to collect Bob Tieson; he's working late at his office in the Docklands. I'm collecting Alex Lynton from the theatre – I hope the performance hasn't started! And last but not least, Matthew Wilson is flying into Heathrow. He's been working in Frankfurt. I've arranged for him to be met by a colleague and taken through Immigration and Customs the VIP way.'

'Excellent,' said Rafi with a smile.

Jeremy called across to Kate. 'Do we have any cars left?'

'Of course, but heaven only knows where,' came the reply. 'If you go down to reception I'll get you one.'

'Thanks.'

Rafi sat there, thinking. Would this team of five plus Aidan have sufficient gravitas to stand up to the new Chancellor of the Exchequer? He was a serious politician, but with only a few months' experience of the job, it was difficult to predict whether he had become influenced by the highly PR conscious Treasury team. And how would he react when the chips were down? Would he understand the seriousness of the huge risks facing the country, or opt for the easier strategy of procrastinating?

'Where have we got to on the London property front?' asked Kate.

'I've been trying to find out the address of the London or South of England property that HFFF own,' replied Emma. 'I've spoken to the Land Registry Office again. Sadly, their system isn't set up for this type of general enquiry. I spoke to Justin again and he's been trawling through their property databases. He says that there are too many permutations, even if you try to narrow down the search criteria, and that it's likely the deal would have been done subject to a confidentiality clause, so wouldn't even be on the databases!'

'Emma,' Kate called across to her, 'the immigration officer, Roger Harewood – the man who keeps the notebooks – is en route back from the West coast of the United States. Could you find the airline and flight number? There can't be many long haul planes from the USA landing at Manchester Airport early tomorrow morning. Then arrange for us to speak to him, in case he can remember something.'

'I'll get straight on to it.'

There was a momentary lull. Rafi leant back in his chair. What else could he be doing on the property front? What seemed like moments later, but was in fact half an hour, he was woken by Kate, standing over him and calling his name.

Rafi looked up into her hazel eyes. A sight to lift the spirits, he thought to himself.

'I thought you'd better be left to your short power nap. Here's a cup of coffee. The first two members of your economics team should be here in five minutes,' said Kate.

Jeremy and John arrived almost simultaneously. They had two very angry individuals with them: Bob Tieson and Alex Lynton. They were taken up to the fourth floor interview room.

'I think that you'd better placate your two friends,' said John as he walked into the office. 'Even though we told them otherwise, they still think they've been arrested. Bob definitely didn't want to come. I had to threaten him with handcuffs. I told him he could speak to his lawyer, if he wanted, when he got here.'

Jeremy came off his mobile phone. 'Saara is making excellent progress down the M1 and Matthew has landed at Heathrow where his reception committee is waiting for him on the tarmac. They should both be here within the hour, hopefully sooner. We caught up with Donald on the A303. His helicopter is en route to the rugby pitch at the Honourable Artillery Company, just around the corner.'

'You better go and greet your two irritable friends. Jeremy no doubt has arranged for fresh coffee and something or other as a peace offering. And Aidan is on his way – says he's finished his filing!' said Kate.

Alex and Bob were sitting in silence awaiting their fate.

Rafi walked in with Kate and Aidan following close behind him. He realised that he probably looked like someone who had been dragged through a bush backwards and sensed that they feared the worst – being implicated as one of his friends. He sat down opposite the two irate individuals, who eyed him suspiciously. Kate sat to his left and Aidan to his right.

Kate started the conversation. 'We will shortly be joined by Donald Hollingsworth, Matthew Wilson and a fifth person who is winging her way down the M1 as we speak. You know Rafi and Aidan Gilchrist? Good. No doubt you want to know why we've hauled you in here. Rafi was quietly released from Paddington Green police station earlier this week and has been helping us to unravel a terrorist plot. It's probably simplest if I get Rafi here to explain what is going on and how you can help us.'

Rafi observed the two of them: Alex Lynton, the economist, sat uneasily, whilst Bob Tieson looked as if the father of all black clouds was hovering over his head. Rafi guessed he still had a lot of work to do on the IPO he was launching in a few days' time and didn't appreciate being dragged away from his office, even at this hour of the evening.

'If it makes you feel any better,' said Rafi in a calm and collected tone, 'in ten minutes' time a home office minister, the Defence Secretary, and the heads of MI5 and the armed forces are meeting with the commissioner two floors up. Like you, they have been asked in for a briefing, and like you, have dropped whatever they were doing . . . We have uncovered a terrorist plot to attack a number of key energy and nuclear facilities in the UK. They are also planning to cause havoc in the financial markets where they have built up massive positions in the derivatives markets. To cut a long story short, we believe the terrorist attacks will severely knock market sentiment and the closing of their derivative positions will turn the falling markets into a rout.' Rafi paused then went on. 'We have to stop the markets gaining any major downward momentum.'

The silence was interrupted by Bob. 'What do you want us to do? The impossible? Or should we man the printing presses, print money out of thin air and then wave our magic wands?'

'Not quite,' Rafi replied. 'What we need is a plan that can be put in place to calm the markets.'

'Boy, that would be pulling a rabbit and a half out of a hat,' said Alex.

Aidan cut in. 'Rafi has a plan, which we believe you and your colleagues can make a reality. We believe there is the possibility to create listed Government property vehicles – REITs – and use share issues to mop up the liabilities that the Government may face, and to finance gilts buy-backs.'

At that moment a flustered Donald Hollingsworth appeared through the door. Rafi got up and walked over to greet him.

'Bloody hell, Rafi, you look truly awful!'

'Yes, thank you Donald. Sorry to have ruined your weekend away. Let me introduce you to the other members of the team who beat you here. In the next fifteen minutes you'll be joined by Matthew Wilson – who I believe you know – and by a Dr Saara Khan, who you won't.'

Aidan stood up. 'In straightforward terms, gentlemen, your mission, should you wish to accept it, is to come up with a credible strategy that the Bank of England and Treasury can adopt to avert a financial meltdown. Coffee is on its way. I will bring you up to speed with the minutiae as soon as the others arrive. In a moment Detective Constable Emma Jessop will join us and help us turn this room into our office.'

Rafi could sense that they were hooked – their body language had visibly relaxed and there was determination in their eyes.

'If you'll excuse us, Kate and I have a number of things to attend to. Thank you for helping,' said Rafi. 'In case you are worried about the attacks, there is a team upstairs planning how the SAS can neutralise them.'

B ack in the office there was a quiet knock at the door. Standing outside was Rafi's sister. She broke into a run and flung her arms around him.

'I've been so worried.'

'Thanks Sis. Me too! Meet Kate, who I'm working with.'

'You're not under arrest?'

'No,' said Kate, 'your brother is working with us – he's a godsend.'

Rafi looked at his little sister. She smiled a smile that he wouldn't forget in a long time – its intensity was wonderful. 'I'm sorry to drag you away from home, but we need someone with a clear, logical mind who can act as an independent thinker amongst a team of financial experts.'

166

'But finance is a blank in my book.'

'Yes, but you know how to structure a hypothesis and set up tests to prove or disprove it. Come and get a cup of coffee and let me introduce you to the team,' said Rafi.

They entered the interview room; it was buzzing and exuded a sense of teamwork and urgency. The conversation paused and Rafi introduced his sister to Aidan's team. 'Saara is here to be your devil's advocate. Forgive her if she asks any naive questions on the finance front; I promise you she'll be worth her weight in gold by the time you finish. Aidan here will explain what's going on.'

Bob enquired, 'What are the chances of nipping back to the office to collect some papers and download some files?'

'No problem,' replied Kate. We'll assign you Constable Peter Ashby to act as your chauffeur. Is the gravity of the position understood? *No one* outside this building other that MI5 and the SAS have a clue what's going on. Absolutely *no* talking to anyone! *Got that?*'

'Of course,' said Bob.

'When Bob gets back could I borrow Constable Ashby?' asked Alex.

'Me too,' said Matthew.

'Emma will make the arrangements for you.'

'Aidan, whilst the others are out could you bring Donald and Saara up to speed, please?' asked Rafi.

'Will do.'

Rafi left to rejoin Kate. He re-entered the office that had become his home.

She looked across at him. 'You look bloody awful,' she said with a soft smile.

'You don't look too good yourself,' Rafi replied gently. 'Where do we go from here?'

'Time to ring Rick Feldon in Manchester,' said Kate.

After a long wait Kate was put through.

'Sorry to keep you. I was about to phone you. Wesson, the valuer, is one sandwich short of a picnic; he's really messed up. It's like walking on eggshells. When our word search on the PCs came up with nothing, I spoke to the MI5 suits and they have gone through the secretaries' paper files. The good news is they have just found the letter. No wonder the word search revealed zilch – the letter was never saved on the computer. It's being faxed to you as we speak. The good news is that it gives you two more properties.'

Kate smiled. 'Good work Rick; it's just what we needed. Thanks.'

Rafi sat on the edge of his chair; he couldn't wait to get his hands on the fax.

'Oh, by the way, Rick, we think that we're missing one more property,' said Kate. 'One in the South East or London area. It might be worth trying to chat to your man about it.'

'I'll see what I can do,' said Rick, 'and sorry again for not finding the letter sooner.'

'We've got it and that's what matters,' said Kate.

Moments later the fax arrived. Rafi read it. It was very straightforward. It confirmed that the value of two properties exceeded their book cost of £7.4 million. Rafi looked at the addresses: development land at Park Avenue, Wasdale Road, Gosforth, and Marfleet Lane, Kingston-upon-Hull.

Rafi went back to his desk and pulled up Google Maps on the screen. He typed in Gosforth and was given the option of Gosforth NE3 or Gosforth CA20. Rafi clicked on the CA20 link and a large scale map appeared on the screen. Rafi reduced the scale by a couple of clicks so he could scan the surrounding area. Oh hell! He recognised the location; it was close to Sellafield nuclear reprocessing plant.

'Kate,' he called across, 'do you have a spare moment?' He showed her the map. 'We've found another location. The terrorists have a property within a couple of miles of Sellafield,'

'Oh shit,' said Kate. 'This isn't what we wanted.'

'But at least now we know where to look,' added John.

Rafi typed in the address of the Hull property and looked at the map.

Kate, standing over his shoulder, said, 'Go east a bit. Thought so – it's just down the road from Easington, where there is the vast gas terminal and storage facility.' She looked pleased. 'So, by my calculations, seven down, three to go! As long as none of the missing three are nuclear installations, I reckon we're in with a chance.'

'Or seven down and one to go, if we can get confirmation that the fifth missile launcher is on board *Golden Sundancer*. That would leave only *one* more to find.' Rafi looked apprehensive.

'Now we've got this new information under our belt, could you help me with a bit of photocopying?' Kate asked Rafi. 'I'm putting together corroborating evidence to support what we believe is going on – in case we get a frosty reception upstairs.'

U pstairs, Giles and David were preparing for the 8 o'clock meeting.

Air Chief Marshal Sir Nigel Hawser and the head of MI5, Ewan
Thorn, were booked to come; however, it was proving more difficult
to get the Government ministers to the meeting without telling them
why.

Giles had phoned the Defence Secretary. He introduced himself and
immediately cut to the chase. 'I've arranged a meeting for 8 o'clock
this evening. It is of vital importance; can you attend please?'

'What's it about?' answered a frosty voice. 'I have a social engagement – Covent Garden with the wife. The tickets are like gold dust.'

'I can't talk over the phone, but we would value your input
alongside that of the head of the armed forces and the head of MI5.'

'Oh, I see. Yes, I'll be there.'

'Thank you, sir.' Giles gave the minister the details of the venue and
put the phone down. He looked relieved; the Defence Secretary,
though new to the department, was a level-headed man and a
renowned stickler for the minutiae. Once brought on side, he would
be an invaluable asset to the team.

His next phone call, Giles mused, was likely to be interesting. The
stand-in Home Secretary was a different ball game altogether. He
phoned the Home Office, asked to speak to the minister covering for
the Home Secretary and was put through to the minister's personal
assistant.

'The minister is in a strategy meeting and has left instructions not to
be disturbed.'

'This is extremely important; I would have spoken to the Home
Secretary but he's out of the country,' said Giles.

'Let me have a word with the minister,' said the secretary.

What seemed like ages later, the minister's voice came on the phone.
He sounded peeved.

'What, may I ask, is the purpose of this call?' he asked bluntly.

'When we met at the Bishopsgate bomb location you mentioned
you would be available to help 24/7. I have arranged a meeting for
8 o'clock this evening; it is of vital importance. Can you attend
please?'

'I'm sorry but I'm busy. I could send my assistant, or we could have
the meeting tomorrow morning, say, at 11 a.m.,' said the Minister.

'Sir, under normal circumstances I would have asked the Home
Secretary,' said Giles politely, hoping the minister would get the point
that the meeting was crucial.

169

'If I am to consider rearranging my diary, I'd have to know why it's so important I attend. I'm booked to give a keynote speech. I'm spearheading the launch of our new data collection unit on immigration statistics. The press will be there. I've prepared an excellent speech and it's already been distributed for tomorrow's papers. Unfortunately, I'll have to decline your offer of a meeting.'

'Sir, this is sufficiently sensitive that I can't tell you about it until we meet, but it is of utmost importance.'

'No. I've made my mind up; you can have my assistant or you can see me at my office tomorrow morning,' added the minister uncompromisingly.

Giles raised his eyebrows, perplexed. 'But it *is* important.'

The Minister wasn't pleased. 'Damn it! You won't be getting me to your meeting at this short notice. Do you *know* who you're speaking to? My press conference is far too important an opportunity to miss, particularly as our newly formatted statistics look excellent. Good evening to you.' The phone line went dead.

The commissioner didn't rise to the provocation; it was as if he was dealing with a petulant teenager. He dialled the 10 Downing Street hotline, got straight through to the PM office and asked to speak to the Prime Minister regarding the recent bombing. Within a minute the PM came on the phone.

'How may I help you?'

'Prime Minister, we have a situation developing. It would be helpful if we had your or the Home Secretary's input, alongside that of the Defence Secretary, the head of the armed forces and the head of MI5. I have spoken to the minister covering for the Home Secretary and have been informed that his prior engagement means he's unavailable. I was hoping . . .'

'When do you want to see me?' came the businesslike reply.

'8 o'clock this evening at Wood Street, please.'

'I will have to put you on hold – bear with me; I need to speak to my secretary.'

Giles waited, fingers crossed. The recent General Election meant the Prime Minister was working with a wafer-thin majority and had a lot to contend with.

The PM's voice came back on the line. 'My secretary has rescheduled my diary. Traffic permitting, I shouldn't be more than five minutes late.'

Giles was grinning when he put the phone down. 'There are times when a politician can restore one's faith in the system.'

'You couldn't have asked for a better group of people to pitch our problems to,' said David, who was also smiling.

A couple of minutes later the phone rang: it was a very disgruntled Home Office minister. 'Regarding your recent phone call . . . For the record, I wish to repeat that I am unwilling to drop this press briefing, unless you explain to me in detail why it is so important I attend.'

David sensed that Giles wanted to get him off the line as quickly as possible, in case the topic of the PM was brought up.

Giles said very politely, 'I've been considering your offer of a meeting tomorrow morning; perhaps I could come over and brief you. Would 11 o'clock at your office be acceptable?'

'Er . . . yes, that should be fine. Do phone my personal assistant first thing to check the time and venue and that my diary is still free, though,' came the reply.

'Thank you, Minister.'

Giles couldn't put the phone down quickly enough. 'Don't repeat me, but that man is a self-obsessed pillock of the first order. Heaven help the country if he ever gets a department to run. Can you see if Kate has made any progress with the missing information? Thanks. I'm going to pay Greg a visit, implement our emergency plans and get a command centre set up.'

Kate and Rafi were collating their supporting information for the 8 o'clock meeting.

Down the corridor Aidan and the economics team had transformed the interview room into their base. Beyond them, the rooms that had been the offices of Chief Superintendent David Pryke and his team had been cleared. Greg and his team were working on turning them into an operations room. A group of desks had been put back-to-back in the centre of the room, with a row of phones and networked PCs with flat screens down the middle. Video conferencing and LCD screens were being mounted on the walls and secure phone and video links to the SAS command centre, the HQ of the paratroopers and the army's command centre in Wiltshire were being set up. The PM's hotlines were being installed in an adjoining office.

Greg was looking concerned – his assistant was having problems getting two video links and the large LCD touch screen up and running. It seemed that one of their big video screens had developed an electrical gremlin, whereas the other simply didn't want to work and the touch screen was playing up intermittently.

Aidan and Emma came down the corridor to chat to Greg about their PC and printer needs. As they walked through the door, they saw it was a bad moment.

Greg turned Aidan. 'Could I ask you a question, please?'

'Of course,' said Aidan. 'What's up?'

'Bloody wiring . . .' came the reply. 'We are a large video screen, a video conferencing unit and a touch screen down.'

'Can I have a look?' asked Aidan.

Greg waved him across and asked Emma quietly, 'Don't tell me he has a degree in electrical engineering as well?' which Aidan overheard.

'No, I'm afraid not – just as I thought: the same leads in and out. What you have here is an older version of what we have in the office. Emma, see if you can find Rafi; he'll know.'

Moments later Emma reappeared with Rafi in tow.

'Rafi, what do you think? It's similar to the stuff we've got in our conference rooms, isn't it? The leads look the same; it's just the screen and the kit that's older.'

'Rafi looked at the leads. 'You're right.'

'Thanks, mate,' said Aidan. He turned and spoke to Greg. 'I just need to make a quick call.'

Aidan spoke briefly to his boss, a main board director of Maine Leadbetter.

'Hi, Russell, it's your erstwhile colleague Aidan here . . . Yes, I've been working hard . . . No, I'm not off somewhere with a bit of fluff . . . Yes, I aim to be back in the office tomorrow, probably by 10.30 a.m.; sorry, I'll miss the morning meeting and the early trading. Don't worry, if I get what I'm doing right, it'll be excellent news for the firm.' Aidan paused. 'This brings me to the reason for my call: I've a pitch to some wealthy players first thing tomorrow and I need to knock the socks off them. I've got a favour to ask. Would you ring the security guards on reception and authorise my borrowing the screen in the small conference room and a little bit of associated kit?'

Silence – Greg and Rafi could tell from Aidan's face that his boss wasn't keen.

'OK, let's say that if it's not back in time, I'll buy a new one. You *do* trust me, don't you? Oh, good. Thanks. Yes, I know I take liberties! See you tomorrow.' Aidan put down the phone. 'I hope he won't mind the small white lie. There's no bloody way that what I'm planning to borrow will be back in time. As the markets will be closed, they won't be much good to him anyway! Greg, if you could find a van, would you and one of your assistants like to pay my office a visit?'

172

Greg's face changed from a scowl to a beaming smile. 'Give me a couple of minutes to draw up a list of what I need and I'll meet you in the rear car park.'

Rafi looked at Aidan, 'Good move! I hope you've got what he needs.'

'Oh, I don't think that there should be too much of a problem. We have a basement storeroom full of last year's kit which makes this lot look steam age in comparison. This should be fun. I'm willing to bet Greg will think he's visiting Santa's Grotto!'

Kate put her head around the corner of the door.

'So this is where you are! Rafi I thought you might like to listen in; we've got the captain of the Nimrod, tracking *Golden Sundancer*, on the blower and he has some news for us.'

As they scurried back to the office, Kate brought Rafi up to speed. 'Twenty minutes ago the captain of the Nimrod radioed in and spoke to John to report that *Golden Sundancer* was on a converging course with a trawler around 250 miles from Iceland, north-west of the Faeroes, in the middle of nowhere.'

'Any more news from the MI5 agent in Reykjavík?' asked Rafi

'No, he's drawn a blank,' replied Kate.

The Nimrod captain came back on the phone – his radio had been patched through. 'Good evening, is that the City of London Police?'

'Yes,' replied Kate who introduced herself and sent John's apologies.

'Your boat, *Golden Sundancer*, has hove to in close proximity to a fishing vessel, which we've identified as an Estonian trawler. Her name is *Anu Riina*. The captain of the trawler launched an inflatable dinghy over the stern a couple of minutes ago and fired a line across to the motorboat. There's a big swell down there and the temperatures are sub-zero. The line has been secured aboard *Golden Sundancer* and her captain is manoeuvring to get the dinghy into the lee of the wind to make it easier to get it on board. We've started to get enhanced images from our high magnification camera . . . Bloody hell! It looks like there are two wooden coffins lashed into the dinghy. The trawler has disengaged, turned south-east and looks as though it's heading for home. The dinghy and the two boxes are, as we speak, being pulled on board *Golden Sundancer*.'

'What speed has *Golden Sundancer* been cruising at?'

'Between thirty-seven and forty-one knots – very respectable given the conditions down there. Their de-icing system seems to be working well; unusual, though, for this type of boat.'

'How many do you reckon are on board?'

'Two men; the captain and a crew member are all we've seen. Give me a moment and I'll send through the pictures.'

'While you're at it, could you include any markings on the wooden boxes?' asked Kate.

'Will do.'

'Is there any chance of them picking you up on their radar, seeing or hearing you?' asked Kate.

'Don't worry; we're as good as invisible as we've got our radar-cloaking device on.' He paused. 'They've completed the unloading of the dinghy and the two boxes have been safely stowed on board.' After a moment's silence he went on, '*Golden Sundancer* is returning to her bearing of 152° and is getting back up to her previous speed. I'll keep you posted if she alters speed or course, or has another rendezvous. Out.'

Kate looked up. 'Emma have you got the pictures?'

'Yep,' came the reply. 'The boxes and their markings are just what we wanted.'

'Brilliant; these confirm the whereabouts of our missing Kornet missile launcher. Now we've only got one missile target to find, not three!' Kate picked up the phone and relayed the good news to the commissioner's assistant, Beverley.

John, who was back in the room, raised his coffee cup towards Kate, toasting her.

'Here's to your eclectic team. Twenty-four hours ago I wouldn't have given you a cat in hell chance. Now – who knows? – we might beat the buggers, yet.'

Alex entered the room. 'I thought I'd see how the other half lived. My goodness, it's cosy in here!'

'You should have seen it thirty-six hours ago – none of this mess was here,' replied Rafi.

'No,' said Emma, 'it was all tidied away into the filing cabinets!'

Alex walked across to Rafi's desk and pulled up a chair. 'I am so pleased that you are OK. Might I ask why you chose me when you could have picked one of the high-profile City economists?'

Rafi looked at Alex. 'It was a no-brainer. How are you getting on with your colleagues?'

'Really well.'

'There's your answer,' he said with a broad smile.

'Thank you. Thank you for choosing me. Oh, by the way, your little sister is proving an inspired choice; she's a bright cookie and has us all organised. Chat to you later.' With that Alex turned and left.

Kate looked across at Rafi. 'You don't by any chance have a brother? If so, I'd like to meet him, please.'

'Afraid not.'

She looked at Rafi, her head slightly to one side. 'You're proving to be a most resourceful guy with some great friends. I'm pleased that I allowed David to bully me into getting you out of Paddington Green!'

As Kate and Rafi were finalising the background materials for the presentation to the Chiefs upstairs, Jeremy bounced into the room.

'Well done tracking down the fifth missile launcher; at last we've something to celebrate.'

How he managed to keep up to date amazed Rafi.

'Talking of fun, we've been over to Aidan's office. Greg has had a field day, borrowed three large state-of-the-art video conferencing screens, a large plasma screen and various other useful gismos. The basement store proved to be a real Aladdin's cave. Aidan did a brilliant job of distracting his two security guards and he even got them to lock up the conference rooms before he left, saying that they were to remain locked until 8 a.m. tomorrow. Greg is down the corridor setting up his new toys now. How long has the meeting been going on upstairs?'

'Almost an hour, I reckon,' replied Emma. 'The PM arrived a bit late.'

'My inside line,' said Jeremy, 'is that we can expect the politicians to play it slow and to insist that COBRA – the normal emergency committee – is brought into session as soon as the meeting finishes, and they will ignore MI5's concerns about there being sleepers. This flap will really test the PM.'

Rafi nodded – the PM would be in uncharted waters – and wondered how he would react.

Kate had finished her collating and crossed over to her desk. 'Well, I seem to be ready. How are you feeling, Rafi?'

'Given the circumstances, not that bad, thanks. At least my brain is still working; the rest of me feels due for a refit and needs a bit of TLC.'

Kate smiled and whispered, 'When all this is over, I'll see what I can do – as a small thank you.'

'A thank you for what?' Rafi replied.

'Bloody hell, you're impossible! What planet are you on? If it hadn't been for you, I'd be having a normal night, oblivious to the fact that tomorrow would be hell.'

'Sorry.' Rafi, still deep in thought, walked off down the corridor to the interview room. He wondered how the economics team were

175

getting on. He put his head around the door. The six occupants had reorganised the room, with a group of desks in the middle. Alex and Donald were sitting next to each other, opposite Matthew and Bob. Saara was at one end and Aidan at the other. On one side of the room were a couple of PCs and a printer photocopier. A whiteboard, now covered with writing, had been hung on the opposite wall. Plates littered the table. The room definitely had a 'work-in-progress' air to it.

'Just thought I'd drop by to see how you were getting on and to let you know that we currently have a good idea where seven of the eight terrorist targets are.'

'And they've traced the two suicide bombers and the journalist Shah to the outskirts of Aldermaston, not far from the Nuclear Weapons Research Establishment, as Emma predicted.' added Kate who had arrived just behind Rafi.

Matthew spoke up. 'Emma and Aidan have filled us in on what the terrorists are planning. My view is that you're understating the financial downside.'

'But at least we have advance warning,' said Aidan.

Rafi smiled at his sister.

'They're being very tolerant of my lack of finance skills,' she said.

'Have none of it Rafi; this young lady could join my team any day!' said Donald, Rafi's former boss, with a smile.

Rafi turned to leave and heard the soft voice of Saara follow him down the corridor. 'Rafi, look after yourself.'

Back at his desk, Rafi was feeling depressed and downright irritable. He'd been chatting with one of John's team, who had been working on the properties the terrorists were involved with. He too had come to the same conclusion as Rafi, but had spoilt it by saying, 'I'm glad my head isn't on the block on this one. Your hunch seems logical and you seem to sense how they'd operate, but bugger me, talk about pissing in the wind!'

'Thank you for those well-chosen words of wisdom.' Rafi replied.

Kate stood next to him. 'Don't for one moment feel sorry for yourself. How you manage to think straight, let alone sort out this bloody jigsaw puzzle after what you've been through, amazes me – not long now,' she said in a caring tone.

Rafi was halfway through a sandwich when Kate's phone rang. 'We're on. Time to face the music!'

As they went down the corridor, Kate put her head around the door of the interview room and asked Aidan to join them.

They walked past a positively beaming Greg, who by the looks of things had the Ops Room fully up and running. He gave a thumbs up sign to Aidan, who acknowledged it with a wave and a grin.

The walk up the back stairs took him back to his school days; it conjured up memories of visiting his house master – the gloomy lighting and the greying wall paint added to his apprehension.

Part 5

T he team walked into the commissioner's anteroom, where Beverley was at her desk. 'Giles is ready for you. Do go straight in.'
The commissioner's conference room had a very businesslike air to it.

'Good evening,' said Giles, standing up as Kate entered the room.
'Please be seated. John and Jeremy, would you let Rafi, Kate and
Aidan sit at the table and pull up two chairs behind them? Thank you,'
said Giles. 'Sorry it's a bit of a squeeze, but I reckon we can manage.
Time for some introductions: Prime Minister, Secretary of State for
Defence, Air Chief Marshal Sir Nigel Hawser, head of the armed
services, and Ewan Thorn, head of MI5. It's my pleasure to introduce
to you: Jeremy Welby of MI5, Detective Chief Inspector John Dowsing of Special Branch, Detective Inspector Kate Adams of our Economic Crime Department, Aidan Gilchrist of Maine Leadbetter – a
derivatives expert – and Rafi Khan.'

Giles continued. 'We have had a fruitful discussion, but before we
go any further the Prime Minister and his Defence Secretary would
like to ask you some questions.'

'Thank you, Commissioner,' said the PM in a measured voice.
'Three hours ago I had envisaged spending the evening dealing with
mundane matters. Suffice it to say, Giles's revelations have come as a
serious shock – the intricacy and scope of the terrorists' threat to our
energy supplies, our financial system and our country's economic
welfare is every bit as grave as anything we've faced since the Second
World War,' he looked at Giles reassuringly. 'I'm not going to shoot
the messenger. Indeed, I understand that you've been working day and
night since Monday. To have come this far with your investigations in
such a short time deserves my considerable gratitude.'

The PM paused and looked around the room. 'Unfortunately, all
you have accomplished will come to nought unless our next steps are
the right ones. As has most eloquently been pointed out to me, we have
to be proactive and not reactive in the face of these heinous threats.'
He looked at his Defence Secretary, then continued. 'There are a

number of questions to which we would appreciate candid answers. First of all, why do you believe that COBRA is not the right way forward at this point in time?'

Kate looked across at the PM. 'I wish it were, sir,' she said slightly shakily. She paused and fully regained her composure. 'MI5's and our worry is that the terrorists could have contingency plans. At this point in time we've a lead on all except one of the expected terrorist targets. We know that we're up against well-trained and battle-hardened mercenaries. If they were to be tipped off, such is the transportability of their missile launchers that they might simply switch to a plan "B". To answer your question, whilst the chances are small, the downside hazard is too large.' Kate paused.

'Where precisely is the threat of an internal tip-off?' asked the PM.

Kate pulled out some stapled sheets of paper from the small bundle in front of her and passed one to each of the individuals around the table.

'In front of you are the names of individuals we and MI5 can place within the terrorists' web of companies. To put it bluntly, all these individuals are on the terrorists' payroll – whether they know it or not. You will note that there is an executive officer of a metropolitan authority on that list, which falls within the London disaster planning area. On page four is a list of the organisations which the terrorists have infiltrated through their huge outsourcing service business and the limited liability partnerships they run. The list includes: the Ministry of Defence, GCHQ, Paddington Green police station, the Home Office—'

'Thank you,' cut in the PM.

'This list is impressive, but can it be verified?' asked the Defence Secretary.

'The names come from Companies House and have been given the once-over by MI5.'

'Let us be clear; you're suggesting,' the PM turned the sheet over, 'that a special adviser to me at Number 10, whom I was with not four hours ago, is on their payroll, as are two individuals who provide support to COBRA. Is that correct?'

Kate looked straight at the PM and said, 'Yes, sir.'

'The problem is that we believe we have identified two potential moles in COBRA, but we can't be 100% sure that we haven't missed a third,' said Ewan.

The PM looked at Ewan, the head of MI5. 'This is very disturbing; why the hell didn't I know about this sooner?'

'Unfortunately, we've only just uncovered them. They're "sleepers", put in place to carry out one or more specific activities. Up to that point, they are in effect invisible. I've seen the documentation relating to one of the limited liability partnerships controlled by the terrorists, on which an MP sits as a non-executive. He gets paid £40,000 per annum for attending four half-day meetings a year. Although the sum is disclosed in the Members' Register, there's nothing there about the fact that his daily rate is £20,000. The going rate for an individual with little business experience would be less than one-tenth of what he's being paid. The fact that this MP sits on a couple of sensitive committees is what concerns us at MI5. Following our investigations into the activities of Maryam Vynckt we have become aware that many on the list could be receiving large payments offshore via Gulf Trade Bank. The problem is that to all intents and purposes these offshore payments are very hard to trace unless one knows exactly where to look. For the time being, it's difficult to confirm that the list is comprehensive.'

The Defence Secretary kept quiet, but looked agitated.

'So, it's a matter of timing?' asked the PM. 'Whilst the terrorists have their Kornet missiles and remain at large, you believe COBRA should not be activated?'

'Precisely, sir.'

The Prime Minister looked thoughtful. Rafi sensed he didn't agree.

'Thank you,' said the Prime Minister, 'that answers my first question. My second question is: how certain are we that the terrorists have Kornet missiles?'

Kate flicked through her bundle of papers, pulled out copies of the digitally enhanced photo of the two wooden boxes strapped into the inflatable dinghy and passed them around the table.

'This photo was taken under an hour ago. The markings on the boxes in the picture correspond to those for the Kornet missile launcher and its missiles. The boats involved are owned by the terrorists. Similar boxes were seen by the manager of the terrorists' warehouse in Tallinn. The Russian Security Service has confirmed that five missile launchers and twenty missiles have been stolen. The markings on the boxes match those mislaid by the Russians.'

'Thank you. Now for question number three. Could you please tell me why you are so confident that the four Chechen mercenaries have two targets each?'

'A combination of things, Prime Minister. Firstly we have confirmation that they took delivery of five Kornet missile launchers and twenty missiles, four of which we know have been fired. This leaves them with sixteen missiles. The photos we have just received indicate that a launcher and probably four missiles are now on board *Golden Sundancer*. This leaves the four Chechen terrorists with a launcher and three missiles each. We have been talking to the army; the launcher, its tripod and the missiles are cumbersome for one man to move around quickly. We therefore believe the Kornet launcher will be used to fire three missiles and then left behind. Each terrorist will then move on to where they have hidden a Vektor mortar and use it to attack their second target. Our Estonian friends have confirmed that the terrorist have taken delivery of four such mortars with eighty high-explosive shells.'

Kate paused to let what she had just said sink in, and was about to carry on when the Defence Secretary enquired, 'Could they not use the mortars first?'

'Yes that is entirely possible. Our thinking was simply that the Kornet missiles would inflict more damage, so would be used first,' replied Kate.

The Defence Secretary nodded and she continued. 'If we consider the types of targets close to the terrorists' vacant properties and their weapons – they correspond. The Kornet missiles will be used on the substantially built targets – the nuclear power stations – and the Vektor mortars will attack lighter-weight targets – the oil and gas facilities.'

'OK. Question number four: when and where do you believe that the terrorist attacks will come?'

'Our educated guess is that the attacks will be tomorrow between 7.30 and 8.00 a.m. – from first light to when the Stock Exchange opens. This will maximise the news coverage and the adverse impact on the markets. This theory is supported by the information we have from the local harbour masters who have informed us that the trawlers are all due to slip their berths tomorrow between late morning and early afternoon.'

Kate passed across more sheets of paper detailing where they believed the attacks would take place.

The PM looked around at his colleagues, who were deep in thought. 'Any questions or shall I carry on?' After a short pause, he moved on to his fifth question. 'Why do you want us to let the terrorists escape and make them believe that they've successfully hit their targets?'

Kate looked behind her at John and Jeremy. Neither showed any desire to tackle this question so she carried on.

'It's our desire to catch the four main ringleaders: Sheikh Tufayl, Basel Talal, Jameel Furud and Maryam Vynckt and any other people who have been helping them,' said Kate. She paused momentarily to collect her thoughts.

'Perhaps I can shed light on this Prime Minister,' said Ewan. 'Our intelligence unit tells me that the four main ringleaders and the escaping terrorists will meet up. We believe that their destination is Morocco. Jameel is there and confirmation has come through that the sheikh's private jet has filed a flight plan to Marrakech airport. It's scheduled to land at 12.45 p.m. on Monday. We believe the terrorists will leave Britain on the trawlers and rendezvous with their fast motor vessel, *Golden Sundancer*, which will then sail to Morocco.'

'What are the extradition procedures like from Morocco?' asked the Defence Secretary.

'They're a diplomatically friendly country. We have successfully extradited the £50m Securitas robber from there.' Ewan paused. 'However, the procedure is long-winded and the evidence has to be watertight and well-documented. Put bluntly, time wouldn't be on our side. Sheikh Tufayl, a Muslim, is very wealthy and very well-connected. He has the ability to slip the net if he winds up in the hands of the Moroccan authorities.'

'How important do we think that these people are?' asked the PM.

'Very,' replied Ewan. 'We're dealing with international players who are in the vanguard of financing terrorist activities. Their bank accounts are in both neutral countries and some less than neutral. Deals struck in the financial and derivatives markets can easily be done via intermediaries – something like the Banco de "we launder your money for a fee". The turnover in the derivative markets is vast. Tracking down such transactions would take time and the profits made would rapidly become untraceable. We believe that we need positive proof of the ringleaders' involvement and can't afford to let them slip away to fight another day. Capturing them *in flagrante delicto* would make it far simpler to freeze their assets and then have them confiscated. If they think that they've been successful, they and their accomplices will be less likely to go to ground.'

Ewan looked at the PM. 'In addition, there would be a feel-good factor from the news coverage following their capture. However, our priority is to scupper their plans and then apprehend them.'

Kate spoke up. 'It's worth remembering that the four Chechens are dangerous killers. If we were to corner them with people around, all hell could break loose and the collateral damage could be large. If we follow them we can pick them up well away from others. I should make it very clear that we would only wish them to be allowed to escape to the trawlers *if* and only *if* their Kornet and Vektor weapons are out of action.'

The PM paused after Kate had finished. He thought carefully about what she had said.

'My last question is: could you please explain your fears relating to the financial markets?'

Rafi glanced at Kate and Aidan. They nodded at him. 'Could I answer that one, please, Prime Minister?'

'Yes, go ahead.'

Rafi thought for a moment about where it would be best to start and eventually decided to start at the beginning, with the description of their three PhD theses. 'John and Jeremy discussed the ringleaders' work with a senior lecturer who was a contemporary of theirs; he described their dissertations as being incisive and of exemplary standard. To quote him: "If one puts them together, they're rather like the instruction kit for building a financial atomic bomb."'

The PM shifted uncomfortably in his chair.

'Sheikh Tufayl is conservatively worth $10 billion,' continued Rafi. 'Jameel Furud, through his control of Prima Terra Fund Managers, has around £30 billion of funds under his management; Maryam has, we estimate, a similar sum under her control. Talal, in contrast, has been using the sheikh's money to build up their terrorist infrastructure. They have billions of pounds at their disposal. They are seeking to undermine the Government's finances,' he paused, letting the point sink home. 'The terrorist activities should be viewed in the context of the recent stock market crash and the continuing uneasiness in investor sentiment. Their aim is to trigger – amongst other things – price falls in long gilts and large rises in long interest rates, which will enable them to make *massive* profits from their positions in the derivative markets.'

Rafi stopped and looked around the table to check that the guests had taken on board what he'd been saying. 'Aidan has been doing excellent work on the scale of their intervention into these derivative markets.' He leant forward and looked past Kate at Aidan.

'Yes, Prime Minister; in a nutshell, if they achieve their ambition they'll saddle the derivatives markets with losses in the region of £50-100 billion,' added Aidan. 'I have identified a sufficient number of contracts to confirm the scale of the numbers involved.'

The Prime Minister looked at Rafi and then at Aidan. 'Well, there's an uncomplicated answer: we close down the market and unwind the positions in the derivative contracts.'

Rafi looked at the PM. 'Might I enlarge, please?' he enquired politely.

'Yes,' came the slightly clipped reply.

'The terrorists have identified a number of areas where Government guarantees exist. Their aim is to bring billions of pounds of debts and liabilities back on to the Government's balance sheet. In particular they are targeting the accelerated decommissioning and clean-up costs of nuclear power stations, *and* the money that will be required to stop the outsourced public sector services that they control from collapsing. This would put the weakened Government finances into a very nasty position,' concluded Rafi.

'This all seems rather far-fetched if you ask me,' said the Defence Secretary. 'My view is that the greedy bastards want to make a financial killing, nothing more nothing less. Let's stop the trading in the contracts that Aidan has identified and get on with catching them.'

The PM looked at Aidan and Rafi. 'Do you believe that the Government's finances are in peril?'

'Yes sir. These terrorists aren't just financially astute and used to dealing with huge sums of money; they are also exceedingly devious and clever. They seem hell-bent on inflicting as much damage as possible to our country. It is as if they have declared war on our economy.'

Rafi sensed that the Defence Secretary disagreed. 'In the limited time available to us, we've looked at the two most obvious derivatives contracts and can confirm that they have big positions. I strongly believe there will be others and they will have been trading in Frankfurt and Chicago. It would be nigh on impossible to unwind the myriad of positions they and possibly their associates have built up.'

'This is bloody preposterous!' burst out the Defence Secretary. 'This is all too much. You're exaggerating – trying to play things up for your own self-importance! Have none of this Prime Minister – get on and stop the terrorist attacks. We can let the Treasury and the Bank of England sort out the financial problems next week, as and when they occur.'

Aidan was doing an excellent impression of a boiler building up a head of steam: his ears had gone red and his eyes had narrowed. He was close to telling the Defence Secretary exactly what he thought of him.

'Do you have a solution?' asked the Prime Minister.

'We believe that we do, sir. All we ask is that the authorities don't procrastinate. We're working on a detailed report for the Chancellor of the Exchequer, his Treasury team and the Board of the Bank of England as to how these financial problems can be contained. All we're asking is to be allowed to put these proposals in front of them tomorrow as soon as we know how badly or otherwise things are going to be. In light of the impending attacks it's our suggestion that the London financial markets do not open tomorrow. This will give us—'

'That's exactly what I suggested!' burst out the Defence Secretary.

'Not quite,' Aidan added quietly. 'Your suggestion was to unwind derivatives transactions; ours is to close the market for a day to give us time to counter the terrorists' financial attacks. What we have to avoid is procrastination; if the markets pass the point of no return, I'm absolutely certain that financial Armageddon will become an unstoppable reality for the UK economy.

The Prime Minister looked perturbed.

The Air Chief Marshal spoke. 'Prime Minister, might I make a suggestion? I hear what our friends here have been saying. As I see it, they are experts in their field and we're not. If what they say is correct, it could have damaging consequences that far outweigh the physical damage that the terrorists might inflict. Without a prosperous economy and a fully operational banking sector our democracy would be undermined. Let us focus on stopping the terrorists – their missile and suicide bomber attacks – but at the same time we should run with Mr Khan and Mr Gilchrist's assertions and get the experts and the top decision makers at the Treasury and the Bank to consider their grave predictions, as soon as practical.'

The PM nodded. 'Thank you, Sir Nigel; that makes good sense.'

The commissioner cast his eyes in Rafi's direction. 'You had something else to say, I believe.'

'Not more bloody financial pessimism!' exclaimed the Defence Secretary in an irritated tone.

Rafi smiled. 'No sir, some good news for once. If we can stop the markets from falling and hold long interest rates where they are until, say, the middle of next week, the terrorists' positions in the derivative markets will become untenable. Their margin calls will become larger and larger, and they'll be financially wiped out. This will eliminate several billion pounds from their coffers, damage many of the shadier banks and set back the terrorist cause by months if not years.'

He stopped and glanced at the PM. 'We have a plan.' he paused. 'Government real estate investment trusts could be created, thus providing the Government with a source of finance that will enable it to meet such financial obligations as and when they arise. It will remove the need to tap the gilts markets, and help the Government refinance its increased borrowings resulting from the bail out of the UK banking system.'

'Why didn't you say that sooner?' interjected the tetchy Defence Secretary.

The Prime Minister smiled. 'So there's a silver lining – as long as we take on board your solution and you get it right.'

'Yes, Prime Minister.'

'Right, back to matters at hand,' said the PM. 'The outstanding question that we need to answer is: do the terrorists have a contingency plan "B" in place? And if so, how much damage might a Kornet missile inflict? I'd be very interested to hear your views, Air Chief Marshal.'

'The damage could be extensive. If MI5 are confident that they know where the terrorists are going to attack in all but one of the locations, why give them a second chance?'

'Ewan?'

'From MI5's standpoint we can't believe our good fortune in finding where the attacks are likely to come from. Why risk tipping the terrorists off?'

'Defence Secretary?'

'We've everything in place to run such an operation from COBRA. And how certain are we anyway that these properties are where the terrorists will be located rather than just decoys? I believe that the two moles in COBRA should be apprehended so that we can get COBRA up and running, using the advantages that its set up will give us. I'd be willing to take the seemingly minute risk that there isn't a third mole. However, I will fall into line if everyone else believes COBRA isn't the right way forward at this point in time.'

'Commissioner, what are your views on COBRA?'

'The consequences of the terrorists swapping to a plan "B" are, in my opinion, too great a risk to contemplate whilst they and the four Kornet missile launchers are at large. Perhaps, sir, you might like to take a look at the emergency operations room we've set up downstairs before you make up your mind?'

The PM turned to Ewan. 'Please arrange for the two suspect COBRA individuals to be brought in *without* tipping off the terrorists, and see if you can discover how they were going to contact the terrorists.'

'Yes, sir. We have them under surveillance.'

The PM looked at Kate and her team.

'We owe you a great debt of gratitude for all your work and insight into the terrorists' activities, and thank you for placing our troubles into context. Mr Khan, thank you for your tenacity. And thank you to the rest of you.'

Kate took that as the invitation to leave. Her team filed out of the room.

T hey didn't have to wait long. Jeremy received a call on his mobile. 'Bloody hell, no! Well, I'm damned.' He listened a little longer and then said, 'Thank you.'

Jeremy looked across at John. 'My colleagues have interviewed one of the COBRA suspects. He gave them the phone number he was to ring and the phrase he was to use each time COBRA was activated. They traced the landline number as the ex-directory number of a special press adviser. However, the call was to be redirected through to the voicemail box of a mobile phone. And – would you bloody well believe it? – the mobile is currently located on the outskirts of Aldermaston, 200 metres away from where the suicide bombers are holed up in the horsebox. It's a bit of luck; we had assumed that they were all together.'

K ate and Rafi settled down and went through their paperwork to see if they had missed anything that could lead them to the missing target. Hours later they had still found nothing.

Rafi felt exhausted. He turned to Kate. 'I need sleep.'

'Would you like me to come and tuck you in?' she asked with a mischievous smile.

'Not tonight, thank you,' he replied. 'Could you wake me at 4 a.m., or earlier if I'm needed?

'Will do,' replied Kate. Rafi walked down the back stairs to the basement, grabbed a blanket and pillow and lay down on his cell bed. His mind started to clear. He got up, knelt down and for the first time in over a week said his prayers. Back on the bed, within moments, he was out for the count.

J ust before 4 a.m. Rafi was woken by Jeremy. He was groggy and struggled to get his brain back into gear. Strong black coffee was waiting for him upstairs.

'Hey, you still look rough,' said Kate cheerily as Rafi walked in. 'You've chosen a good time to join us. Things are hotting up in the Ops Room. It's like a game of chess. If you come down the corridor with me, I'll bring you up to speed.'

Kate started putting him in the picture. 'Emma, Peter and John are catching up on some sleep down in the cells, as is the economics team. The duty sergeant has never known the cells to be so full of sober people. The Defence Secretary's mood has improved; it seems first impressions are deceiving – in fact he's conducting himself rather well.' She paused. 'As you'll see, the Air Chief Marshal has brought in a specialist anti-terrorism expert and a couple of senior officers to act as coordinators.'

Rafi tentatively entered the Ops Room. It was buzzing. Kate and he stood out of the way to one side. The video conference screen to his left was linked up with the SAS command centre. The Air Chief Marshal, Brigadier Harold Sparkman and Colonel Paul Gray were discussing the first operation – the capture of the two suicide bombers and Kaleem Shah at Aldermaston. The colonel gave instructions and two teams, red and blue, were deployed. The plan was to overwhelm the suicide bombers and the journalist at precisely the same moment.

The two suicide bombers were not expected to be much of a problem. They were not professional soldiers, but they did have two large bombs in their horsebox. Speed and an element of caution were going to be critical.

The SAS commander reported that the two bombers were, to all intents and purposes, tucked up in the living quarters of the horsebox and appeared to be sleeping fitfully.

Kaleem Shah was a different matter. He had many years' experience of working in war zones. He was undoubtedly a cautious and capable soldier. The fact that he'd opted to sleep a couple of hundred metres away from the two terrorists suggested that he was expecting the unexpected.

The infrared sensors had identified the journalist as lying quietly across the back seat of the large Jeep. The vehicle was positioned such that it had a line of sight through to the horsebox and a second 4x4, but was largely screened by twiggy vegetation and small saplings.

It was all quiet in and around the large Jeep and the horsebox. The two SAS teams silently approached the two vehicles and waited for their orders.

Rafi watched, totally caught up in the proceedings. Unlike watching TV, this was real. He felt his heart pounding.

Just then Colonel Gray gave the command for the two assaults. There was a short delay and then from the video link there was the sound of two muffled explosions. The speaker crackled as it picked up the voice of the red team leader who was commanding a team of three against the journalist and his Jeep. 'We've secured the vehicle and have captured the journalist. He didn't put up a struggle. We found two booby traps outside the vehicle. Nothing too sophisticated, but nasty enough to take off a leg.'

The blue team simultaneously descended on the horsebox, found nothing untoward protecting it and seized the two suicide bombers, dragging them from their sleeping bags out into the open.

At that moment a loud bang echoed around the room. The horsebox erupted into a fireball.

'Shit! The bastard had a radio-controlled device up his sleeve,' was heard from the speaker.

'Blue team, come in blue team!' There was silence.

Two further loud explosions were heard as the terrorists' explosives went up.

The Air Chief Marshal looked at the colonel. 'Not a good start Harold, is it?'

The silence was followed by a muffled voice across the video link.

'Jesus, that was close,' said a shaky voice. 'Two of us are singed, but otherwise fine; two have suffered minor injuries from flying debris, but my corporal has an eighteen-inch piece of aluminium sticking out of his thigh. The two suicide bombers are in a bad way – one has a piece of shrapnel in his chest. They had no protective clothing on and both are badly burnt.'

'Get the three terrorists out of there and into protective custody. As far as everyone is concerned, the two suicide bombers are dead, got that?' ordered Colonel Gray.

'Yes sir.'

The journalist had attached a small radio-controlled explosive device to the fuel tank of the horsebox, which had ignited around 100 litres of diesel.

Colonel Gray gave the order, 'Initiate phase two.' The dull thud of an explosion in the distance was audible. The video screen showed a section of Aldermaston's outer fence with a gaping hole and a nearby building on fire, billowing black smoke.

'Not bad, eh?' said Jeremy, who had materialised from nowhere and was standing next to Rafi. 'Gives the impression to the other terrorists that they were successful, doesn't it?'

'Good work,' said the Air Chief Marshal.

The SAS command centre came online. 'Some plans and a spare timer for a detonator were found in Kaleem Shah's vehicle. The plans mark two buildings that were to be attacked. Both contained low-level radioactive materials; nothing really nasty, but sufficient to close the plant if released. Odd though, the timer had been tampered with. Whatever the setting, it would have gone off after about five seconds. The blue team leader saw the explosives; they weren't packed into vests but rucksacks, just like at Bishopsgate.'

'Thank you,' said Colonel Gray.

The commissioner was thoughtful. 'Well, that explains why the bomber at Bishopsgate got caught in the blast. He thought that he'd far more time to get away. A five-second stroll from the bomb's location to where his body was found fits in with the time delay on the fuse – so he wasn't a suicide bomber, just a servant set up by his masters!'

'Interesting,' mused Ewan. 'Ergo, the bombers at Aldermaston were expecting to escape!' he went quiet for a moment – deep in thought. 'I wonder if this attack has anything to do with the Iranians and the UK's escalation of its Trident nuclear weapons programme – supporting Iran's cause would have given them a safe place to hide after the attacks . . .'

'Oh bloody hell!' The Air Chief Marshal looked concerned. 'Don't go there! Ewan, let's just pray that there isn't a link between the terrorist leaders and the Iranians.'

Ewan shrugged his shoulders. 'Sorry, just trying to put two and two together.'

He turned to the brigadier beside him. 'Now for phase three; the news and the TV crews are all yours, Harold.'

Brigadier Sparkman nodded and called a member of the Ministry's press team, who was sound asleep. 'I've arranged a press conference for you at 7 a.m. near to the Aldermaston explosion. When you're dressed and have had a cup of coffee, I'll brief you.'

'What's happened, sir?'

'Have a strong cup of coffee, get your brain into gear and then we'll talk,' said the brigadier.

'Yes sir.'

Colonel Gray, meanwhile, was giving orders to the SAS red and blue team leaders. 'Arrange for the journalist's vehicle to be removed and the area cleaned. Can you please confirm the journalist is with the MI5 operatives?'

'Yes sir.'

'Good. They know what to do with him. Well done. How serious are the injuries your team sustained, blue leader?'

'Relatively minor, sir. Corporal Evans looks a bit like a hedgehog, but he can be patched up! Corporal Winderson suffered concussion when he struck his head in the explosion, but he's a thick-skulled bugger – give him a few hours and he'll be right as rain.'

'Thank you blue leader. All fit members of your unit are to join the red team. A helicopter is on its way.'

Rafi looked at the clock on the wall; everything had happened so quickly. It was only 4.20 a.m., Friday morning.

The brigadier turned to the Air Chief Marshal. 'Press briefing arranged, sir. Our boys on the ground have been told to keep the buildings smoking as you ordered, sir.'

Shortly after the Ops Room had become operational, the PM, the Defence Secretary, the Air Chief Marshal, Colonel Paul Gray and Ewan Thorn had gone into a conclave. It was a meeting each of them would remember for years to come. On the table in front of them was a list showing the sum total of all the special forces, marines, paratroopers and army units with urban warfare experience – plus the crack anti-terrorist personnel – that were available. The country's defences were stretched to breaking point. The conflicts overseas and tight budgets had left a gaping hole in the numbers available. A decision had to be made. Their terrorist adversaries were highly trained and experienced in the deadly art of urban warfare and concealment; therefore they agreed that quality rather than quantity had to be the order of the day.

The considered view was that the terrorists wouldn't make their move in the dead of night. And the command centre didn't want them to be tipped off by reconnaissance teams being spotted; accordingly, only cursory inspections of the properties and the surrounding areas were done.

'No sign of any of the four terrorists,' came over the speaker. 'We will wait until all our special forces, marines and paratrooper teams are in position.'

'I hope to God we've got this right,' the Air Chief Marshal murmured apprehensively under his breath.

The PM pondered quietly to himself as he listened to the discussion over the allocation of their scarce recourses. He, too, now appreciated just how overstretched they were. Resources were being allocated according to the perceived size of the latent hazard – priority was given to protecting the nuclear installations, leaving the defence of the gas and oil plants bordering on threadbare.

'I t's now time to see whether the terrorists are where we think they should be,' called out the Air Chief Marshal.

Rafi felt a wave of apprehension flow through him. If he was wrong about the properties and they drew a blank, it was game over. The butterflies in his stomach turned into a dull ache. He looked at the screens in the Ops Room; they were focused on the nuclear installations. There was an air of twilight in the pictures from the infrared cameras which gave a distant feel as to what was going on.

The Air Chief Marshal addressed his team. 'Brigadier Sparkman, as discussed, you'll coordinate the SAS and the Paras at Hartlepool, Hull and Easington.'

Then he turned to Colonel Turner and enquired, 'Is all in place at the Peterhead properties, St Fergus and Cruden Bay?'

'Yes, sir.'

His next question was addressed to Colonel Gray. 'All ready to go at North Walsham, Bacton, Grays and Sizewell?'

'Yes, sir.'

'Ewan, is all in place at Troon, Peterhead and Great Yarmouth docks?'

'Yes, sir.'

'That leaves me with Sellafield, Prestwick and Heysham.' The Air Chief Marshal spoke via his headphones to his SAS contact, glanced across to the video conferencing screen which linked their Ops Room with the SAS command centre and then at the screen next to it, which showed the paratroopers' command centre.

'Gentlemen, are we ready to go in five minutes?' Affirmative replies came in.

The die is cast, thought Rafi. He touched Kate's shoulder.

She was standing in front of him, gazing at the screens. She turned; her face was white with tiredness. 'This is it,' she said apprehensively. 'We'll soon find out if our hunches were right or if we've got it completely wrong!'

'Hunches . . . I hope they're a lot more than that!'

'Your confidence is most refreshing,' said Kate. Rafi found his hand next to hers; he gave it an affectionate squeeze. She took half a step backwards and let her body rest against his. She kept hold of his hand as she watched the three screens intently and listened to all that was going on.

The waiting was nail-biting. There were, Rafi estimated, twenty teams of special forces, paratroopers and anti-terrorist personnel out there in the darkness, stalking their prey. Behind them provisions had been made for their support. The scope of the mobilisation made it one of the largest peacetime operations on record.

Rafi held his breath.

Then the five minutes were up.

'Go, go, go,' came over the speakers. The troops swung into action.

On the screens Rafi could see the shadowy terrain over which the soldiers were navigating. Greg would have been pleased: his makeshift Ops Room was working well.

At Heysham, a squad of paratroopers were supporting a team of three SAS soldiers. The building had been under observation for the previous five hours. There was no sign of movement and no telltale infrared heat signatures showing where the terrorist was. It was a tall property, to one side of the industrial estate. It was being refurbished and sections were covered in tarpaulins. At the back of the flat roof there was a new scaffolding tower. The SAS soldiers inched forward, carefully checking for booby traps. Eventually the first SAS soldier reached the bottom of the scaffolding tower. He gave a thumbs up sign and pointed to the top of the tower.

His signals were relayed back to the command centre, which briefed the Ops Room. It was then that Rafi heard, 'Infrared shows the target to be lying on the scaffolding boards under the tarpaulins. He's going to be bloody difficult to get at without giving our presence away.'

There was a flurry of movement in a number of the small frames on the screens as the units' progress was fed back to the Ops Room.

The brigadier called out, 'Terrorist located at the Hartlepool property. He's under camouflage netting in the gully of the roof. He has a clear line of sight across to the nuclear power plant. The team on the ground is working out how best to tackle him.'

Rafi felt his hand being gently squeezed, as if to say, 'We weren't wrong!'

'No sign of the terrorists at Cruden Bay, St Fergus or Peterhead,' shouted Colonel Bill Turner.

'No sign of the missiles or of terrorists at North Walsham, Bacton, Sizewell and Grays,' added Colonel Gray, abruptly. 'Wait! A Vektor mortar and twenty shells have just been found on a motorbike parked at the back of the North Walsham property.'

Colonel Bill Turner spoke. 'An unattended utility van three kilometres from St Fergus has been investigated and a mortar with twenty shells has been recovered. No sign of the terrorist and nothing to report at Cruden Bay.'

The Air Chief Marshal called out, 'They've located a mortar and twenty shells in the panniers of a BMW motorbike parked in an old container on the building site at Gosforth, near Sellafield.'

This was quickly followed by the brigadier. 'A mortar and twenty shells have been uncovered at the Hull property.'

Rafi's pulse was racing. He did a quick calculation: two terrorists and their Kornet missile launchers were still unaccounted for. All four Vektor mortars had been recovered. They were almost there; just two launchers or two terrorists to neutralise. The smile on his face evaporated, as he realised it was too soon to be complacent. Just one missile hitting a nuclear target and it could be game over.

Rafi listened to the Air Chief Marshal being briefed. The SAS soldiers at Heysham couldn't get at the terrorist on top of the scaffolding without alerting him to their presence. After a short conference, a decision was taken and a message went back. 'Take him out. At all costs stop him firing a Kornet missile.'

The SAS assaulter at Heysham waited unmoving in the darkness. He had advised command that he couldn't guarantee to immobilise the terrorist with his compact 9 mm sub-machine gun. The SAS snipers behind him also had no clear shot.

He waited for his orders and then moved forward silently. The scaffolding tower had four main legs. He approached the furthest pair, reached into one of the pockets of his assault vest and pulled out a couple of small packages – the special services own blend of plastic explosive – which were spot on for cutting structural supports. Without a sound, he expertly set the charges, then moved back to the other pair of legs and repeated the process. He heard a person moving above him. His pulse rate stayed steady. The terrorist had no line of sight to him and the SAS soldier knew that he'd been as stealthy as a summer breeze; silently, he backtracked around the corner of the building.

He gave the signal that he was clear of the detonation zone and waited for the order from command. When it came, he pressed the miniature magneto in his hand and felt the shock waves of the four explosions ripple through his body. Each of the tower's legs was now missing a section. The tower remained motionless for a moment and

195

then gravity took hold. The scaffolding wall ties had no chance of holding the load. The tower arced outwards from the building and crashed into the ground. The terrorist, who had been under the tarpaulin on the top, spilled out and did a dead cat bounce on the tarmac. Three darkly clothed SAS men descended on him and stripped him of his weaponry. The Kornet missile launcher and three missiles lay on the ground close to him.

'Beware of any remote controlled devices,' barked the commanding SAS soldier.

In the Ops Room the capture of the Kornet launcher, its three missiles and the terrorist was greeted with cheers. The terrorist was still alive, but unconscious and looked to be in a bad state.

Suddenly, on the screen in front of him, to his horror Rafi saw flames erupt near to the Heysham nuclear power plant. There was dense billowing smoke. Then he remembered it was the army at work, giving the impression that a terrorist attack had occurred.

Kate was still leaning against Rafi. She felt a release of pent-up anxiety. She turned her head and looked into his eyes. 'Your instincts were bang on. You're a star.'

He felt the warmth of her body. 'More like good teamwork,' he replied, holding her gaze with a big grin.

The action at the Hartlepool property distracted them.

The brigadier received confirmation that the SAS soldiers couldn't safely capture the terrorist. 'Has the terrorist got a clear view of the nuclear power station?' he asked his opposite number in the command centre.

'Yes, sir. Good news is that an SAS sniper has outflanked him and has him in his sights.

'Take him out. Just don't risk him firing a missile.'

'Yes, sir!'

A few moments later, confirmation came over the speaker.

'Terrorist taken out.'

The brigadier turned to Colonel Gray. 'Crikey! The sappers have been busy – that was a massive explosion at Hartlepool nuclear power station; I wonder what they've found to blow up?'

Rafi watched the flames darting high into the air, followed by thick smoke engulfing the area around the nuclear power station. He looked across the screens. The army's pyrotechnic skills were being shown off at Aldermaston, and now at Hartlepool and Heysham. The TV cameras would make a meal of this!

Daylight would reveal damage to a non-nuclear building at Aldermaston, a smoking zinc factory next to Hartlepool nuclear power station and fire and smoke coming from the abandoned visitor centre on the perimeter of the nuclear compound at Heysham.

Rafi and Kate were on tenterhooks. Two terrorists with Kornets were still out there. The good news was that at least one of the likely targets wasn't nuclear – the oil pumping station at Cruden Bay – but where on earth was the other target?

'Nothing to report on and around the three trawlers,' called out Ewan.

There was a lull in the proceedings. Time ticked by slowly; the remaining two terrorists were conspicuous by their absence.

Rafi and Kate hurried back to their office. They looked again through their paperwork, but still couldn't find any clues as to where the missing location might be.

Rafi was worried. Had he let the side down and missed something obvious which could have pointed them to the missing target? The very possibility haunted him.

The Air Chief Marshal took the PM, the Defence Secretary and the head of MI5 to one side. 'I would like your permission to mobilise the entire military. We've passed the point of no return. I should have asked for this hours earlier. Unfortunately, at the time I was preoccupied with coordinating the limited resources we had available. He looked at the PM. 'Sir, we *have* to have a cast-iron insurance policy in place should one of these bloody missiles get through to something nuclear. Our ability to deal with a nuclear incident isn't what it should be. We have two terrorists with Kornet missile launchers on the loose. Who knows if they now suspect that we're on to them? We must prepare for the worst eventuality: a nuclear disaster.'

The PM agreed and, on his authority, at 4.45 a.m. all armed services' leave was rescinded. All personnel, including part-time territorial soldiers, all available medical and support Corps, were called to their barracks and put in a state of readiness. Every hospital with an Accident & Emergency Department within 100 miles of a nuclear plant was told to be fully staffed up by 6 a.m. The Home Secretary was contacted and advised to catch the first flight back to London. His ETA in Downing Street was 9.30 a.m.

Every barrack and hospital was told that this was a surprise training exercise, sanctioned by the Prime Minister to test their readiness to respond to a national emergency. The message went out to senior officers that the new Prime Minister wanted to use the exercise as a way of seeing where the problems might be and whether they had the right resources available.

Those in command were left in no doubt that they should prepare for a sizeable disaster or conflict and that, in order for the training exercise to be effective, secrecy was of paramount importance.

The Air Chief Marshal turned to Brigadier Sparkman and Colonel Turner who were standing close by. 'There are contingency plans in place for attacks on nuclear installations. What I want from the two of you is a plan – we'll call it "Operation Counterpane" – which will deal with a serious nuclear emission, contaminating, say, ten to twenty square miles of a densely populated urban area. On your agenda there need to be provisions on how to get a nuclear leak covered from the air, arrangements for an exclusion zone with a guarded perimeter, decontamination and triage units, medical facilities, an evacuation and rehousing plan, and a system to monitor the identities of all those displaced. Basically, take what is already there and make it work – big time.'

The Air Chief Marshal was looking perturbed. 'Probably best if you include Len Thunhurst, commissioner of the Metropolitan Police, in your plans. Giles here has brought him up to speed with all our problems and he's aware of the need for secrecy.' He paused. 'The transportation front is what really concerns me. We are a couple of squadrons of transport helicopters short. Without them, logistical support in an urban disaster area will be a nightmare. There'll be blocked roads and restricted access at a time when speed will be paramount. The number of operational workhorse helicopters in the UK is far below what we'll need.'

The beginnings of a smile appeared on Air Chief Marshal's face. 'I think I'll have a quiet chat with a close friend of mine who runs the Royal Netherlands Air Force. Colonel Turner, you're a logistics expert, please coordinate with Ewan and get him to draw up a list of the whereabouts of all private helicopter fleets around the UK. Tell the operators that all helicopters capable of carrying four or more people are subject to a requisition order for the next twenty-four hours. Their helicopters should be fully fuelled, with pilots on immediate standby and ready to join a UK task force as soon as possible, but preferably by 6 a.m. They will be held on call for the rest of the day. Full compensation will be paid if requested. Inconvenienced clients should only be advised that their helicopter is on loan for a rescue operation.'

As of 5.35 a.m. the Royal Netherlands Air Force's base at Gilze-Rijen, fifty kilometres west of Eindhoven, was on full standby and over half of the Dutch military helicopter fleet had been offered to assist the Royal Air Force.

The Air Chief Marshal breathed a sigh of relief on hearing the news – the Royal Netherlands Air Force had one of the most modern fleets in Europe and its helicopters were only an hour away from the east coast of England. Twenty-nine helicopters – Chinooks, Eurocopters and Apache Combat helicopters – were on standby and a direct link had been established with their operations room. This, in one stroke, had more than doubled the number of military helicopters available. He walked over to the PM to warn him that if deployment of the military became necessary, it might well throw up a number of glitches and the level of overstretch of domestic UK armed forces would be laid bare within the next twelve hours.

The PM nodded. 'Up until a few hours ago, I had only placed importance on our forces countering terrorism, peacekeeping and fending off challenges faced by rogue states. I believe I've missed a very obvious threat to our well-being: energy terrorism. Without guaranteed access to energy, we, or rather our people, face an uncertain and potentially bleak future, Air Chief Marshal,' the PM said, looking carefully at him. 'When this is over, please draw together a team of experts and provide the Cabinet with a briefing paper on how we should build the armed forces so that they're fit-for-purpose in terms of protecting our country's interests at home. I have no wish for us to become a police state, but the possibility of a small but well-funded terrorist cell attacking the heart of our energy supplies has greatly perturbed me.'

Back in the office, Rafi was still racking his brains about the two missing locations. He would have put good money on one of them being the crude oil pumping station at Cruden Bay – its location and its importance to the economy put it right at the top. Then for the other there was Sizewell nuclear power station or Grays liquid natural gas storage depot, but the special forces had still found nothing.

Kate and he had been exploring whether the location could be linked to HFFF's new London cold store. They had checked to see if the terrorists' property company had used any specific firm of lawyers. Unfortunately, they used a different firm for each transaction. They had spoken with Land Registry, but drawn a blank.

Neil had arranged a special visit to PREH's offices an hour earlier. They were empty. It transpired that they were being moved from London to Manchester. All their computers and files were in transit and MI5 were not surprised to find that they were unable to trace the removals firm.

As a last resort, the commissioner had decided there was nothing for it, but to pull in PREH's directors. There were four of them. Basel Talal was at large in the North Atlantic on board *Golden Sundancer* and the other three, it transpired from one of the director's wives, were on a corporate bonding week with their staff in the Caribbean. The tour company advised that they had chartered a crewed yacht. No one in the marina from which they had sailed knew where they were heading. Their ship-to-shore radio was switched off, as were their mobile phones. They were incommunicado.

The yacht had left the marina twenty-four hours earlier with the wind a comfortable force three, gusting four. The US Coast Guard advised that with an average speed of eight knots the yacht could be anywhere within a couple of hundred mile radius, equivalent to an area of around 100,000 square miles. Neil had spoken to his opposite number at the US Homeland Security. Four US navy helicopters and all available coastal patrol vessels were dispatched to reconnoitre the possible area. They would try the captain's usual haunts first but, given the scale of the area to be covered, they didn't have high hopes of finding the yacht.

Meanwhile, Kate had rung Rick in Manchester. Wesson was asleep. Rick described the man as unhinged, with a persecution complex – he was still being totally uncooperative. Rick promised to wake Mr Wesson early and see if he could get anything more out of him.

John had tracked down Roger Harewood's – the immigration officer's – flight. He made contact with the airline and had, eventually, got through to the captain of the 747 and to Roger, who sounded surprised and dazed. 'Er . . . Good morning, or is it evening? To what do I owe the pleasure?'

John explained about HFFF and the need to find their new cold store in London.

Roger sounded very apologetic. 'I seem to recall making a jotting or two. It's hard to keep track of people entering through the immigration fast track process. Sorry, I can't recall any details. We're asked to process rather a lot of people.'

'Steve said that information in your notebooks might help us,' said John.

'Yes; I've a drawer full of cheap notebooks in which I make miscellaneous notes. As soon as we land I'll go straight to the office and try to find my scribbles on HFFF. I hope I didn't throw them away. All I can remember is that the location was somewhere in London. Sorry, I can't recall anything more. We aren't encouraged to muddy the waters. My scribbles aren't welcomed on the files. Just a habit I suppose.'

'A good one,' said John. 'We'll arrange to have you picked up from the plane and taken to your office when you land. Will your wife and family be OK?'

'Yes, no problem there; Felicity is well-organised.'

'If you should remember anything in the meantime, do please let us know. When you get to the office, if for any reason you can't get through on the phone, please fax us with anything you have. The fax comes through to the middle of our office. Steve has put the numbers on your desk. Safe journey.'

John asked to speak to the captain.

'How can I be of assistance?'

'Mr Harewood is going to be helping us with important enquiries when he gets back to Manchester. He seems to have unwittingly uncovered a piece of information that might help us solve a serious crime. We could do with him being as alert as possible when he lands. Could you . . .'

The pilot didn't need to hear the rest of the sentence. 'I'll arrange for him and his family to be moved to first class for the remainder of the flight.'

'Thank you. When you land I will arrange for Mr Harewood to be collected from the boarding gate. Could you ask the control tower to give you landing priority, or should I?'

'No problem, I can do that.'

'This is hush-hush so another excuse would be appreciated. Thanks, for your help,' said John.

John thought for a moment, picked up the phone and spoke to Phil Scott, Rick's assistant. 'Sorry to wake you. I could do with a favour, please. I need to get a Roger Harewood from Manchester Airport to Sheffield when his plane lands just after 9 o'clock this morning. Time will be of the essence.'

'It's forty miles and at that time of the morning the traffic will be awful. I've got an idea. Can I ring you back?' said Phil.

'No problem.'

A few minutes later, Phil came on the phone. 'I've pulled some strings and booked the police helicopter to be at Manchester airport, and I've arranged for an airport security car to take Roger from the plane across to it.'

'Perfect, thanks very much,' said John.

It was now a matter of waiting. Rafi looked at Kate. It was obvious that neither of them was optimistic.

'What else can we do? How about we get the large scale London maps out again and see if we've missed anything?'

Kate gave Rafi a concerned looked. 'I don't know how you do it. You've suffered more stress in the last week than most people deal with in their lives and you still keep going with a smile on your face. I'm absolutely shattered.'

He looked at Kate and saw a different, softer side to her.

'It's the company I keep and an overwhelming desire to stop the terrorists,' he replied.

Kate smiled at him. 'You think the company is tolerable?'

'Yes,' he smiled, 'when you walked into the interview room at Paddington Green, I doubt if you knew how close I was to folding. I shall be in your debt for—' Rafi paused, trying to think how best to express his feelings, but, before he could finish his sentence, Kate cut in.

'It was David who said I should back you. For my part, I'd have left you to the wolves. I'm glad my first instincts were wrong,' said Kate.

In the Ops Room the planning of 'Operation Counterpane' continued at a feverish pace.

Time had slipped by – dawn would soon be breaking.

'They're professionals, hardened in the tactics of guerrilla warfare,' said Colonel Gray to his team. 'If they're half as good as the Russian Security Service say, we can expect them to be invisible right up to the last moment.'

At Cruden Bay in North Scotland, the expectation was for an attack shortly after daybreak. The SAS and paratroopers were waiting, but there was still no sign of the terrorist. However, the indications were that a terrorist was in the vicinity. An outbuilding behind the vacant industrial unit in Peterhead had been occupied the previous day. Someone had been sloppy. Numerous cigarette ends were found on the floor. In themselves they were nothing out of the ordinary, but in the circumstances they were like manna from heaven. In the FSB files was a miscellaneous comment on Sergy Kowshaya – he was a chain-smoker.

The brigadier's two adjutants were having an increasingly frenetic time coordinating the Ministry of Defence's press team and the release of information to the news desks.

The message they were trying to put across was: 'Yes, there have been three terrorist attacks, but this is a matter for the armed forces and the police, not the politicians. The attacks have been partially successful. Thankfully, no nuclear material has been released. Security has been stepped up at all UK nuclear installations. Another attack couldn't be ruled out. Nothing is being taken for granted and the military has been called in to provide a defensive ring around key installations. This is what the armed forces are trained for and the public should remain calm.'

The Air Chief Marshal spoke to those around him in the Ops Room and those on the video links. 'Daylight will bring with it the real danger as the terrorists will be able to see their targets more clearly and the news cameras will capture any scenes of destruction. Be prepared for anything to happen. We've two bloody dangerous terrorists out there. We have to find them and stop them.'

It was cold at Cruden Bay. A swirling sea mist lapped around the bulbous twin tanks of the oil pumping station, cloaking them in a soft, white blanket. The outline of the buildings was barely visible, making an accurate attack by a terrorist difficult.

Suddenly there was activity. A suspicious movement had been detected one and a half kilometres from the perimeter of the oil pumping station. From nowhere, there was the feint infrared image of an individual kneeling on the ground out in the open, with a missile launcher at his side. The enhanced pictures showed that in the blink of an eye the terrorist had the launcher up on its tripod and was ready to fire at the pumping station. It was clear he knew exactly what he was doing. The nearest SAS soldier was 500 metres to the terrorist's left but, unfortunately, his line of sight was partially obscured by a small undulation in the terrain.

It was too late – there was a *whooshing* sound and seconds later one of the two oil storage tanks erupted into a fireball that lit up the grassland for miles around. The explosion was followed by a series of smaller explosions. It was like a gargantuan Chinese firecracker going off, one explosion after another. Thick, grey smoke engulfed the whole facility.

The soldier broke cover and moved rapidly to a point where he could clearly see the terrorist in the distance. On the run, he opened fire. The terrorist seemed unfazed by the bullets whistling around him and fired a second missile into the thick pall of smoke. Another explosion was heard, but this time it lacked the cataclysmic intensity of the first. The dark, clawing smoke belched up into the sky. Anyone downwind was going to have an unpleasant time.

The terrorist's position looked hopeless; three SAS soldiers with their automatic fire had him pinned down in his foxhole. Suddenly the ground around the terrorist started belching out thick white smoke, creating a smokescreen which rapidly obscured him from the view of the SAS – he was well prepared.

Then, from within the blanket of white smoke, the engine of a powerful motorbike could be heard – it had been stowed under a nearby camouflage net. The terrorist had abandoned the missile launcher and was making a quick getaway.

He appeared at speed from his protective smokescreen, handling the bike with skill. He slipped unharmed through the security force's net and now had an unhindered run to Peterhead and then towards the St Fergus gas terminal. He had foreseen that the security would be tight given the location, but was surprised by the speed of the response.

The team in the Ops Room were briefed on the events: the oil pumping facility had been extensively damaged.

Rafi recalled Emma's earlier comment: 'It's not size that matters, but the throughput of the pumping station. Cruden Bay is where the Forties Pipeline System has its landfall. It can pump over one million barrels of oil a day from the offshore oil fields and send them to the inland processing terminal at Kinneil. Without Cruden Bay the lion's share of the UK's daily crude oil supplies would stop.'

The Air Chief Marshal looked across to the Prime Minister. 'So, four of the five Kornet missile launchers and all four Vektor mortars are accounted for. Unfortunately, we have incurred some major structural damage at Cruden Bay, but thankfully there are no civilian casualties or injuries. The sappers are doing a great job at Heysham, Aldermaston and Hartlepool. To those not in the know, it's been a bloody awful night. It's as if World War III has broken out in our back yard. Thankfully we know better.' He paused. 'As a matter of utmost priority we've got to find the fourth Chechen terrorist or his Kornet missile launcher.'

The commissioner, who had been watching quietly, leant across and said to the Prime Minister and the Air Chief Marshal, 'I think it's time for me to advise the London financial markets not to open.' He picked up the phone and first spoke to his contact at the Stock Exchange, and then to Euronext.liffe. Two minutes later, both exchanges had posted on their dealing screens that they would not be opening due to terrorist threats. Then, as an afterthought, he picked up the phone and spoke to the heads of the derivatives exchanges in Frankfurt and Chicago. To his relief they both agreed to postpone the opening of their exchanges.

It was 6.45 a.m. at Sizewell – the grey February dawn was still forty minutes away; the cutting east wind was blowing over the coastal marshland and was forecast to veer around and come from the southeast. Dick Newton and his co-driver, Ted Dyer, had received notice the day before from their controller that their run to the marshalling yard at Willesden Junction in north London had been brought forward by two and a half hours and that they would be going straight through to Sellafield.

The heightened anxiety of terrorist threats over the past year had resulted in Dick and Ted's timetable being subject to frequent changes. Gone were the days of a regular schedule. But that didn't seem to worry them, as they were well looked after. This morning, however, was a first. Never before had they been on the move in darkness and never before had they gone further than Willesden.

It was cold outside as Dick and Ted undertook their final inspection of the train and the two carriages transporting the spent nuclear fuel casks. The radioactivity coming from the sweating casks was within the guidelines. Dick radioed through to control confirming that the freight train was ready to depart at its allotted time.

They had been operating the Sizewell–Willesden Junction run for several years and it had become a regular feature of both their lives. They knew the routine like clockwork and the safety procedures as prescribed by their employers had become second nature.

In the warmth of the train's cab, Dick handed his empty coffee mug to Ted and waited for the last few minutes to tick by before their departure time. At 6.50 a.m. precisely, Dick reported in to his controller, released the brake and eased the train out of the sidings. The train made light work of its two fifty-tonne reinforced canisters and gathered speed – on the old rails and wooden sleepers – down the branch line from Leiston to Saxmundham.

A few years earlier an early morning start would not have been possible. The 45 mph speed limit imposed on the nuclear freight trains meant that peak rush hours had to be avoided as they caused too much congestion for the commuter trains. Behind the scenes, the speed limit had unofficially been raised to 60 mph. The result was that if Dick and Ted timed their slot correctly when they joined the mainline at Ipswich and went behind the Norwich to London express, they would cause hardly any disruption to the passenger train schedules. In any event, the reliability of the early morning commuter trains was far from good and it was not unusual for their journey to be delayed by one of the many problems encountered by the long-suffering commuters.

There was no real hurry to get to the junction at Saxmundham, where they joined the Lowestoft–Ipswich line. They were scheduled to go after the two-carriage diesel passenger train which was timetabled to stop at Saxmundham at 7.31 a.m. But, as this morning it was running a few minutes late, Dick brought the train to a gentle stop outside Saxmundham station and they waited for the passenger train to come and go. It was 7.38 a.m. when the nuclear freight train passed through Saxmundham. They were four minutes behind schedule, but in the scale of things this was well within the bounds of normality.

Over the years Dick had become used to Ted's running commentary of the places they went by and his interpretation of what they were. The descriptions rarely changed. It helped the time slip by. There was the llama farm and then the small market town of Woodbridge, nestling on the banks of the river Deben, a favourite of Ted's. He would recall how the Viking burial ship at Sutton Hoo on the other side of the river was worth a visit. Then it was on to Ipswich to wait for their slot behind the Norwich to London express train. The intercity train was on time. Dick eased his train through Ipswich station and the tunnel beyond. After that, it was a straight run down to Stratford on the north-eastern outskirts of London, where they would leave the main line for the North London line which would take them around London, past the marshalling yards at Willesden Junction and on to the north-west line towards Sellafield.

When their speed limit had been 45 mph, the seventy miles from Ipswich to Stratford had taken two and a half hours, with a couple of stops to let passenger trains past. At 60 mph, the journey would be almost an hour faster and they would need only one stop to let an intercity commuter train through.

I t was approaching 8 o'clock. The early morning news channels had wall-to-wall coverage of the four terrorist attacks. The infernos and the tall columns of acrid black smoke filled the TV screens.

When one of the journalists queried why they were being briefed by the Ministry of Defence and not the Prime Minister's office or COBRA, they were told that the PM was on top of things and that he had scheduled an imminent COBRA meeting.

In the Ops Room, the PM stood next to the Air Chief Marshal; he looked drawn and tired. He turned and spoke to those around him.

'I'm sorry that we let a couple of missiles get through. I suppose we should be grateful that the damage has been far less than it might have been, and that our nuclear facilities are 100% intact.'

The PM paused and looked across at his Defence Secretary. 'We have just one terrorist and one Kornet missile launcher unaccounted for. As we don't know where he is or what his target is, plan "A" or plan "B" has become immaterial. I've phoned the Permanent Secretary for Intelligence Security and Resilience and the director of Civil Contingencies. COBRA will be in session as of 9 a.m. I have told them to have experts on CBRN – chemical biological radiological nuclear – in attendance. And to have all members of ACPO (TAM) – Association of Chief Police Officers (Terrorism and Allied Matters) – available via video conference links. The Defence Secretary and I ought to get a move on so we can be there to brief them.'

The Prime Minister turned to the chief of the armed forces. 'Sir Nigel, I shall leave this Ops Room in your command. Your remit is to take out the fourth terrorist and disable his missile launcher. And please keep all the fleeing terrorists under close observation.'

The PM and the Defence Secretary walked around the Ops Room and shook the hands of everyone there before leaving for Downing Street.

He stopped briefly to have a word with the brigadier. 'Any news from Sizewell or Grays?'

'Nothing sir. We believe both are clear.'

'Thank you.'

I t was an uneventful journey down towards London. Ted kept up his almost constant commentary which was broken only by short conversations with the manager or his assistant at the control centre. They discussed the terrorist attacks. The nuclear train convoys weren't being stopped, just the timetables changed. The new strategy had been approved by their bosses, who deemed that 'Their cargo posed too difficult a target and was thus an insignificant risk,' according to the control room manager.

The controller was in a grumpy mood; he'd been trying unsuccessfully to give up smoking and had succumbed. In his absence for a cigarette break or two, Ted spent time chatting with his assistant, a newcomer who had only started working for the nuclear transport company the Monday before. Ted was beginning to wonder if the young lad was thick. He was charming, but seemed to have little grasp of the importance of his job.

Dick was pleased to find that the intercity train behind them was running late because that meant they could proceed to Shenfield before pulling in to let it and a commuter train pass. They were on the outskirts of London when the young assistant controller came on the radio. 'My boss has nipped out to his car to get another packet of cigarettes and have a smoke.'

Ted sensed unease in the young lad's voice. 'Are you alright?' he enquired.

'Yes, it's just that I wish my boss would get back. I need to go for my morning constitutional – I think it was the vindaloo I had last night!'

Ted looked across at Dick and muttered, 'I suppose that means he's desperate for the loo.'

The freight train passed through Romford; it wouldn't be long before they left the main line and started on the next leg of their journey.

The desperate voice of the assistant came on the radio. 'It's no good, I can't wait any longer. My boss should be back soon!'

Dick raised his eyebrows and was going to speak, when Ted cut in. 'Ah well, so long as he's quick no one will ever know that the control centre was temporarily unmanned.' He thought back to when he'd first driven the nuclear waste trains. The manpower involved in those early days dwarfed the lean, efficient teams that had become the norm. Spare capacity was a thing of the past. Forty uneventful years of safe nuclear rail transport had not given rise to complacency, but rather a sense of the mundane had permeated the system and dulled the minds of many involved.

The train was approaching Stratford station. Ted radioed through to the Control Room. There was no reply; the manager hadn't returned from his smoke and the young lad was presumably still otherwise engaged.

As they arrived at Stratford station, the signal for the branch line turned red. Dick brought the train to a halt. As they waited, he noticed that the platforms were almost deserted. After a couple of minutes' wait the light turned green and the train slowly trundled on to the branch line to start its way around suburban London.

Dick smiled. It had been a good run down from Suffolk. He was looking forward to his extended journey up the west coast and wondered if Ted would, for the first time, be lost for words.

In Manchester, Detective Inspector Rick Feldon was having a chat over breakfast with William Wesson. His fifteen years of interrogation experience told him that there was still at least one more nugget of information to be drawn from this despicable man. Wesson continued to ignore his questions – he was in denial and his defence was to shower verbal abuse on those around him. Rick was getting nowhere.

Wesson had finished his food and was sipping his coffee. 'Shall we see what's going on in the world?' asked Rick.

A small TV was brought into the interview room. The channels were filled with special news bulletins showing wall-to-wall pictures of the plumes of smoke resulting from the terrorist attacks. Wesson looked without any apparent interest at the pictures. The detective inspector asked him more questions without receiving any response. It was getting hopeless. He was going round and round in circles. Time was ebbing away. Rick had an idea. It was time for some creative thinking. He left the room and reappeared a few minutes later with three photographs.

Rick laid a photo of a young woman down on the table in front of Wesson. 'She's beautiful, isn't she?'

There was no reply.

'She was working in the labs at Cruden Bay and suffered lethal burns. She was the wife of a man your age.'

Then Rick turned over a picture of a random middle-aged woman on the table. 'She's about the same age as your mother, isn't she? She was a good woman, strived all her life to bring up her family – a boy and a girl – by herself. She worked as a cleaner in the offices at Heysham. She was killed by flying shrapnel. A slow and painful death, I understand. Her two teenage children have no close family to look after them. What would you and your younger sister have done if your mother had been killed when you were that young?'

Rick paused. 'How would you have felt if you and your sister had been fostered away from the love of your parents?' He had tugged at an invisible chord within Wesson, who broke down in front of him. Howls of tears and sobbing came from the insufferable little man. Rick had no sympathy for him at all. He had one aim and that was to get out of him the missing pieces of information. The torrent of tears began to subside. This man is a real drama queen, thought the Inspector. It was time to up the ante. 'Your mother rang. She wants to help.'

Wesson raised his head.

'Why couldn't she have been the person killed by the shrapnel? She always stopped me from doing the things I wanted to and her tongue is as sharp as a carving knife. I don't want to speak to her. In fact, I'd be happy if I never saw her again.'

Oh shit, thought Rick, I got that one wrong. He took a deep breath.

'You valued all the properties which turned out to be close to where the terrorist attacks took place. We're missing one more address; you can help us stop the next attack.' Wesson didn't move.

'How do you think your sister, who you've protected all these years, will survive as the sister of a terrorist collaborator who was responsible for the deaths of innocent people? She won't get any sympathy from her mother, will she? If you continue to be uncooperative you'll be charged with complicity and the book will be thrown at you. How will your sister survive against your mother, without you to defend her? Think about it.'

Rick watched the turmoil bubbling up inside the young man in front of him. '*Now* would be a good time to tell me the address of the property we don't know about.'

Wesson didn't raise his eyes. 'All I know is that they found this property and it's being refurbished for HFFF to occupy later this year. I don't know whether it's freehold or leasehold or its full address other than it's in Stratford, East London – I'll probably have to value it for the next set of accounts.'

The detective inspector looked at the broken young man in front of him. 'You must tell me more!'

'I can't! That's as much as I know. You see, I accidentally overheard Talal and his property director discussing this property. They said it had been bought by PREH in such a way that no one would be able to trace it. Talal described it as the "jewel in the crown"; it was to be refurbished and converted into a cold store. Its location was one where they'd make a killing. They didn't realise I was in the room behind them. When Talal saw me – his eyes were like my father's before he lashed out and beat my sister or me. He was livid and said, "Never repeat what you've heard if you value your sister's life!" '

Wesson got up, staggered over to the corner of the interview room and threw up. Rick thought for a moment and concluded that Wesson had told him all he knew. 'Constable, escort Mr Wesson back to his cell. Make sure he's got at least one person watching him twenty-four hours a day, understood?'

Rick left the room, raced upstairs, picked up the phone and rang Kate's direct line. After several rings the call was diverted to the switchboard.

'I need to speak to DI Adams, please. It's urgent – very urgent.'

'I'll see if I can locate her; she's not answering her phone.'

The seconds ticked by as if they were the last grains in an hourglass. The telephonist came back on the line. 'I'm sorry she's in a meeting with a minister from the Home Office.'

'I need your help, please,' said Rick calmly. 'How can I get a message through to her or her colleague, John, as of now?'

'He's in the meeting too, I'm afraid.'

'Could you write something down for me? It's simple, just: "Urgent. Ring Me. Now! DI Feldon." As a matter of life and death, please give this message to DI Adams.'

'I'm not allowed to leave my post unless I've cover.'

'Of course you're not technically, but we're trying to stop the bastards who planned the Bishopsgate bomb from letting another one off. Understood?'

'Yes, sir, I'll personally give your message to DI Adams straight away.'

The phone went dead.

In his chauffeur-driven car en route to Downing Street, the Prime Minister thought about the events of the night. Had he been right in not activating COBRA earlier? The Ops Room at Wood Street had served its purpose and had worked well. Yes, now was the right time to get COBRA up and running.

He mused about the far-ranging powers that the Civil Contingencies Act gave this committee. To all intents and purposes, when sitting it became all powerful. In the first instance he chaired the committee, but if he wasn't available, it fell on the Home Secretary or his deputy to take his place. He smiled, his mind wandering briefly to how COBRA had got its name thanks to the room where the meetings were held: Cabinet Office Briefing Room A, which was deep under Number 10, Downing Street.

The PM's thoughts turned to his Home Secretary, whom he had chosen in order to placate the wing of his party he found most difficult to deal with. As he leaned back on the soft leather car seat, he wondered whether the Home Secretary and his department spent too much time courting favourable headlines and news coverage. In the few months since taking power he had realised that he had become increasingly anxious as to his Home Secretary's motivation. The press painted him as good party leadership material and liked his and his ministers' charm offensive. Perhaps his party's wafer-thin majority had prompted his spin offensive and he was jockeying for position in case the PM slipped up.

The PM's attention refocused on the previous week's COBRA meeting, which had been convened to sort out the mess left by the Bishopsgate bombing and to foil any follow-up attacks. The minutes showed it had been a straightforward meeting. It had been chaired by the number two at the Home Office, a loyal supporter of the Home Secretary, with liaison officers from the MoD, the police, MI5, MI6 and the Metropolitan police. This meeting was going to be considerably more difficult. He personally would take the chair.

Deep under Number 10, with the Home Secretary away, his number two had taken the chair. He'd arrived at COBRA early, sensing it was his opportunity to take control. By 8.45 a.m. he had a quorum. Against the advice of the permanent secretary, he called the meeting to order and had COBRA up and running. He almost caught MI5 with their trousers down. They had the video link, relaying what was going on at COBRA to the Ops Room, working only seconds later.

The minister chairing COBRA appeared very concerned about the impact of the adverse TV coverage and asked for suggestions on how the news stories and the TV pictures could be made to look less grim.

The army at Hartlepool in particular were doing an impressive job. The zinc factory next to the nuclear power station was belching out acrid smoke. Elsewhere, in the words of one TV commentator at Cruden Bay, 'The locals must think that they are on the edge of a war zone, what with all the explosions and the dense smoke.' Aldermaston and Heysham also looked grim.

The Home Office minister got a buzz from his time in the spotlight in front of the members of COBRA. He cleared his throat. 'First, we counter these awful pictures with something that will prevent us from looking feeble and, second, we consider what the terrorists will do next and what can be done to stop them. The second part, I shall leave to the PM who will be joining us shortly.'

Neil Gunton, Jeremy's boss, had, unexpectedly, been asked to attend the meeting. He was sitting there getting more and more annoyed by the self-obsessed minister's lack of progress, but managed to disguise his feelings reasonably well.

The minister turned to the Metropolitan Police representative and asked, 'What do we know of these terrorist attacks and the likely direction of future attacks?'

'I'm unable to brief you fully. The anti-terrorist response is being conducted by the City of London police and MI5. We do not yet have the full details,' came the reply.

The minister didn't like that answer. 'I've been getting reports that the armed forces are on full alert in response to a large, nil-notice training exercise ordered by the PM. Is this true?' he asked irritably. Turning to the special services officer sitting next to Neil, he asked, 'Would you know anything about this?'

The SAS officer shrugged his shoulders and remained silent.

The minister turned his attention back to Neil. 'You and your boss were at Wood Street last night, weren't you?' It sounded like an accusation.

'No, sir,' came the reply, 'I was interviewing two suspects at MI5.'

'Can you enlighten us as to what's going on?' added the minister.

'Things are rather sketchy at the moment,' replied Neil.

The minister was not pleased; the tone of his voice betrayed his annoyance. 'When can we expect the Prime Minister to brief us?'

Neil left the answer to the permanent secretary.

'I am informed he'll be here at 9 o'clock, Minister.'

'We need a distraction to deflect the TV coverage and show the public that we're playing hard ball with the terrorists. I have a colleague working on this. Do I hear any other suggestions?'

'Perhaps COBRA should start vetting everything going on air, as was the case in Iraq?'

The minister thought that this was a good idea. 'We should implement this now.' He turned to his colleague, a junior minister, who had come up with the idea. 'Derek, would you please look after this personally?'

'Yes, sir.'

Derek stood up to leave, when the door opened and the Prime Minister walked in with the Defence Secretary and his personal secretary at his side. The PM, as the screen at Wood Street showed, beckoned Derek to sit down, strode over and stood facing the minister.

The room fell silent.

'Minister, am I right in believing that last night you declined an invitation as the Home Secretary's stand-in to meet with the commissioner of the City of London police force and three very high ranking officers of the State?'

The minister looked most put out and went into bluster mode.

'But I wasn't told who would be there and I was extremely busy. I had a speech to make. I'd already issued a press release and I knew that there would be excellent press coverage. Anyway, I rearranged the meeting for this morning. So no harm was done!'

The Prime Minister's voice took on a steely tone.

'Your judgement call was fundamentally flawed. Events have over-taken you. You should have been a safe pair of hands on which the commissioner could have relied. Instead you placed personal spin above the needs of your country.'

'That's quite untrue, Prime Minister; the press conference was for the good of the Government.'

The PM beckoned to his personal secretary, who was sitting to one side. He stood up, walked over to the minister and placed a typed letter in front of him.

'For your signature,' said the PM.

The minister read the short letter and looked up at the PM, his eyes exuding animosity.

'Why should I resign at this of all times when I'm needed here?'

The PM looked at him as if he were a grouchy schoolboy. 'That meeting you were too busy to attend last night is still going on. It has been coordinating twenty plus special forces, paratroopers and anti-terrorist units who, between them, have since the early hours of this morning foiled seven terrorist attacks. The terrorists had a success at Cruden Bay, but the rest of what you see on the television is an act of fiction, thanks to the army's pyrotechnic skills. We have had to maintain a high level of secrecy as our intelligence uncovered a web of collaborators and sleepers. It has been crucial not to let the terrorists know we were on to them as we had intelligence concerning their primary targets, but no idea what their alternative plans might be. We have had to be very careful. Their weaponry is such that they have the wherewithal to cause catastrophic damage.'

'But why wasn't I told?'

'You were, but you chose to ignore it,' replied the PM in an even voice.

'Why the hell did you deduce that I might let slip what was really happening – that's downright slander!'

'The stakes have been so high that we haven't been able to trust anyone unless they've been within a secure intelligence-monitored environment. Suffice it to say that the two gentlemen missing from this meeting aren't the only moles we've found in senior places.'

'But *I* am needed here.'

'The Home Secretary will be here within the hour. Sign the letter or I will be forced to fire you.'

The minister hesitated, signed and stood up. He was livid and intent on letting everybody know just how furious he was.

He was escorted out of the room by the PM's personal secretary. At the door the minister turned and with venom in his voice spoke directly to the PM, 'This isn't the last you'll be hearing of this outrage.' And with that, chaperoned by a waiting MI5 man, he was gone.

The Prime Minister looked at the set of statue-like faces around the room. 'I think that we can now get back to business as usual. Let me put you in the picture as to the events of the past thirty-six hours. However, lest you worry that things are being left to drift, let me assure you that a fully-staffed Operations Room has been up and running since yesterday evening and is dealing with matters as we speak. The Defence Secretary and I spent the night there. We left the Ops Room less than an hour ago.'

The PM, with input from the Defence Secretary, gave a detailed description of the events of the past thirty-six hours and the strategy that had been put in place for dealing with the terrorists.

A little earlier, back at Wood Street, at 9.39 a.m. Kate's phone rang. It was the main desk.

'A junior minister from the Home Office is here to see a Mr Khan. I'm advised that you might know something about his whereabouts? He wants to see him, with two senior officers, in an interview room now!'

'Leave this to me,' said John. 'I'll tell him this is an inconvenient time.'

Kate looked at Rafi. They were now alone in the room. 'How are you holding up?' she enquired in a concerned manner.

'OK, but I wish we could find the last terrorist. I'm on tenterhooks with this waiting for Rick or Roger to get back to us.'

Kate's phone rang. It was a very disgruntled John. 'The junior minister is insisting that he sees Mr Khan. Says he has a direct order from the Chair of COBRA, his boss. It seems he hauled himself and his press entourage over to Paddington Green police station only to be kept waiting and to find Mr Khan wasn't there. He was redirected to MI5 headquarters and they sent him here. He's extremely pissed off.

He says he'll throw the book at us unless we let him see Rafi immediately. He refuses to understand that things are at a very delicate stage and won't take no for an answer. He's told me that he'll use his powers under the Civil Contingencies Act to make us cooperate, or else.

'I've spoken to Beverley; Giles and David have gone to a meeting with the deputy commissioner of the Metropolitan Police to brief the Met's COBRA liaison unit and can't be disturbed. I can't find Ewan. It's down to us. The minister keeps saying that he has to find out how much more Mr Khan can tell him about the Bishopsgate bombing and the recent attacks. Basically, I reckon all the self-obsessed plonker wants is a smokescreen: a story to tell the news teams outside in order to deflect all the bad publicity the Government is getting.'

'Why the hell now?' blurted out Kate.

'Because the man doesn't live in the real world!' Tiredness had reduced John's ability to remain calm.

'Sounds like the old saying: "They came to do good; they stayed to do well",' added Rafi weakly.

'Thank you, Rafi,' said Kate in a frustrated tone.

'Anyway,' continued John, 'I suppose we'll have no option but to let him see Rafi.'

'OK, but we keep the interview as short as possible,' Kate replied.

Over the phone she heard John shouting to the duty officer at the reception desk.

'Bloody hell! Get those bloody journalists away from here. Get the bloody area outside the station cordoned off and keep the bloody press away – at least fifty bloody yards from the front door.'

'Yes, sir,' came the prompt reply.

'Sorry about that,' said John. 'You and Rafi – meet me in the third floor interview room. I'll bring the junior minister up.'

'This had better not take long,' said Kate to Rafi, who sensed her nervousness.

In the stairwell she stopped him, put her hand on his head and roughed up his hair.

'We can't have you looking kempt.' She pulled his rugby shirt out of the back of his tracksuit trousers and looked at him. 'You'd better take your shoes off.'

'Seriously? My socks stink!'

'Don't worry; it's all part of the illusion.' Kate looked him over. 'Yep, you'll do. You look bloody awful, and yes, your socks reek!' To his surprise, she leant forward and planted an affectionate kiss on his cheek. 'No doubt you'll be worth knowing after a wash and brush up!'

They were the first to arrive at the interview room so sat down and waited. Minutes later John and the politician arrived.

'Sorry for the delay,' said John. 'The junior minister had to wash his hands.'

The junior minister, flanked by John and Kate, sat opposite Rafi.

'I went to see you at Paddington Green this morning only to find you weren't there. I was redirected to MI5 headquarters – most irregular – and they said I'd have to come here for the full story. I've wasted much valuable time and am in no mood to be messed around. Mr Khan, what I need to know is why you aren't helping the police with their search for the terrorists,' said the frustrated junior minister.

Rafi looked blankly across the table and remained silent.

'Thanks to you we had more terrorist attacks last night. Your resistance and reluctance to help is setting a bad example to the Muslim community. I'm advised that a growing number of extremist youngsters are becoming your followers. This is bad for the country. I'm here to give you an ultimatum: either you cooperate or I'll throw the book at you and your family, do you hear? What do you have to say?'

Rafi looked at the junior minister: at his pale blue double-cuffed shirt, the light pink tie, the immaculate grey suit and his perfectly combed hair. If things weren't so serious he would have laughed at his pomposity and the bizarre nature of the interview.

'Are you threatening me and my family?'

'Damn right I am! Your type should know what they're up against when they tangle with the Government. You're outside the laws that protect decent and innocent Englishmen. You should be sent home.'

Rafi's temper was rising – valuable time was being wasted. 'I'm dark-skinned and a Muslim. Why does that make me and my family undesirable? Answer me that and I'll help you with your questions.'

The junior minister was silent for a moment. 'It's your bloody fundamentalism that's the problem – only permitting one God.' He paused. 'You debase all other religions and criminalise the pursuit of wealth or personal advancement. Your brand of fundamentalism is myopic and detrimental to a modern society. You're all the same: out to undermine our democracy. We will stop you, you know. Your approach to life will be stamped out and the likes of you will be removed from this country.'

Rafi sensed the junior minister was spouting forth a well-rehearsed monologue. 'Is that your view or the view of others?'

'My boss, a senior minister in the Home Office, agrees with me. Fanatical Muslims have no place here. Once our backs are turned, all you want to do is to bring down our democracy.'

Rafi wanted out. Time was ticking away and the idiot on the other side of the table was being irrational.

'Sir,' said Rafi, 'I'm innocent until proved guilty. Find the evidence and then try me.'

The junior minister lost his cool. 'Of course you're bloody guilty – we all know that. The CCTV footage alone will convict you. I've the press outside waiting for me. I need something to tell them which will make a good story to deflect the coverage of all the horrors you've caused. Will you cooperate? Or shall I personally make your life and your family's not worth living?'

Rafi sat there, too annoyed to answer.

Unexpectedly, John stood up. 'Sir, you're not getting anywhere. Mr Khan is obviously not going to help you.'

'What the hell are you talking about, Inspector? Don't you know who I am? I'm your boss's boss! I won't take orders from anyone, let alone a junior policeman!'

John kept his cool.

There was a knock at the door. The telephonist burst in.

'DI Adams, I've an urgent message for you.' She passed the piece of paper across the table to her.

The junior minister grabbed it. 'I'll see that.'

Kate looked at the telephonist. 'What did it say?'

'Rick someone asked for you to call him urgently.'

'Oh hell!' said Kate and dashed for the door.

The junior minister was taken aback. He shouted after her. 'You can't leave until I've finished with you. Come back here this instant!'

Kate was long gone.

John stood up and looked piercingly at the junior minister. 'I strongly suggest you stay here,' he said authoritatively. 'The constable outside and I will escort Mr Khan back to his cell – in case he does any *more* damage. You should see the mess he made of the three guards at Paddington Green – nearly killed one of them. He's a third dan karate black belt. See his right wrist? He felled a nineteen-stone guard and fractured his jaw.'

'Why didn't you tell me this before?' squealed the ruffled junior minister. Rafi stood up and moved towards him.

'No, get back,' shouted John. 'He isn't worth it.'

'Get him out of here!' shouted the squirming junior minister.

'Yes, sir. I'll take Mr Kahn to the cells and return to discuss how we can give your press friends a good story.'

'Do that and don't be long.'

John and Rafi left. John locked the door, turned to the police constable and handed him the key.

'Under no circumstances let him out until the commissioner or I get here. Understood? Whatever the minister says, ignore him!'

'Yes sir. But what about Mr Khan here? Will you be safe with him?'

'Of course.'

'But, what about his karate skills?'

'You shouldn't believe everything you hear!'

'Sorry, sir.'

'Rafi, go and help Kate; I must contact the commissioner before the minister gets on his mobile and does something even more crass.'

Rafi raced back to the office. Kate was on the phone to Rick; she switched on the speaker.

'I've had another go at interviewing Mr Wesson,' said Rick. 'By accident, Wesson overheard Basel Talal and his property director discussing a building in Stratford, which they said would be untraceable. Basel described it as the jewel in the crown and added that its location was one where they'd make a killing. You're looking for an industrial property in Stratford, East London; it's undergoing refurbishment.'

'Thanks,' said Kate, 'you're a star!'

She hung up and rushed out of the room. Rafi was about to follow her when her phone rang. It was the switchboard.

'There's an urgent message from Roger Harewood; he wanted to check that you got the fax.'

Rafi hung up, rushed over to the fax machine, scooped up the sheet of paper sitting there and ran to the Ops Room, oblivious to all his aches and pains – and his lack of shoes. He briefly looked at the contents of the fax as he ran. It read: 'URGENT – I tried to phone. My notes are sketchy, sorry. The HFFF cold store is a large industrial building between Billingsgate and the A12 in East London. It's being refurbished. Hope this helps. Roger.'

As he passed the meeting room where Emma was, he banged on the door and called for her to follow. Seconds later he barged into the Ops Room, skidded to a halt and shouted to Kate, waving the fax in his hand.

'Roger confirms: it's between Billingsgate and the A12; a large industrial property being refurbished.'

Rafi prayed that they weren't too late and that the valuable minutes wasted with the junior minister would not be their undoing.

At 9.56 a.m. the PM finished briefing COBRA on the events of the past thirty-six hours.

The video conference link showing the Wood Street Ops Room was switched on. The PM introduced the Air Chief Marshal, Sir Nigel Hawser, and asked him to update COBRA on the whereabouts of the missing terrorist.

Suddenly, the Ops Room door burst open and in charged DI Adams closely followed by a dark-skinned individual with an unshaven face in a Harlequins rugby shirt, waving a piece of paper and shouting.

Kate and Rafi didn't stand on ceremony and cut across the PM.

'We've found the location of the last terrorist. He's at a large industrial property in Stratford, East London, between the A12 and Billingsgate fish market. It's being refurbished. I hope it won't be too difficult to spot from the air.'

'What's the target at Stratford?' asked the PM.

'Could there be a nuclear waste train in transit near there?' suggested Emma, who had arrived at the door. 'It is the only thing left on our list that could fit.'

'Find out,' said the Air Chief Marshal to Colonel Turner. 'Let's find the building and then the target should become obvious.'

At that moment they were joined by John. He sidled over to Rafi and passed him the tape of the interview with the junior minister. He said quietly, 'I thought that you might like to have the tape as a memento.'

'Thanks. Good news – we've found the last location; it's Stratford, in East London,' said Rafi.

The Air Chief Marshal was on the scrambler. 'What air cover do we have? A fighter over Sizewell in Suffolk? Excellent! Get it over Stratford as quickly as is physically possible.'

'There's also a Tornado preparing to land at Marham, in Norfolk,' said the squadron leader on the video link with the Ops Room.

'Get it over Stratford in double quick time,' ordered the Air Chief Marshal.

'Commissioner, alert the nearest police helicopter and get it to Stratford. The first to arrive will have to locate and take out the terrorist.'

The brigadier called across. 'The Tornado will be at Stratford in seven minutes and the Jaguar from Suffolk will be there in eight and a half minutes. I've alerted the nearest anti-terrorist squad and they'll be in the area in twenty-two minutes.'

'Tell the pilots to look for a scaffolding tower, or a platform on the roof of an industrial building; it could well be overlooking the railway tracks,' ordered the brigadier.

The colonel meanwhile was having a frustrating time finding out where the nearest nuclear waste train was. The clock showed it was just after 9.58 a.m. He was looking agitated. He'd dialled through on the direct line of the control room coordinating nuclear trains, but he was being given the runaround by the computer-controlled switchboard.

'Oh sod it!' he said. 'Bloody lift music! Who the hell do they think that they are – some poncey retail store?'

A woman answered and apologised for the delay. 'If you've come through to me, it means that either the phones in the control room are engaged or the people are busy.'

'Do you work in the same building as the control room for the nuclear trains?' enquired the colonel.

'Yes; they're on the floor above me.'

'Excellent! Go right now and get someone in authority to pick up my call immediately. There's an accident waiting to happen. This is vitally important – do it now!'

With that the phone reverted back to what the colonel described as 'bloody bog music'. His face had gone from a normal shade of pink through the spectrum to a bright red. A meek voice came on the phone a minute later.

'Sorry, you caught me with my trousers down. How can I help?' came the response.

'Do you know the whereabouts of any nuclear trains near Stratford?'

'Er . . . yes and no,' came an uncertain reply. 'Sorry I'm not that sure; this is only my first week here. The board shows that there's one scheduled to pass through Stratford. My boss has gone outside for a moment.'

'Is there anyone else with you who can help us?'

'Sorry, no,' came the reply.

'Find your boss as quickly as possible.'

'He won't like being disturbed,' came the unfortunate reply.

'Get him now; tell him there's an emergency and you've COBRA on the phone.'

221

'You what?'

'Just get him, now. Tell him it's a matter of life and death.'

'Will do!'

Rafi looked up at the clock; it was 10 o'clock. He looked around the room. Everyone was holding their breath; there was a deathly hush. Moments later, the voice of an aggravated man came on the phone.

'What the hell do you want?' he barked.

'Do you have a nuclear train anywhere near Stratford?' The colonel barked back.

'Who the hell are you?' came the abrupt reply.

'Colonel Bill Turner of the anti-terrorist squad; I have the Prime Minister alongside me.'

'No shit!' was the reply.

'Do as he says, now!' commanded the PM in a stern voice. 'Before you ask, yes, I am the Prime Minister.'

'Hold on a moment. Yes, the Sizewell train is running slightly late; it's just left Stratford station and is entering the Stratford branch line.'

The Colonel shouted down the phone, 'Tell them to do an emergency stop!'

The voice of the controller was heard over the speaker. 'Dick, stop your train immediately; there's a terrorist threat . . . The train is coming to a halt about 600 metres down the spur line past Stratford.'

'Get the train to back up to Stratford station and up the main line.'

'That's against the rules; I can't do that!'

'Do as he says,' came the uncompromising voice of the PM.

The colonel continued, 'Get all the trains on the main line stopped.'

'One bloody thing at a time.'

'Get them to back up now,' barked the Colonel. 'Get them to do it before it's too late.'

'Keep your hair on! They're starting to back up as we speak.'

There was an expletive heard over the phone, followed by a couple of sentences heavily laced with choice words.

'Did I hear you say that your train has disappeared off the screen and the radio connection with them has been lost?'

'Yes,' stammered the coordinator. 'There was a loud bang and they've effing disappeared off the screen.'

Rafi looked across at the clock; it read 10.02 a.m.

The shaky voice of the controller came back on the line. 'I can confirm that I've lost contact with the driver and the satellite positioning marker is no longer functioning.'

222

The brigadier interrupted the silence. 'The Tornado is one and a half minutes away.'

Rafi felt spellbound and sick with apprehension. They'd found the missing piece of the jigsaw, but were they seconds too late?

The voice of the Tornado fighter pilot came over the loudspeaker. 'There's been one – now two – explosions! The target is a train, just west of Stratford station.'

The Ops Room meanwhile had been patched into the pilot's on-board camera showing an orange ball of flames erupting high into the air. Under it, for all to see plainly, was the devastated wreck of the train strewn across the track – one of the nuclear canisters was missing its front half and the top of the second canister was no longer there. Black smoke spiralled up into the sky, drifting north-west in the light wind.

The Air Chief Marshal spoke to the fighter pilot, who had received the grid reference for the property.

'Can you identify the terrorist's position?'

'Yes, sir,' came the reply.

'Is the building occupied or unoccupied?'

'Hard to tell sir – looks vacant.'

'If you have him on visual, take him out in case he fires another missile.'

The terrorist looked across at the devastated train from the top of a scaffolding tower. Radiation would soon be all around him. He launched himself over the side of the tower and abseiled from view.

You could have heard a pin drop. That was what they were after – London – the business capital of Europe and the venue of the 2012 Olympics.

It was a calamity.

Having foiled the other attacks, Rafi found it hard to take on board the impact of this terrorist success. He had known that the stakes were high and the consequences would be grave if a nuclear catastrophe occurred – the reality was numbing.

The voice of the Tornado pilot could be heard again. 'Sir we've a major nuclear incident here. One canister has a gaping hole in it and the second has been ripped apart.'

Emma looked at Kate and Rafi. 'Sweet Jesus help us! That's around two tonnes of spent nuclear fuel in the air,' said Emma, with a lump in her throat, 'which is something like 20 kg of plutonium and 40 kg of other radioactive particles on the loose.'

Rafi looked around the room. The service chiefs had been trained to work under pressure and they were already making plans to deal with the calamity.

Rafi's thoughts were still fixated on the scale of the horror unfolding in front of him.

The Air Chief Marshal spoke via the video links to the Army HQ at Wilton and then to the colonel standing next to him.

'Activate "Operation Counterpane". I repeat, activate "Operation Counterpane". Brigadier, advise the Royal Netherlands Air Force that we need every helicopter they can spare, pronto.'

Colonel Gray spoke to the Prime Minister, who had turned a whiter shade of pale.

'Sir, I suggest that you activate LESLP – London Emergency Services Liaison Panel – immediately. The Metropolitan police are on standby. Although control rests with you and your colleagues at COBRA in the first instance, sir, I suggest that you ask us to coordinate the military element required to contain the disaster, and oversee the evacuation and the decontamination process for the time being.'

'Carry on,' replied the PM. 'I have two nuclear experts with me who will advise you on the size of the exclusion zone.'

'Thank you, sir.' The video link camera swung round and two middle-aged professors came on to the screen. They spoke to the Air Chief Marshal and explained what data they would require.

En route to the nuclear train, from Colchester Barracks, was a helicopter equipped with radioactivity-sensing devices. Like many others, it had been placed on standby by the brigadier in the early hours of the morning as part of "Operation Counterpane". The helicopter pilot radioed through that he would be over the train in seventeen minutes.

'For the time being, gentlemen,' said the professors, 'we recommend an exclusion zone of one mile upwind and four miles downwind. We will give you the precise figures shortly after we have the data in from the helicopter.'

The Ops Room was like a hornets' nest. The scale of the operation dwarfed anything that had ever been attempted in peacetime.

At last, the helicopter flying at 1,000 feet started to collect and send the data on the radioactivity levels through to COBRA. The professors fed the data, in real time, into the impressive-looking laptop computers in front of them. As the helicopter flew over the smouldering train, the operator of the radioactivity-sensing equipment let out an expletive and advised the pilot to give the train a wide berth next time. The pilot carried on with a predetermined series of flyovers and sweeps of the vicinity on a grid basis. As the volume of data fed back to the professors increased, it became obvious from their faces that the news was far from good – they had turned an ashen colour.

After what seemed like an age, but in reality was only a matter of minutes, the younger of the two professors started speaking.

'We need to know, Prime Minister, what acceptable mortality rate to put into our models. The scale of the radioactive leak is very large. What level of increased cancer mortality is acceptable? Should we take one additional death per 100,000 people every ten years, or what?'

There was a discussion amongst the COBRA team; a number was agreed on and keyed into their computer model. The younger of the two professors spoke up hesitantly.

'I hope you're sitting down. On the basis of the data, gentlemen, the exclusion zone is: two miles upwind of the train, ten miles downwind and the ellipse at its widest point is six miles wide.'

Rafi looked at the map. A vast swathe of London, from Enfield to West Ham and from Stoke Newington across to Woodford, was now destined for dereliction in perpetuity. It seemed completely unreal – like something out of a disaster movie.

'Air Chief Marshal, we have emailed you the perimeter line of the exclusion zone. It can be superimposed on your maps.'

A hush fell over the two rooms. The second professor spoke solemnly. 'The exclusion zone has an area of fifty-seven square miles and the length of the perimeter is close to thirty miles.'

Rafi looked at Kate. 'I've had enough.' He felt gutted and disheartened. All his attempts had proved to be inadequate. The terrorists had won through. Tears welled up in his eyes. They'd pulled the big one off. Over fifty square miles of one of the most densely populated parts of Europe would have to be abandoned and many people would face horrible deaths.

Haunting thoughts flooded through his mind. If they'd told the junior minister to 'sod off', they could have got the information on the last property to the Ops Room minutes earlier. Valuable time had been squandered. If the nuclear train had been stopped just a few hundred metres sooner the terrorist wouldn't have had a clear line of sight. The knot in his stomach tightened.

Rafi turned and walked down the corridor to break the bad news to Aidan's team. The ball would now be in their court. He opened the door and in a monotone told them of the missile attack at Stratford, and that one of their team should liaise with the Ops Room to be briefed on the scale of the radiation contamination. He left their room and noticed Kate still standing by the door to the Ops Room.

Rafi walked over to her and took hold of her hand. She turned and looked at him with tears in her eyes. 'Come on, let's go; there isn't much we can do here.' But she didn't move. She stood captivated by the screens, like a rabbit caught in the headlights.

'In a few minutes, please,' she replied. 'I would like to see what happens next, if I am not in the way.'

P lugging the gaping holes in what was left of the spent fuel containers was the immediate task. Access by air was the quickest and safest way to get materials in to cover the ruptured containers. The imperative was to stop further hazardous and highly toxic radioactive waste escaping by entombing the train in concrete.

"Operation Counterpane" was under way. The army's HQ Land Command based at Wilton, near Salisbury, had been in a state of full readiness and within minutes of the train being hit by the first missile it was already coordinating troop movements, working closely with those in the Ops Room.

Colonel Turner had passed across a long list of all the available UK civilian helicopters. These were now under the command of the Royal Air Force.

All helicopters within 250 miles and powerful enough to lift a concrete hopper were en route to Stratford. The workhorse Chinook helicopters would be the best at transporting the concrete, but as at 10.45 a.m. the nearest was still forty minutes flying time away. The demands of the armed intervention in the Middle East had seriously depleted the modest size of the services' ageing helicopter fleet. On paper, the numbers of helicopters remaining in the UK looked significant, but in practice the majority were out of action, undergoing repairs or modifications. Thankfully, the helicopter squadron from the Netherlands was now only fifty-five minutes away.

Colonel Turner's team had identified seventeen large building sites with cranes and concrete hoppers. There was a local property development boom going on thanks to the impending 2012 Olympics. Each helicopter was directed to a property development site, where they could pick up a concrete hopper and a crane driver.

It was going to be a dangerous operation, particularly for the first four or five sorties which would be the most at risk when they jettisoned their loads in close proximity to the hot radioactive contents below. In theory, it would be best to use the biggest helicopters first, but in practical terms the colonel opted for a first-come-first-served basis. An added complication was getting the calculations right as to the maximum payload which each helicopter could carry.

The reaction time of the coastguard helicopters was far faster than anything the colonel could have hoped for. The first collected its hopper of concrete within forty-one minutes of the request going out. Having a modest lifting capacity, it was only able to take the hopper a third full, but it was a start.

The pilot and his two crew members were joined by the crane driver and took off with the hopper slung under the helicopter's belly, heading for the plume of dark smoke which was clearly visible in the overcast February daylight. The pilot made his approach from the south-east – upwind. Half a mile from the train, the helicopter gained altitude and the hopper was lowered to the full length of its steel wires. Hovering over a specified spot was second nature to the pilot – even in a force eight gale. This time, it was different. The risks were unseen.

'Bombs away!' shouted the crane driver pulling the mechanical release cord. 'Now comes the slow bit,' he shouted. 'I reckon we'll be here for sixty to seventy seconds.'

'Shout when we can bugger off,' said the pilot. Seventy-five seconds later their task was completed. The empty tubular steel hopper and hawser were ditched; the helicopter banked and headed south.

The co-pilot called back to those behind him. 'What were the readings?'

'OK-ish,' came the reply. 'No more dentist's X-rays for some while, I reckon. We're still below the maximum limit and a bit more shouldn't do us any real harm; just fry a few cells here or there.'

'Are you willing do a second run?' enquired the pilot.

'If no one else is around and we can help stop the radioactivity escaping, do we have a choice?' said the crane driver.

The co-pilot radioed through to the Ops Room and spoke to the colonel. 'Load safely deposited. Our radioactivity gauge shows that we can do another run. Where's the next helicopter?'

'It's five minutes behind you, followed by two more shortly after that, then there's . . .' he hesitated, 'a bit of a gap.'

'Sign us up for that slot. Where do we get our next load of concrete from, please?'

The colonel studied the map. His adjutant beside him pointed at a mark on the map, saying, 'I suggest this one,' and relayed the coordinates. The pilot moved on to the new course.

'What did it look like?' asked the colonel.

'Devastation,' replied the pilot. 'There's a river and a canal nearby. You're no doubt aware of where the water goes?'

'Yes,' replied the colonel. 'We're working on how to stop the radioactivity getting into the water courses and the leaching into the water table.'

Multitasking was the order of the day. Kate was roped in by the colonel. 'Find me a good location to set up a decontamination unit for the helicopter crews and where we can put the helicopters that have been exposed; ideally a small local airfield away from the public gaze. When you've found it, get the RAF command centre to set up a decontamination unit and field hospital there.'

'Yes, sir,' came the reply.

A private airfield and flying club was found at Stapleford, near the M25/M11 intersection and less than fifteen miles away. She passed the details on to the RAF Control Centre.

'Let me look it up,' said the voice at the other end of the phone. 'Good choice – its main runway will take transport planes. Tell them to expect a couple of Hercules planes within the next forty-five minutes. Get them to clear the area to the west of their runway number 28/10. We'll put the contaminated helicopters there.'

Kate phoned the flight centre, half expecting the phone to be answered by an unhelpful individual. It was answered by the manager of their Club House. Kate explained that the RAF needed to borrow their facilities.

'No problem. We've been listening to the flurry of radio traffic for the past half an hour. Is it as bad as they say?'

'I'm afraid so,' replied Kate.

'What can we do to help?'

'You can expect two Hercules transport planes carrying medical supplies within the hour. They won't be staying long, as they've other deliveries to make,' said Kate, who went on to give details of their requirements.

'We'll clear out the student accommodation block. It'll make a good medical block and decontamination facility. I've only one favour to ask: if you could ask the transport planes to land on the tarmac part of the main runway and not on the grass section it would be much appreciated,' said the manager.

Back at the train, the first five sorties flown by the lighter coastguard helicopters had all but covered the ruptured canisters with concrete.

'Bloody pyramids!' commented the adjutant. 'The train line is on an embankment and the concrete pours down off the carriage on to the sloping ground. The base layer of the concrete gets wider and wider but the pile doesn't get much higher.'

The crane driver in the back of the first coastguard helicopter overheard this conversation and shouted to the pilot, 'Suggest they add a setting agent or salt to the concrete; it'll speed up the setting time.'

The first heavy-duty Chinook helicopter did the sixth run and took almost two full hoppers. This was closely followed by eleven more Chinook sorties. By midday, the ruptured canister and train were no longer visible, buried beneath a small hill of concrete. Phase One had been completed successfully.

Meanwhile, the irate junior minister had been let out of the interview room and was now en route to 10 Downing Street, where he had been summoned to attend a meeting with the head of PR at the Cabinet Office.

Phase Two, which had commenced simultaneously with Phase One, involved the establishment of the exclusion zone.

Four Apache helicopters were tasked with marking the thirty-mile long boundary of the exclusion zone and the location of the fourteen decontamination centres. They used a combination of electronic and smoke beacons.

From listening to the conversations, Rafi had gleaned that the main problem was the large amount of radioactive material that the south-easterly wind had picked up and was depositing over a wide area.

The Kornet missiles had thermobaric warheads. These, it seemed, were different to conventional explosive weapons and used the oxygen in the air instead of carrying an oxidizer in their explosives. As one of the army officers explained, 'They produce more bang for their bucks. Unfortunately there's water surrounding the spent fuel rods. The thermobaric explosion will have extracted the oxygen from the water and liberated hydrogen gas, which will have made the bang even bigger. The ferocity of the blast will have vaporised much of the radioactive material and catapulted it high into the sky. The radio-active plutonium is heavier than lead, so thankfully won't travel far. It's the lighter and more highly radioactive isotopes in the spent fuel that will cause the problems. They will stay airborne far longer and are responsible for the unexpectedly large size of the exclusion zone.'

16 Air Assault Brigade, the army's premier rapid reaction fighting brigade from nearby Colchester Garrison, Rock Barracks, near Woodbridge and Wattisham Airfield, parachuted in 750 troops using Hercules and transport planes. They were joined by soldiers from the 1st Royal Tank Regiment's Nuclear Biological and Chemical Unit, stationed alongside RAF Honnington in Suffolk, who landed at London City Airport within fifty minutes of the first missile exploding. They were transferred by helicopter to the locations of the fourteen decontamination centres and were tasked with helping clear the ground.

The soldiers on the ground had already started securing the perimeter of the exclusion zone: they were stopping people from entering and directing those leaving the exclusion zone towards the nearest decontamination centre. The public were left in no doubt that the soldiers carried live ammunition and were prepared to use it, if necessary.

Meanwhile, 3,000 soldiers were being airlifted in from all round the UK to reinforce the cordon around the perimeter as quickly as possible. Commercial planes had been commandeered to assist in the troop movements.

Companies of soldiers were tasked with supervising the evacuees and corralling them into the holding areas, located adjacent to each of the fourteen embryonic decontamination centres and the adjoining medical centres which were triaging the casualties and dispensing radiation tablets.

It was calculated that over 1,000 decontamination shower units would be required to process the majority of the 900,000 people in around ten hours. Rafi couldn't work out where all the planes and people came from. The screens showed the skies full of parachutes. Rapidly, it all became a blur. He stood watching but taking little in.

One question that had been exercising COBRA was how to make certain that the inner exclusion zone was completely cleared of people. A 90% rule was adopted. Speed was of the essence. Those who could be moved quickly were dealt with first. Reluctant individuals would be strongly encouraged to leave later in the afternoon.

The squadron of twenty-six helicopters that had flown in from the Netherlands, combined with the armada of private helicopters, were a godsend. Every available decontamination unit and the associated medical support teams within their range were commandeered and delivered to one of the fourteen decontamination centres. The ingenuity of the Royal Engineers and the soldiers from the Royal School of Military Engineering at Chatham and at Minley in erecting the decontamination centres tipped the balance. By the early afternoon 1,250 decontamination shower units were up and running.

Specialist army units moved in to coordinate the mammoth task of clearing the exclusion zone. They were joined by the Territorial Army's Medical Services and Veterinary Corps.

Thanks to the forward planning, 'Operation Counterpane' had sufficient numbers of paratroopers on the tarmac on runways around the UK waiting to take off. Within eighty minutes of the missile explosion the thirty-mile perimeter had a significant military presence guarding the electronically tagged line. The line in the densely built-up areas was zigzag in shape. The smoke beacons marking the locations of the fourteen decontamination centres were clearly visible.

600 Regular and Territorial personnel from the Royal Military Police, Provost Staff and Guard Service arrived to work alongside the local police forces and emergency services. Their first job, with the paratroopers, had been to systematically block all the roads and side streets out of the exclusion zone so that no vehicles at all could leave the area. Lorries and cars were commandeered and used as barricades. Tempers flared as people were forced to walk to safety.

A one-way road system was established to funnel the traffic away from the exclusion zone. In the opposite direction the local police assisted by the Territorial Army established express ways to enable troops, the emergency services and their equipment to get to the perimeter of the exclusion zone. To stop the civilian movement of traffic and keep the roads moving for emergency vehicles, a curfew was imposed on the whole of the Home Counties.

One of the hardest parts of the operation was to stop panic setting in. All radio, cable and TV stations carried the same content. There was a message from the Prime Minister, followed by an explanation as to what was going on and what people should do.

Appeals for help with the rehousing of those dispossessed went out to councils and people living away from the exclusion zone.

The helicopters that had completed their sorties collecting the decontamination equipment and medics were tasked with flying in Territorial and Regular Army soldiers in protective clothing to work with the paratroopers to create corridors within the exclusion zone. These corridors channelled people towards their nearest decontamination centre. Those who couldn't walk were transported by army vehicles. The longest walk was three miles; thankfully most people had less than a mile.

The brigadier and his team were in charge of identifying and unblocking bottlenecks. The decontamination centres were their main headache. They implemented a fast track system. At the holding areas alongside the decontamination centres, units were set up, screening people for alpha, beta and gamma radiation. Where 'Within nominal' readings were detected, people were given potassium iodate tablets, sent away from the exclusion zone and told that they didn't need to be decontaminated.

Initially, those people from the fringes of the exclusion zone were found to have negligible levels of radiation and were sent on their way, but soon the contamination levels rose as the radioactivity travelled with the wind and a point was reached where everyone had to undergo decontamination. Logistical problems were experienced as families found that they were being split up in the process. Contaminated children not of school age were allowed to have a parent with them. All other schoolchildren separated from their parents were fast tracked and moved to nearby schools to be reunited with their families as quickly as possible.

It was a bitterly cold day. Thankfully, many of those who had been out in the open had the benefit of wearing heavy winter clothing and much of the radioactive material was removed by simply stripping them of their clothes.

Once naked, the radiation readings were taken again. For those with external contamination and whose skin was intact, it was a relatively uncomplicated procedure: a wash under a shower of warm water and a good scrubbing with a soft brush or surgical sponge. These soon ran out and were replaced with strips of towel. The small proportion with more severe contamination was moved on to a second decontamination section for more thorough treatment.

The brigadier and his team had devised a processing system which enabled those running the holding areas and the decontamination centres to keep track of people's identities. Bar coded hospital wrist and ankle tags were used and these gave details of whether the person's identity had been confirmed before they had been parted from all their belongings. This data was cross referenced with a central database, along with their digital photograph and their basic bio-metric details.

London City Airport was turned into a transport logistics centre. It was cleared of all its civilian traffic and became a military airport. The runway, at 1,319 metres, was long enough for it to take the CN-235 tactical military transport and Hercules planes. Its close proximity to the exclusion zone was a stroke of luck.

Nearby, on the southern edge of the exclusion zone, the army had set up its field HQ. The coordination of people's movements, prioritising the casualties and the problems of the long queues at the emergency decontamination units were an administrative nightmare. Logjams became common place as the newly-built system struggled to deal with the huge numbers. Nevertheless, substantial progress was being made.

An SOS had gone out to all neighbouring countries which could get decontamination equipment into London City Airport within three hours. The Belgians, Dutch, French, Germans and Irish all contributed to this urgent request from COBRA. By midday their transport planes started landing with their cargoes of decontamination equipment, medics and medical supplies. By early afternoon, planes were stacked high above the southern approaches to the airport, waiting for a landing slot.

P hase Three was proving more difficult. How were the watercourses to be dealt with? Radioactive particles had been thrown violently into the air by the explosion. Those that entered the nearby canal, the River Lea, or the water table would be transported slowly towards Docklands in the City of London. Unless they were stopped quickly, the scale of the exclusion zone would have to be widened, threatening Docklands and the eastern fringes of the City of London. Colonel Gray's team was given responsibility for coordinating this.

R afi and Kate stood at the side of the Ops Room looking on in awe. The Air Chief Marshal's military machine was an impressive sight. The scale of the operation beggared belief. By early afternoon the last task given to the Wood Street Ops Room in respect of Stratford had been completed and an exhausted Air Chief Marshal handed over to COBRA and the command centre in Wilton, near Salisbury.

Under the watchful eye of the brigadier, the focus of the Ops Room moved back to coordinating the capture of the terrorists.

Rafi was feeling gutted and his sense of guilt refused to go away. He became aware that Ewan was standing next to him.

Ewan had a good idea of what was going through Rafi's mind and put his arm around his shoulder. 'You know, had it not been for your

233

early warning, we would be faced with a catastrophic disaster far bigger than anything we are witnessing. Your forewarning gave the Air Chief Marshal the opportunity to take the unprecedented step of putting the whole UK military machine into a state of readiness a full five and a half hours before the train was hit. Your determination to beat the terrorists has enabled us to have a response time we could never have dared dream of. I know it won't make you feel much better, but thank you.'

W hilst all eyes were on the unfolding disaster at Stratford, MI5 had been tasked with the surveillance of the two Chechen terrorists who were on the run. Without their Kornet and Vektor missile launchers they no longer posed a serious threat to national security. The PM, in approving the plan to let the terrorists run, had made it crystal clear that if they posed *any* danger to the public they should be stopped by whatever means necessary. The object of the exercise now was to round up the terrorists, their associates and their ringleaders.

Sergy Kowshaya, fired up by the success of his missile attack at Cruden Bay and his escape from the hail of bullets, had in a well-executed move swapped his motorbike for an elderly-looking car. Unbeknown to him, however, he was being observed. He opted for a circuitous route up the coast to retrieve the Vektor mortar he'd left in the utility van the afternoon before. The van was parked on a grass verge in front of a terrace of cottages, 2.5 km to the north-west of the St Fergus gas terminal.

Sergy made good time to the van and, 300 metres short of it, he steered over to the bushes at the side of the road, stopped dead and inspected the scene in front of him. All was quiet. He felt under his leather jacket for his Stechkin automatic pistol. He paused and then continued on his way towards the van. Adrenalin pumped through his veins. He knew he would be vulnerable as he approached the van. If the security services were on the ball, there was the possibility that they could have pieced together the location of his second target. If so, they would be watching the surrounding area like a hawk for all unexplained movements.

He stopped his car in front of the van, pulled out a set of keys from his jacket pocket, walked over and opened the van's sliding side door. On the floor were two heavy-duty workman's tool bags. He lifted them up, turned and made for the small gap in the hedgerow a few metres away. He dropped to his knees, opened the first bag and lifted out the Vektor mortar. In moments it was pointing through the gap towards the St Fergus gas facility and storage tanks over the slight hill in the distance. He had already calculated the sets of angles of trajectory and compass settings required in ballistic mode. The missiles would explode above the main storage tanks.

In the second tool bag, lying next to the mortar, were twenty missiles. He pulled opened the top of the bag, picked up a missile and in a fluid movement dropped it down the barrel of the mortar.

'Svoloch!' he swore in Russian. The bloody thing had misfired; either the firing pin was damaged – but he'd checked it the day before – or it was a bad missile. There was an outside chance that the missile could go off at any moment. The odds were that the missile was a dud, but did he want to risk it exploding as he got it out of the barrel?

Sergy then did what he would never have done on the battlefield: he left the mortar where it was, put his hand into a side pocket of his jacket, fished out a small explosive with a timing device, armed it and placed it in the bag with the nineteen remaining missiles. He stood up, returned to his car and left the scene, heading towards a small industrial unit on the outskirts of Peterhead.

He was in contemplative mood; he was £3 million richer after his success at Cruden Bay, but destroying the St Fergus facility would have earned him a further £1 million. He abhorred the sense of failure, but whether he had £3 million or £4 million in the bank made little difference – he was now richer than in his wildest dreams.

Moments after Sergy's car has disappeared out of sight, the three special services men who had been watching his every move broke cover. They had known that the terrorist would suffer a misfire, as they had removed the firing pin, and had watched Sergy place an explosive in the bag with the missiles. The nearest soldier was seventy-five metres away. He spoke with his commander. It was agreed that the terrorist had left an explosive with a time delay to cover his tracks. It was now time to decide whether to investigate or wait for the big bang. The SAS soldier ran crouching close to the ground. If it had been him, he would have set the device to explode in ten minutes in order to give him time to get away from the scene before it went off.

He opened the bag. His eyes locked on to the small explosive device. It was a small but lethal piece of plastic explosive with a sophisticated timing device. The digital readout showed 0:37. Delicately, he picked it up and walked fifteen paces out into the field, placed it on the ground, turned and ran for cover.

Sergy wound down his window; it was a bitterly cold day and the heater of his old car barely made an impression on the wintry air flooding inside. He heard the dull bang of the explosion; it was far quieter than he'd anticipated. His mind put two and two together. Koit, the Russian bastard, had sold them duds. He wound up the window and thought unspeakable thoughts. Suddenly, not having the full £4 million rankled.

Twenty-five minutes later and still thinking foul thoughts, Sergy arrived at the industrial property that had been his base for the past twenty-four hours.

Away from prying eyes, he swapped his car for an old moped and changed into scruffy sailor's clothes. Unbeknown to him, the front of the property was being watched. It was one of those on Rafi's list.

Sergy opened the back door to the industrial unit and left via an overgrown dirt track on a short cut through an adjoining property. He came close to losing those watching him, but as he turned into Catto Drive his moped chugged straight past the nondescript MI5 communications vehicle coordinating his surveillance. Instead of heading straight for the harbour he went to a truckers' café a mile away. Here he consumed a hearty English breakfast washed down with several cups of coffee, read a tabloid newspaper and watched, with pleasure, the awful news on the small television secured to the wall. The team watching his every move kept their distance.

Just before noon he paid, got on his moped and headed slowly towards the docks. He counted three police cars with lights flashing pass by. They paid not one jot of interest in him. At the docks, he parked a short distance away from the trawler *Northern Rose*, went into a warehouse and came out moments later carrying a crate of supplies. He headed towards the trawler and climbed on board, as she was slipping her mooring lines.

Sergy stood on the deck for a few moments, as if he was looking for a colleague, then went below deck. *Northern Rose* motored out to sea then steered northwards on to a course that would take her safely past Rattray Head. An hour later she changed course to north-north-west, heading towards Duncansby Head, the Orkney Islands and the Pentland Firth.

The MI5 team were pleased to see Sergy safely on board. He was away from the public and the prospect of collateral damage had receded.

Meanwhile, the Nimrod aircraft tracking *Golden Sundancer* picked up *Northern Rose* as she headed northwards. The navigator spoke to the Ops Room and COBRA, and gave a predicted rendezvous between the trawler and *Golden Sundancer* north-west of the Pentland Firth, around 18:00 hours.

D akka Dudayev, the terrorist who had caused all the carnage at Stratford, had evaded detection and left the industrial building in a sports hatchback. The team tasked with tracking Dudayev had become worried; he was thought to be making for North Walsham, but, an hour and a half after the Stratford attack, his precise location was still not known.

There were sighs of relief when he was seen turning off the M11 on to the A11. Dudayev motored up the A140 to Aylsham and on to North Walsham.

When Dudayev entered the industrial estate he saw smoke and flames coming from the industrial unit, two down from where he'd stored his Vektor mortar and the twenty high-explosive shells. Parked right in front of his factory were a fire engine and a police car. The whole area had been cordoned off. He didn't hesitate. He casually turned his car around and headed for Great Yarmouth.

Those watching him were pleased to see him leave.

On the outskirts of the town, he slipped off the main road into a housing estate and headed for a lock-up garage. After swapping his casual attire for nondescript fisherman's clothing consisting of a duffle coat and patched trousers, and his sports car for a moped, he slowly made his way to the ship repair yard.

At the docks, Dudayev left his moped a couple of hundred metres away from where *Rosemarie* was berthed. He walked calmly down the road, through the ship repair yard, past the dry dock, on to the dock side and stepped aboard *Rosemarie* as her mooring lines were being cast off.

At just after 4 p.m. *Rosemarie* motored out to sea, turned south on to a bearing of 179° and ratcheted her speed up to an impressive fourteen knots. She, it was thought, was heading for the Straights of Dover, with a likely rendezvous point with *Golden Sundancer* somewhere beyond the Isles of Scilly.

A second Nimrod was on station to monitor *Rosemarie*'s progress in case she put into port to offload her human cargo.

I n Scotland, the industrial property at Prestwick had been under surveillance by a special forces and MI5 unit since the early hours of the morning. Alistair Hartnell, Basel Talal's number two, had been identified as a passenger on an internal flight from London Stansted to Prestwick the night before. Hartnell was lying low in the industrial property. He had been joined by an unidentified man late in the evening. His colleague, it transpired, was Kim Chindriani, the man responsible for running the offices of UKSOIL and recruiting potential suicide bombers.

Neither was viewed as particularly dangerous, but rather as two rats abandoning the sinking ship. Just before midday they were observed leaving the property in a small car and were followed to the dry dock and ship repair facility just up the coast at Troon harbour. They left their car in the ferry car park and casually sauntered across to the ship repairer's quay where they boarded *Highland Belle* a whisker after 1 o'clock. A few minutes later, the trawler set sail and settled on to a course of 233° at a speed of thirteen knots. She was heading for the North Channel. No doubt she would leave the Mull of Kintyre to starboard and head north-west out into the Atlantic to her rendezvous with *Golden Sundancer* in the early hours of the following morning.

On board the trawlers there was sadness that some of their colleagues hadn't made it. The terrorists had been operating independently and had only been briefed on their targets, but had found out from the news channels that two of their colleagues had been killed at the scene of the attacks. The TV coverage asserted that their weapons had malfunctioned and this led the remaining terrorists to question how well the operation had been planned. However, the coverage was music to their ears. The combined effect of their attacks sounded devastating. The fires were still burning at Cruden Bay; dark plumes of smoke were coming from Aldermaston, Hartlepool and Heysham, and at Stratford they'd hit the jackpot.

The sheikh and Maryam were also being closely watched. MI6 had sent a team to find Miti Lakhani, but had no news of his location.

In Luxembourg, Maryam was acting as if it was a normal working day. She was due to remain there until Tuesday, when she was booked to fly back to the Gulf. The reports were that she was looking very pleased with herself.

The sheikh, likewise, was doing nothing out of the ordinary and had spent much of the day at his palatial home, sunning himself by the pool.

In silence, Kate and Rafi had left the Ops Room to get a coffee and something to eat. They weren't feeling very hungry, but had missed breakfast and lunch. After a short break they ventured back. The commissioner saw them enter and walked over to speak to them.

'I thought that you might like to know that we still have the three trawlers under observation and they don't realise that we're on to them.' He looked at Rafi with tired and slightly bloodshot eyes. 'I see that the weight of the world is on your shoulders. You should be congratulated and not feeling guilty! Only two out of nine attacks got through. Cruden Bay pumping station will be out of action for a number of months, but it will be brought back on stream.'

'But we let Stratford slip though the net,' said Kate.

'It wasn't your fault that the Stratford missiles got through – understand that! The information came in sufficient time. It was the system that screwed up and not you two – please remember that.'

He looked carefully at Kate. 'Time the two of you got some well-earned rest. Rafi, your flat in its present state wouldn't be very welcoming. My sincere apologies for turning your life upside down. We totally misjudged you. Perhaps we could put you up at a hotel?'

'Thank you,' he replied.

'Have a rest. But then, I'd appreciate it if you could come back and listen to what your economics team has to say. They have a meeting scheduled with the PM and the Chancellor of the Exchequer this evening, followed by the Bank of England early tomorrow afternoon. If you could be back in action by, say, 6.30 p.m. it would be appreciated.'

'Yes, sir,' replied Rafi.

Giles turned to go back to his allotted space on the central desk, when he caught sight of Saara, who was in deep conversation with the brigadier. 'Your little sister is quite remarkable! For an un-assuming person she packs one hell of a punch. Her understanding of things nuclear and her ability to decipher the experts' suggestions is impressive. If your parents were around they would be very proud of you both. Kate, please look after Rafi. The outside world still views him as public enemy number one. He deserves some proper TLC. Remember, we need him fighting in our corner until all the terrorists have been rounded up and the financial gremlins have been slain.'

Rafi was ready to drop. His head ached and his eyes hurt. He was finding it increasingly difficult to take in what was going on around him. Kate gently tugged at his sleeve.

'You've been working non-stop for nearly four days. Time to get some shut-eye. First, though, we need to pay a visit to accounts. They'll arrange for the hotel to bill the station. Let's sort out some accommodation for you.'

As they walked down the back stairs towards the accounts office, the prospect of being booked into a tourist or cheap business hotel filled Rafi with horror.

'Are my credit cards working?' he inquired.

'Should be by tomorrow,' Kate replied. 'I'll ask Jeremy to arrange for them to be returned to you as soon as is practical.'

They arrived at the accounts department. 'Hi,' said Kate. 'Let me introduce you to Rafi Khan.' Kate explained their requirements and the importance of confidentiality.

Rafi interrupted her. 'What I need, please, is a comfortable hotel where I can pay the bill in a couple of days' time. Unfortunately, my credit cards are still with MI5.'

Rafi thought for a moment. 'Could you please book me into a suite at the Savoy?'

'That'll cost a flaming fortune,' commented Kate.

He looked at her. 'I'm exhausted. I could do with somewhere where I know it'll be really comfortable and quiet, and the service will get whatever I want. The prospect of a soft, comfy bed and a luxurious duvet at the moment is worth its weight in gold. Don't worry, as soon as you've got my credit card working again, I'll pay for it.'

'The Savoy shouldn't be a problem,' said the accounts woman. 'Although I can't say that we've ever used them before. Let's give them a ring.' She found the number, dialled and began talking to their corporate reservations department. In a matter of minutes she had everything lined up. To Rafi's surprise she booked a two-room suite in Kate's name. 'It's the Commissioner's suggestion; he said you could both do with a rest and Rafi will need someone to vouch for him as, in the eyes of the public, he is still a terrorist.'

It slowly dawned on Rafi that he'd been oblivious to all the press coverage of the past week and the vilification he would have been subjected to.

'Fine,' said Kate with a gleam in her eye. 'Good idea. Come on, let's go.'

On their way to the rear car park, Kate picked up an old pork-pie hat and a scarf.

As they were getting into the car driven by Peter, Neil arrived on his way back from COBRA. He beckoned to Kate and Rafi. 'What a bugger! We so nearly stopped them from doing any serious damage. Stratford will be a defining point in the history of this country. I'm willing to bet that people will soon be talking in terms of BS and AS – Before Stratford and After Stratford. Even in my book, the sheer scale of Stratford is mind-blowing. Sadly, though, I doubt if people will ever appreciate how much carnage your actions prevented. I was talking to a boffin at COBRA; he described what a thermobaric warhead could have done to a waste storage pool at a nuclear power station. In his words, "It would have made Stratford seem like a modest inconvenience." ' He gave Rafi a pat on the back, shrugged his shoulders and went on his way.

Part 6

Peter was waiting for them in the rear car park. Thanks to the curfew, the traffic was unprecedentedly light. On their arrival at the Savoy Hotel, Kate went in and sorted out the formalities, whilst Peter and Rafi waited in the car. She returned clutching a key card.

Rafi put on the pork-pie hat and wrapped the scarf around his neck and lower face. He felt a bit of a berk. They said their thanks and goodbyes to Peter and made their way to a separate door opposite the main entrance. The foyer in front of the lifts was quiet.

'Are you very, very wealthy?' Kate asked, as they were waiting for the lift. 'One night here costs about the same as my monthly mortgage payment.'

Rafi was too tired to explain that he simply wanted comfort and was prepared to pay any price. The last week had been worse than anything he had ever known and he yearned to put it behind him.

They arrived at the door to the suite. Kate opened it. 'Wow! This looks fantastic. Do you normally live like this?'

'No, I have a two-bedroom flat in north London. This is the first time for me as well.'

Kate looked at him with a smile. 'What makes you think that I haven't stayed in a place like this before?' Nervousness came over her. 'I have a confession to make. I hope you don't mind but I've changed our suite from a two-bedroom to a single bedroom, as this lets them give our booking to a displaced family.'

Kate looked at him anxiously, waiting for his reply. She felt as if she'd been caught doing something wrong at school.

He was too tired to care – he just wanted to get some sleep. He smiled at her as she opened the door. 'Fine by me,' he replied in a deadbeat manner.

The apartment was opulent; a modest entrance hall gave way to a spacious sitting room, with windows overlooking the Thames below and the Millennium Wheel down the river to the right. To one side of the sitting room was a door leading into a spacious bedroom containing the father of all king-size beds and a large en suite bathroom.

They were travelling light; they didn't even have a toothbrush between them.

Kate went to explore the bedroom and bathroom and came back proudly clutching a sumptuous white towelling robe in one hand and a toothbrush in the other.

'What more could a girl want?' she said, eyes shining. Where she'd got her second wind from, Rafi didn't know. He needed to crash out.

'I'm ready to drop; let's toss for who's going to use the bathroom first,' he said.

'No need to do that,' said Kate, 'women and children first. In the meantime, will you order something easy to eat?'

Rafi looked at her. 'I'm too tired for food; can we see what's in the bar?'

Unlike other hotel rooms he had been in, this hotel apartment had its own bar area. He opened the refrigerator. 'What would you like? Gin and tonic, fresh orange juice, wine, smart mineral water – you name it we've got it.'

'Orange juice and a large gin and tonic, please.'

'There's some great-looking chocolate and the nuts look good; how about cashew nuts, crisps or chocolates with your drink?' asked Rafi.

Kate took her two drinks, placed them by the side of the bath and returned for the chocolate and nuts.

'I won't be long,' she said. 'If I fall asleep in the bath, feel free to wake me. In the meantime, I suggest you make yourself comfortable and have a stiff drink or two.'

Rafi looked at her. 'You can do the drinking for both of us.'

'Oh, sorry, I didn't realise you didn't drink.' And with that, she turned and walked off towards the bathroom. As she went, she unclipped her tortoiseshell hairclip and gave her head a shake. A mass of deep auburn hair sprang out.

It was the first time Rafi had seen her with her hair down. He gazed at her. She looked after herself well – her slight frame, though not curvaceous, was nicely proportioned and well toned. Her shoulder-length wavy hair looked soft and would undoubtedly be a stunning feature when washed and brushed. He was too tired to think any further.

Kate was smiling. 'Thank you for all you've done. I hope when this is over we'll be able to get to know one another better.'

What was that about? pondered Rafi. He was too tired to consider whether it was an offer of friendship or something more.

The sound of the running water stopped. Soothing splashes washed through the air. He poured himself a second, large glass of fresh orange juice and looked out of the window. London seemed calm and still.

He mulled over the twist of fate – this part of London had been spared the ravages of the explosion at Stratford. His mind wandered – had the wind been blowing in the opposite direction, it would have covered the City, and for that matter the West End of London, under a deadly blanket of radioactivity. Would the closure of the City of London have stopped the terrorist leaders' from cashing in on their profits? Of course not; they would also have positions in Frankfurt and Chicago. His tired brain left it there.

Rafi drank his orange juice, just standing there gazing out over the Thames, enjoying the tranquillity. He heard the bathroom door open and turned to see Kate snuggled into a soft white bathrobe, clutching an empty glass in her hand.

'This is my idea of heaven,' she said.

Rafi looked at her approvingly and replied, 'Mine too. Would you like a top-up?'

'I think I can do that, thanks. You can have that bath you deserve and undoubtedly need,' she said, holding her fingers over her nose like a clothes peg.

As he walked past her to the bathroom he smelt a sweet orange aroma and made a mental note to use the body wash.

The bathroom had the same smell, which now reminded him of her. He smiled as he discarded his scruffy clothing. He was looking forward to getting back to his normal clothes.

The hot, gushing water of the shower was wonderful. He eventually got out and, after wrapping himself in the luxurious towel, walked back into the bedroom. The room was peaceful; Kate had turned off all the lights except for the small lamp on his side of the large bed. She was sound asleep, her wild damp hair framing her face against the background of the white duvet and pillow. Lying on the floor was her bathrobe. She stirred slightly; she looked beautiful – stunningly beautiful. She snuggled further under the duvet and continued her well-earned sleep. Rafi slipped off the bath towel, slid under the crisp duvet and turned the light out.

As he drifted off to sleep, he reflected that something good had come out of the worst week of his life.

Rafi awoke to find the curtains half open and noticed it was dark outside. Kate was sitting at a small table by the window in her bathrobe; her mass of hair was neatly brushed and resting strikingly on her shoulders. He looked carefully at her face and the splashes of freckles on her cheeks and across her nose – she had an innocent schoolgirl-like quality. Very gamine. That was the word he'd been looking for. He liked what he saw.

'Late lunch is served,' she said. 'Hope you like my cooking! I've ordered a selection of things: a couple of starters – smoked salmon or pâté – followed by medium-rare steak or Dover sole, and a delicious-looking gooey chocolate pudding . . . And loads of fruit.'

Rafi opted for the pâté and the fish, letting Kate finish off both chocolate puddings.

Whilst they were eating, Kate thought about the person sitting opposite her. What was it about Rafi that made her want to be in his company? His inner strength? Perhaps they were soulmates? She hoped so. She worried that she had shown her feelings too soon.

'I hope that was alright changing suites,' said Kate, coyly.

Rafi looked across at her lovely face. He'd been working alongside her for almost four days and hadn't fully taken in how beautiful she was. 'Sorry I wasn't more enthusiastic earlier. I didn't know whether I was coming or going with tiredness.' As an afterthought, in case his comment sounded less than enthusiastic, he added, 'A nice move.'

She smiled and poured a cup of steaming coffee. They sat there, sipping their coffee and enjoying each other's company.

When they had finished their late lunch Kate got up and, looking at Rafi, said, 'I have some bad news. Well, not that bad . . . Our time here is running short. We've been asked to be back by 6.15 p.m. That gives us forty-five minutes. But before we go, I think we should get that off,' she said, pointing at him.

Rafi raised his eyebrows.

She smiled a beaming smile. 'No, not what you are thinking. I meant that dirty Elastoplast bandage. Whilst you were asleep, I asked the manager for a medical kit and some clothes.' She opened the first aid box and pulled out a pair of scissors and a roll of bandage. She leant forward, took his hand and carefully cut the plaster from top to bottom. She finished and moved closer.

'I fear this is going to hurt. If it's anything like strip wax, it'll hurt like hell – sorry.'

She pulled the plaster with a sharp, prolonged tug of her hand. There was a quiet ripping noise as it pulled the hairs out of his arm.

This was accompanied by the sharp hissing sound of Rafi sucking air in through his teeth.

As Kate moved back, her bathrobe fell open across her chest, revealing a lovely and distracting sight. 'That wasn't too bad, was it?' she said.

'It was an eye-opener,' he replied.

'I'm here to please,' she quipped and then realised why Rafi had gone quiet and was staring at her. She leant across and kissed him delicately on the cheek.

'All in good time; unfortunately, we have things to do.'

'Queen and Country and all that,' he mocked.

'You've got it in one,' she said, pulling her bathrobe closed. 'Let's get you bandaged up.'

Adeptly and tenderly she strapped his wrist. 'Your bruises still look very impressive. Are they painful?'

He smiled at her. 'In comparison to your strip wax treatment, not really!'

'Time to get dressed,' said Kate. 'The manager has sent up a selection of clothes for both of us. They've hung them in the wardrobe. Have a look and see what you think. I've got a bit of tidying up to do in the bathroom.'

They dressed in casual but smart new clothes. Rafi chose a white shirt, charcoal grey flannel trousers, dark blue blazer, black moccasin shoes and a smart blue wool overcoat, in case he had reason to venture outside. Kate opted for a light camel-coloured trouser suit, a creamy-white open neck shirt and a dark brown wool and cashmere overcoat. She looked stunning.

'I hope your credit card is going to be working soon; there's no way that mine will withstand the damage that I've run up since we got here!' said Kate.

'Don't worry,' he said, 'we can sort it out mañana.'

'It must be nice to be rich,' Kate replied.

'Yes, it must be. Unfortunately, this isn't how I normally live,' replied Rafi.

'Well, I'll want to be with you when it is like this.' Kate chuckled and winked playfully at him.

Rafi looked down at the clean dressing on his wrist. 'And whenever I need cheering up all I've got to do is look at this bandage and think of you!' He pointed to the old hat and stripy scarf draped over the back of the sofa.

'Will I need these?'

'How about these?' said Kate, pointing to a dark blue scarf and trilby hat, then adding, 'We must get going. Jeremy and John are waiting for us downstairs.'

Sure enough, a large unmarked police car was waiting outside.

They sped through an eerily quiet London.

'The curfew is still in place,' said John. 'Thankfully, almost everyone is keeping their heads down. The people from COBRA and the PM have been on radio and television to stop people panicking and advising them to stay indoors.'

John turned left at Trafalgar Square, into Whitehall. 'I hope you're going to be on your best behaviour,' he said as he turned right and stopped the car in front of the tall metal gates guarding Downing Street. John showed his police warrant card to the armed guards standing at the gate and they were let through.

'We've been asked to act as your minders,' said Jeremy. 'Heaven only knows how long it'll be before you get to see the Prime Minister. It must be chaos in there.'

John stopped the car in front of Number 10. Kate and Rafi were ushered in.

To Rafi's utter surprise, they were met in the front entrance hall by the Prime Minister, with outstretched hands. He then led them through to the inner sanctum of Number 10. As they started walking he looked at Rafi. 'I like the disguise,' he said with a grin. 'You'd make a good gangster – I am afraid that there's rather a lot going on at the moment. Kate, I need Rafi for half an hour or so. Would you and your colleagues see how things are progressing downstairs in the COBRA meeting?'

Kate nodded.

'Mr Palmer here will show you the way.'

A dark-suited young man beckoned Kate to follow him.

'Rafi, I've arranged for you and your economics team to meet here at 7.30 to discuss your concerns. We'll be joined by the Chancellor of the Exchequer and a couple of people from his team.'

The PM strode on, with Rafi following close behind. They arrived at the door to his study and the PM beckoned him into the room. They'd been in there for only a few seconds when the phone rang.

The Prime Minister took the call. 'I'm sorry, Rafi. I have the Mayor of London on the line. Why don't you find DI Adams and catch up on what's been happening? If you go next door, I'll arrange for someone to show you the way.'

Rafi walked into the empty, adjoining office. He looked around, plumped for the comfiest chair, sat down and waited.

A smart, but soberly dressed woman appeared several minutes later.

'Sorry to have kept you,' she said with a hesitant smile. 'I've been asked to show you the way to COBRA. Please come this way.'

'Thank you,' said Rafi, getting up unsteadily.

They passed through a further set of security checks and descended some sets of stairs.

Rafi looked at the woman he was following. She had eye-catching blonde hair which was in stark contrast to her clean-cut, formal white shirt and black skirt.

When they arrived at their destination the woman turned. 'I'll come and get you when the PM is free.' Her businesslike face was transformed by a fleeting smile.

Rafi saw Kate chatting to a swarthy-looking man and went over to join them.

'I was updating Kate on our progress,' he said. 'We're making headway, but it's one hell of a large task. No doubt you want to know about the escaping terrorists? Sorry, I should introduce myself. I'm Craig – MI5.'

The young officer looked the opposite of Jeremy: short, thickset, dark haired – almost uncouth.

'*Golden Sundancer* is currently going like a bat out of hell round the Western Isles of Scotland, averaging almost forty knots. Her rendezvous with *Northern Rose*, north-west of Pentland Firth, went without a hitch. We now expect her to rendezvous with *Highland Belle* west of Stanton Banks, just before dawn tomorrow.'

'*Rosemarie* is heading for the Straights of Dover. We estimate she'll rendezvous with *Golden Sundancer* south of the Isles of Scilly, in the early hours of Sunday morning. The question is, are we right in believing that she'll head for Morocco?'

He fell silent for a moment and looked at them, working out how much he should tell them.

'The Navy has checked what vessels it has between the Scilly Isles and Morocco. At Gibraltar, they have HMS *Scimitar* and *Sabre*: two sixteen-metre fast patrol boats, capable of thirty knots plus. There's nothing else in the vicinity which can match *Golden Sundancer*'s speed. I understand that the boffins at the Admiralty are currently hatching a plan.'

Craig paused. 'Jameel is still in Marrakech where we've an agent keeping an eye on him. The sheikh's private jet is scheduled to land there at 12.45 p.m. on Monday. He has hired a helicopter for the afternoon and his plane is scheduled to take off again at 22.30 that evening.'

Kate nodded.

He continued. 'We've looked at all the ports within range of the helicopter from Marrakech, in the time available. The Moroccan Atlantic coastline is long, but thankfully there are only three ports that we believe fit the situation: Safi, Mohammedia and Casablanca. For a number of reasons, Safi is the one our anoraks confidently predict they will use.'

'So, how are you going to capture them?' asked Kate.

'The Prime Minister wants them captured alive,' said Craig. 'The bosses believe there's a better chance of success if we seize them when they are all in one place.' He looked at Kate as if what he was about to say was strictly confidential. 'The plan is to have a vessel, with SBS personnel aboard, waiting for *Golden Sundancer* in Safi. They overpower them and whisk them away to a waiting submarine.'

'So quite simple, really,' said Kate, with a grin.

'Why aren't they using the SAS?' Rafi queried.

'The special boat service, or SBS,' replied Craig, 'is the Royal Navy's special forces unit – it's part of the Royal Marines and they have their own anti-terrorist squad. The SBS are every bit as formidable as the SAS, but, in essence, are the aquatic version. In many quarters they're rated more highly!'

'Things will have to be done quickly, which could complicate matters. The terrorists and their masters will probably be in our grasp for only a few hours. At *Golden Sundancer*'s present rate of progress, she'll arrive in Safi early Monday afternoon, which gives us only twenty-four hours to prepare an appropriate welcoming party.'

'How's the plan going?' Rafi asked.

'Hold on a moment,' said Craig, 'let me make a call.' Several minutes later he put down the phone.

'It seems we've arranged for two resourceful female Naval Lieutenants – Anna Gregson and Janet Steiner – to be flown to Gibraltar. They're on their way as we speak, together with some special kit for our SBS friends.'

Craig continued explaining the plan. 'Obviously, we don't want to scare the terrorists' leaders away. A fast motorboat moored in Gibraltar has been identified. We ruled out HMS *Sabre*, as there's no way we can disguise her military parentage – one sight of her and the terrorists would run a mile. Furthermore, the Moroccan Authorities wouldn't take kindly to the Royal Navy operating within their territorial waters. So we're renting, or purchasing if we cock up, a Sunseeker Manhattan 56 called *Puddle Jumper*. She has a top speed of some thirty-two knots and is fast enough to get down there before them. The British owners have reluctantly agreed to let us use her. She's being given the once-over and provisioned right now.'

Craig paused, as if searching for an elusive word. 'The awkward bit is that we have a hiccup or two on the resources front. SBS's M Squadron, which deals with maritime counterterrorism, should be on standby. They're, er . . . rather busy at the moment. They're in action in the Middle East. The Air Chief Marshal has secured the services of two of their team who are cutting short their current operation and will be joining those on board *Puddle Jumper*. We had hoped for more, but so be it. The special forces command centre is sending SAS soldiers to Marrakech Airport and to the ports of Safi, Mohammedia and Casablanca. The last two, just in case our intelligence has ballsed up.'

A grin spread across Craig's face, his white teeth framed by his tanned face. 'A bright spark at the Admiralty has dreamt up a cunning plan. Our two naval officers and two SBS operatives on board *Puddle Jumper* are to be joined by two retired civilians.'

Kate tilted her head to one side in surprise.

'Yes, I know you must think that they're off their rockers. The Navy has trawled through their records for recently retired naval officers who had seen active service and who could go along as parent figures to keep up the illusion that those on board are civilians. The retirement age for many very able officers is early fifties.' Craig grinned. 'They couldn't believe their luck. They found a couple who are both still fleet of foot: a highly experienced retired commander, Adrian Bell, who's a master navigator and has seen active service. Furthermore, as a youngster he commanded one of the three HMS *Scimitar* class, fast training craft during the Cod War in the North Atlantic. They were at that time the fastest wet hulled military craft in the world. And it gets better: the commander's wife, Helen, also has twenty years' experience in the Navy. So we have two capable "parents" to look after our boisterous rabble. The two naval officers will become their "daughters" and the two SBS operatives will be the "boyfriends".'

'Not surprisingly,' continued Craig, 'the husband and wife were a bit taken aback to be volunteered. They were at home in their garage, varnishing their dinghy. They're currently packing their sailing gear. Two, twin-seat Harrier jump jets are waiting for them at the nearby Thorney Island army facility and will fly them to Gibraltar.'

'The two "parents", as I call them, together with the two naval officers, will arrive in Gibraltar in the next couple of hours. *Puddle Jumper* should put to sea an hour after they land. The SBS officers should rendezvous with her sometime in the next twelve hours. I understand a wet jump is planned.' Craig paused.

'As I was saying, the terrorists' boat, at her current rate of progress, should make Safi by Monday early afternoon. Our team on *Puddle Jumper* plan to arrive under the cover of darkness, late on Sunday night.'

A frown fell across Craig's face. 'Getting them away is also proving difficult. It is rather embarrassing as a world power, but we seem to have all our submarines in, er . . . the wrong places or in dry dock for repairs, and the four new Astute class submarines are still not in service. The cutback in numbers, without the new replacements, has left the Navy decidedly short. The earliest any submarine can be off the coast of Safi is 15.40 on Monday. However, those at the Admiralty are a tad uncomfortable – well, that's an understatement – as the only one that could get there on time is one of our Trident Class nuclear submarines with all its nuclear missiles on board. It seems that the prospect of taking our terrorists on board her is beyond the Admiralty's comfort zone. Out of the frying pan and into the fire! However, they have been won over by the PM. She's broken off from her current manoeuvres and is sailing at full speed to be on station Monday afternoon.'

Rafi was about to ask a couple of questions, when his guide appeared at the door and beckoned him over.

'The Prime Minister will see you now,' said the secretary.

Rafi was ushered up the claustrophobic stairs to the PM's meeting room. He wondered how Aidan and his team of five were getting on, and whether the PM and his new Chancellor of the Exchequer would tackle the impending financial problems head-on. His thoughts were on the huge risks now faced by the markets which were still reeling from the after-effects of the credit crunch.

Rafi stopped outside the meeting room – he felt apprehensive. What if they'd reached mental overload and wanted none of his bad news? The future would be bleak.

As he entered, he was greeted by the sight of fourteen tired and slightly dishevelled-looking people. Aidan and his team were sitting along one side of the table. There was an unoccupied chair next to Aidan, to which Rafi was shown.

The PM stood up to greet Rafi. He looked pale and in need of some well-earned rest. On one side he was flanked by his private secretary, the head of press communications and the Defence Secretary, and on the other side, by his Chancellor and three people from his Treasury team. The PM did the introductions.

Rafi looked around the shiny, dark wooden table. There was a grim feel to the room. His eyes caught those of Saara's. They exchanged brief smiles – she seemed at ease in the exalted company. Aidan and his team's faces looked strained, as if they were expecting a hard time.

The PM called the meeting to order. He was forthright. 'Gentlemen, we're here at the request of Mr Khan. Yesterday he asked me to consider the risk our weakened financial markets are now facing and, if we agree with his predictions, he's asked that we listen to a strategy to stop our markets going into meltdown when they reopen on Tuesday. Mr Khan advises me that the main item on the terrorists' agenda isn't the physical disruption of our energy supplies, but financial chaos.'

The PM turned to his Chancellor. 'I appreciate that it is only a few months since you took up your post. The final decision as to how we proceed rests with you. I shall back your judgement and the proposals you put before the Cabinet tomorrow, in advance of our statements to the Commons on Monday afternoon.'

The PM looked around the table. 'Before we start, I must reiterate that we're here as a group seeking to work as a team.' He paused. 'If Mr Khan is correct, the challenge that faces us is gargantuan. He has made it clear to me that the terrorists expect us to hesitate and to drag our feet before we react. If we do, Mr Khan has in no uncertain terms advised me that we may not regain control of the financial markets. We have to consider whether Mr Khan's hypothesis has substance. We must not shirk our duty, even if it means that we get bad press for taking a robust approach when others are unable to see the dangers facing us.'

The mood of the room was sombre. 'Before we start,' said the PM, 'I should like to thank Mr Khan for his foresightedness and Mr Gilchrist and his team from the City and academia for their Herculean efforts. You have been able to focus on the financial problems at hand without being overwhelmed by the practical and human issues that we face as politicians. Gentlemen, the stakes are high.' He then turned to his Chancellor. 'Is there anything you would like to add before we listen to Aidan and his team's concerns and recommendations?'

'Not at the moment, thank you.'

'What then, please, are your proposals?'

Aidan spent a few moments detailing the expertise of those sitting alongside him and turned to Rafi's former boss, Donald, to make the presentation.

Donald stood up and walked over to a whiteboard which had been set up at the end of the room. He was confident, without being arrogant.

'Our objective, gentlemen, in these uncertain times, is to provide the financial markets with a sense of certainty and confidence. We are facing two problems. Firstly, the terrorists have created a black hole in the Government's finances and, secondly, Aidan has proved beyond all doubt that the terrorists have built up large put positions in the derivative markets.'

Aidan nodded.

'The costs that will be incurred following the Stratford catastrophe will be sizeable,' continued Donald. 'The scale of these liabilities when added to the recent surge in Government debt, if not neutralised, will alarm the financial markets.'

An understatement if ever there was one, Rafi thought.

'The results will be falling gilt and bond prices and a significant rise in interest rates across the board.' Donald paused and cast a glance around the room. They were following his every word intently. Even the Defence Secretary, whom he'd been warned about, was nodding his head sagely.

'Added to this we have the terrorists' derivative positions, which are mainly in the financial futures and traded options contracts for gilts and Sterling interest rates. As things stand, if gilt yields and interest rates were to rise significantly, it would furnish the terrorists with massive profits. By massive, we're talking in terms of tens of billions of pounds – our top estimate is £100 billion. The derivatives market is a zero-sum game: they win – others pay up, which would send a shock wave through the banking and insurance sectors, bringing many financial institutions to their knees. We have seen what contagion can do with the recent banking crisis,' Donald paused.

The room was totally silent.

'Currently the Government's finances are stretched to the point where international investors are truly wary and there is a high probability that they will be unwilling to finance the new demands for Government borrowings unless they are offered unprecedentedly high rates of interest, and even then many will view the Government as a risk too far.' Roger sensed that he had just put the fear of God into his audience.

'All is not lost; we believe that there are ways to neutralise the threat. The terrorists are playing with a two-edged sword. If we can keep the markets stable or even cause interest rates to fall, the terrorists and their financial intermediaries will be wiped out, financially speaking.'

He looked at the Chancellor and, in a measured tone, asked, 'Could I run through where the pressure on the public purse will come from, before I talk about the proposed way forward?'

The Chancellor nodded.

'On the expenditure side we have the costs associated with Stratford, plus the accelerated decommissioning of the UK's nuclear plants; then there will be compensation costs relating to the Olympics and the Eurostar Stratford link. Both sit within the exclusion zone. Also the mess at the outsourcing company PSSAF will need sorting or else many public sector services will self-implode. If we add these costs up we get a total of £220-250 billion.'

The figures were met by a stunned silence.

Donald looked at the faces scrutinising him. They were looking far from happy and for the time being things were not going to get any more palatable. 'I should now like to turn your attention to the problems that the growing Balance of Payments deficit pose. In particular it makes it very difficult to defend a run on our currency and it will make interest rate reductions tricky, if not impossible.' He paused and beckoned to Saara. 'Last on our list is energy.'

She stood up. 'The UK's prospective energy deficit has to be resolved or it will unnerve the markets,' she said. 'The nuclear switch-off will result in the loss of around 20% of the country's electricity generating capacity and will accelerate the energy shortfall. Against a backdrop of tight, Continental–European energy markets, more gas-fired power stations cannot provide the solution. We need to encourage the development of, and research into, alternative and environmentally-friendly energy sources. This will cost money up front, which might be seen as a brave move in the current financial climate, but in our view would be money well spent. We believe tax breaks to kick-start clean coal, carbon capture and alternative environmentally-friendly energy sources would cost the Treasury less than £1 billion and would have a short payback period. It would give the UK the wherewithal to become a leader in the sector.'

'Thank you, Dr Khan,' said the PM, 'your point is well noted. I am pleased to say that Number 11 has taken this on board and has scheduled a meeting of energy experts for tomorrow morning. They will be briefing the Chancellor and me tomorrow afternoon. I can assure you we share your concerns.'

'Thank you,' said Saara, sitting down.

Donald carried on. 'In summary, the key is to persuade the financial markets that the supply side of Government debt won't mushroom out of control in meeting all the liabilities.' He paused, then continued, 'Increased taxes and new issues of gilts won't bring in sufficient funds to meet the financial shortfall and, in our view, would send out totally the wrong message.'

There was complete silence as Donald waited for a few moments to allow the scale and complexity of the problem to sink in.

'Let me now propose how the position can be addressed,' he said, with the beginnings of a small smile.

'It is the immediate short term that concerns us. If we can keep gilts prices and interest rates stable, the terrorists' derivative positions will, in the space of a week, become untenable. If we could engineer a fall in interest rates and a small rise in gilts prices, within 24–72 hours the terrorists would be financially wiped out. The short term is driven by sentiment; what the markets will need is a transparent, robust and believable game plan.'

'Step one. We take a leaf out of the Swedish Government's book and transfer a significant proportion of the State's and the public sector's £500 billion plus of property and tangible assets into Real Estate Investment Trusts – REITs – and list them on the London Stock Exchange. Initially the shares would be owned by the Government. Share sales would be used to finance the expenditure I have just outlined. Currently these assets are valued on either a cost or an existing use, vacant possession, basis, but sitting in an REIT as investments let to the Government, their values would be *much* higher. We believe these Government REITs would give a war chest of over £400 billion.'

'So we wouldn't have to tap the gilts market?' asked the Chancellor.

'Precisely,' replied Donald. 'Now for the clever bit. For Government REITs to be successful, a liquid aftermarket is needed, so we propose that REITs be classified as a suitable alternative to annuities. Relative to annuities, REITs would provide pensioners with an enhanced real income stream. We have set out our analysis in the handouts.'

'Would I be right in suggesting that offering REITs as an alternative to annuities would reduce pension fund deficits?' asked the Chancellor – who thought a bit more – 'and additional REIT sales could be used to reduce the Government's debt and reduce the money supply?'

'Yes, you would,' replied Donald.

The Chancellor smiled.

'We suggest that a statement is issued, declaring that some of the REITs' sales would be used to buy back long dated gilts. This would underpin market sentiment and support long gilt prices,' continued Donald.

'Now I come to a thorny issue.' Donald paused. 'Sterling will come under immense pressure and its steep decline will cause unfortunate and painful long-term consequences. The solution we propose is for Sterling to join the Euro. This would stop Sterling being targeted by speculators and enable the Bank of England to bring UK interest rates in line with Euro rates, thus boosting the economy and market sentiment. Our thoughts on the entry rate are set out in the supporting documents. Representatives of the Bank of England should meet with the heads of the leading central banks and explain the risks which the global financial system is facing, such that the Chancellor on Monday can announce wide-ranging international support for Sterling, pending its entry into the Euro.'

'The next area for consideration is the superfluous Trident missile programme. Stratford has shown how radioactive contamination can blight a vast area. The UK has thousands of tons of highly toxic radioactive materials in storage. Trident should be replaced by "dirty" missiles designed to contaminate an area of several square kilometres. The threat of being able to detonate a "dirty" missile in the middle of an aggressor's city will, post-Stratford, be as strong a deterrent as annihilating it with a Trident missile. The cancelling of the next generation of Trident missiles and switching to "dirty" missiles would save billions. We advise that this money should be invested in higher education and academic research and development activities, which will assist the long-term growth of our economy.'

'Finally, we would like to draw your attention to the problem of a Government guarantee which hitherto has been swept under the carpet. Its superficial invisibility, in these dire times, will be called into question by the international financial markets.' Donald looked around the room. 'I am talking of the *public sector pensions deficit*, which is estimated by top actuarial firms to exceed *£1,000 billion*. It dwarfs even the monumental costs of the Stratford disaster. To put

257

this deficit into context, next fiscal year it will be equivalent to one-third of the revenue generated by basic rate income tax. And worse still, this annual liability is growing. Its scale is such that in these perilous financial times it must be addressed as part of the process of getting the economy back on track. It is too large for us to deal with it in one go but, given the circumstances, we believe a start *has* to be made. I repeat, the financial markets will go through *ALL* the Government's financial liabilities and look for items which could jeopardise the country's economic fight back. Unfunded public sector pensions are precisely the potential spanner in the works that could seriously damage the country's credit rating. At this point, no exact figures need to be given: just a framework for change. Our proposals are straightforward. The guaranteed pension element should be up to a specified percentage of average wages. Where employees have incomes above this, their pension relating to the higher amount should be funded by unit-linked pensions. This unit-linked fund could be enhanced by injecting into it a number of Government REIT shares. Our supporting appendices show how our proposals will significantly reduce the Treasury's subsidies and liabilities in this area. I'd like to point out that sorting this problem out would produce savings that are greater than all the costs associated with Stratford.'

Aidan got up and went to a couple of large boxes in the corner of the room from which he pulled out smartly bound reports. 'Gentlemen,' he said as he handed them across the table, 'you'll find in these the numbers behind our proposals.'

Donald meanwhile walked back to the table and sat down.

'I am grateful to you for your incisive work,' said the PM. 'Any questions?'

'Just one,' said the Chancellor. 'Timing is going to be tight. You and I will be making our announcements to the House on Monday afternoon. Am I right is assuming that we don't want the terrorists to know we're on to their conspiracy, whilst they're still at large?'

'Yes,' replied the PM.

'So, the financial rescue plan shouldn't be revealed until the terrorists have been captured, which is expected to be . . . when?'

'Around 3.30 p.m. on Monday afternoon,' said the PM.

'So that means we must speak for at least ninety minutes before being able to make any concrete announcements?' queried the Chancellor.

'Possibly longer, if the capture of the terrorists doesn't go to plan,' replied the PM.

The Chancellor looked thoughtfully at him. 'If you were to set the scene and explain how the Government is tackling the enormous problems associated with Stratford, and what the future holds, then I could run through the financial issues. Would that be OK?'

'Yes, that's about it,' agreed the PM.

'Then if things are delayed, I shall just have to make sure that I have some other worthy proposals I can talk about, which will use up time,' said the Chancellor with a small frown. 'I have been given a lot to consider. Mr Gilchrist, I am extremely grateful to you and your team for letting me have advance warning of what's in the wind. I hope I can live up to your expectations.' He glanced back at the PM. 'Perhaps I could retire with my team to work on Monday's speech. Shall I report to Cabinet tomorrow evening?'

'Yes, please,' replied the PM. 'Is there anything else?'

'I have an observation,' said Rafi. 'If the wind had been blowing in the opposite direction, the City of London would have become the no-go area. I believe the terrorists would have thought of this, so my thinking is that they could have sizeable positions in both the Frankfurt and Chicago derivatives markets. We suggest that they be asked not to open on Monday.'

'Good point,' said the Chancellor. 'Leave that with me.'

The meeting had finished. The PM spoke to Aidan's team. 'Would any of you like to watch Monday's proceedings from the Gallery?'

'If it's all right with you, sir,' Aidan replied, 'we would prefer to watch with a couple of trading screens in front of us in order to see what the other markets make of the speeches.'

Saara spoke up. 'I would like to take up your offer, please. I'm ashamed to say that I've never been into the Houses of Parliament. This would make a good first time, I think.'

'Of course.'

'If you'll excuse me,' said the Chancellor. He picked up his papers and, deep in thought, headed for the door, followed by his team.

Aidan hovered by the door. 'How did you manage to get all that documentation together so quickly?' Rafi asked.

'It was a close run thing. We brought in a couple of Donald's team to help with the word processing behind the scenes, plus a lot of copying and pasting from existing documents. We shipped a couple of large printer–photocopiers in from my offices and in the end borrowed the PM's secretarial team for the collation and binding of the documents. I reckon we did quite a good job!' answered Aidan proudly.

'Bloody outstanding considering the circumstances,' replied Rafi. 'Would you like to join us for a quick bite to eat?'

Rafi was about to say yes when the PM beckoned him to stay behind with his permanent secretary.

'I'm afraid I still have a few things to do. Let's get together for lunch soon, though.'

The tense atmosphere that had characterised the previous meeting remained. The PM picked up the phone and Kate was shown in. 'Sorry, I don't have that much time; I have another meeting due to start in five minutes. I wanted to speak to you both. I had considered leaving it until this was all over, but it didn't seem appropriate given all you've both gone through and done.' The PM drew breath. 'It's not possible for me to fully express my gratitude. Your foresight has given us the opportunity to come out of this disaster with some vestige of hope for the future.'

He had a serious look on his tired face. 'Mr Khan and Inspector Adams, were I to be in a position to grant you a request or two, what would they be?'

Rafi looked at the Prime Minister and then across to Kate. He sensed that his first wish had been granted. He had found someone with whom he would enjoy spending time; hopefully lots of time. Rafi returned his gaze to the Prime Minister. 'I'm not certain whether I need anything, thank you, sir.'

'But come now, there must be something?'

Rafi thought for no more than a few seconds. It dawned on him that here was an opportunity of a lifetime – he could do something that would have made his hard-working parents proud. Rafi took a deep breath.

'Well, here goes,' he said. 'Would it be possible for there to be a Royal Garden Party at Buckingham Palace, where those invited are drawn from Muslim communities throughout the United Kingdom? Not the movers and shakers, but rather the quiet, hard-working, first-class citizens who help to make this country tick. For too long they've been unappreciated and disenfranchised.'

The Prime Minister thought for a moment. 'I like your idea of acknowledging those who quietly get things done.'

'Also, it would be much appreciated if my flat could be given a bit of a tidy up!'

The PM smiled and nodded. 'Consider it done.'

'Detective Inspector, is there anything we might do for you?'

Kate thought for a moment. 'Could I have a couple of weeks' leave starting as of Monday evening? I'd like to recharge my batteries and get to know someone I've recently met,' she said with a grin.

Rafi felt a warm glow building inside him. He looked across at Kate approvingly. The Prime Minister nodded. 'I suggest that you speak to your boss and say that I asked you to spend a couple of weeks overseeing Mr Khan's recuperation, following the unfortunate events at Paddington Green.'

'Sir, there is one other thing,' said Rafi. 'It's more a comment rather than a wish. I'm not a vindictive man; however, in my experience as a fund manager, the vast majority of people in positions of influence get there because they're good at their job or, in a few cases, because no one else is willing to pick up a poisoned chalice.'

Rafi put his hand into his pocket and pulled out a tape. 'I have here the interview between a junior minister and me. He was sent with a press entourage by the stand-in Home Secretary to interview me valuable minutes before the Stratford missiles were launched – no doubt to use his actions as spin to deflect what was going on elsewhere. This is the original tape. There are no copies.'

Rafi hesitated. 'The contents, I believe, are political dynamite. On second thoughts, Prime Minister, you would be better off not listening to it. Hypothetically speaking, if it transpired that the Stratford missile attack could have been averted had it not been for an obsession with spin which fatally delayed key information getting through, it would damage politicians and politics irreparably. And currently, there's more than enough to sort out – starting a blame game would only be counterproductive.' Rafi hesitated. 'As I see it, a growing number of politicians spout forth initiatives and policies, but have little or no idea of change management and the workings of the real world. They've become obsessed with spin and looking good in the eyes of the media and have forgotten about implementation.'

The PM looked concerned.

'What I ask,' continued Rafi, 'is that whoever listens to this tape should consider whether or not spin interfered with the course of events. For example, without the obsession with spin, would the train have been stopped sooner and thus been outside the terrorist's line of sight? If they agree that the Stratford attack could have been prevented, I ask you to set up a task force to report on how the Civil Service can change the way *they* and *politicians* deal with the media, such that the current practice of spinning, giving misleading information and part-truths becomes a thing of the past. As I see it, at the moment too many senior politicians have little more than political research and think tank experience, and have become obsessed with perception rather than practicalities and substance.'

The Prime Minister looked at Rafi. 'Are you telling me that this tape is evidence that spin by a member of my Government prevented you from stopping a terrorist attack? And that tape in your hand is the only copy?'

Rafi nodded and said, 'I couldn't possibly comment Prime Minister, but I can assure you, you don't want to hear the contents of the tape.'

The PM thought for a few moments. 'I shall do as you request and if the head of the Civil Service confirms that the contents are as inflammatory as you say, I shall indeed ask him to undertake a full root and branch review of how politicians, their spokespeople and the Civil Service deal with the media.' He stopped, deep in thought, for what seemed like a long time, but was probably no more than a few seconds.

'I will go further; if spin has corrupted the system, I will introduce an independent verification process.' The PM paused. 'It will be overseen by a select committee, whose members will be chosen by a secret ballot of MPs. This committee will be tasked with bringing into the open blatant spin, barefaced lies, half-truths and white lies. Offenders will have to face this committee and if they are not cleared of wrongdoing, they will have to make a public apology and correct their errors on the record. Furthermore, their apologies will be added alongside the relevant sections of Hansard requiring amendment or clarification. The committee will have teeth to investigate and bring people to account; these powers will include the ability to suspend members of both Houses and, in extremis, debar the individual from public service.' The PM went silent for a moment, then went on, 'On reflection, I am prepared to go further and widen the powers of the committee to include all public officials who blatantly deceive in order to further their or their party's own ends.'

'Thank you Prime Minister.'

The door to the office opened. 'Your next meeting is ready to start, Prime Minister.'

'Thank you, SJ.'

The PM looked at Kate and Rafi, and held out his hand. 'It's time for me to be elsewhere. Thank you both again for your help.'

They shook his hand and left.

B ack in the hotel suite, Kate put her arms around Rafi's neck, her warm brown eyes gazing into his.

'What now?' said Rafi.

'Silly question! How about we get some food – I'm starving – and turn in for an early night?' she said with a wicked glint in her eyes.

'Great idea. What do you want to eat? The room service menu is impressive.'

'I'm glad you're paying,' she said with a smile. 'I could eat out for ages on some of these prices.'

'We deserve some pampering, or at least I thought your orders were: lots of TLC.'

'That,' said Kate, 'could be on the menu for dessert.'

They settled for a light supper. After the meal they snuggled up on the large sofa, enjoying the tranquillity.

'Would you mind if we paid an impromptu visit to my brother Marcus and my parents on Sunday?' asked Kate. 'I think they need a bit of reassuring after the past few days.'

'Sounds like a great idea. Are you sure we aren't wanted elsewhere, though?'

'We'll no doubt be required tomorrow, but we should be able to slip away on Sunday. I'll fill you in on my family on the way.'

'Where exactly do they live?'

'Just outside Colchester.'

'Sounds like an excellent idea,' said Rafi.

The conversation moved on to what they could do during Kate's two-week break, which was scheduled to start as soon as the terrorist leaders were in captivity.

'I don't feel like going far away,' Kate said.

'Before this all happened, I'd booked a suite at a hotel in Cornwall for ten days. What do you think?' enquired Rafi.

'Is it a very smart hotel?'

'It's family run – by all accounts it's comfortable and has good food,' said Rafi.

'But what about the beds?' queried Kate.

'They should be fine,' he replied.

'They?' said Kate sleepily. 'Would it be too forward if we continue to share a bed?' Kate planted a kiss on his cheek and snuggled up.

Rafi smiled. The prospect of having Kate as a girlfriend appealed.

'I'd like that,' he replied. 'I'll ring the hotel in the morning.' He didn't get a reply; Kate was sound asleep in his arms.

Rafi awoke to the buzzing sound of the bedside phone. He reached over and picked it up. His watch showed the time to be 8.45 a.m. He recognised the voice at the other end but couldn't initially place who it was. The quietly-spoken woman introduced herself as SJ from Number 10.

'Could you come in to see the Prime Minister again, please? I've arranged for a car to collect you. It'll be waiting outside your hotel in thirty minutes. Could you make it here for 9.30?'

'No problem,' Rafi replied, replaced the phone and sat up.

Rays of daylight crept in though the edges of the curtains and cast a soft warm light around the room. Kate was sound asleep next to him. She looked very comfortable and beautiful. He fought against the urge to give her a hug. They'd been sleeping side by side for two nights and hadn't even got as far as a cuddle. With regret, he slowly slipped out of bed and made for the bathroom.

On his way out Rafi scribbled Kate a note telling her where he had gone. By 9.10 a.m. he was sitting in a car on his way to Number 10. He arrived early. There was practised calmness in the way people moved around, which disguised the telltale signs of people working under considerable stress.

SJ, whom Rafi had seen several times the day before, apologised, saying that the Prime Minister was running late. 'Would you like a cup of coffee while you wait?'

'That would be nice. I seem to have missed breakfast,' replied Rafi.

'I'll see what I can do,' she said with a smile.

She returned a few minutes later with a tray. On it was a cup of coffee and a croissant. 'I hope this will help.'

Rafi beamed. 'Thanks, just what I needed.' He settled down to the welcome sustenance.

Ten minutes later SJ reappeared. 'The PM is snowed under at the moment. He'll see you as soon as he can. I've been asked to slot you in ahead of his next meeting. Can I get you another coffee?'

'No, thanks, I'm fine.'

She bent forward to pick up the tray from the low table just in front of Rafi.

To his surprise, he wondered how such a primly dressed secretary could look so provocative.

'Do let me know if you need . . . something,' she said as she stood up and turned to leave.

'Thank you, I will,' said Rafi. A few minutes later his thoughts were interrupted by SJ returning.

'The PM is wrapping up his meeting and will see you as soon as his visitors leave. He's given me strict instructions to look after you whilst you're in Downing Street. My offer still stands: if you need someone to help you with anything, please ask,' she said with a lovely smile. Her soft blue-green eyes made fleeting contact with his.

Rafi looked at her and wondered whether she'd just tried a discrete chat up line or was simply doing her job diligently.

The door to the adjoining room opened. The PM was standing there ready to greet him – he looked deadbeat. 'I'm sorry I had to call you in again.'

Rafi had to smile. Despite everything, the PM's manners were still impeccable.

'Please take a seat.' The PM sat opposite him. 'Rafi, I'd be grateful if you would do me a favour.'

'Anything, Prime Minister.'

The PM looked at Rafi carefully. 'The Chancellor and I have brought together a group of energy experts to advise us on where the UK stands post-Stratford. Their brief is to provide us with a coherent new energy strategy.'

He paused to collect his thoughts. 'If I could explain the problem, we can then discuss how you might be able help. As your friends pointed out last night, the next couple of days will be won or lost on the perception of what we are going to do in the future – the reality will be another matter. We have to get across clear strategies and joined-up thinking. There is no scope for doubt and disagreement. Obviously, we have to deliver the strategies, but inevitably there will be some fine-tuning before they become reality. Firstly, we must get the big picture right and regain the public's confidence. It is my Cabinet's opinion that nuclear power has become redundant. I shall be telling the House of Commons on Monday that all our nuclear power stations will be decommissioned as quickly as is feasible and that this process will commence next week. We have to find long-term, environmentally-friendly alternatives and have a solution that does not make us dependent on fickle, or politically corrupt third party energy suppliers. The committee of leading energy experts I spoke of is meeting next door in Number 11. What I am asking of them is a tall order. They have until tomorrow evening to provide the Cabinet with a briefing paper. By the time I stand up in the House on Monday afternoon, I must have a clear view in my mind as to what is possible and practical, and what is not.'

'How can I help?'

'This energy committee comprises the movers and shakers in the energy industry together with representatives from the environmentalist and renewables arenas. They have been given the authority to co-opt whoever they deem necessary. The problem is they are not making any headway. I should be grateful if you would join their meeting and see what you can do to get them to work as a team.'

Rafi looked at the PM in a questioning manner.

He picked up on Rafi's hesitation. 'Are you wondering why I'm asking you and not someone else? Firstly, you've had longer than anyone else to think through the consequences of having no solutions post-Stratford. Secondly, you have proved to be good at thinking under pressure and coming up with workable, practical answers. Thirdly, I am advised that as a fund manager you've got a good knowledge of the energy sector and the players in it.'

Rafi nodded.

'Excellent! Please stir them into action and get them to see the importance of working as a team to produce a coherent strategy – and soon!'

The study door opened and SJ reappeared. Rafi left with his guide. As he was leaving, the PM called across in a quiet voice, 'Good luck!'

His courteous guide took him through the corridors to Number 11. 'Here we are,' she said. 'Please, give me a ring if I can be of assistance. Just ask the switchboard for SJ and they will find me.'

Rafi looked at her and smiled. 'Will do,' he replied. He knocked and entered a sombre room. The room itself was bright, but it was the overpowering solemnity of its occupants that struck him.

'Good morning,' he said, 'I understand you're expecting me.'

The chairman, a man in his fifties, got up. Rafi had met him before, as his funds had invested in the chairman's oil company.

'Welcome. Let me do the introductions.' The chairman then went on to introduce Rafi to each person sitting around the table.

'Before we start, Rafi, I'd like to extend to you my thanks and gratitude. Your actions, in addition to saving many lives, have saved my company many hundreds of millions of pounds.'

The chairman sensed that several of those around the table were questioning why Mr Khan was there. 'It may seem odd to have Mr Khan, a former terrorist suspect, join us. He is here on a strictly confidential basis. The terrorists still believe he is locked up in prison. Rafi has been instrumental in helping the authorities close in on the terrorists. But in case you are still wondering why he is here, let me assure you that he sits amongst us as an equal. As a senior equities fund manager, his knowledge of the financial markets and of the energy sector is substantial.'

He smiled as he looked at Rafi. 'I bet Mr Khan could tell me what my company's pre-tax profits were last year and give me its current and prospective earnings per share.'

Rafi looked at the chairman and nodded.

The chairman chuckled. 'He should do, as his funds are big investors in the energy sector.'

This broke the ice and Rafi breathed a sigh of relief.

The chairman started to brief him. 'We seem to have reached a bit of an impasse. The impact of Cruden Bay being out of action will have a knock-on affect on downstream products, but thankfully alternative arrangements can be made to cover the shortfall whilst the rebuilding and essential repairs are completed.'

He paused. 'Our first problem rests with the cessation of nuclear power generation. This will produce a 20% shortfall in electricity generating capacity. Our second problem rests with providing environmentally-friendly solutions to make the UK energy self-sufficient. Put the two together and we need to find alternatives to about half the UK's energy needs. Mr Khan, before we continue our deliberations, do you have any ideas or observations?'

Rafi hesitated – never before had he been asked to work with such a morose-looking group. He was used to interviewing the chairmen, managing and finance directors of major UK companies, but not to lead their discussions and get a group of hitherto fierce competitors working as a proper team. He looked around the room. The committee members were sitting in their suit jackets around a large oval, mahogany table. The formality was stifling. He sensed that the deadlock was a matter of vested interests and pride. Rafi leant across and asked the chairman, 'Could we begin with a short break? I have a couple of proposals I'd like to discuss.'

The chairman stood up. 'I suggest we have a fifteen-minute tea break whilst I bring Mr Khan fully up to speed.'

Rafi noticed one or two members of the committee did not seem pleased by this interruption.

After everybody had left the room he turned to Rafi and said, 'So, Mr Khan, what do you suggest?'

'Where have you got to in your discussions?'

'Well, we've resolved the short-term position and are confident that the shortfalls following the attack at Cruden Bay can be met by existing spare capacity and additional short-term imports. But, how to plug the *huge* medium- to long-term energy gap is *the* big issue.'

'Right; here is what I think.' Rafi hesitated as he gathered together his ideas. 'Firstly, I think that the atmosphere in here is too formal. I suggest that your committee members be encouraged to take off their jackets and ties.'

The chairman nodded.

'Also, how's about we get rid of the large table and replace it with four or five tables, and get people working in small teams? That way, they should generate more ideas and feelings of competition and hostility should be reduced. Thirdly, let's give each table a flip chart or whiteboard to keep track of what's being discussed.'

Rafi thought for a short while, then went on to illustrate his other suggestions. 'I believe your committee will need more resources. How about all those whose companies have in-house research teams arrange for their key staff and researchers to be on call in their offices asap in order to enable them to access data as and when required? Also, we should put like-minded people to work together in small teams, ask them to come up with their ideal solution to the problem and identify any issues associated with their solution. Finally, we should see whether we have the beginnings of a strategy and start the debate in earnest!'

Rafi waited for the rebuff but it didn't come. The chairman looked at Rafi. 'I'd heard that you were a bright and incisive individual, but I had no idea you were this good!' He turned to the civil servant who was standing next to him. 'Please arrange all Mr Khan has proposed.' He turned to Rafi and said, 'I'll brief the committee on what you've suggested whilst they finish their coffee. Perhaps, while I'm doing the rounds, you could take the attendance list and the name cards, and group people according to how you'd like them to sit.'

Rafi nodded.

He stacked the name cards in front of him. On the first table he planned to put the two other oil and gas company directors and the head of a large gas-fired power station. On the second, he placed the two owner–managers of UK coal pits, the two former coal union bosses, the boss of a coal-fired power station and the tax specialist. On the third, he grouped the three environmentalists and the two renewable energy experts, whereas on the fourth there would be the committee chairman, the director of a nuclear power company and himself. On the fifth, he would bring on board some senior civil servants to act as expert minute takers, who could come up with their own views on the political practicalities of the proposals.

Rafi spoke to one of the staff tidying the room and asked him to find the chairman. He arrived a few moments later. Rafi put forward the idea of adding three senior civil servants to the existing group.

'Good call,' said the chairman. He spoke quietly to the civil servant who had been hovering in the background and left the room with him.

The tables were rearranged. Rafi walked around them, distributed the name cards and straightened the chairs. The room was transformed: the dark mahogany table had gone and been replaced by five circular tables with crisp, white tablecloths.

The chairman ushered his dismal flock back in, some of whom now looked mildly intrigued. He introduced the first newcomer – a permanent secretary from the Treasury – and explained that they would shortly be joined by a colleague from the Energy Ministry and a member of the PM's staff.

It didn't take very long for everyone to settle down in their places. The chairman stood up.

'Gentlemen – apologies – lady and gentlemen, as you'll see, during the break there have been a few changes. I'd like to ask each group to discuss the three things required of us by our political masters: first of all, how, following the switch-off of nuclear power, can a 20% shortfall in electricity generating capacity be replaced by environmentally-friendly sources? Secondly, what can be done to make up the other 30% shortfall necessary to make the UK energy self-sufficient over the next five years? And, finally, what are your views on the timescales involved in bringing on board this new capacity?'

'Each table,' he continued, 'is to come up with their ideal solution and must identify such problems that will have to be overcome in order to implement their plan. Let's see where we are in, say, ninety minutes. Oh, one last thing. Before you proceed with your discussions, please give a thought as to what support, in terms of data and research material, you might need and who is in the best position to deliver it to you. Please pass the names and contact details to Barney here, who will arrange for those named to go into their offices so as to be at your beck and call.' With that the chairman got up. 'If you will excuse me, I have a couple of matters to sort out,' he said and left the room

Rafi was left sitting close to the nuclear power expert. His body language suggested that he would have preferred to have been miles away. He was looking out of sorts. Understandably, thought Rafi, although he couldn't work out whether it was him or those in the meeting room he wished to avoid. It would be interesting to hear what his suggestions might be.

Rafi started the conversation. 'How about we start by looking at things from the nuclear perspective, pre-Stratford? Could you list the sources of energy that your industry viewed as being competitors and their pros and cons? Then perhaps we could move on to the timescale for taking nuclear offline.'

The nuclear scientist carefully studied the dark-skinned man sitting next to him. There was an uncomfortable silence which was suddenly broken by his flat-pitched voice.

'Good idea. If you could give me a bit of time, I'll write down my thoughts.' He grimaced, pulled out a blue enamel Waterman pen from his breast pocket and started to scribble something. Whilst his head was down, Rafi took the opportunity to look around the room. The atmosphere had changed from one of overpowering sullenness to one more typical of a quiz night.

The oil and gas company directors had their smartly ironed sleeves rolled up. The youngest of the three, who Rafi reckoned to be in his mid-forties, had been made their spokesman and sat alongside their flip chart, scribbling hard. They were brainstorming, jotting down the key issues as they saw them, in whatever order they occurred to them.

The tone of the second table, which comprised the two former mine workers, the two coal barons, the boss of the coal-fired power station and the tax expert, surprised Rafi. They'd agreed to shelve all past hostilities and were working together to promote the benefits of a revitalised coal industry with the aim of supplying a new generation of power stations. At the top of their flip chart they had written: 'Why Coal?' and at the bottom: 'Why Not Coal?' – across the middle was a dotted line. It looked like they'd set themselves a target of writing down more pros than cons. Rafi noted a couple of their scribbled notes: 'The UK has a couple of centuries of supplies – 100 countries export coal – so we can't be held to ransom'; 'Clean coal technology (CCT) and carbon sequestration have to be the rallying call'; 'We have the technology – tax incentives are needed'.

Rafi's eyes temporarily skipped the third table and rested on the fifth table, where the Treasury permanent secretary had been joined by a balding red-haired man with an immaculately kept moustache, and a smartly dressed woman. They greeted each other like long-lost friends. The Treasury official was in the throes of updating his colleague from the Energy Ministry and the woman from the PM's office as to what was expected of them. They gave the impression that they were definitely up for the challenge.

Rafi's gaze turned to the third table. The three environmentalists and the two experts on renewable energy were still discussing who was to be their team leader and what they should do next. They were getting nowhere. Rafi stretched across and picked up the blue felt-tip pen which was lying in the tray at the bottom of the flip chart, ripped off the top sheet and tore it into five strips. On one he put a blue tick and proceeded to fold up the five pieces of paper.

He got up and walked over to the third table. As he approached he heard one of the environmentalists say, 'Why me? Surely you'd be better at putting our point of view across?'

'How goes it?' Rafi asked.

'Well,' replied George, a renewables expert, 'we're still trying to sort out where to start.'

'I've got an idea,' Rafi said. He put the five folded paper rectangles on the table. 'Why don't each of you pick one and the person with the blue mark on their paper becomes your team leader?' There was silence among them as no one seemed willing to make the first move.

'OK, on the count of three each of you picks up a piece of paper. One, two, three!'

The unfolded pieces of paper were picked up. The winner was an elderly-looking environmentalist.

'All yours,' Rafi said to him.

The old man smiled. 'Thank you, Mr Khan.'

On returning to his table Rafi passed the three civil servants. Their flip chart was now headed: 'Delivery Constraints' and under this title there were a number of neat bullet points. 'Change management', 'Planning regimes' and 'Tax incentives' were underlined. Rafi overheard one of them say, 'It'll be down to giving the people a sense of ownership of the solutions,' which made him smile.

Back at his table the nuclear expert had lost none of his downtrodden frown. He was scribbling energetically on his pad and barely acknowledged Rafi's return. 'I'm almost there,' he said apologetically. 'If you could give me, say, ten more minutes, please?'

The chairman nodded his approval. 'Where did you pick up your team management skills?' he quietly asked Rafi.

'At Business School, I reckon,' Rafi replied. 'We spent a lot of time on problem solving and being treated like mushrooms.'

'Mushrooms?'

'Yes: being kept in the dark as to what the overall picture was and being fed on—'

'Alright! I get the picture,' he interjected.

The nuclear expert raised his head. 'OK, I'm ready when you are,' he said. His apprehension was starting to recede. 'I've listed the energy sources used in electricity power generation and, given the self-sufficiency brief, I've ranked them according to their availability in the UK, with a note on their cost effectiveness, environmental friendliness and potential amount that they could supply. And I've also put down my thoughts on a realistic timescale for switching off the nuclear power plants.'

Time had flown by. Each table in the room was deep in discussion and the whole atmosphere had changed; there was dynamism in the way people were working.

The chairman looked at the nuclear expert. 'Would you be willing to start the ball rolling?'

'Happy to.'

The chairman stood up. 'You've had your ninety minutes. I'm giving you a further ten to draw your thoughts together, get a cup of tea or coffee and have a pit stop if required. Then we'll start on the next leg of our work. Don't worry if you still have some loose ends. We'll sort them out as we go, or come back to them at an appropriate time. When we return, our nuclear expert, Edgar, will kick things off. We're going to do this in a friendly but robust manner. Each table will put forward their thoughts. Our three civil servants will work with us to pull together a coherent list of topics we have to agree on and from this—'

There was a knock at the door and SJ walked in. She passed the chairman a handwritten note. He read it, raised his eyebrows and looked at Rafi. 'It seems, Mr Khan, that your time is up; your presence is requested next door. Thank you for your input. Do call by if you get a spare moment later.'

Rafi said his goodbyes and left with SJ.

As they walked down the corridor, she turned to him and said, 'You're booked to see the PM in seventy-five minutes' time. The PM is grateful to you for getting them moving, but thought that you'd now prefer to be brought up to speed on the terrorists' whereabouts. It's back to the dungeons to pay COBRA a visit.'

She looked at Rafi and felt she couldn't work him out. His mugshot had been plastered all over the papers as 'public enemy number one', but he seemed to be one of the good guys. He'd had a rough time by the looks of things, but his eyes told another story. They were alive and bright.

A few minutes later they arrived at the door to the COBRA meeting room. As Rafi walked in he sensed a new feel to the room. The urgency and horror of the day before had given way to a businesslike atmosphere. Inside the door was a face he'd got to know very well over the past few days. Jeremy greeted him warmly and they fell into conversation.

SJ smiled. 'I'll come and get you in seventy minutes,' she said, turned and left.

J eremy looked at Rafi. 'Where would you like me to start?'
'*Golden Sundancer* and the three trawlers, please.'
'It's all go at sea and up in the air with the two Nimrods tracking them. The Great Yarmouth trawler left port at 16.00 hours on Friday and, as you know, turned south. She entered the Straights of Dover around 22.30 yesterday and is currently heading towards the Lizard Point off Cornwall. On board is Dakka Dudayev, the Stratford bomber; a real hard case.'

'The trawler from Peterhead offloaded Rudnik Miromov, the Cruden Bay terrorist, on to *Golden Sundancer* north-west of the Pentland Firth at 5 p.m. yesterday evening. She then headed at speed around the Western Isles. The Troon trawler rendezvoused with her at 03.00 south-west of Stanton Banks where she picked up Talal's number two, Alistair Hartnell, and the recruiter of the suicide bombers, Kim Chindriani. Since then *Golden Sundancer* has been flying down the west coast of Ireland at a bloody impressive 40–46 knots. She's currently just west of Bantry Bay. Our calculations point to the Great Yarmouth trawler, *Rosemarie*, and *Golden Sundancer* rendezvousing at 19.00 hours this evening south-west of the Isles of Scilly. From there, we believe that they'll head for Morocco and the port of Safi.'

'What's Maryam up to?'
'She's carrying on as usual in Luxembourg, playing at being a real socialite. Wining and dining seem to be her middle names. The commissioner is arranging a visit to Luxembourg to tie in with the

capture of the other terrorists on Monday afternoon.' Jeremy drew breath and pointed to the screens around the room. 'On the home front, the army's pyrotechnics continue to be impressive: there's still a good mix of dark smoke, explosions and flames from Cruden Bay, Aldermaston, Hartlepool and Heysham. Even though numerous announcements have been made that no radioactivity has been released and the terrorists missed their nuclear targets, the TV crews love it. I feel sorry for the local residents, but at least it's in a good cause.'

'How's it progressing at Stratford?' asked Rafi.

'Basically, it's a bugger and is still taking up masses of resources. Thankfully, – Operation Counterpane – got most people away from the exclusion zone relatively quickly. The genius part was getting others to look after them. It's worked magically. The reaction of the provincial cities, and in particular the rural communities, has been beyond anyone's expectations. Trains have been running constantly from the London termini since Friday morning transporting the refugees to their destinations. Fleets of coaches have poured into London from across the country, with offers of accommodation and homes for those who got on board them. The logistics of the major retailers have stood up well. In some instances people have been getting on their coaches with a blanket, duvet or just a towel or coat around them. En route to their destination, stop-offs to department stores have been arranged to fully clothe and re-equip the travellers. The Dunkirk spirit has been unbelievable. Only a small minority of those dispossessed have caused trouble; the vast, vast majority have been grateful for the help and to be evacuated. The police and the army have been dealing with the minority in a calm but firm manner,' said Jeremy.

'What are the radiation levels like?' Rafi enquired, concerned.

'The experts got their initial calculations for the exclusion zone spot on. The Royal Engineers, with the help of specialist building contractors, have completed the demarcation and the clearing of the perimeter of the exclusion zone and I understand that plans are afoot for work to start tomorrow on the foundations for the perimeter wall. There have been attempts at looting and to get items that are now, of course, radioactive out of the exclusion zone. The army patrols have been up to their task and clamped down firmly on such activities. There are 3,000 battle-hardened troops with experience of Iraq and Afghanistan policing the perimeter – next to nothing has got out.' Jeremy paused.

'The scientists have put together plans to counter the problems of the leaching of the radioactive materials into the water table. Fingers crossed they'll get it right, or else the City of London and Docklands will be in trouble.'

Jeremy chatted at length, detailing how the exclusion zone was being cleared of people and how the location of London City Airport was a godsend. 'It must be a nightmare for the air traffic controllers, what with all the transport plane movements. Thankfully, only one pilot has got his approach wrong and nearly ended up in the water,' he recalled.

Jeremy hesitated. 'Your interrogator, Andy, phoned me earlier today.'

Rafi involuntarily tensed up.

'Nothing untoward,' reassured Jeremy, sensing Rafi's unease. 'In his investigations he came across an individual who paid your family money every month for over fifteen years.' Jeremy passed him a piece of paper with a name and phone number on it. 'I think you might know him?'

Rafi looked in surprise at the name: Major Charlie Staveley. Then he smiled. 'Yes I remember him well. He was my maths teacher at Haileybury.'

'Andy interviewed him about the money he paid to your grand-father and then to you father. All he would say was, "It was a long time ago and Haileybury had strong connections with the Stepney Boys Club which assisted East End of London families – this was my way of helping." Andy reckons that the major was hiding something. You might like to drop by and have a chat with him one of these days, just in case.'

'Thanks,' said Rafi, still faintly puzzled, 'I'll do that.'

Their conversation returned to Stratford and the terrorists.

Out of the corner of his eye Rafi saw SJ enter the room and realised his time with Jeremy was up. It had flown by.

Rafi felt a delicate tap on his shoulder, turned and saw her smiling face just behind him. 'Time to come with me,' she said with a grin.

Rafi nodded, said his goodbyes to Jeremy and followed her up to the ground floor of Number 10 and the PM's anteroom.

'You must be beginning to get to know this room rather well,' SJ commented in a friendly manner.

'Yes, I can recommend the service – it's excellent,' Rafi grinned. He seemed to have said the right thing. SJ nonchalantly preened her hair, turned with a little wiggle of her hips and left the room. A few minutes later she was back holding a tray with a cup of tea and some chocolate biscuits.

'Thank you.'

She smiled. 'I only try to please. The PM will be ready to see you soon.'

After only a few moments Rafi was shown by SJ into the adjoining room.

The PM got straight to the point. 'Rafi, the head of the Civil Service has listened to your tape,' he began and then paused. 'He says that if I heard its contents I could not, with a clear conscience, deny knowledge of what went on, should it ever get out into the public domain. He confirms that it's political dynamite. It's clear that the Home Office and a number of its ministers took spin to an unprecedented level of crassness. Thank you for bringing this matter to our attention. What transpired, I agree, is best left in the past.'

Rafi nodded.

'I have commissioned a report on "Media briefings and dissemination of information and data by ministers and public servants". I have asked for proposals from the head of the Civil Service for a select committee to monitor this area. We have to make those who use lies, half-truths and false statistics as tools of their trade openly accountable,' said the PM.

'Thank you,' replied Rafi.

'I'm truly sorry; it seems you and Kate came within a whisker of averting the Stratford disaster, only to have people who should have known better mess things up for you. By the way, the junior minister in question has resigned his seat. I understand he's going to try his hand at something well away from the public gaze.'

With that the meeting was over and Rafi was ushered into the entrance hall of Number 10 where he found Kate waiting for him.

'Have you had a useful morning? I missed you. Your friend SJ,' she said with a wink, 'phoned. She asked if I could come and collect you. So here I am. There's a car outside and if it's OK with you, our next port of call is Wood Street.'

Rafi nodded; he was becoming accustomed to being at people's beck and call.

'We're going to give John, Jeremy and the team a hand with the logistics for rounding up all those suspected of being on the terrorists' payroll. Actually, that's a bit of a white lie; they want me and I rather like your company – hence the we,' she said with a big grin. 'I reckon

I'll get withdrawal symptoms when this is all over. Will you come with me?' asked Kate, slightly flummoxed by Rafi's deadpan expression. 'Don't worry; if you don't want to tag along I can easily drop you off at the hotel on the way.'

'I'll come . . . I'd love to. Sorry for being slow, it's just that my thoughts were with what the PM had just told me.'

Rafi leant forward and gave Kate a peck on the cheek. 'Come on, we can't keep the car waiting. Remember you promised me some TLC and I'm going to enjoy cashing it in . . . with interest!'

They had been in the Ops Room at Wood Street for less than five minutes when Jeremy appeared. 'I thought I might update you. The list of very highly paid non-executives on the terrorists' payroll is quite something. Several of the names are dynamite. For example, we've identified six Members of Parliament who have been implicated.'

Jeremy yawned. 'Apologies for that – where was I? Yep, we've checked through the bank accounts of the two COBRA members caught with their snouts in the terrorists' trough. It seems that they received their money from our old friend the Gulf Trade Bank. They've been bloody naïve and stupid. Thankfully, they weren't sophisticated enough to use an offshore account. The bungs went straight into Building Society accounts. Those who *have* been using offshore accounts will be harder to pin down and no doubt they will be the ones really worth catching – *c'est la guerre!*' He smiled and added, 'John and his team have done great work; the fun bit is going to be hauling the culprits in.'

'Have you looked at ESSA and the people they placed in the financial dealing teams, and the people running HFFF?' Rafi asked.

Jeremy nodded. 'We've got them on our list. The bosses at MI5 are gobsmacked by how much John and his team have turned up in such a short time. They have people working around the clock going through bank statements and corroborating the evidence. There's a real buzz down there. One of these days I must show you around!'

'Who do you think ran the UK end of the slush fund?' Kate asked.

'Maryam, we reckon, looked after the money side of things via bank accounts funded by the sheikh. At the moment we aren't sure who did the recruiting and management of those in their pay. My hunch is it was someone working for one of their private companies, like SPAD – Security Protection & Defence.'

'When will the arrests take place?' asked Rafi.

'As soon as the terrorist leaders are in our custody,' replied Jeremy. 'Oh – by the way – you remember that a BlueKnite employee turned a blind eye and let the bomber in at Bishopsgate? Well, it also seems that the controller looking after the nuclear trains only joined a year ago and was on the terrorists' payroll. Last week he received £15,000 from the Gulf Trade Bank; one hell of a coincidence or what? No wonder he took so long to get back to the control room and employed such a plonker to work with him.'

'Thanks for the update; now, if you'll excuse me, I've got a few loose ends to tidy up.' Kate winked at Rafi and added, 'Do make yourself at home!'

Rafi's attention turned to the large screens on the walls. One showed a press conference, describing the full impact of the nuclear sabotage. It included a report on what had happened in the previous twenty-four hours and on the progress being made. All roads into the exclusion zone were now dead ends. The one-way – out only – system was being enforced rigidly at the army-controlled checkpoints.

Rafi felt a shiver go down his spine as he saw pictures, from the previous day, of masses of people corralled in one of the open air holding areas. The footage followed the process of decontamination; people were stripped of all their belongings and clothes, and taken to a purpose-built shower marquee, next to a prefabricated building. Large signs in many languages had on them: 'Radiation risk – NOTHING to be taken beyond here.'

The TV cameras showed heart-rending footage of people arriving at the checkpoint and being forced to give up all their possessions. The pictures included those of a confused little girl being made to give up her favourite teddy – she was crying and couldn't comprehend what was going on. The scene brought a tear to Rafi's eye.

The report contained footage of mobile phones being handed out to each individual or family. The mobile phone companies had literally cleared their warehouses and the stocks in their shops. Free pay-as-you-go phones with credit vouchers for calls were issued to those coming out of the decontamination centres. Those with missing family members were given a phone number they could call to give information about the people they had lost. A number of local sports halls became rendezvous points for the missing people.

The TV commentator commended the Dunkirk spirit. The attitude wasn't 'How much is this going to cost?', but rather, 'What can we do to help those who have lost everything?'. The newscaster then announced that there would be a public holiday on the Monday, to respect the loss of life and the suffering.

Rafi watched a piece on how the National Health Service was holding up. All the hospitals within 200 miles of the disaster area were flooded with people. A number of five star hotels had been requisitioned and turned into specialist cancer treatment units. Those with radiation poisoning were sent on to one of these new specialist hospitals, with instructions from on high that everything should be done to make them feel comfortable. Elsewhere patients were seen on trolleys and makeshift beds. Against the odds, the system held up.

The armed forces were stretched beyond anything anyone could ever have envisaged. By late Friday afternoon, 10,300 troops and specialist professionals had been brought in to enforce the perimeter of the exclusion zone, to run the decontamination centres and to clear the exclusion zone of people. All military bases remained on full alert.

The RSPCA worked with the armed forces and Territorial Army's veterinary teams to deal humanely with those animals found in the exclusion zone. It was a gruesome and gruelling task. The RSPCA gained permission to run their own decontamination units for mildly contaminated pets where the owners could be identified.

Rafi was enthralled when the bulletin turned to the problems associated with the leaching of the radioactive materials into the water table. In particular the River Lee and its canal were near to the wrecked train. An ingenious solution had come from a company based just south of Newcastle, which made a polymer for – amongst other things – nappies. It rapidly turned liquids into jelly which would remain stable for over a month. They had dispatched eight lorry loads with a police escort and arrived in London late on Friday afternoon. Their cargo was applied to the flowing water in and around the exclusion zone. The main problem related to the River Lee which flowed through it. Short term, a decision had been taken to divert the Lee into the King George reservoir just to the north of the exclusion zone and from there the water was to be pumped straight into the mains as, unfortunately, the large Coppermills water treatment plant, a mile to the south, was now contaminated.

According to the reporter, decisions were being taken on how the River Lee could be redirected long-term. He listed the few solutions which were being considered – including diverting it into the River Roding – and concluded that drinking water shortages would be a feature for months to come. However, the good news was that the critical problems were being resolved and there were high hopes that radioactive materials would not leach out of the exclusion zone.

Rafi spotted Colonel Turner and his team looking at a screen showing a large chart. Curious, he went over to investigate. The screen showed the precise location of *Golden Sundancer*. She was still heading south.

It was late afternoon. Tiredness was rapidly overcoming Rafi – he felt ready to drop. The pressures and excesses of the last week had caught up with him again. He'd lost track of where Kate was, so he left a message for her and cadged a lift back to the hotel. Once there he grabbed a cold drink, had a quick shower, climbed into bed and turned the lights out. Sleep came quickly.

He awoke on Sunday morning to find it was almost 9.30 a.m. He had slept for fifteen hours – a welcome relief. Kate was already up and about and dressed.

'Hi there, sleepyhead; your timing is perfect. I've ordered breakfast and the hire car is waiting for us downstairs.'

They enjoyed their breakfast, and by 10.15 a.m. were on their way.

Rafi took his trilby and cashmere scarf and a couple of the Sunday newspapers with him.

The curfew that had been imposed on Friday morning had been lifted at midnight on Saturday. The roads were unduly busy and the exclusion zone severed the usual roads towards East Anglia.

Their destination was the Suffolk–Essex border, where Kate's family lived. They talked about her family and about her early childhood years. It became obvious that she'd had a very happy time living in Kenya, where her parents had been farmers.

'Then the carefree days ended,' Kate recalled with sadness in her voice. 'When I was twelve my grandfather died. We returned to England so that my father could sort out his affairs. The death duties were far larger than my father had expected and a decision had to be taken. Sell up in England to meet the huge tax bill and return to Kenya, or sell up in Kenya and live in the family home in Suffolk. My father chose the latter and following that decision much of the happiness in my life evaporated. My school changed from a relaxed private school to a large state school. My friends in Kenya loved outdoor activities: riding and hunting for creepy crawlies. Everything was tame in England. The weather was awful for five months of the year and people spent so much time indoors.'

'Was it that bad?'

'I had nothing in common with my new peer group at school,' she said. 'I was teased for my strange accent. My parents had promised that I would go to a smart girls' public school but it wasn't to be. My brother, Marcus, and I were sent to the local comprehensive school. It was only meant to be for the first year while my father sorted out the family's finances. However, it soon became apparent that money was very tight due to the size of the Estate Duty tax bill and the large running costs of our house.'

Kate paused. 'Mark is fifteen months younger than me. He contracted diphtheria as a child and was on death's door for over a week. He pulled through, but the illness had made him partially deaf. In Kenya he grew up as if poor hearing was a minor hindrance. He was well catered for at his school and had the full attention of his own nanny to work with him at home. Sadly, in England things were totally different. Marcus didn't fit into the education system which lacked the flexibility to cater for his special needs.

'I remember,' continued Kate, 'my parents discussing our education. Basically, they felt that I needed to stay at the same school as Marcus, as he relied on me to protect him from bullies. So I stayed there for my A levels,' she sighed. 'I spent my gap year helping my father, working for the family business. It was then that my relationship with my parents crumbled. They had expected me to go off to university to read business studies or agricultural economics and return to the family business. I didn't do that.'

'Why not?'

'I had other ideas. I wanted to become a policewoman. I had a massive row with my parents, left home and joined the police training college. But at last, I had found something I really enjoyed doing. I shouldn't brag, but I sailed through with flying colours. Like my brother, I have a flair for figures. Whilst I was a young constable I studied part-time at the Open University Business School and five years later graduated with a BSc in Business Studies and Accounting. It was hard work, but in my heart I guessed that one day I'd want to go back to Suffolk and work alongside my brother, helping the family business, so I chose a degree I could use when I returned home.'

Kate paused. 'Sadly, things went from bad to worse with my parents. While I was at the police college I became friendly with Maurice. My parents didn't approve of him as my boyfriend. I refused to back down and after a stormy weekend at home they disowned me.

'I was working long hours. Maurice wanted us to socialise and party more and in the end we went our separate ways. I moved from the Met and joined the City of London police force and focused on my work and studies.

'When I graduated, only my brother Marcus turned up to the ceremony. My relationship with my parents by that stage had dwindled to an exchange of Christmas cards and that was all. Since then I've been working for David and my social life has been practically non-existent.'

They had reached the Suffolk border. 'Are we getting close?' Rafi asked.

'Yes, not long now,' replied Kate, who noticed Rafi was deep in thought. 'Are you OK?'

'Yes, sorry, I was just thinking about family and friends. I was wondering if on our way back into London we could drop in and see an old teacher friend of mine, Major Charlie Staveley. Would you mind doing that? He lives just outside Hertingfordbury, in Great Amwell.'

'Good plan – why don't you give him a ring now?' replied Kate.

His phone call successfully completed, Rafi saw National Trust signs to Leverthorne Hall and Leverthorne Vineyard, which they seemed to be following. Alongside the roadside was a tall brick wall. A large splayed back entrance, with impressive black wrought iron gates appeared. To Rafi's surprise they drove through the gates up a tree-lined driveway. Leverthorne Hall was nowhere to be seen.

'Would you like to see where I grew up?' enquired Kate with an impish grin, as they turned a corner. In the distance was a large Georgian mansion which could be described as impressive by anyone's standards.

'Not bad eh?' said Kate. 'Marcus and his family live in the west wing. My parents have the coach house and stable block. My brother has let most of the main house to the National Trust on a peppercorn rent. Says it makes life much simpler and lets him get on with the running of the estate and its businesses as a proper commercial venture.'

Rafi looked at Kate. 'So, all along, things like the suite at the Savoy were second nature to you!'

'If only! As far back as I can remember, living here was a continuous round of penny-pinching. Just try to imagine: two acres of roof, rising damp, old wiring and cranky central heating . . . To name but a few of the house's redeeming features – they all cost a fortune.'

Kate glanced at Rafi; there was sadness in her eyes. 'This is going to be difficult. I haven't seen, let alone spoken, to my parents for many years. In the beginning I tried, but they wouldn't answer my calls. I have kept in touch with Marcus. It was especially difficult when he found a girlfriend and wanted to get married, but my parents refused to let him have the reception here if I attended. In the end, he and Susannah decided not to get married. That, as far as my parents were concerned, was the final straw. The last time I went home was with Maurice. This time it's with you in tow. Please don't be surprised if this is a very short and fiery family reunion.'

'I don't have the luxury of having a family,' commented Rafi. 'It's got to be worth a shot at patching things up between you and your parents. It's a shame that all you've been doing has to be kept quiet until the terrorists are caught.'

'A blaze of publicity might have been useful,' mused Kate, 'but this way we'll see if there's any real affection left for me.'

The car stopped.

'Whatever happens, you've still added one extra person to your life: me.'

Kate turned her head and looked at Rafi. He could see the beginnings of tears welling up in her gorgeous eyes. She leant over and kissed him.

'Right, let the charm offensive begin.' Rafi groaned as he eased himself out of the car seat. His bruised lower back had not liked the prolonged car journey.

Kate smiled. 'Be your normal self. They get us warts and all.' She gave his hand a squeeze and headed for the open front door. Rafi followed, with his trilby tilted over his eyes and the scarf round his neck and lower face.

He marvelled as he stepped inside. The entrance hall could have contained his flat. They approached the National Trust booth where a kindly woman greeted Kate with a big smile.

'Hello, Mrs Hindmarsh; sorry I didn't recognise you straight away.'

'Don't worry dear – it's been over ten years.'

'How's . . .' Kate hesitated, 'Danny?'

'On excellent form, thank you. I have three grandchildren. He works in Sudbury now, has a shop opposite the church. He would be pleased to see you, so do drop by.'

'Thank you, Mrs Hindmarsh, I'll do that next time I'm up here. Today is a bit of a fleeting visit.'

Mrs Hindmarsh nodded in a knowing manner and they proceeded on their way.

They walked into a cavernous central hall. It was devoid of furniture. Its stone floor had small squares of black stone inlay to give it a criss-cross pattern. The main feature in the central hall was the grand sweeping staircase. There was a pair of large double doors to the left which led through to an impressively furnished drawing room. In front of Rafi the open double doors framed a view through what looked like a music room and on to the largest set of French windows he could ever recall seeing, with a vista down to a lake and a gazebo. To the right of the hall was a grand dining room.

'How many could you seat?' he asked.

'Oh, I think we had about sixty in there for my twenty-first,' she replied nonchalantly. 'Come on, enough of the sightseeing; let's find somewhere more comfortable.'

Kate took hold of his hand and led Rafi off to the right of the dining room, past a winding, back staircase, past a billiards room, down a long passage and past the kitchens. They climbed up a second set of back stairs and there in front of them was a normal-looking front door.

'Welcome to my brother's flat,' said Kate with a broad smile. She rang the doorbell.

They were greeted by a beaming Marcus. 'Great to see you, Kate. And if I remember correctly from your phone call, this must be Rafi?'

'Yes,' said Kate.

'Susannah will be with us shortly; she's sorting out the final touches to lunch. Let's find Mother and Father. I have told them that you've a boyfriend with you, but not that it's Rafi! Sorry, but I thought it might be simpler for you to explain how your boyfriend has gone from being a terrorist to a good guy.'

They walked down a small corridor, the walls covered in pictures of Africa. Marcus looked at Kate. 'Happy memories!'

'Yes,' came the reply, 'the best.'

They came to a cosy sitting room with an open log fire brightening the cold February day. On the other side of the room was a large sofa and parked in the middle of it were two elderly people, who stood up slowly. They weren't doddery but time had started to take its toll. There was an apprehensive look on their faces. Kate walked forward and gave her mother a kiss on the cheek, followed by a hug. She turned to her father, stretched out to shake his hand, had second thoughts and gave him a peck on the cheek and a hug. Rafi sensed that her parents had been surprised by Kate's attempt at showing reconciliation. They sat down. Not a word had been spoken. Marcus did the introductions.

'Mr Rafi Khan, it's my pleasure to introduce you to our parents: Major Sir Percy Gant-Adams and Lady Yvonne Gant-Adams.'

'This, Mummy and Daddy, is Rafi. You'll no doubt have seen his picture in the papers recently. He's been working undercover for us. The full story will come out next week. We've only known one another for a week but I can assure you he's a real catch and my first boyfriend in ages.' And with that Kate planted a caring kiss on Rafi's cheek.

Wow, that was brave, Rafi thought. Talk about light the blue touchpaper and stand well back!

The tension eased as Susannah walked in carrying a tray with a bottle of champagne and some orange juice. She exclaimed in delight when she saw Kate. The tray was put down next to Marcus, who uncorked the bottle with a pleasing pop, charged the glasses and passed them around.

The major lifted his glass, looked at the bubbles and took a sniff of the bouquet. Then he stopped, looked at his daughter and said, 'Please forgive me for not standing up, but I would like to propose a toast.' He raised his glass in the direction of Marcus and Susannah.

'First I should like to toast our hosts without whom this reunion would not have happened – thank you both.' The glasses were raised and an appreciative sip was taken by all. The major turned his gaze to Kate.

'The second toast is to Kate, my long-lost daughter. Your mother and I look forward to you telling us what you've been up to. Marcus tells me that you've been heading up a team involved with the Bishopsgate bombing?'

'Yes, Daddy – and a bit more besides.' The conversation stopped in its tracks. It was as if Kate's career was of little interest to her father.

Rafi felt annoyed, but tried not to show it. He looked carefully at the major. In his youth he must have been a dashing and well-built man, and his wife must once have been, he guessed, a slightly willowier version of Kate. She had the same hair and warm brown eyes.

Susannah looked at her watch. 'Lunch will be in ten minutes. Please excuse me while I put the vegetables on.'

There was a silence. Rafi waited for someone to break the ice. Kate's mother beat him to it. 'Tell me Kate,' she said in a frail voice, 'I have been reading the papers. I am confused. How precisely did you manage in the space of a week to turn a terrorist suspect into a boyfriend?'

'It's a long story, Mummy. Rafi was set up. I was sent to see if he had information that could help us prevent more terrorist attacks. That was last Monday. Since then Rafi and I have been working flat out unravelling their conspiracy. Rafi helped us uncover a number of terrorist attacks.'

'I see, dear,' came her mother's uncertain reply.

Marcus got up and recharged the glasses.

'Don't you drink?' asked the major.

'No, sir,' replied Rafi. The major looked at him and hesitated before saying, 'Do please call me Percy; it will make things less formal.'

Rafi sensed that uttering those few words had taken courage.

'Thank you, sir.'

The major continued. 'Where do you come from?'

'It's not a very interesting story,' Rafi replied, but was encouraged to continue.

Rafi took a mouthful of the orange juice and then began. 'My father owned a bakery in the East End of London. I was educated at Haileybury and then studied for my Bachelors and Masters degrees in London.'

The major nodded, hoping for more.

'Up to a week ago, I was a senior fund manager in the City of London. The rest, as they say, is history.'

Kate skilfully switched the conversation to Leverthorne Hall and its vineyards. It transpired that Marcus had studied through the Open University Business School and had specialised on the marketing and product development side of Business Studies.

In the words of his mother, Marcus had turned the estate around. 'There is now a small rural business park with a growing number of successful cottage industries and he has found an excellent farm manager to run the 3,500-acre farm.'

'How big is 3,500 acres?' Rafi enquired.

Kate looked at Rafi as if acres to square miles was a ratio he should have known, and replied, 'Five and a half square miles.'

'Oh, really!' exclaimed Rafi. There was laughter. He sensed that the tide had turned.

'Lunch is ready,' echoed through from the dining room, where Rafi soon found himself sitting between Lady Yvonne and Kate, and opposite the major.

Given the circumstances, lunch was a relatively jolly affair. There were a few hesitant pauses in the conversation, but the sheer joy of Kate and her brother being back together again, under the roof of the family home, was plain for all to see. They sat next to each other and chatted away at ten to the dozen.

After lunch, the small talk continued over coffee. Rafi found himself the centre of the conversation. It seemed her parents found it simpler to talk to him rather than to Kate, lest they unintentionally reopened hidden wounds.

Rafi's background, education, hobbies, work and involvement in uncovering the terrorist plots were all discussed.

Kate looked across at her parents. 'Did I tell you that I have also met Rafi's sister, Saara? When I saw the two of them together, it reminded me how much fun we had when we were living in Kenya and all the grief of the last decade seemed irrelevant; I just wished we could be as happy again.'

Kate paused and fell silent. Her parents, who were comfortably slumped on the sofa, seemed overcome by emotions. The major looked at Kate and then his wife.

'Kate,' he said, 'I agree; we did have a good time in Kenya. I am sorry that moving here caused friction and hardship. Yes, we should strive to find that happiness again.'

'But with a few more coats and jumpers,' added Marcus with a laugh.

Coffee had long been finished. There was a lull in the conversation. Kate looked at her watch – time had flown by; it was coming up to 3.30 p.m. She explained that they had a second visit to make on their way back to London, as a teacher-friend of Rafi's, Major Charlie Staveley, had invited them for tea.

They said their goodbyes and promised to be back soon.

Back in the car, Kate looked radiant. 'Thank you for being so patient and courteous through all the interrogations.'

Rafi looked into her warm eyes. 'My pleasure; it was fun, and I am hugely relieved it all worked out.'

'Yes; after a shaky start – I can't believe how well it went,' said Kate.

They had an uneventful journey and in what seemed like no time at all they were pulling into Gypsy Lane. They stopped in front of a red brick house. Great Amwell was only a couple of miles from Haileybury College.

The major's front garden was well-kept. They went up to the front door, rang the bell and stood there, holding hands.

A stooping silver-haired man answered the door. Rafi instantly recognised him – he had aged well, but was looking a little unsteady on his pins.

They were greeted by a jovial, 'Come on in, come on in, it must be cold standing out there.'

'Thank you,' said Rafi and went on to introduce Kate.

They entered the modest-sized home and headed for the sitting room, where they were greeted by a roaring open fire.

Charlie beckoned Rafi to sit on the sofa next to the fire.

'Your timing is excellent – the kettle has just boiled. Let me look at you first, young Rafi, it's been too long since I last laid eyes on you.' He stood there gazing at him. 'Thank you for your phone call. I'm sorry that you got caught up in this terrorist mess. I wondered whether you might make contact after I had a visit from MI5,' he said and then paused as if uncertain what to say next. 'Why don't you have a look at some photos whilst Kate and I get the tea?'

Charlie picked up an old leather-bound photo album from the sideboard and handed it to Rafi, then disappeared with Kate into the kitchen.

Rafi opened it. It contained pictures of the major's life. There were a couple of early photos of him at Haileybury: one of him playing cricket, which rekindled memories of Rafi standing in almost the same spot, bowling his right arm off breaks. The chapel and the large central courtyard looked just the same.

He moved on a few pages to see a very handsome, young man with a dark brown moustache and closely cropped wavy brown hair dressed in a smart army uniform. The sparse text under the photos showed that he'd been posted to Palestine and had initially served under Allenby, before being posted to India.

He turned the page and there was a picture of a beautiful Indian woman in a nurse's uniform standing in front of a large hospital. This was followed by a series of casual snaps of him and her taken during their outings. Rafi looked carefully at the photos; 1945–46 seemed to have been a very special and happy time for them. Then there was a sun-bleached photo showing the nurse and her family, all dressed up in their finest, looking very splendid in palatial surroundings. In the centre was the person he assumed to be the head of the family; he looked intimidating. A couple of photos of a kindly-looking servant carrying a tray laden with glasses, cups and saucers followed.

'What?' Rafi exclaimed. He recognised the servant as his grand-father. He then looked carefully at the picture of the nurse. It couldn't be! He couldn't believe it – it was his grandmother in her early twenties. He was confused. Why was Charlie holding hands with his grandmother in many of the pictures? The last photo showed Charlie and Rafi's grandmother standing formally next to each other. There was a look of sadness in their faces.

Rafi turned the page and there seemed to be no more pictures. The rest of the pages were blank, except the penultimate page on which there was a photo of Charlie standing next to a young lad, with his arm around his shoulder, a beaming smile across his face. Rafi remembered the occasion. It was taken in the summer near the end of his third year at Haileybury. He had taken four or five wickets in an inter-house cricket match. Charlie, who had been watching, insisted that a photo be taken for posterity. Rafi hadn't seen the photo until now. He sat deep in thought without comprehending the situation.

He was interrupted by the clattering of an old-looking trolley on which the afternoon tea had been placed. Charlie and Kate sat down and passed around the tea.

Charlie looked carefully at Rafi's face. 'I'm sorry,' he said. 'I wish I could have remained with your grandmother. Sadly for both of us, it wasn't to be. In those days, family honour ranked above individual feelings and sensibilities.'

'Pardon?' said Rafi.

'There's no easy way to say this,' said Charlie. 'I met Lateefa, your grandmother, in India just before its partitioning with Pakistan. We fell in love and then calamity struck: she told me that our relationship had to end, but she would not tell me why. I didn't find out until later that she was carrying my child and had been disowned by her family. Had it not been for your grandfather, Mansur, a servant in her household, it would have been a disaster. He sought me out and explained why Lateefa had broken off our relationship.'

Rafi could see the beginning of tears in Charlie's eyes.

'I had been transferred to the Green Howards and was being posted to Sudan. I had so wanted to go back and see Lateefa, but there wasn't time. To have become a deserter from the army would have only made things worse. When I told Mansur why I had to go, I had expected him to be angry with me. Instead he smiled and asked if he could help. It transpired that he had been in love with Lateefa since their childhood.'

Charlie looked sadly at Rafi. 'The partitioning caused large-scale and violent cross-border migration of Muslims, Hindus and Sikhs. It was this upheaval and Lateefa being without family support that prompted Mansur to find me. I was impressed – he had it all planned. He asked me to arrange passes for Lateefa and him to get to England. Mansur then found Lateefa and they emigrated there. I helped them with what little money I could.'

'So my father was your son?' Rafi exclaimed, finally understanding what Charlie was trying to tell him.

'Yes.'

'Why on earth didn't you tell me?'

'I promised your parents that I would not interfere,' said Charlie.

'Hold on a minute!' said Rafi. 'Did you have anything to do with my going to Haileybury and Saara going to a private day school?'

Charlie nodded. 'After decommissioning I went back to my studies, became a teacher and then accepted a job at Haileybury. Several years later, I had been visiting a school in Stepney, with which Haileybury had long-standing links and, as good fortune would have it, on the way home I stopped off at a local bakery in the East End. I unexpectedly met Mansur again. He looked much older, but I recognised him instantly.'

Charlie poignantly related how he had returned the following weekend and had met Lateefa and Mansur. 'It was a tear-filled reunion. We talked about Jansher, their only son and decided that the past should remain in the past – it wouldn't have been fair on them for me to come back into their lives. I asked if I could help them with their finances. They were too proud to accept any help. In the end, they allowed me to help with the education of any grandchildren that they might have.'

Rafi smiled. 'Which explains why I went from an underperforming state school to a smart boarding school!' He was overcome by emotion.

'I'm sorry,' said Charlie.

'I'm not,' replied Rafi. 'As of today my close family relatives have grown by a factor of two. Let me give you a hug.'

Rafi sat back down. 'I always knew Mansur as grandpa. Could I call you grandfather?'

Beaming, Charlie nodded, not trusting his voice.

'Saara will be delighted; I can't wait to tell her face to face.'

'Unexpectedly, Mansur wrote to me once or twice a year keeping me up to date as to what your father, Jansher, was doing. It was just like him to be so thoughtful,' said Charlie. 'After your grandmother's death he wrote saying he had told Jansher, your father, about me, and they had decided not to tell you or your sister.'

Over tea, the conversation drifted back to when Charlie had first met Lateefa, Rafi's grandmother. 'She came from an immensely powerful and wealthy family. They commanded respect for tens if not hundreds of miles around,' said Charlie. He went on to describe the close-knit community in India before independence, the partitioning and painful birth of Pakistan. Charlie talked about the British Army families – the nannies and the family helpers – and about Lateefa. 'Our relationship should have progressed to marriage,' Charlie's voice faltered. 'It broke my heart to lose her.'

The conversation moved on to Rafi's father, Jansher. 'He worked with Mansur in the bakery, leaving school at fifteen. Sorry – of course you know all that, but perhaps there are elements that you might not be aware of,' said Charlie.

He paused, topped up the cups of tea and continued. 'By the time Jansher was twenty, Lateefa had become increasingly feeble and he took over the day to day running of the bakery to enable Mansur to spend more time looking after her. She died, just after your father's twenty-first birthday, leaving Mansur heartbroken and increasingly reclusive.'

Charlie hesitated. 'Then, quite out of the blue, the family in Pakistan made contact with Mansur, seeking an arranged marriage for a cousin, with Jansher. Mansur had initially been against it, but relented when he heard she was bright, lively and a real beauty. The eldest son of the head of the family – the heir apparent – had fallen for her, but his parents wanted their son to marry the daughter of a wealthy merchant. Mansur was told by the head of the family that he would be doing them a large favour and that the marriage would right the wrongs of the past. Mansur agreed, but on one condition: your mother, Ameena, would have to come to stay for a couple of months as a guest and your father was not to know about the suggestion of an arranged marriage. Your parents enjoyed each other's company and it didn't take long for their love to flourish. They got married seven months later in a small ceremony.'

'I was so pleased when Mansur wrote saying they had you and then your sister,' said Charlie. 'I was given a new lease of life when you arrived at Haileybury. I was sad that I saw very little of your sister, but at least I managed to slip into a back seat and see her graduation ceremony.'

Charlie paused and looked at Rafi. 'I was devastated to hear of the deaths of Jansher and Ameena in that dreadful car crash.'

'Thank you. Could you tell me about my family in Pakistan?' asked Rafi.

'Your cousins are very powerful people. Their fiefdom stretches over an area of thousands of square miles. Perhaps you should pay them a visit one day,' suggested Charlie.

It was approaching 8 o'clock.

'We should be going,' said Rafi, 'it's getting late and tomorrow we have an early start.'

'Don't you want to stay for a quick bite of supper?' said Charlie hopefully.

Rafi was about to decline the offer when Kate interjected, 'That sounds like a nice idea.'

The conversation switched to Kate, her family reunion and her teaming up with Rafi to track down the terrorists.

Rafi talked about Saara and he promised to visit with her. After lengthy and fond goodbyes, they finally left at 10 o'clock.

The journey back into London was slow but straightforward and they arrived at the packed hotel just after midnight.

Rafi opened the door to their room and found a white envelope lying on the carpet. It contained two messages: one from Kate's boss and one from Saara.

Kate picked up the phone and spoke to David. It was a short call. 'We'll be picked up from the front of the hotel at 8 a.m. He wants me at work early.'

She passed the phone to Rafi who dialled his sister's number. There was a delay before the phone was answered. He guessed he'd woken her up.

They chatted briefly and she updated him on the meetings she and Aidan's economics team had had with the Chancellor of the Exchequer and representatives of the Bank of England.

'They're playing their cards very close to their chests. Heaven only knows what the Chancellor is going to do and say tomorrow. At least it's a bank holiday and the markets will have to wait until Tuesday morning to digest things,' said Saara. 'I'm going back to Birmingham tomorrow evening. I've missed a couple of deadlines and don't want to let my colleagues down . . . And I'm missing Steve.'

'How are you getting home?'

'Coach of course,' came the reply. 'I got the ticket booked for me earlier today by a helpful man at Number 11. I can't wait to get back to normality. Let's talk soon when things are calmer. Please give my love and a hug to Kate. Tell her Steve and I look forward to seeing you both in Birmingham. Bye.' He put the phone down. He felt guilty, as he had not told Saara about their grandfather. He wanted to tell her face to face, but was it fair to keep the news from her?

Rafi turned around to see where Kate had got to. She'd gone into the bedroom. He switched off the lights in the sitting room and went to join her. The bedroom lights were on, but Kate was in bed, fast asleep. Moments later he slipped into bed and turned off the light. He lay there thinking back over the day. Unexpectedly, it had been a very good day.

Part 7

A fter a good night's sleep and a quick breakfast, Kate and Rafi were at their desks in Wood Street by 8.15 a.m. on Monday.

Soon, though, Rafi found himself alone as Kate had disappeared to work with John and the rest of the team downstairs.

The office felt strange without the pent-up tension of the previous week. Rafi tidied his desk and then browsed the Internet to see how the main overseas markets were trading. He looked at Bloomberg's news page first. There, at the top of the 'Breaking News', was a headline than made him smile: 'International markets closed – in respect for all those who lost their lives in London'. Rafi clicked on the link to read the story. It explained how the chairmen of the major international banks operating in London had got together and asked their home stock and derivatives exchanges not to open for the day as a mark of respect, and the idea had snowballed. Rafi smiled; the Chancellor had arranged things in a very appropriate manner.

After forty minutes he'd run out of things to do so decided to see how things were progressing in the Ops Room. There Rafi was greeted as one of the team – basically no one took much notice of him! He looked at the screens and listened to the discussions going on.

Puddle Jumper had arrived at Safi in the early hours of the morning with its crew of six and they had cleared customs. *Golden Sundancer* and the sheikh's plane were some five hours away.

The atmosphere ratcheted up a notch as Giles and David walked in, accompanied by Len Thunhurst, the Commissioner of the Metropolitan Police, John, Kate and the rest of their teams.

Rafi noticed that video links had been established with regional police command centres. Those around him spoke of Operation 'Dry Clean' and explained it would be the largest series of coordinated arrests ever undertaken.

Giles started the video link briefing. 'The need for secrecy is absolute. Details of the arrests and the names of the intended targets won't be released until Len Thunhurst is satisfied that it's safe to do so. The terrorists' network of contacts should not be underestimated – let's not forget that two members of COBRA have been arrested. Operation "Dry Clean" will commence as soon as we receive confirmation that the ringleaders have been apprehended. There will be hell to pay if the terrorists are tipped off and give us the slip at the last moment. The capture of the terrorists is scheduled for 3.30 this afternoon, give or take a bit. Until then we must keep our actions under wraps. Len Thunhurst will be in charge of the UK arrests and I shall be overseeing the arrest of Maryam Vynckt in Luxembourg.'

Len took up the proceedings. He congratulated Giles and his team on their work and turned to Emma. 'The floor is all yours.'

Emma looked worn out. She was a little hesitant at first, but soon got into her stride. She pointed to the electronic presentation on a second screen, which was linked to the conference rooms of those listening. Emma explained, using the diagrams on the screen, the relationship between Basel's AGVC, Jameel's Prima Terra, Maryam's Gulf Trade Bank and the sheikh, who was the chief financier. She also mentioned the clandestine nominee holdings and the raft of public and private companies controlled and manipulated by the terrorist leaders. Jeremy nodded approvingly.

Emma paused to take questions and then put a new image up on the screen. This contained a very lengthy list of names and addresses linked, where available, to mugshots of the people involved. She turned to Jeremy. 'Thanks to the work of MI5, so far we've been able to trace 289 of the 323 people we're interested in. MI5 will be seeking your assistance to find the missing individuals.

'For those on our list,' she continued, 'we've adopted a colour coding of red, blue and black. The names in red are individuals who have been complicit in the recent terrorist activities and for whom we have more than sufficient evidence for a prosecution. The blues have direct connections with the recent activities, but more evidence has to be gathered before we've got a watertight case; for example, we may need to find their overseas bank account or where they've received their monies from the terrorists. The names in black are circumstantially linked: while we believe that they've been very much involved in the terrorists' plans, we need more information before we can confirm their involvement. The red names are our first priority. However, all the names are important as they'll complete the picture of what the terrorists have been planning and corroborate the case against those we're going to prosecute.'

Emma pointed to the screen. 'As soon as we have a person in custody, we'll give their name on our list a yellow background. That way we can quickly see how things are progressing.'

'Thank you, Emma,' said Len turning to the video camera, as he took over. 'Many of the people you will be arresting are sleepers. Do not feel any sympathy for them – they are all implicated. Once in custody, we need to build a complete picture and identify any loose ends we have missed. Emma and her team, with the help of MI5, John and his team, have prepared a dossier on those you'll be arresting. It will provide you with background details of what these individuals have been doing and how they've crossed the line. I do stress that each and every one of them should be treated with caution.' Len paused to let his last statement sink in.

'The resources of this terrorist operation have been likened by MI5 to those of a small- to medium-sized country. They have on their payroll some of the most dangerous mercenaries we have ever had the misfortune to deal with. Be warned: some of the people on this list may be truly nasty and please be aware that these sleepers or invisibles who would usually go unnoticed are valuable to us. The fact that we don't catch them with a smoking gun should not lessen the gravity of their involvement,' said Len.

The commissioner turned to Jack Fisher; one of John's team. Jack blushed as he stood up. His voice started as a quiet squeak. John passed him a glass of water and gave him an encouraging smile. 'Jack has spent the last couple of days, with the help of MI5, unravelling the terrorists' network of outsourcing companies working for the public sector. What he and the rest of the team have unearthed makes for unpalatable reading.'

The commissioner nodded towards Jack, who had recovered his composure. 'You'll see there is also an extensive list of companies, limited partnerships and businesses. These are controlled by the terrorists. Key individuals in these companies have been listed above. Also, their paper and electronic records will be needed so that we can identify the internal chains of command and see exactly what they have been doing.'

Len concluded matters with a stark warning. 'We have good reason to believe that several of those on the list have a direct line of contact with the terrorist leaders. Until we've got all the key leaders in custody we must under *no* circumstances – I repeat, under no circumstances – let the cat out of the bag that operation "Dry Clean" exists. Is that clearly understood?'

Fifteen minutes later, after a series of searching questions, the video links were turned off and connection was re-established with those tracking *Golden Sundancer* and the sheikh's plane, and those planning the capture of Maryam in Luxembourg.

Colonels Turner and Gray and a reduced team came back into the room, which was rapidly reverting to a mini war room. On the central screen there now was a large electronic map showing Morocco and the north-west coast of Africa.

The clock on the wall gave the time as 11.06 a.m. The PM was scheduled to stand up in front of the House of Commons in less than three hours. Even though it was a bank holiday, these were exceptional times and the House was in emergency session.

Rafi turned his attention to the activities in Morocco. The chart showed a red blob which was making its way across the screen following a thin yellow line towards Marrakech. It was about 700 miles away. There was a second red dot 100 miles offshore following a thin yellow line along the coast towards the port of Safi. Then he spotted another red dot by Marrakech and a number of blue dots.

Kate tugged at his arm; she was also looking at the central screen. 'I reckon those red dots are the sheikh's plane, *Golden Sundancer* and Jameel. The blue ones must be the good guys. So the blue one in Safi must be showing our friends on board *Puddle Jumper*.'

Rafi pointed to the fine yellow line which stopped about fifteen miles off the coast. 'That, I presume, is where the submarine is to rendezvous with *Puddle Jumper*.'

One of the colonel's adjutants walked over to chat to Kate. 'It's all starting to come together nicely. The next few hours should be interesting! We've patched into the SBS command centre which is overseeing the operation at Safi. There's a Nimrod many miles off-shore at 40,000 feet monitoring the location of *Golden Sundancer*. She has her cloaking device on so she'll be invisible to the terrorists. She'll pick up the video pictures and radio communications from the SBS men on board *Puddle Jumper* and the SAS teams on the ground and relay them to the command centre where they'll bounce them on to us.'

The adjutant looked concerned. '*Golden Sundancer*, at her current speed, should reach Safi between 1.30 and 1.45 p.m. our time this afternoon. She's slowed down a bit; it seems she's sailing into a steep swell. The sheikh's plane is scheduled to land at Menara airport, Marrakech, at 1 o'clock. If the switch to the helicopter goes quickly it could be at Safi shortly after 2 o'clock our time. We would prefer there to be more of a gap before the helicopter arrives.'

'Are they going to be well guarded?' asked Rafi.

'The terrorists still seem blissfully unaware that we're on to them,' continued the adjutant. 'The two SAS operatives we have undercover at Marrakech Airport have reported that the helicopter is unguarded, with just the pilot waiting. The sheikh has two minders with him on board his jet. Both are big gorillas of men, but definitely not in the same league as the two Chechen mercenaries on *Golden Sundancer*. The two SAS soldiers in Safi have identified four heavies watching the harbour and if they're anything like the Chechen mercenaries, the SAS will have a proper skirmish on their hands. Thankfully, the industrial part of the port is relatively deserted. In contrast, the nearby fishing boat quays are a hive of activity. From the location of the four thugs, we believe that the helicopter plans to land on the quay in the industrial part of the harbour, about 50–100 metres from where *Golden Sundancer* is likely to berth. As good fortune would have it, our friends on board *Puddle Jumper* seem to be in the right place: nearby, with a good view across the harbour, but not so close as to raise any suspicions. Now that we're certain Safi is the rendezvous point, the three SAS men at Mohammedia and the three at Casablanca are, as we speak, driving down the N1 to Safi. Roads permitting, they'll be there in good time.'

'What's Jameel up to?' asked Kate.

'He finished a round of golf half an hour ago and is currently in the hotel bar. He's packed his bags and ordered a taxi to the airport ten minutes ago. He's the proud possessor of a couple of tracking devices: one in his shoe, which he left unattended whilst playing golf, and another in his hand luggage!'

On board *Puddle Jumper* the atmosphere was calm and relaxed. The retired commander and his wife were sitting on the aft deck, enjoying mugs of tea. They were joined by a scantily clad Lieutenant Anna Gregson, with a colourful caftan wrapped around her waist. She was followed by a similarly dressed Lieutenant Janet Steiner.

'Been enjoying the sun?' enquired their "mother".

'It's fantastic up on the foredeck,' replied Anna.

'Any idea where your "boyfriend" Clive is?' the commander asked.

'Yes; he and Jim have gone on a bimble – said they had to see a man about a dog,' replied Janet.

The commander nodded. 'We've got about two and a half hours before we will have company, according to our friends.'

'In which case,' said Janet, 'time for a bit more sun on the foredeck.'

'Remember the sunscreen,' said their "mother" tossing a bottle of lotion in Anna's direction.

'Thanks "mum"!'

As the two women left for the bow of the boat, Jim and Clive climbed back on board and walked over to chat to the commander.

'That was quick; I thought you were chatting to your SAS friends?'

'We were and we've sorted out what equipment we have between us. They're rather well tooled-up. As long as a small army doesn't arrive, they should give us more than enough cover.'

'What do they make of the four minders guarding the helicopter landing area?' asked the commander.

'Piece of piss!' said Clive. 'The way they handle themselves and their guns, they're no more than local hoodlums. All they do is smoke cigarettes; none of them has even done a recce, which is good news.'

'It's the two Chechens on board *Golden Sundancer* that we have to be careful of,' said Jim. 'Oh, by the way, we reckon that *Golden Sundancer* will moor up 100 metres across from where we are.'

I n the Ops Room, Rafi turned his attention to the flat screen TV. He watched the commentary preceding the PM's speech in the House of Commons, where a political correspondent was standing inside the Houses of Parliament with a senior opposition MP on either side of her.

'Gentlemen,' asked the interviewer, 'what do you believe the chances are of the Prime Minister surviving this afternoon, and there not being a call for a vote of no confidence?'

'My party will want to find out why things have gone so badly wrong and will wish to see those who have let this country down take responsibility for their negligence,' replied the first MP.

The interviewer turned to the second politician. 'It's going to be very difficult for the PM and his Chancellor to put a lid on the financial fallout from Stratford, isn't it?'

'Undoubtedly. It's going to cost the country tens if not hundreds of billions of pounds. This could sink our economy, our currency and scare the living daylights out of the markets. The last thing we need is political uncertainty. I hope that the PM will find a way of getting the opposition parties involved with the process of getting the country out of this mess.'

The interviewer looked at the first MP. 'If there's a call for a vote of no confidence, what will the implications be?'

'The Government has a tiny majority and will seek to tough things out. It's more likely that pigs will fly than a recently elected Government to give up its reins on power.'

'Thank you, gentlemen, and with that we return to the studio,' concluded the political correspondent.

T he special forces command centre and the Air Chief Marshal were in discussion with Clive and Jim. As things currently stood, the helicopter would land in Safi only minutes after *Golden Sundancer* berthed. Jim asked whether it might to possible to get them more time to overpower those on board before the helicopter arrived.

Accordingly, at Marrakech airport, a quick-thinking and inventive SAS operative borrowed the jacket of an airport worker and walked up to the helicopter. He had a water bottle filled with oil hidden in his pocket. The bottle had a tube – commandeered from a drinks machine – tightly inserted into its top which went down his trouser leg.

The disguised SAS man sauntered over to the pilot to enquire whether the helicopter would be requiring the help of a baggage handler. He was summarily sent away. As he left, he walked towards the back of the aircraft and stopped to tie his shoelace under the tail's rotary engine. Job done. He got up and walked off. On the concrete apron behind him was a fresh puddle of oil.

The SAS man walked back to the airport buildings and found an airport security man. He explained that the helicopter he'd visited seemed to be leaking hydraulic fluid from its engine.

'It's probably nothing, but should someone look at it? We don't want it to fall out of the sky.'

The security man had shrugged his shoulders and begrudgingly gone off to tell his boss. Nothing happened for some while. It seemed that the message hadn't got through.

A relieved SAS man reported that a man dressed in overalls was on his way towards the helicopter. The conversation between the man and the helicopter pilot looked animated. The pilot eventually got out, looked at the fluid on the concrete and with a shrug of his shoulders agreed to let the man look at the engine. This entailed the engineer walking back to collect his tools and a stepladder.

There was a noticeable smile on the face of the officer in the special services command centre; the engineer was in no hurry and was slowing things up, just as required.

The sheikh's plane landed at Marrakech Airport on time. It parked away from the passenger planes, next to a group of small private aircraft not far from the helicopter. Those on board were quickly cleared through customs and immigration. The sheikh met Jameel on the tarmac and they were seen smiling in the hot sunshine, next to their two heavily-built security guards. However, on hearing the news of the delay, the sheikh hunched his shoulders and scowled.

A t Safi, *Golden Sundancer* had turned on to the final approach to the harbour. As things stood, she would now arrive comfortably ahead of the helicopter.

Jim and Clive, with assistance from the two SAS soldiers, had three groups of people to take care of: six on board *Golden Sundancer*, the four thugs on the harbour side and the five people on the helicopter – fifteen hostile people. It was the two Chechen mercenaries on board *Golden Sundancer* and the two bodyguards with the sheikh to whom they would have to pay special attention.

The command centre made it clear that the mission was to capture all the terrorists alive. Casualties, if at all possible, should be avoided, but in the last resort be limited to the bodyguards and the thugs on the dockside. The politicians wanted the terrorists unharmed.

T he Prime Minister was due to stand up in the Commons in less than fifteen minutes. The tension was rising in the packed chamber.

B ack at Safi, preparations were complete. The plan was straight-forward. When *Golden Sundancer* arrived, the two female naval officers would act as attractive distractions; meanwhile, the two SBS officers would slip on board *Golden Sundancer* via the swimming platform at the stern, neutralise those on board, then wait for the sheikh and his entourage to board the vessel and overpower them too. The SAS would take care of the four heavies on the dockside.

The commander was standing next to the radar screen on *Puddle Jumper*. 'I can see them on our radar; they're approaching the outer harbour,' he said to Jim and Clive. 'ETA: four minutes.'

Over the radio, one of the SAS soldiers confirmed that he'd got *Golden Sundancer* in his binoculars. 'The captain plus one are on the flybridge and two people are sitting on the foredeck, leaving two people below deck.'

B ig Ben struck twice. Rafi, who had been following events in Safi on the screens, switched his attention across to the TV.

The Speaker of the House called: 'Order, Order! Pray silence for the Prime Minister.'

The Prime Minister rose and moved to the dispatch box in front of him. He waited a few seconds. A hush fell over the packed House of Commons. Uncharacteristically, he took off his wristwatch and placed it face up on the dispatch box. The estimate he had been given was for the submarine to pick up of the captured terrorists at around 3.30 p.m. Maryam meanwhile would be smuggled out of Luxembourg. Only then could he reveal what had been going on. So much could go wrong. There were bound to be delays. It would therefore be something like two hours before he and his Chancellor could announce the full story.

There was a sense of anticipation in the air. The future of the Government lay in his hands. The next couple of hours would be crucial.

'I come before the House with a heavy heart. The Stratford disaster will haunt us for years to come.' The PM's demeanour mirrored his words.

'My Government and I wish to pay our humble respects to all those who have suffered from this disaster and to all those who will suffer from radiation poisoning in the future. I am mindful of all those who have lost everything. The efforts of the police, the armed services, doctors, nurses and emergency services deserve our thanks and praise. I pay tribute to all those who have played a role in the rehousing of those who lost their homes. In recognition of the deeds and acts of friendship, in future, the second Monday in February will be a public holiday. It will be a day to remember all those who suffered and a day to reflect. I hope Stratford Day will become a day of community and good deeds.'

One could have heard a pin drop.

'The financial implications of the disaster will be explained by the Chancellor of the Exchequer shortly. He will set out what the Government will be doing to help those who have been caught up in this heinous and barbaric attack.'

The PM paused. 'The trials and tribulations that now face our country are greater than at any time since the end of the last World War. It is imperative that unity and common purpose prevail.'

303

R afi listened to the PM give an update on the tragedy, which included details on the dead, the dying, the dispossessed, the army's progress in guarding and clearing the exclusion zone, its size and the problems they had overcome to stop radioactive materials polluting the water table and travelling down the River Lee.

The PM moved on to his policy initiatives. 'The General Election, which was held less than three months ago, produced a finely balanced result. The number of votes cast for the two main parties was almost identical and the vote for the Liberal Democrats gave them a creditable third place. 95% of the votes cast at the election were for the three main parties. The manifestos on which the election was fought were as similar as the political pundits could remember; indeed some called for a hung Parliament to bring in the dynamism and skills of the opposition parties.'

He paused to collect his thoughts. 'The recent exploits of a few of my former ministers have highlighted the misguided and muddled thought processes of political apparatchiks. Their goal was to ingratiate themselves with the news gatherers and the media rather than to focus on doing their jobs well. For this I am deeply sorry. We were elected to run the country on behalf of the people and not to look good and score points as if we were on a TV game show. Last week, presidential style, single-party politics were the order of the day. As of Friday morning this all changed. It is our duty to pull together, work in harmony and deal with the aftermath of this tragedy. Therefore, this afternoon, my Chancellor and I shall be setting out my Government's proposals which are designed to take us forward, with one voice.'

The PM glanced across at the opposition benches as he spoke. 'Until such time as the country has recovered and its economy is prosperous again, I will be forming a Coalition Government and a new collective Cabinet drawn from across the political spectrum of this House. The Cabinet's composition will be along the lines of Parliamentary committees. This morning I had an audience with the Queen and I also met with the leaders of Her Majesty's two main opposition parties. We have agreed to identify a range of topics which will henceforth be outside the Punch & Judy nature of politics, which will become a matter for consensus between the leading political parties. This will enable us to deliver long-term strategies and not quick fixes. The country will require this, if it is to fully recover its dynamism.'

The PM had the complete attention of those listening to him.

'A State of Emergency will continue until such time as the after-effects of Stratford have diminished. Lest those of you sitting on the back benches or in the Upper Chamber feel left out, Parliament will have a major role to play in scrutinising the legislation that will be put forward by the Coalition Government – a National Government. Transparency and genuine debate will be key elements of this process.'

The PM hesitated and looked across to the Speaker of the House. 'This Government recognises that responsibility has to be taken for the disaster. The air has to be cleared to forestall any accusations that there might be in this House. I have accepted the resignations from the Home Secretary, a minister and two junior ministers in the Home Office. I will talk about their replacements shortly.'

The PM continued resolutely. 'I have also accepted resignations from all those public servants in charge of nuclear safety matters and the board members of the company responsible for running the nuclear freight trains. My Cabinet has arranged for senior executives from leading energy and industrial companies to be seconded to take their places in the short to medium term. I am pleased to report to the House that a distinguished former leader of an opposition party has agreed to work with the new Home Secretary, as the Home Office minister with responsibility for Homeland Security. He has put on hold all his private business activities and speaking engagements. Some might say that the Home Office is a poisoned chalice; others might view it as an opportunity to do something good for the country. I am pleased that the former party leader takes the latter view.'

The PM paused and took a sip of water, looked at his watch, and continued. 'I shall be announcing the details of my Cabinet reshuffle over the next twenty-four hours; this will include the name of the new Home Secretary and the other key ministers of State. I have not asked them yet, as many of them sit on the benches opposite me and today their role is to hold this Government to account. In picking the new members of the Cabinet, I have borne in mind that there is no substitute for real world experience. The pendulum has swung too far. Too many members of the Government have little or no experience outside the political arena. This is unhealthy and undesirable.'

The camera swung around the House. The brooding menace which had been in the air over the opposition benches had lessened. The inclusive proposals had taken those in the Chamber by surprise – so far so good.

G olden Sundancer had her fenders out on her port side. With a delicate touch, she was brought alongside the harbour wall about eighty metres across from Puddle Jumper. The captain and

Basel were on the flybridge. The muscular frame of Dakka Dudayev, the Stratford terrorist, could be seen standing at the stern. The slight figure of Kim Chindriani, one of the recruiters of the bombers, was at the bow. They threw lines to the two heavies waiting at the edge of the harbour wall. The ropes were passed round heavy metal bollards and back on board. Bow and stern springs were attached and a gangway was put in place.

'That leaves Sergy Kowshaya, the Chechen terrorist, and Alistair Hartnell, Basel's number two, below deck,' said the SAS soldier over the radio from the shadows on the harbour side. 'What are the odds that they're suffering from seasickness?'

As if on cue, two very dishevelled and grey-looking men stumbled on deck and walked shakily up the gangway to dry land, both dropping to their knees and kissing the ground.

'Excellent, excellent,' said a voice from the command centre. 'Kowshaya definitely looks below par.'

Meanwhile, the retired commander, his wife and two "daughters" had come out on to the foredeck of *Puddle Jumper* to watch the arrival of their neighbour. Janet waved to the man standing on the harbour side by the bow of *Golden Sundancer*. Unnoticed, Clive and Jim slipped over the stern in their grey, lightweight wetsuits, their sleek air tanks strapped to their backs.

The command centre had briefed the two SBS men. 'We've identified a blind spot, three to four metres from the stern of *Golden Sundancer* at her waterline, on her starboard side. Suggest you wait there.'

The two men slid out of sight below the water, hugged the harbour wall and quietly surfaced at the specified blind spot. They shed their air tanks and flippers, and waited for the signal that the coast was clear and it was safe to climb on board via the swimming platform.

The two minders who had helped *Golden Sundancer* berth walked to where the helicopter was expected and started chatting to their colleagues.

The command centre received confirmation from the two SAS men onshore that they were in place to take out all four heavies, if required.

The Prime Minister was now thirty minutes into his speech. He was talking about nuclear power and the importance of the UK being self-sufficient in energy terms. 'The security of our energy supplies is crucial. In a modern society, energy is a cornerstone on which the foundations of a civilised way of life are built. We have suffered the devastating impact of a nuclear disaster. Maintaining the status quo is no longer an option. In the last Parliament a decision was taken which seemed to be the simplest and most convenient zero carbon option.' He paused and looked around the House. 'The go-ahead was given for £50 billion to be spent on a new generation of nuclear power stations for the 2020s. This, in hindsight, was ill-conceived and a monumental miscalculation. Nuclear power has an infinitesimal probability of things going wrong, but when they do, the hazards are so extreme that they dwarf the benefits. The debate should have been focused on how self-sufficiency can be achieved without nuclear power.

'With this in mind, a Ministry for Energy and Scarce Resources will be created. It will be tasked with moving forward energy savings, the development of sustainable and efficient renewable energy technology and the efficient use of this country's energy resources. It will work with the Treasury and provide the stimuli required to make us use our existing natural resources wisely. The Treasury's role will be central to our move to energy self-sufficiency and nuclear-free electricity generation. Accordingly, I have commissioned a report from a panel of experts on how Britain can deal with the impending 50% energy shortfall. Their detailed findings will be published the day after tomorrow, after having been discussed with my new Cabinet, and we shall place our proposals before Parliament at the earliest opportunity.'

The PM paused, looked down at his watch and continued. 'In particular, the panel is considering clean coal technology and carbon capture and sequestration techniques. The Victorians recognised the importance of sanitation and built a network of sewers to counter the threats of disease. We now recognise the threat of global warming. With this in mind the panel is looking at the benefits of building a network of pipelines to collect carbon dioxide from the largest carbon polluters so that it can be stored cost-effectively underground.' He rearranged his papers, looked at his watch again and continued. 'Coal is an energy source steeped in political connotations. It transformed our country's economy during the Industrial Revolution and it is a valuable resource which we have prematurely discarded. The country has a couple of hundred years of retrievable reserves and, unlike oil and gas where exporters act like a cartel, with coal there is a free market with over 100 countries exporting it. Clean coal will play an integral part in our future and our ability to become energy self-sufficient and environmentally responsible.'

A movement on the main screen caught Rafi's eye and his attention shifted. The Air Chief Marshal was speaking to the SBS command centre.

News had just come in from the six SAS soldiers travelling to Safi. Two trucks had collided on the bridge at Azemmour, blocking the road to all traffic. Unexpectedly they were facing a slow 45 km detour via the next bridge upriver at Maachou and were likely to miss the party. Colonel Gray was not pleased.

The PM had moved on to a new topic. 'On the Homeland Security front, we must of course make sure that coordinated attacks as suffered on Friday never happen again. Over the past few years the security associated with airport travel has been tightened up. However, the security associated with our land borders has been shown to be unfit for purpose. Our immigration rules and methods of identifying who is legitimately in this country and who is here illegally are too lax and seriously wanting. I am not a believer in identity cards or in Orwellian Big Brother-style interference in people's lives. However, the system must be improved.'

The PM glanced across to the opposition benches. 'I will ask the new Home Office minister in charge of Homeland Security to draw up proposals which will provide transparency as to who is in our country. Biometrics will be used for the unique identification of individuals. The software, I am advised, is available to facilitate this. I repeat: this is *not* the thin end of the wedge for the full-scale issuance of identity cards. One secure biometric database will be created and it will be used to confirm a person's identity. Name, date of birth, contact address, photograph, fingerprints, iris scan and such other biometric data as appropriate will be stored on the database. Biometric information will be gathered at police stations and specialist Homeland Security offices free of charge. Visitors to the UK will be required to provide biometric data at their point of entry.'

The PM paused. 'This database will be available online for a restricted number of users, so that they can confirm a person's identity. However, these users will only be able to confirm that the individual is who they say they are by checking their biometric details online. We have become accustomed to having our PIN number checked when we withdraw cash – this will be a broadly similar process. No part, I repeat, *no part* of the database will be available for downloading. In the future, an individual's biometric information will be checked as part of the process of obtaining a passport or driving licence and verification will be real time, online at an official office. Furthermore, as from 1 September, all new car insurance policies will require named drivers – each of whose identity will need to be verified against the biometric database.'

'Over a relatively short period of time, users of public services such as, for example, the National Health Service, social and local authority services, tax offices and the Electoral Register will be required to be on the biometric database. However, I stress that each database will remain separate. It is *fundamental* that they do. The State does not wish to invade people's privacy, but it does need to know the names of the people in our country, have a point of contact for them and the basis on which they are here. It is currently not possible for the Home Office to give an accurate estimate of the people in the UK. *Too* many people are off the radar screen. The numbers run into hundreds of thousands. This is totally unacceptable. Those who are here illegally or without the appropriate documentation will be identified. There will be duplicates and anomalies, and these will be investigated by the authorities.'

The PM paused to let what he had just said sink in. The Chamber remained quiet. 'The introduction of this biometric database cannot be done overnight. It will be brought on board incrementally and rigorously. At one end of the spectrum we live in a free country which values civil liberties; at the other, there needs to be a way in which we can identify those amongst us who have no right to be here. With this in mind, a new arm of the judiciary – Homeland Courts – independent of the Government will be created. Homeland Courts will preside over disputes. For example, issues relating to whether individuals have the right to be here – how to deal with those in possession of no or falsified documents and those who have aided and abetted the latter. These Courts and their judges will preside over requests by the police and security services for information held on the biometric database. Explicit approval of a Homeland Court judge will be required before such information can be released.'

The PM shot a glance at his watch. 'Too many people have created multiple identities and, currently, are able to get away with it. In future they will have to decide which *one* they will use, or they will be caught out. In the few instances where people have identical names and dates of birth, they will be asked to provide an additional forename or given name to differentiate them. Furthermore, the Homeland Courts will preside over issues relating to privacy, bugging and the scope of the Information Commissioner and the Data Protection Agency. These courts will champion the freedom of the individual, whilst being mindful of the threats posed by criminals.'

The PM's voice gained a steely note. 'We shall *never* give in to terrorism; however, we *have* to accept the painful truth that our trusting attitude has enabled terrorists to prosper unchallenged in our society.'

O nce again Rafi's attention shifted to the action on the big screen and he stopped following the events in the House of Commons in order to focus on Safi.

Dakka Dudayev had left *Golden Sundancer* and was enjoying a cigarette on the quayside. Janet and Anna waved at him and his brief acknowledgement was taken by them as an invitation to approach him. They hopped off *Puddle Jumper* and, in a carefree manner, walked around the harbour towards Dakka, with their caftans flowing in the wind. The material was bunched up and tied around their waists, thus obscuring the small pistols that were tucked into their bikini bottoms. Under their hair, out of sight, were miniature headphones, and tiny microphones were hidden in their bikini tops.

Janet approached Dakka as if he was the first red-blooded male she'd seen for a long while. Anna stood nearby, looking on shyly. The two women giggled like teenage girls. They looked beautiful, flirty and helpless.

A t the airport, the sheikh was beginning to get annoyed by the delay. He pulled out a wad of banknotes and gave them to one of his bodyguards, with instructions to hurry the mechanic up. Minutes later, as if by magic, the mechanic reappeared carrying an aluminium stepladder on his shoulder and a large toolbox. He set up his ladder and climbed up to the rotary engine, then removed a side panel and looked in. He stood there for a minute, seemingly tinkering around. He closed the panel, gave the pilot the thumbs up and walked slowly back to the buildings.

The helicopter was ready to get on its way to Safi. The thirty-minute delay was all that had been needed.

O n *Golden Sundancer*, the captain and Basel were still on the flybridge, while Dakka was on the quayside. This left the three remaining individuals below deck. It would soon be time for Clive and Jim to make their move.

Over the radio came the voice of the SAS man. 'The captain is calling up the harbour master about refuelling. There's no reply. He's sending Sergy to investigate.'

Sergy walked up the gangway, stopped, spoke briefly with Dakka and walked off hesitantly down the harbour side. As he passed *Puddle Jumper*, he received a friendly 'Good afternoon' from the commander's wife who was sitting in the sun on the aft deck.

Sergy was about to discover the problem. The harbour master was lying unconscious at his desk – he had had a visit from the second SAS soldier who had also bugged the room and placed a small gismo looking like a Coke can in the rubbish bin. It was a radio-controlled device containing some of the strongest knockout gas known.

R afi's attention switched back to the TV. The PM was in his stride. His sound bites were excellent.

'After Stratford, nuclear weapons have become an irrelevance for this country. Worldwide, people are now aware of what a few kilograms of radiotoxins can do in a built-up area. The additional destructive power of a nuclear bomb has become superfluous. As a country we have many tonnes of plutonium and radioactive fission by-products. We also have proven delivery mechanisms that give us the wherewithal to explode a "dirty" missile anywhere in the world. This will be a sufficient deterrent in itself and therefore Trident missiles are overkill and will no longer be required by us. And this will bring massive financial savings.'

The atmosphere in the House was starting to thaw. 'These savings will not be wasted. They will go directly to benefit the country and will be invested in our higher education system; in particular university research and development with science, the environment, engineering and linguistic departments at the forefront. Higher education has suffered from underinvestment over the past three decades, and we have seen the relative rankings of our universities on the global stage slip. Despite this, fourteen of our universities are in the top 100 in the world; twenty-five are in the top 200 and forty-three are in the top 500. These are figures we can be proud of. UK higher education is an area of international excellence. We shall build on this excellence and it will benefit our economy.'

The PM then paused and again looked at his watch. It was coming up to 14.45 – he and the Chancellor still had a lot more talking to do.

K ate nudged Rafi and pointed towards the screens.
The SAS officer watching *Golden Sundancer* had given the all-clear.

Clive and Jim slipped quietly on to the bathing platform. They peeled off their waterproof suits to reveal dry clothes underneath. Silently, they moved forward, their automatic pistols drawn. Talal and the captain were on the flybridge, chatting, whereas Sergy and Dakka were ashore. That left Chindriani and Hartnell below deck.

The SAS soldier's monitoring device pinpointed the location of the two people in the cabins. Clive and Jim crept silently through the boat's main stateroom and proceeded down the stairs to the cabins. They were directed towards the two men on their bunks.

Forty-five nail-biting seconds later Jim's voice came over the speaker: 'Both men are inoperative. They are gagged and tied up. Please advise when we should expect our next customer.'

Two terrorists down, six more terrorists and six bodyguards to go, Rafi thought to himself.

A long the quay, Sergy arrived at the harbour master's office. He quietly approached the shabby front door, which was closed. His hand was tucked under his loosely fitting shirt. Forty metres away, the concealed SAS man noted that he was undoubtedly armed. Sergy looked around before he pushed the door open and entered the tired-looking building. He closed it behind him. A torrent of what Rafi could only imagine were Chechen swearwords were picked up by the listening device.

Sergy was obviously far from pleased. He pulled out a small walkie-talkie. The bug picked up his conversation with the captain. 'The harbour master is pissed out of his mind; sprawled out cold across his desk with an empty bottle of Scotch in his hand. I'll sober him up and come back to the boat. Out!'

The SAS officer listening in pressed the red button on the small grey box in his hand. The knockout gas in what looked like a Coke can was released into the room. Six seconds later there was a resounding thump as the Chechen's body hit the floor.

The SAS officer moved unobtrusively from his hiding place and skirted around the back of the harbour master's office, out of the line of sight of those on *Golden Sundancer*. He slipped on a clear plastic gas mask, pulled out from his back pocket a scrunched-up flannel hat and placed it on his head. He stood there, waiting for the all-clear signal from his colleague who was observing the captain on the flybridge. As Talal turned to descend the stairs to the main deck level, the SAS man casually walked around to the front of the harbour master's office, quietly slipping inside.

A minute later Sergy was trussed up like a Christmas turkey, as was the harbour master, just in case either woke up, which, given the circumstances, was highly improbable. Both men would be out for at least two hours; far longer if either of them suffered from a weak heart or asthma.

The SAS officer radioed in that the two had been tied up and, on hearing that the coast was still clear, slipped out of the office, making sure the door was left slightly ajar to let fresh air in to disperse the knockout gas. He then walked around the back of the buildings to join his colleague watching the minders waiting for the helicopter.

As Sergy was being tied up in the harbour master's scruffy office, the second SAS operative warned Clive and Jim of the imminent arrival of Talal below deck.

Talal was on his way to his cabin when he was ambushed. Not being trained in unarmed combat, he didn't stand a chance and didn't see what was coming. Unconscious and securely trussed up, he was left by Jim in his cabin, propped up in a chair.

Outside, on the quay, Janet and Anna were doing their best to chat up Dakka.

He was interested in them, but his training told him that there would be time later. He spotted the captain descending from the flybridge and turned to leave.

In their earpieces the two women received an order: 'Slow him down; we don't want him on board for a couple of minutes. Will advise when it's safe for him to board.'

Janet called after Dakka. 'Before you go, would you by any chance have a bottle of vodka we could borrow? Our parents are so boring; they don't like people drinking on board. Please, please; we would make it worth your while!'

Dakka stopped and gave the two attractive women an appraising look. 'Wait there and I'll see what I can find.'

Janet moved alongside him and followed him towards the gangplank.

'We need another thirty seconds – don't let him board,' came an urgent voice over the communications link. Anna broke into a run, caught up with Janet, tripped and went flying on to the concrete quayside. She let out a howl and a series of expletives. Janet bent over her friend who was spreadeagled on the ground. 'Sis, are you alright?'

'Oow, I've really hurt my knee.'

Dakka stayed where he was, watching.

Janet helped Anna to sit up. Blood was streaming down her leg from a nasty gash in her knee.

Dakka looked down at Anna and watched, then said in a matter-of-fact manner, 'I'll fetch the first aid kit.' He paused briefly and then added, 'And a bottle of vodka. Wait here.'

Moments earlier the SAS lookout had sent a warning to Jim and Clive that the captain was on his way below deck.

The captain sensed something was wrong as he was about to enter his cabin. As he turned to investigate, he was felled by a strong blow to the side of his neck.

'Bloody hell, Clive,' said Jim, 'you nearly took his head off.'

'Yep, I didn't know he was going to turn around.'

The captain was securely bound up and dragged to his cabin, where he was dumped on his bed.

Clive and Jim waited silently and out of sight at the bottom of the stairs.

Dakka went to a cupboard in the stateroom and pulled out a bottle of vodka, then turned and collected the first aid box from the stern deck. He walked up the gangplank to the two women huddled on the quayside. He handed them the bottle and the box. 'Put the box on the gangway when you've finished. I'm busy now. I'll come over and see you later for my reward.'

Meanwhile, Clive and Jim had climbed the stairs and were waiting in the stateroom. Their earpieces kept them informed of where their target was. Dakka walked down the gangplank and through the open door into the stateroom. His sixth sense told him he wasn't alone. He spun around to see Jim coming at him. Instinctively, he shifted his weight from one foot to another and let fly a lethal drop kick which caught Jim just below the shoulder, knocking him backwards. Jim started to pick himself up, but was too slow: Dakka was on him, his powerful hands locked around Jim's neck, pinning him to the floor.

There was an almighty crash. Dakka slumped unconscious across Jim's body. The remnants of a heavy glass decanter were scattered across the carpet.

Jim struggled to regain his breath, as Clive hauled the muscled man off him. Moments later, Clive had Dakka's arms tightly secured behind his back with reinforced plastic handcuffs.

'Thanks mate,' said Jim, as Clive carried on with securing the terrorist's immobilisation.

Jim got up slowly. 'For a heavy man, he sure moved quickly! I reckon the bugger has either broken my collarbone or dislocated my shoulder.'

'No good asking you for a hand in getting him down below, then?' Clive dragged Dakka across the stateroom and, with a series of loud bumps, down the stairs, and reappeared a few minutes later.

'I've put him with the captain. Right, let's have a look at you.' Jim stood in front of Clive.

'Lift you arm as high as you can. Is that all you can manage? Does it hurt here?' he asked, as he prodded his collarbone area.

'Not much.'

'Turn around and think of something nice; your girlfriend with no clothes on – got the picture?'

Jim nodded.

Clive took hold of his arm and with a quick upward motion relocated his shoulder back into place.

'Jesus!' screeched Jim, 'That was bloody painful.'

'Come on, let's see what you can do with your manky arm. Can you hold a gun?'

Jim nodded.

'You'll be useless in a fight unless the opposition has a blouse on,' commented Clive.

Rafi smiled. Six out of six accounted for on the boat. This left the four minders on the quayside and the five in the helicopter.

The helicopter was about fifteen minutes away. The communications equipment in the Nimrod picked up the mobile phone conversation between the helicopter and one of the heavies on the quayside.

The sheikh's bodyguard was saying, 'Is everything OK? I've tried to ring the captain but there's no answer.'

The heavy standing on the quayside looked across at *Golden Sundancer*. 'All quiet here. The captain has gone below; probably getting ready to meet you.'

'Good. We'll be with you in about fifteen minutes.'

Rafi made a mental calculation. The operation was running about twenty minutes behind schedule. He hoped the PM and his Chancellor had sufficient material to keep talking, then noticed that the PM was handed a folded piece of paper.

315

Colonel Gray, standing nearby in the Ops Room, had arranged for its delivery only a few minutes earlier. The note read: 'Terrorists on boat at Safi have been captured. The helicopter with sheikh and Jameel is en route to Safi and expected to land in next fifteen minutes. We estimate it will take sixty to seventy-five minutes to wrap things up.'

The Prime Minister paused to read the message – his face gave nothing away – turned and passed it across to his Chancellor, who read it, smiled and tapped the pile of files in his lap. The PM took a deep breath and carried on. He was a professional, carrying on as if his prolonged speech was the most natural thing in the world.

'The role of our armed forces has to be reconsidered. Our military forces must be properly equipped to defend us against terrorist attacks. We have to change our strategy and start fighting not with brute force but with minds and souls. Post-Iraq we have surrendered the moral high ground. Our international image is tarnished. We must rebuild the trust in ourselves and our country.'

The PM was in flowing form. 'It is time to restore our sense of fair play and equity. Warfare has changed. Warfare is moving from the macro level and large theatres of war, to the micro level and local operations. We need to refocus our military prowess and twin our military might with our anti-terrorist expertise. Stratford has been the wake-up call to end all wake-up calls. We have to be able to counter terrorist attacks on our own soil and have the wherewithal to deal with major calamities should they ever arise again. We must have personnel and equipment fit for purpose; I have asked the head of the armed forces and the Defence Minister to prepare a briefing note to this end for Cabinet. Part of their brief will be to consider the valuable role that the Territorial Army and former military personnel can play. In particular, they will look at the specialist skills they can offer, and will advise on how they might be appropriately rewarded for their part-time commitment to our military activities.'

Anna's knee was patched up by Janet. The two women slowly walked back to *Puddle Jumper* clutching the first aid box and the bottle of vodka. They had been informed via their earpieces that Dakka had been overpowered.

Anna smiled; the gash to her knee had been worthwhile.

On board *Puddle Jumper*, Anna was given a hot cup of tea by the commander's wife. The commander was deep in thought, looking over the charts in front of him.

'What are you looking at?' asked Janet.

'I reckon it's always a good idea to know exactly where everything is, just in case things turn interesting and one has to leave in a hurry,' came the reply.

The sound of an approaching helicopter caught their attention and that of the four heavies.

Across on *Golden Sundancer*, a mobile phone started ringing in the cabin where Basel had been stowed. Clive opened the door and pulled the phone out of Basel's trouser pocket.

It was Jameel. 'Baz, Jamie here; we'll be landing in a couple of minutes. The sheikh is most pleased and wants to congratulate you personally. He says he's looking forward to the London markets reopening tomorrow. He says after tomorrow he'll have jumped up the world's rich list by umpteen places. His positions in Frankfurt and Chicago should also show fantastic profits; he's going to close the lot tomorrow and send the markets spiralling down. We're all going to be so bloody rich it'll be difficult to count the noughts! Baz, are you there?' Jameel heard the sound of a loo flushing and a muffled voice.

Clive hung up and smiled.

The helicopter hovered over the area next to where the minders were standing, preparing to land.

Clive and Jim rummaged around in the captain's and Basel's cupboards. Jim found a panama hat and gaudy striped shirt. He slowly took off his top and replaced it with the loud shirt, put the hat on his head and walked up to the stateroom to join Clive, who was wearing the captain's hat and a tight-fitting white jacket.

They pulled up two chairs and positioned them partially facing away from the open door, yet visible from where the helicopter was landing. They could be seen, from the quayside, enjoying a drink. It was as though the captain and Basel were casually waiting for their guests to arrive.

The two SAS men, who had been patiently watching the two of the four heavies standing in the shadows, spoke quietly to each other.

'I can see my targets, but can't get near them,' said one SAS soldier.

'Not much cover to help me either,' said the other.

A crisp voice from the command centre cut in. 'If necessary take them out and move on – and provide backup for Jim and Clive. Remember it's the sheikh and Jameel we want unharmed. If the others get in the way, so be it. Got that?'

Under the noise of the helicopter landing, the quiet pops of the silenced guns were inaudible. The two heavies who had moved back to the nearby buildings slumped to the ground with bullet holes to the chest and forehead.

Rafi winced, but told himself that the stakes were too high for niceties. It all felt a bit unreal.

The two SAS officers shifted their location to get a better line of sight of the two remaining minders, the helicopter and the walk across to *Golden Sundancer*.

If they smelled a rat and tried to take off, the pilot would be their next target. They stayed hidden.

The rotors were still whirring when the two remaining heavies, with their heads held low, ran forward and opened the side doors. The two bodyguards were the first to step out; they were closely followed by Jameel and the sheikh. The group started walking towards *Golden Sundancer*. Jameel and the sheikh were at ease, smiling and talking to each other. They didn't notice anything untoward, until it was far, far too late.

Jim, with the brim of his panama hat pulled down at a jaunty angle and his bright shirt catching the light, waved energetically to Jameel, raised his glass in the air and returned to his conversation with the 'captain'.

Anna and Janet stepped off *Puddle Jumper* and made their way back towards *Golden Sundancer* with the first aid box. They arrived at *Golden Sundancer* just before the group from the helicopter. Their flimsy flowing kaftans caught the eye of Jameel.

The sheikh and the two bodyguards headed towards the gangway.

One of the minders meanwhile turned to check where his colleagues were and, seeing them lying on the ground, let out a loud warning shout.

The sheikh's bodyguards turned with their guns raised to see what the commotion was.

Over the radio came the command from the closest SAS soldier: 'They've gone hostile. Take them out.'

There was a spluttering of the silenced guns. The sheikh's two bodyguards fell on the spot. Only seconds later, the two remaining heavies slumped to the ground. The helicopter pilot, sensing danger, fired up his engine, but wasn't fast enough. The closest SAS soldier broke cover, sprinted across and with his gun pointing through the window, beckoned the pilot to turn the engine off. The sound from the rotor blades faded.

The sheikh lunged forward to grab his bodyguard's gun, which was lying nearby on the ground.

'I wouldn't do that if I was you,' said Clive, who was standing at the bottom of the gangway, his gun trained on the sheikh. 'Move once and you lose your manhood; move twice and you lose your mobility!' The sheikh froze. Clive slowly walked down the gangway towards him.

'What do you want?' he growled.

'Maryam sends her best wishes. She's set you up; her freedom for yours. She has all your account details and, with you behind bars, she gets everything,' he said, enjoying the wind-up.

'The devious little bitch,' spat out the sheikh.

Clive swung him round and tightly secured his hands behind his back with plastic handcuffs. He spoke to the command centre. 'The sheikh has been apprehended.'

Anna, meanwhile, had been standing less than three metres from Jameel when the SAS opened fire. Jameel stood there, transfixed, watching as those around him fell to the ground. He returned his gaze to the beautiful woman standing near him. There, in the palm of her hand was a small shiny revolver.

'Don't move,' she ordered. 'At this range I can choose whether I hit you in the heart or perhaps the eye. Either way, if you move you're dead.'

Jameel stood still. 'Who are you?' he said.

'Silence – or you leave here in a box.'

'What's going on?'

'Silence!' ordered Janet. 'You'll get explanations in good time.'

Jim walked over to Anna. 'Need a hand?' he enquired.

He didn't wait for an answer. He swivelled Jameel around and with a firm grip secured his hands behind his back with a pair of handcuffs, and then proceeded to frisk him. 'He isn't armed; he's all yours.'

'Thanks,' said Anna, 'why do you boys get all the fun?'

Jameel looked from Anna to Jim. 'Who are you?'

'Friends of Maryam,' came Jim's reply.

At that moment, an urgent message came through to the command centre from the Nimrod. 'Moroccan air traffic control has picked up a distress message from the helicopter pilot.'

They played it back. 'Sheikh Tufayl, a worthy friend of Mohammed, has been kidnapped by hijackers at Safi docks. The hijackers have a large motor vessel and are set to escape out to sea. There has been shooting and killings; we are all in grave danger.'

The pilot had started to repeat his message, facing away from the

SAS man, when he heard the thump of the butt of his gun against the window. When he turned and looked down the barrel of his gun he stopped talking.

'Moroccan air traffic control has informed the police and the Royal Moroccan Air Force,' came the message from the Nimrod.

'Time to get out,' ordered the command centre. 'We suggest you take *Golden Sundancer*. Get out of there quick. You probably have less than five minutes before the local police arrive and less than half an hour before fighter planes come to have a look.'

Clive shouted to the SAS officer. 'We have to get Sergy. I left him trussed up in a cupboard in the harbour master's office.'

The two men left for the office at a sprint.

The command centre was speaking to the commander on *Puddle Jumper*. 'There isn't time to transfer the prisoners to your vessel. Take *Golden Sundancer*; check she has enough fuel and prepare her for immediate departure. Suggest you take your local charts with you and leave now.'

Meanwhile, Jim, Anna and Janet had frogmarched the sheikh and Jameel on board. They were taken below, tied up and left in a cabin.

The commander grabbed his charts and a few personal belongings and called across to his wife to gather up all she needed quickly. They ran as fast as they could in the direction of *Golden Sundancer*.

The PM was winding down his speech. 'I have set the scene for the next phase of British politics. It will be consensus politics. The three largest political parties speak for 95% of those who voted in the recent general election and their representatives in the Cabinet will have much work to do.' He paused as the members of the minority parties stirred with disaffection. 'However, I recognise that it would not be a good idea to leave out members of the minority parties, especially those representing the regions.'

The PM looked across to the minority parties and their representatives. 'I am aware that there are some very able people who sit in this House who are not members of one of the three main parties. Rest assured you will have a role to play. I have been heartened by the generous offers of help that have come from Scotland, Wales and Northern Ireland. As part of the Union, all parts of the UK will have responsibility in shaping our countries' future. London has been the powerhouse that has driven the UK economy for decades. Post-Stratford, it is an inevitable truth that London's economy will struggle, with nearly one-sixth of its population displaced and almost one-twentieth of its land now unfit for human habitation. Our capital must now be joined by cities across the UK in the quest to regain our competitive and prosperous economy. Regional cities must pick up the baton and push our economy forward.'

He glanced to his left towards the Speaker. 'These are exceptional times. I propose to break with tradition, if the Speaker permits, and ask the Chancellor of the Exchequer to follow me with his proposals on how to get this great Country back on its feet. After the Honourable Member has set out his proposals, I shall face any questions the Members of this House might wish to put.'

The Speaker nodded and the PM picked up his watch.

Rafi looked at the clock on the wall. If all went to plan the Chancellor would need to speak for just less than fifty minutes plus the time it took to capture Maryam. Then the news of the terrorists' capture could be made public and the round-up of those associated with the terrorists could begin.

As the PM stood aside to let the Chancellor rise and move to the dispatch box, Rafi noticed him whisper into the Chancellor's ear. The Chancellor took off his watch and placed it to one side in front of him. He had with him his notes and a small pile of different coloured wallet files, which he stacked neatly next to the dispatch box. Rafi wondered what was in them.

The polite silence continued for the Chancellor. Rafi sensed that the fireworks were being reserved for the questions after the Chancellor's speech.

The Chancellor's face was strained and unsmiling. His voice was unruffled, but sombre. 'Our economy and the Government's finances have suffered a second massive blow. Just as we thought we were coming to terms with the first shock to the system – the debilitating effects of the global credit crunch – we have been hit by a nuclear catastrophe. We face financially perilous times which will necessitate significant changes in order to steer our economy back to safe waters.'

Those in the Chamber sat in shocked silence as they waited for the gravity of the position to be fully revealed. 'I will, this afternoon, set out how the Government plans to remedy the position and I shall be introducing a range of initiatives to facilitate the rebuilding of our economy . . .'

The commander had reached *Golden Sundancer* – a big sister to *Puddle Jumper*. He bounded up on to her fly deck. 'Phew!' The ignition key was still in place.

He turned the key and pressed the ignition buttons. The turbo diesels roared into life. He ran through the checks.

He was talking to himself under his breath. 'The auxiliary fuel tanks are both empty, but the main tank is probably good for 100, maybe 150 miles. That should be more than enough. This is going to be fun.' He never dreamt that he would find such heavy duty power again. 'It's going to be like the Sabre class vessels; one hell of a way to feel young again!'

He called across to Lieutenant Anna Gregson. 'Cast off and stow the fore and aft springs – then man the bow line.'

In the direction of Lieutenant Janet Steiner he shouted, 'Prepare to stow the gangway. And Jim, man the stern line.'

The commander saw the door to the harbour master's office swing open. Clive and his SAS colleague were carrying the deadweight of the bear-like terrorist; they had an arm under each of his shoulders, leaving his feet to drag along the ground. They were doing something more than a trot, but they were still over 200 metres away. The commander did some mental arithmetic.

The two SAS soldiers had handcuffed the helicopter pilot to his joystick and as a parting gesture fired a couple of bullets into the helicopter's radio and fuel tank. For the time being at least the helicopter would be going nowhere. They then tidied up the bodies of the six bodyguards and left them sitting on the concrete with their guns on their laps.

The commander called across to the two SAS officers. 'Come and join us.' He then shouted to Jim, 'Move the stern painter to the starboard side and make certain it can run freely around the bollard on the quayside. Stand by the cleat until you receive further orders.'

'Aye, aye, sir. Runs freely,' came the reply.

'Lieutenant Gregson, check that the bow painter runs freely and prepare to cast off.'

'Runs freely, sir.'

The commander turned to his wife who was standing behind him. 'Darling, would you please find a boat hook and when I say "Cast off bow", push hard at the quayside wall and swing the bow out into the harbour?'

He turned and looked astern. 'Jim, when I call "Cast off bow", let out three metres of mooring line – no more – and hold her until I say "Cast off stern". Mind there are no knots to snag the rope and watch your fingers.'

'Aye, aye, sir.'

In the distance there was the wailing of police sirens. They were getting closer. The two special services men were making good progress carrying the unconscious terrorist. They only had a few metres to go. The commander waited patiently for them to reach the gangway. Sergy was unceremoniously dragged on board by the SAS officer and Clive.

The commander shouted, 'Stow gangway, cast off bow, let out stern line and, darling, push!' He then eased the control for the port engine forward and the starboard engine slightly into reverse. The boat, which was still secured to the quayside with a stern line to her starboard side, turned on a sixpence. At that moment he caught sight of the first police car. Moments later, the bow was facing the opposite side of the harbour and was swinging round to face out to sea.

The commander called out, 'Cast off stern!'

Jim, thinking of his fingers and the taught rope, took out his razor-sharp knife and cut the lines secured to the rear stanchion. At that moment the commander pushed forward the throttles to both engines. The vessel was like a wild stallion that had been tied down and suddenly allowed to run free. With the engines roaring, the stern dug deep into the water. The commander by now had the throttles towards their maximum revs.

The commander shouted, 'Lieutenants: stow the fenders and prepare for sea.'

The harbour water was like a millpond. *Golden Sundancer*, with the power of her two turbo engines propelling her forward, gracefully lifted her bow up out of the water and on to the plane.

The commander looked over his shoulder and saw that the first police car was 150 metres away. *Golden Sundancer* was almost up to her cruising speed. He smiled. He was enjoying the feeling of the immense power beneath his feet.

'I'll give a prize,' shouted out the commander, 'to the first man or woman who can cause a distraction on the quayside. A car's petrol tank perhaps? We want them to keep their heads down until we get out of range.'

Clive passed Anna his rifle. 'See if you can hit something.'

With the skill of a trained professional, she picked up the rifle and loosed off a shot in the direction of the nearest police car. At that moment there was a huge explosion which ripped apart the nearest harbour building, followed by a second explosion further down the quayside. The quayside was torn apart and a plume of dark smoke erupted from the tall storage tank behind the buildings. The police car screeched to a halt and the policemen dived for cover.

Clive shot a glance at the SAS soldier standing nearby and laughed. 'Bloody good shooting!' he exclaimed and gave Anna a firm pat on the back. Her bemused smile stretched from ear to ear.

Hidden from view, in the palm of the of the SAS soldier's hand, was a small radio-controlled transmitter which had set off the explosions. He grinned at Clive, 'So nice, for once, to be properly prepared for a retreat.'

The commander called down. 'See if you can hole *Puddle Jumper*'s hull. She's the next fastest vessel in the area and we don't want her coming after us.'

Anna and the two SAS soldiers trained their rifles on *Puddle Jumper*. Flecks of spray appeared along her waterline as the shots reached their target.

The commander on the flybridge had the engine throttles forward to their maximum. He looked at the rev counters. The port engine had crept into the red. He eased it back to below the red and at the same time balanced the revs on the starboard engine. *Golden Sundancer* was making forty-nine knots. She was pure poetry in motion. He cast an eye over to the chart which he had been studying carefully earlier in the day. The channel posed few pro-blems. Phase one was complete. It was time for phase two: getting out of Moroccan territorial waters, into the freedom of international waters and on to the rendezvous with the submarine twenty miles off the coast.

Jim, who had climbed up on to the flybridge, called out, 'Permission to come on to the bridge, commander,' as he climbed the last step.

The commander turned around. 'Yes. Jim, could you sort out the radio? I need to find out from command centre what the incoming Moroccan Air Force is up to. In a few minutes we'll be in open water. I need to know which direction they're approaching from.'

Jim sat down next to the radio and changed the settings.

'Here you are, commander.'

'It's all yours Jim; I've the charts to work on.' The commander called down to his wife. 'Darling, could you come up to the flybridge?' She bounced up the stairs like a young rating and he gave her some instructions: 'Right, your task is to steer a course of due west and to keep an eye on the two rev counters, the temperature and oil pressure dials. Anything untoward, please shout! We're making straight for international waters.'

The swell in the Atlantic Ocean had eased and the waves, though several metres tall, were long and well spaced out. *Golden Sundancer* was creaming through the sea; being light on fuel helped. These were the type of conditions on which she thrived. She looked and felt spectacular – like a thoroughbred. The commander's wife delicately adjusted the throttle, applying a little more power, lifting the revs to a fine whisker below the red. The roar decreased a few decibels as she eased back the throttle to a point where the pitch of the engines sounded pleasing and not laboured. They were doing a very respectable forty-eight knots.

The commander recalled that Morocco had signed up to the international convention. Their territorial waters ended twelve nautical miles from land. It was an easy calculation: fifteen minutes to freedom – then he could start to breathe a small sigh of relief.

'Jim, what's the position regarding the fighter planes, please? And also enquire about the weather – those clouds look like rain in the offing.'

The radio crackled; it was the control centre. 'Are you receiving me, commander?'

'Jim here,' came the reply.

'Tell the commander that you'll shortly have company. A Mirage F1 fighter has been scrambled from Sidi Slimane Air Base some 235 nautical miles to your north-east.'

'North-east,' repeated the commander quietly. 'Yes, I have it on the chart.'

'We'll advise when she's airborne: ETA from take-off is eleven minutes. Radio traffic suggests that the pilot is in no hurry – the control tower is telling him to pull his finger out, but the plane hasn't started taxiing to the runway as yet. And an old Northrop F-5E Tiger II has been scrambled from Meknes Airbase, 225 miles north-east of where you are – ETA from take-off is thirteen minutes. We'll advise when airborne. Radio traffic from the control tower suggests that the plane is undertaking its final checks as we speak and could be airborne shortly. To add to your problems, there's a Floréal class frigate at Casablanca. She's received orders to put to sea and has on board a Eurocopter Panther. She's 140 miles away. She'll pose no problem unless she launches her paraffin pigeon which is armed for anti-surface and submarine warfare. You've potentially three bandits to avoid. We're working on a plan.'

The commander reached over and took the microphone from Jim's hand.

'We're heading due west from Safi harbour. We will reach international waters in . . .,' he paused, looked at his watch, then continued, 'in thirteen minutes forty-five seconds. Please advise the submarine to make her rendezvous point fifteen miles due west of Safi harbour. Please advise her ETA.'

It was unheard of for a Trident class nuclear submarine to surface in open water when there were potentially hostile aircraft around – and so close to another country's territorial waters.

The commander surveyed the scene. He was having fun: *Golden Sundancer* was a joy to handle. His mind went into overdrive. He could clearly visualise in his mind's eye where he was and where the three hostiles were going to be approaching from.

The radio crackled to life. 'I've spoken to our pickup vessel; she'll be at the rendezvous point in forty-six minutes. You asked about the weather – expect some rain showers.'

The commander looked at his watch. Yes, that should give him enough time so long as neither of the fighters got their act together and took off within the next three or four minutes. It was going to be a bloody close call. He called across to Jim, 'Get me Clive and the two SAS chaps here; we need a council of war. Tell Lieutenant Steiner to see how many life rafts she can find and ask her to take them to the aft deck. And get Lieutenant Gregson to see if she can find an inflatable dinghy, an outboard, and some life jackets, and to put them on the aft deck as well.'

The commander spoke into the radio. 'Do you have any news for us?'

'Yes, as good planning would have it, they kept back one of the Harrier jump jets that flew you and your wife to Gibraltar. She's fully armed and took off two minutes ago. Her ETA is forty-one minutes.'

'Thank you,' replied the commander. The seconds were ticking by.

The longer it was before the fighters took off, the better their chances. He could pick out dark rain-laden squalls in the distance. A small smile crept across his face.

T he Chancellor was in sombre mood. He was explaining to the House the consequences of the terrorist attack at Stratford and was setting out his proposals to persuade the public and industry to make the best use of energy and to encourage the diversification of the UK's energy resources.

'I shall be announcing a range of tax incentives to encourage the production and use of efficient and renewable energy sources, and to progress carbon sink technology to enable coal-fired power stations to move to zero emissions . . .'

At this point, Rafi's attention was pulled back to the big screen and the running commentary from the command centre.

Jim had returned to the flybridge with Clive and the two SAS men.

'Right,' said the commander, 'we've got ourselves a spot of bother. Two Moroccan fighters have been scrambled to intercept us and a frigate with a Eurocopter on board is putting to sea. In the short term it's the two fighters that concern me.'

The commander pointed at a spot on the map. 'The Trident submarine will reach our rendezvous point here in forty-two minutes. The Moroccan Mirage could be there in nineteen minutes and an elderly Northrop Tiger should follow a couple of minutes later. That will leave us unprotected, with nowhere to hide, for around twenty minutes. How many life rafts do we have?'

'Two five-people rafts,' came the reply from Jim.

'Excellent, get Lieutenant Gregson to inflate them and tell her to keep them tied down! Also, find out from Lieutenant Steiner what is happening with the search for the dinghy and the outboard.'

'She's found a twelve-foot inflatable with a ten horsepower outboard,' called back Clive.

'Perfect! Get it inflated and ready for sea – and make sure that the outboard has petrol in it,' said the commander. He turned his attention to his charts. 'We'll reach international waters in five minutes. A couple of minutes later we should reach that weather front,' he said, pointing to the black clouds over the bow. 'Then we will launch the life rafts and I'll change course and head north towards the two fighter jets.'

Clive raised his eyebrows.

The commander turned to the four special forces men around him. 'Here is the plan. You've got seven minutes from now to get the terrorists into the life rafts. Jim, you and Lieutenant Gregson will remain on board with me and my wife. The rest of you will go with the terrorists in the rafts. Once the rafts are in the water, we'll put as much distance between the rafts and the fighters as possible.'

The commander looked at Jim. 'Have you got anything more in your bag of tricks?'

All the special service men nodded in unison.

'Before I jump ship, could you wire up an explosive device, for which I can set the timing?' asked the commander.

'No problem,' replied Clive.

'Plus another bomb which can be detonated from the dinghy? And can you arrange for there to be a radio so that I can talk to the fighter pilots?'

'No problem.'

'Will one of you please disable the tracking devices in both life rafts and put a radio in each?' ordered the commander.

'Consider it done,' said Jim.

'As soon as the inflatable dinghy is ready we'll launch her, abandon ship and leave *Golden Sundancer* on autopilot heading at top speed up the coast. We'll come back in the inflatable and meet up with the two life rafts. If we can buy ourselves ten minutes before the first fighter spots *Golden Sundancer* she'll put over eight miles between us and the fighters. Anything more is a bonus and will make it harder for them to find us.'

The commander's wife called out, 'Four minutes to international waters.'

The commander turned to Clive, 'Time to get a move on.'

The four special servicemen ran down the steps to the lower deck to fetch the captives, who were bundled on to the floor of the rear deck.

'The two Chechens, Chindriani, Hartnell, you and I,' said Clive pointing to the nearest SAS man, 'will go in one raft. The sheikh, Basel, Jameel, their captain, Lieutenant Steiner and the SAS major will go in the other.'

A minute and a half after they'd entered international waters, they reached the edge of the squall. The sea around them had darkened and the wind had strengthened – the telltale signs of looming heavy rain. Moments later the downpour hit them. The commander brought the vessel to a stop.

The terrorists were manhandled quickly into one life raft, then the other and, with their guards safely on board, the rafts were cast off.

The commander pushed the throttles forward and in seconds *Golden Sundancer* was back planing majestically through the water.

Meanwhile, Lieutenant Gregson had the inflatable fully functional and Jim had rigged up two incendiary bombs.

'We will leave the precise timing until we know the status of the fighter planes,' said the commander.

'Of course,' replied Jim.

The radio crackled back into life. 'The Northrop Tiger has completed its taxiing and is taking off as we speak. ETA thirteen minutes and counting.'

'Right!' shouted the commander. 'Life jackets on. I'll slow the boat down, let you get off, set the autopilot and come and join you.'

Jim looked at the commander. 'Old man, you realise that falling into the "oggin" at fifty knots will feel like hitting wet concrete?'

'Jim, get on your way and set the bomb to go off in twenty minutes. Your concern is noted,' replied the commander.

'Aye, aye, sir.'

'Throw me a life jacket and shout when you're ready to leave ship.'

Seconds later came the call, 'Ready to disembark.'

The commander eased the throttles back and she came to rest in the water. From the back of the flybridge he saw the three quickly and safely climb into the small inflatable dinghy and fire up the outboard engine. He picked up his small hand-held compass and tucked it into his trouser pocket, set the course on autopilot, pressed the throttles forward to the top of their red gauges, turned and bolted down the stairs, heading for the swimming platform.

The commander stood on the edge of the platform, watching the water churning at his feet, held his nose, knelt down and rolled slowly side first into the water. The compass in his pocket dug into his thigh as he hit the rushing water. He felt like a human skimming stone. There was darkness. The next thing he knew, he felt a strong pair of hands holding him as he gasped for breath. The inflatable dinghy was bobbing at his side in the pouring rain. Lieutenant Gregson and Jim, using his one good arm, grabbed him and dragged him on board. His wife put the small outboard into gear, turned the little dinghy and headed for the two life rafts.

Shaking from cold and shock, the commander fished inside his pocket and pulled out the small brass-encased compass. He opened it – it was still in one piece. He handed it to his wife and gave her the course to steer before flopping back down on to the wet floor of the dinghy.

The Ops Room and the command centre were on tenterhooks. The presence of the two Moroccan jets was going to make things very difficult and a major diplomatic row was the last thing the Government needed right now.

Colonel Gray sent a message to the House. The Chancellor was advised that he would have to speak for at least another forty minutes before the PM could reveal his hand.

T he Chancellor leant forward and tapped the pile of folders in front of him, sending an acknowledgement to the Ops Room. He pulled out a red folder. 'I now wish to tackle one of our "sacred cows". It's a matter which has held back our economy and resulted in a disproportionate and inefficient allocation of capital away from production. At the present rate of decline, manufacturing's share of output will soon be less than 10%.'

The silence was broken by MPs shuffling in their seats in anticipation of what was to follow.

'We live in a country where our home is our castle. Where we live is an integral part of our well-being. Those of us with above average salaries have the ability to occupy homes near to where we work and homes that are very comfortable to live in, but they are also very expensive. Too many of those who provide our public services and make our economy and our lives operate efficiently and harmoniously have been priced out of the market. They have been forced either to move long distances away from where they work or to live in substandard accommodation. Furthermore, the lack of appropriate accommodation near to where they work has prompted many individuals to leave their public sector jobs. Nurses, teachers, firemen, street sweepers, policemen and many, many more who work to make our lives better view owning a home as an impossibility; something they would love to afford in the right location, with the right amount of space, but that is financially out of their reach.'

The Chancellor looked up at the camera. 'Our love affair with housing has created exorbitant house prices and a dearth of affordable housing. These two factors are two of the – if not *the* – key factors driving social exclusion and social deprivation.' He paused for effect. 'Why should we have to live in homes which have values far exceeding their building cost? Economists maintain that it's all to do with the immovable laws of supply and demand, but I have a different perspective; one borne out of the necessity to rectify the current inequity. The current housing market solutions for those on low salaries – namely, affordable housing, equity sharing and the like – make house ownership for the less well off a very risky business. Were these shared equity schemes a stock market product, I am sure that they'd be outlawed by the Financial Services Authority as being far, far too risky for a family's largest investment.'

Rafi watched intently as the Chancellor paused and took a sip of water.

'I now turn to another fundamental problem with affordable housing and housing for our armed forces and their families. It *is* low cost. It provides *small* residential units, *not* family homes, and encourages building down to a price, which is environmentally unsound. We are racking up problems for future generations: ghettoisation and the creation of the "haves" and the "have-nots". Our housing, when energy is a scarce resource, must be built to environmentally sound standards. The further we make our key and low paid workers commute, the less environmentally sensible it is – and the less able they are to enjoy their work and their home lives. In London, too many key workers lose over two hours a day commuting, not because they want to but because they have to. For too many, between ten and fifteen hours a week are wasted. This is very poor use of people's time; it spoils people's quality of life and does not foster a contented society.'

The Chancellor moved up another gear. 'This Government will introduce a new ownership structure: *indexhold*. Indexhold is an uncomplicated structure: it simply uses the tried and tested legislation for leasehold property which will form the basis of the legal relationship between the freeholder and the indexholder.' He paused for a moment. 'Key workers and members of the armed forces will be able to purchase indexhold properties. They will be long leasehold interests at a nominal rent. The purchase price for the indexhold interest will be the gross building cost. It is the high cost of land that has pushed up property prices and driven away key workers from city centres. Indexholds will enable people to own their home but at a sensible price, will provide new housing that is environmentally up to standard and will rebalance the fairness of the position.'

Rafi was amazed; what a remarkable concept and so logical, so straightforward. It would, over time, dramatically improve the lifestyle of key workers and be tremendous for the economy – there was a need for hundreds of thousands of new homes and this would provide house builders with an environmentally-friendly product to champion. He listened intently as the Chancellor continued.

'When the owner of an indexhold interest decides to move and sells their home, they will receive their initial purchase price *plus* a sum representing the inflationary increase. The freehold will be owned by a public body or a charity and they will have the first right of purchase on a sale. They can be expected to exercise this option to purchase as the price will be significantly below the open market value. At this point, the indexhold interest will become available for sale to another key worker on another long lease.

'In practical terms, the money raised by selling indexhold interests will be used to build the right types of homes, with high environmental standards, on land owned by the state. This proposal will assist those wishing to live close to their work in our large towns and cities, but will also be extended to rural communities to enable locals who are being priced out of their villages to remain there or get back into them.'

The Chancellor let slip a small smile. 'There will be another benefit. As there is a guaranteed blue-chip purchaser of the indexhold interest, namely the freeholder, mortgage lenders will factor this into their interest rate charges. Gone will be the days when the less wealthy are penalised for having poor credit histories, low salaries or small deposits.'

Rafi realised he had been listening in awe, completely distracted from the events at Safi. Something good *would* come out of the Stratford catastrophe. The Chancellor had, in a single stroke, introduced an initiative that would, over time, improve the lives of hundreds of thousands, if not millions, of people – *and* free up capital which could be deployed in more productive areas of the economy. He listened as the Chancellor ran through an example of the significant benefits indexhold would bring to the family of a key worker with three children.

'Let us consider this family who buy a city centre indexhold flat for £125,000. They live there for ten years and then decide to sell. How much extra will they get? That will depend upon the rate of inflation. Let us say that it has averaged 2.5% per annum – so their indexhold investment will have increased in value over the ten years by £35,011. This tax-free capital gain will have been immune from the shocks and vagaries of the housing market.'

He turned over a couple of pages. 'As for single key workers, even those on modest salaries – health care assistants, for example – would be able to afford a good-sized one-bedroom indexhold flat in close proximity to where they work *and* still be left with a reasonable disposable income. At the heart of indexhold ownership is the ability to provide high quality housing, where it is needed, for those who serve the community.'

'In summary, it will significantly increase disposable incomes of key workers, provide them with a good home in the right location that is theirs *and* remove *all* worries of falling into negative equity.'

The Chancellor quickly glanced at his watch, hoping that no one noticed that he was stalling for time. 'I am conscious that initially there will be more demand than supply for these indexhold properties, as they will be far, far more affordable than freehold properties. This demand will act as a catalyst for the redevelopment of substandard city centre office buildings and of surplus property. In order to assist in the process of releasing property for indexholds, the Government, in consultation with municipal and local authorities, will create residential enterprise zones, in which the planning process for indexhold properties will be simplified and where compulsory purchase powers will be available to buy properties or land which is being under-utilised. I will be forming a cross-party task force to work on and push forward these proposals.'

Rafi was impressed – very impressed. This was a very timely and socially astute initiative. He glanced across to the clock. It had been several minutes since the commander had jumped ship. From the dots on the screen he could see that *Golden Sundancer* was making an excellent turn of speed away from the dinghy and the two life rafts.

Suddenly over the radio came the voice of a fighter pilot in heavily accented English. '*Golden Sundancer* . . . *Golden Sundancer* . . . I have you on my radar – bring your boat to a stop. I say again, bring your boat to a stop.'

In the Ops Room the Air Chief Marshal spoke to the command centre. 'We have to keep the two Moroccan fighters interested in *Golden Sundancer* and looking in the wrong place for about twenty minutes. Get the Harrier pilot to engage the two fighters in conversation and to tell them that there are British nationals amongst the hostages on board *Golden Sundancer* – and that they should shadow the motor vessel. I repeat, we've got to keep them looking in the wrong place. The dinghy and life rafts won't show up on their radar, so they will be safe until the rain clears and the planes fly directly overhead.'

The seconds passed by. The Moroccan pilot would by now have *Golden Sundancer* on visual. What would he do? He had been warned that there were hostages on board. At 48–50 knots *Golden Sundancer* could outrun anything that the Moroccan Navy possessed. A further command was heard.

'Stop or I will open fire.'

'Northrop Tiger, come in Northrop Tiger,' said the Harrier pilot. 'Be advised that there are British Nationals on board . . . *Do not engage!*'

In the rainswept dinghy, the commander leant across to Jim. 'If you hear any cannon fire, please push your little red button. The pilot will think it's all his doing.'

There was silence and a further command to 'Heave to' was heard. *Golden Sundancer* carried on regardless. In the distance there was the distinctive sound of a short burst of gunfire. No doubt the fighter pilot had aimed across the bow.

Jim pressed the little red button. Seconds later the deep boom and shockwave of the explosion reached the dinghy. He squinted through the rain, but could see nothing.

The radio fell silent.

B ack at the command centre there had been initial consternation when the pilot had opened fire and seconds later *Golden Sundancer* had literally disappeared from the Nimrod's screens.

'Sweet Jesus!' the intelligence officer standing beside the team leader was heard to say. He'd just arrived back on duty and had missed out on the recent shenanigans.

Over the speaker came the voice of the Northrop Tiger's pilot. He was calling up helicopter support.

The stern voice of the Harrier pilot meanwhile was demanding to know what the hell the Northrop Tiger pilot thought he was up to.

The Eurocopter on board the frigate *Mohammed V* had taken off to investigate. The sky was going to get busy and the nuclear submarine still had to make its pickup.

'Right,' said the chief in the command centre to the Nimrod, 'where exactly is our Harrier relative to the helicopter?'

'She'll be there in fifteen minutes and the Eurocopter will be there two minutes later.'

'Excellent.'

Meanwhile the Harrier's pilot was demanding that the two Moroccan fighters keep looking for survivors until the helicopter arrived.

I n the wet dinghy, the commander was still dazed. The swell that had hardly inconvenienced *Golden Sundancer* was making life uncomfortable for those in the little open-topped inflatable, which was barely making four knots. Slowly, the commander calculated that they would get back to the life rafts in twelve minutes and the submarine would surface just minutes later.

T he Nimrod continued to pick up the radio traffic between the Moroccan fighter pilots and their control centre. There was consternation. The pilot was describing the size of the explosion.

Jim had placed his explosive charges next to the cool box, which housed the four thermobaric Kornet missiles, which in turn weren't far from the main fuel tanks full of diesel vapour. The overall effect was impressive. One moment *Golden Sundancer* had been there, the next she'd literally disintegrated into a fireball and smoke. Her debris had vaporised. When the smoke and flames cleared there was no sign of her.

A minute later the second Moroccan jet fighter arrived to find nothing but clear ocean. The presence of the RAF Harrier fighter thirteen minutes away, bearing down on their two planes, was causing the Moroccan control centre concern.

R afi listened to the colonel who was talking to the RAF command centre. 'We have the makings of a major diplomatic incident if they piece together what's really going on under their noses. Tell the Harrier to keep talking and to get them to stay where they are . . .'

T he contents of the Chancellor's third coloured folder grabbed Rafi's attention. It was as though he'd been through the Treasury's 'good ideas box' and was bringing them out, one at a time.

The Chancellor started to outline a new corporate structure. 'The *not-for-profit corporation* will primarily be for public sector bodies.' His voice was clear and authoritative.

'The structure of a not–for-profit corporation will be similar to that of a public limited company,' he continued in a businesslike manner. 'Just like a PLC, it will have a Memorandum and Articles of Association. The difference will be that it will have *custodianholders* instead of shareholders. The custodianholders will have limited liability, as is the case in companies limited by guarantee. The custodianholders will have the same role as shareholders, in that they will be responsible for holding the management to account. Custodianholders will be drawn from the managers of the business, its employees, its funders, local organisations, locally elected politicians *and* those who receive the services. The last group, the service users, will have the *largest* number of votes, but no group will have a clear voting majority.'

The Chancellor seemed to be enjoying himself as he went on. 'The custodianholdings can be for different amounts and their limited liability will range from, say, £1 to perhaps a few hundred pounds.

The voting rights will be proportional to the level of limited liability carried. But unlike shareholdings, custodianholdings will be for finite periods of time.'

The Chancellor glanced at his watch. He took a deep breath and continued. 'Instead of having just one board of directors, the not–for–profit corporation will have two: a strategy board and a management board. The strategy board will set out the business framework and will liaise with the Treasury concerning the public money they receive and the delivery of value for money. The management board will deal with the day to day running of the corporation and it will report to the strategy board. However, where the strategy board exercises its powers over the management board, in specified areas, the approval of the custodianholders will be required.'

Rafi was hanging on his every word.

'The custodianholders will hold the strategy board to account, just as shareholders do in companies. However, the custodianholders, for their part, will be expected to bring with them a level of expertise and everyday reality. This reality will include an understanding of how businesses are run. Custodianholders will not necessarily be experts, but will be expected to be more knowledgeable than the so-called person on the "Clapham omnibus".'

'The Prime Minister has already announced that universities will have a key role to play in the advancement of our economy.' The Chancellor paused. 'I will also be giving them additional funding. This will enable them to create units with the specialist expertise that the custodianholders will require. These units will provide the support, training, research and conferences necessary to enable custodian-holders to play a valuable role and appreciate the process of efficient change management. These specialist university units will be charged with working with one another so that they will be able to draw on expertise from each other. They will not be there to tell people what to do, but rather to provide them with the understanding necessary to comprehend the problems and a set of tools to help them find efficient and workable solutions. Public services have become overcentralised. This initiative which will turn public service providers into not-for-profit corporations will make them more aware of their role, which is to benefit society and to provide value for money.'

The Chamber of the House was captivated by the Chancellor's proposals – he was surrounded by the silence of thoughtful listeners.

'I repeat, the not-for-profit corporation structure will primarily be for public sector bodies. However, it will be extended to include

336

building societies, mutual insurance companies, friendly societies, charities, cooperatives and monopoly service providers, such that they will be able to convert if they believe this structure will assist their business plan.'

The Chancellor drew a deep breath. 'I shall now turn to another area fraught with problems – outsourcing. Private companies providing outsourcing services to the public sector have two Achilles heels: the requirement for ever increasing profits *and* the fact that the link between the public body and the end users has been broken. Where it is shown to the minister responsible that these outsourced businesses are operating outside the public good, statutory powers will be put in place to enable the activity to be brought back in-house. For too long the focus has been on financial yardsticks and league tables. The minutiae have been ignored. It is often the little things that make the difference. Public sector organisations have become more interested in glossy brochures, policy statements and the big picture. Strategy has a role to play, but it is at the coalface where battles to help people and society are won and lost. This new structure will provide a framework for accountability. End users – the taxpayers – will henceforth be in a position to influence how they can get the best out of their public services.'

The Chancellor paused, looked at his watch, raised his eyes to the heavens and continued. 'Furthermore, I shall be introducing one further significant change: the accounting regimes for not-for-profit corporations will change to those used by UK public limited companies. This, at a stroke, will make the allocation of public sector resources far more efficient.' The Chancellor hesitated, made a mental calculation on how much longer he might have to speak for and opened up another folder.

'Take, for example, a brand new £10 million facility in an NHS hospital. As things stand, once it has been opened, the money spent becomes invisible. All that subsequently shows up are its running costs, of which wage costs will be a very large proportion. Let us say that the facility needs ten nurses to run it.' He paused and then went on, 'I put before you a not uncommon scenario. Cash becomes tight and this large investment is mothballed. The money no longer paid out on wages shows up as a saving. This is plain crazy – the capital investment has now been wasted. This wouldn't happen in the private sector. A change to private sector accounting regimes would show the £10 million capital expenditure as a fixed asset, which would be depreciated in the accounts over its economic life. If it had, say, a five-year life, this could be represented by a depreciation cost of £2 million per annum. This is equivalent to over £1,500 per hour or the cost of more than *seventy-five* nurses. In this example, either the £10 million facility should have never been created or it should not have been mothballed.'

Rafi detected another small smile as the Chancellor took a brief look at his watch. He moved back to the papers in the previous file. 'I would now like to turn to market forces and the public sector. Takeovers, mergers and demergers are an everyday occurrence for companies listed on the stock exchange. They provide a mechanism for new management to come in and replace poor management. The not-for-profit corporation structure will have such a mechanism, whereby if the business is not meeting its objectives, it will be possible for one or more of the groups of custodianholders to be replaced by those with a proven track record. Such a mechanism will underpin success.'

The Chancellor cast a glance at the leader of the opposition. 'Public sector bodies and organisations receiving significant amounts of public monies will be converted in phases over the next two fiscal years into not-for-profit corporations. This House will debate the optimum size of these businesses and at what point economies of scale are outweighed by bureaucratic inertia. No doubt, some will argue that these new proposals will bring a significant amount of debt on to the Government's balance sheet. Yes, they will. But, to speak frankly, it is already there; it is just that it is being ignored in the statistics. These proposals will improve financial transparency, efficiency and the delivery of our public services. In this hour of need we have to have our public services operating at their best to facilitate our country's recovery.'

The Chancellor leant forward and reached for another folder – an orange one this time. He hoped that some news on the terrorists would be passed to him shortly – and he was waiting for news from the Governor of the Bank of England.

Behind his back he briefly crossed the fingers of his left hand. He pulled out the contents of the folder. He had the Chamber guessing as to what he would do next. He still had to deal with what many saw as a Herculean task: how to pay for the massive costs associated with Stratford.

R afi's attention was pulled back to the action going on off the Moroccan coast. The distant Nimrod reconnaissance plane reported that the dinghy had rejoined the two life rafts. All three specks on the rainswept ocean were ready and waiting for their rendezvous. The squall was clearing and they would soon be clearly visible to a plane flying overhead. Eight miles away the radio traffic between the Harrier and the two Moroccan jet fighters had been concluded. The Moroccans pilots viewed it as job done and had turned back to their bases minutes before the Harrier arrived.

The seconds ticked by.

The Harrier waited, over the spot where *Golden Sundancer* had exploded, for the Moroccan helicopter to get there, so that a final search could be carried out.

The helicopter, in theory, posed a grave threat to the submarine, but with the Harrier in position that threat could be neutralised.

The command centre spoke to the special service personnel on board the life rafts. 'Activate the homing device. You have less than seven minutes to get on board the submarine.'

Jim felt under his shirt and switched on his personal homing device for ten seconds – not 200 metres away, the submarine picked up the signal.

The order went out: 'Make surface and prepare to take on board visitors.'

The sight of the Vanguard class submarine breaking surface at speed surprised those in the dinghy. They knew she was big, but relative to the life rafts she was huge.

'Captain, you have less than six minutes before the helicopter has you on visual,' came the message from the Nimrod. 'The helicopter has you on its radar and has changed course to investigate – the Harrier is shadowing.'

Rafi sensed the tension in the room. It was going to be a close-run thing.

In a flurry of activity, a squad of naval ratings descended on the two life rafts and the dinghy. The ratings and the three special service men hauled the eight uncooperative captives out of the life rafts and manhandled them across the deck to the door at the bottom of the conning tower. They were followed by those from the inflatable dinghy. Meanwhile, Jim had slashed the buoyancy tanks of the dinghy and the life rafts and lashed them together, so they would sink under the weight of the outboard engine.

The Nimrod was tracking the hostile helicopter and speaking to the submarine's commanding officer. 'You have ninety seconds before you're in firing range. The Harrier has taken up a position above and behind the helicopter and continues to shadow her.'

As Jim hurried through the conning tower door, the command, 'Secure hatches' rang out.

With seconds to spare the submarine commenced her dive into obscurity and vanished from the radar screens.

Meanwhile, the Harrier and the helicopter pilots were in conversation.

'The possible vessel has disappeared,' advised the Harrier pilot. 'I suggest we call it a day.'

'We give it, say, ten minutes and we return to base? Yes?'

'Affirmative,' came the Harrier pilot's reply.

Over the speaker Rafi heard, 'All eight terrorists and all eight service personnel safely picked up. Diving and going into silent mode. Will speak later; ETA Devonport in forty-eight hours.'

'Bravo Zulu, out.'

A cheer went up. A sense of relief filled the air.

The submarine was heading back to Plymouth with its cargo safely on board.

The Chancellor was still going strong. He had been going through the contents of the orange folder open in front of him and was explaining how the Government proposed to improve the transparency of corporate ownership. Rafi didn't catch precisely what he was explaining, but from the attentive nature of the faces around him he was still having the impact of a magician pulling rabbits out of a hat. His audience was enthralled.

'Guidelines will be brought in to improve the transparency in our business activities and to stop undesirables running them. All companies, partnerships and business entities operating in the UK will, from 1 June, be required to disclose the true identity of their owners, namely the investors in their equity *and* their debt. This information will be made available in their annual return to Companies House. Before any dividend or interest can be paid or shares transferred, the identity of the ultimate owner or owners must be known to the company. A new division of the Financial Services Authority, working with HM Revenue & Customs, will be formed to assist in these investigations. Where the ultimate ownership of a shareholding or loan is clandestine, these investments together with the dividends and interest paid will be transferred to a special Treasury-controlled escrow account . . .'

In Luxembourg, as soon as *Golden Sundancer* had reached international waters, Giles gave the signal to the local police team. The gendarmerie was waiting outside Maryam's offices. Her arrest had been authorised by the Chief of the Luxembourg police. The evidence he'd been shown was overwhelming and, off the record, he had agreed that a trial in London with the other three terrorists would be the simplest solution. Neither spoke of extradition. A British SWAT team, including a couple of SAS operatives, was standing by.

David was standing next to Rafi. 'Their Chief of Police is being most cooperative,' he commented.

When the knock at the door came, Maryam was found entertaining a group of EU politicians in her boardroom. Their lunch had stretched right through the afternoon. For her part she was celebrating.

Maryam, with the support of her influential guests, put up an impressive verbal fight, protesting her innocence. Things nearly turned ugly when she summoned her two bodyguards. However, the local gendarmes were prepared for resistance and her bodyguards were quickly outnumbered and overpowered.

In the commotion that followed, Maryam was bundled out of the room by two SAS men, down the service lift into a waiting car and transported to the nearby airport. At the same time, a substitute with a coat draped over her head was taken away to the local gendarmerie to keep up the pretence. Nineteen minutes after the main group of terrorists were safely on board the submarine, Maryam was in a private jet taking off for the UK.

A t that moment Colonel Turner gave the order for a message to be passed to the Chancellor of the Exchequer, who was still speaking at the dispatch box.

There was shuffling behind the Chancellor; he was handed a small folded sheet of paper. He finished what he was saying, paused and then opened it out. He read the message twice. All eyes in the Chamber were on him. The silence was deafening.

'Mr Speaker, I have been informed of a development of which I believe this House should be made aware. If the Speaker will permit, I understand that the Prime Minister has received important news.' The Speaker nodded.

Rafi grinned as he thought about the Chancellor's stalling for time and the excellent initiatives he had produced.

The PM was passed the message, stood up and moved to the dispatch box, and read it. As he hesitated, a ripple of uncertainty spread around the Chamber. 'Thank you, Mr Speaker, I have some news. I can inform the House that I have just received information regarding the terrorists who committed the recent atrocities.' He straightened his shoulders and stood upright. The PM looked calm and confident. No doubt under the surface he was jumping for joy, but he was a master of his trade. 'I can inform this House that special forces units have in the past few minutes successfully apprehended nine terrorists. They have captured the four leaders of the terrorist cell, the two mercenaries who wrought the carnage on Stratford and Cruden Bay, a recruiter of the Bishopsgate bomber and two accomplices.'

The PM paused to let the House take in what he had just said. 'Furthermore, I am able to report that the two mercenaries involved in the attacks on Hartlepool and Heysham are safely out of action, as are the three who attacked Aldermaston. I am advised by the intelligence services that we now have in custody the leading players who conspired against us and wrought such terrible damage and grief on our country.'

There was a brief silence as the news sank in. Then, en masse, the MPs sitting behind the PM rose to their feet and started clapping and waving their order papers. Applause and cheers from the other side of the House soon followed. Rafi watched as the Speaker let the House enjoy the moment before calling, 'Order, order; pray let the Prime Minster continue.'

'Whilst the terrorists were at large, I can reveal that we have been waging a war of deception against them. The terrorist attacks on Aldermaston, Heysham and Hartlepool were in fact foiled and what you witnessed on television were the army's pyrotechnic skills being put to use. Attacks on the St Fergus, Bacton and Easington gas facilities were also foiled, as was the attack on the nuclear reprocessing plant at Sellafield. Sadly, the seven successes were overshadowed by the tragic events at Cruden Bay and Stratford. The catastrophic damage suffered at Stratford greatly saddens me. Memories of this attack will haunt me, for ever.'

He paused to let the words of his last sentence sink in. 'As we face up to the enormous losses incurred at Stratford, it is impossible to contemplate what the position might have been had the terrorists succeeded with all their planned attacks. Suffice it to say that we would have lost over 50% of our electricity and gas supplies and would be facing horrendous radioactive contamination in five locations.'

The PM looked up at the camera. 'We owe a debt of gratitude to the commander-in-chief of our armed forces and his colleagues, who in the early hours of Friday morning responded to our intelligence sources and set in motion a vast damage limitation strategy. "Operation Counterpane" was set up to counter the anticipated attacks. It was the commander-in-chief's foresightedness that enabled help to be at Stratford within minutes of the disaster occurring. We owe a huge debt of gratitude to the Royal Netherlands Air Force whose unreserved assistance was outstanding. And the Government's thanks go to all those who ably and promptly came to our aid, in our time of need.'

Applause rippled around the Chamber.

'The terrorists' plotting was uncovered last week by the City of London police, during their investigations into the Bishopsgate bombing. The police and MI5 were helped to a significant degree by a tenacious individual whom they had wrongly arrested in conjunction with the Bishopsgate bombing. There are very many people to whom I would like to pay tribute. Their resolve helped stop the majority of the terrorist attacks and their unstinting work following the Stratford disaster has been beyond the call of duty. They know who they are. They did their jobs not to gain from being in the spotlight and to spin their story, but because it was in their very nature to fight against those who sought to bring this country to its knees. Their identities will be revealed in due course, but for the time being, let them relax in the knowledge that what they have done has been exceptional and beyond what might have been asked of them.'

The Chamber reverberated to loud cheers from all sides.

'The past few days have been doubly difficult. We have been on the trail of the terrorists, but have feared that they might find this out only to disappear off our radar screens and then go on to commit a series of horrendous attacks about which we had no intelligence. The terrorists used their huge wealth to build a network of clandestine informants and to extend their influence far wider than we could hitherto have anticipated. They took advantage of the opaque intricacies of our corporate system and our lax border controls to manipulate and steer events to their own end. The extent of their plotting will be revealed over the next few days.

'It is with humility, regret and deep sadness that I have to report to the House that my Government has been tarnished by this episode. The terrorists used a significant number of people to assist them. I am advised by the police and MI5 that the terrorists had in place a significant number of influential sleepers or moles, who in return for excessive remuneration became their eyes and ears. The identity of these sleepers has caused the intelligence services and me grave concern.'

Gasps echoed around the Chamber.

'For example, MI5 identified two members of COBRA who were on the terrorists' payroll, which is why an Operations Room was set up at the City of London police headquarters in Wood Street. The scale and magnitude of the recent attacks has made me realise how vulnerable we are to those with immense wealth, who take it upon themselves to either attack our society or use their money to influence those around them. Our freedoms, love of material things, and the chasm between the vastly wealthy and the rest of us have made too many people easy and obliging targets. It is with great sadness that I have to report that a large number of people in senior positions took huge sums of money for nominal amounts of work and did not seek to question what was going on – they were in reality working for the terrorists. They should have guessed it was too good to be true. Furthermore, in their greed, many were all too happy to receive this money in secret accounts offshore. Little did they appreciate that they were being groomed and formed part of the terrorists' information network.'

Rafi watched as the PM was forced to pause because the House was reverberating with retorts of: 'Shame, shame!' The noise grew to a crescendo, as the displeasure was voiced in no uncertain terms.

'Silence, silence!' boomed the Speaker of the House.

The PM continued, 'MI5, working with the City of London police force, have identified over 300 well-connected individuals who were on the terrorists' payroll, directly or indirectly.'

More gasps were clearly audible.

The PM paused and looked around the House. 'It is with sadness and displeasure that I have to report to the House that six members sitting in this Chamber succumbed to the terrorists' financial advances and were part of their network.'

A shocked silence gave way to a rising crescendo of calls for justice to be done. It took the Speaker a full four minutes to suppress the noise before the Prime Minister was able to be heard again.

'I should remind everyone that under British Law a person is innocent until proved guilty. Sergeant-at-arms, are you and your colleagues ready?' enquired the Prime Minister.

'Yes sir!' came the clear reply.

'Are you in possession of the list of the Members' names, for whom arrest warrants have been issued by the City of London police in

344

connection with aiding and abetting the terrorists attacks at Stratford and other locations around the UK last Friday?'

'Yes, sir!'

'With the Speaker's permission, I would ask you, please, to proceed.'

The PM sat down while the sergeant-at-arms – the head of Parliament's police force – walked over and passed the arrest warrants to the Speaker who looked at the papers and solemnly asked him to proceed.

The Members' names were read out one by one. They were not in alphabetical order, which only added to the theatrical tension. The six included a newly appointed junior minister and a backbench MP from the Government's party, an MP from each of the two main opposition parties and two MPs from the smaller parties. Protests of innocence rang out around the Chamber. Shock and incredulity spread around the House, as Members who had hitherto been seen as whiter than white had their names called out. Only one MP put up a struggle, whereas the others left with whatever dignity they could muster.

The Prime Minister watched as the door closed behind the last to leave. The hubbub and mutterings gradually subsided. 'If the Speaker will permit, it would be helpful if the Chancellor of the Exchequer could now complete his outline of the Government's financial proposals, before he and I put ourselves before the House to answer questions.'

'Agreed. Pray continue.'

Rafi was on tenterhooks. How much of their advice would the Chancellor take on board? He looked at the faces of the opposition MPs on the TV. They were bewildered.

'Thank you, Prime Minister,' said the Chancellor. 'I have outlined a number of initiatives to enhance economic activity. I will now turn to our proposals of how the Government is to deal with the huge costs associated with the Stratford disaster.' He paused and then went on, 'As Members are no doubt aware, the credit crunch and the various state bail outs have necessitated significant Government guarantees and a substantial increase in borrowings. We shall *not* be undertaking any further borrowings. *Indeed,* as things stand it would *not* be possible to do so without risking the UK's triple 'A' credit rating, steep rises in interest rates and gilt yields, which would be very counterproductive.'

There was utter disbelief on the faces of those opposite him.

'So how then can we pay for all these vast financial liabilities if we do not borrow more money?'

The Chancellor paused whilst those in the Chamber were left to imagine the starkness of the position. 'I am pleased to report that we have a plan. Under this plan the costs associated with the disaster will be met via the issue of shares in *new* Government Real Estate Investment Trusts – REITs. The value of the public sector's property and tangible asset holdings is £900 billion, or thereabouts. A significant proportion of these assets will be transferred into these Government REIT vehicles, which will be listed on the London Stock Exchange. We will compensate each and every person who lost their health, their home, their possessions or their business as a result of the terrorist attacks by transferring to them shares in the Government REITs. A cash alternative will be provided by a consortium of banks who will offer a cost-effective trading facility.

'The sums involved will be large – in addition to the compensation costs there are a number of other significant costs, such as decontamination and decommissioning costs of nuclear plants and the payment of guarantees. At present the best estimate I have for Stratford and the associated costs is £195 billion. A full breakdown will be published by the Treasury in the next twenty-four hours.'

There were gasps around the Chamber – the figure was far larger than anyone had expected. The House fell back into silence and the Chancellor continued.

'I shall *also* make provision for there to be gilts repurchases targeted at the long end of the market, and will use the proceeds of some additional REIT share sales to pay for this,' continued the Chancellor.

Strike one for the terrorists, Rafi thought. This would underpin gilts prices and be the first nail in their financial coffin.

'The Treasury's best estimate is that the cost of the dividends on the Government REIT shares sold to third parties will be no more than £1.5 billion for the next fiscal year, rising to £3 billion in the following year, and will therefore be well within its scope to manage, without recourse to rises in national taxation.' He paused momentarily and looked at the shadow chancellor opposite him.

Strike two: the Government funding requirements would remain within very acceptable bounds. The second nail in the terrorists' financial coffin has been hammered home, thought Rafi.

'I shall also be introducing proposals which will allow pensioners and those planning for their retirement to invest in London listed REITs as an alternative to annuities. This will provide the REITs market with liquidity. Furthermore, I am advised by leading actuaries that the yield advantage of REITs over gilts and their inflation hedging characteristics will reduce the deficits of many pension funds.' The Chancellor let those around him take in what he had said about Government REITs. He now had to move on to a particularly difficult area.

'In the context of pensions, I have asked the Treasury to publish proposals which are designed to resolve the unfunded public sector pension deficits within fifteen years. These deficits are currently costing taxpayers £30 billion a year and represent a total liability in excess of *£1,000 billion*. The Stratford disaster has thrown all the Government's finances into the spotlight, which is why we *have* to tackle this huge liability now, or potentially face the consequences of investors being unwilling to invest in the rebuilding of our economy. I will be publishing a consultation document which will set out our proposals for the introduction of unit-linked pensions for those public sector employees on above average wages, *and* the phased introduction of pensions which start to address the equity of the size of the payout relative to the contributions made. I would ask that the contents of the consultation document on public sector pensions are read in the context of our proposals for the introduction of not-for-profit corporations.'

Rafi grinned; the unfunded pension problem had at last been brought out into the open. The proposals would not be to everyone's liking, but something *had* to be done to reduce the potentially crippling costs, and it seemed that the Chancellor was going to tackle the problem with fairness.

'Our economy,' the Chancellor continued, 'our financial service industries, the City of London and our currency were badly bruised by the recent banking crisis and will be further injured by the nuclear disaster. To rebuild them we need a period of currency and interest rate stability. It is well known that the five criteria for our entry to the Euro have been long debated; this debate has been against the background of a strong currency and a strong economic outlook for the UK. Some eminent economists have argued that Stratford has materially changed the risk–reward relationship. They have advised me that the risks to our well-being and to our economy of being in the Euro are now significantly less than if we were to go it alone and keep Sterling.'

Wait for it . . . thought Rafi.

'I have considered their arguments and have concluded that Sterling is part of our heritage, our identity, and our economic independence, and it should only be given up *in extremis*. So how desperate a position do we find ourselves in? We have found a workable solution to meet all the costs associated with Stratford and this will inject billions of pounds into our economy. We are to make a start at reducing the scale of unfunded public sector pensions, which will improve the Government's finances. The introduction of not-for-profit corporations will make our public sector services more efficient and will reduce the need for future tax increases.'

The Chancellor stopped and looked around the Chamber. People were on the edge of their seats. Back in the Ops Room Rafi suddenly wasn't sure what to expect.

'On the other hand, I have had to consider how much damage speculators might cause if they sought to decimate our currency. Therefore, whether or not we join the Euro rests on whether or not we can hold our currency stable.'

The tension was palpable. So, are we, or are we not going into the Euro? wondered Rafi.

'Early yesterday, senior representatives of the Bank of England flew out to meet with the largest international Central Banks to ask for their help in supporting our currency and to determine the level at which support would be forthcoming. Without this support we would find ourselves in exceptionally difficult times and joining the Euro would become a necessity. The results of these deliberations should be available to me now.'

The Chancellor turned round and was passed a large white envelope by the PM. He opened the envelope, pulled out two sheets of paper and read them. His face gave nothing away. Before he spoke, he pulled out a handkerchief and mopped his brow.

'As of ten minutes ago, the Federal Reserve of America, the European Central Bank, the Chinese, Japanese, Indian, Singaporean, Saudi, UAE and four other Central Banks have all agreed to support and be aggressive purchasers of Sterling until such time as the UK economy has recovered from the recent catastrophe.'

Sighs of relief were heard around the Chamber.

'Furthermore, in order to accommodate a bank base rate cut of fifty basis points, the support rate has been set at a figure 4% below Sterling's trade weighted exchange rate as at close of business Thursday evening. The Bank of England is, as I speak, announcing a 0.5% reduction in interest rates and this will help our manufacturers and businesses.'

The Treasury had taken Aidan's brief *and* added their magic – Sterling was to remain independent! They had done a superb job. Rafi looked at the ceiling, let out a small whistle and smiled. Strike three!

Short interest rates had been reduced and Sterling was to be protected. The third and final nail had been hammered home. The terrorists' positions in the derivatives markets had become untenable and they would be sitting on truly massive losses when the market reopened in the morning.

A weary, but relieved-looking Chancellor surveyed the packed House of Commons. 'Details supporting the initiatives I have set out this afternoon to the House will be published as soon as is practical – the printing presses are running as I speak. The events of the past few days have required much soul-searching and reprioritising.' He paused and looked across at the shadow chancellor. 'I commend these proposals to the House.' He sat down to growing applause from the House, which was taking its time to assimilate all he had put before them.

The Prime Minister rose to take his place at the dispatch box. 'If the Speaker will permit me, I should like to tidy up a few loose ends. The reshuffle I spoke of earlier will be far-reaching. I have scheduled meetings with the leaders of the main opposition parties for later this evening. I will be speaking with many of you over the next twenty-four hours. I have received assurances from the party leaders sitting opposite me that they will place the interests of the country first.'

The PM paused for dramatic effect. 'Where spin rules, reason is wanting, honesty is wanting, public service is wanting and the role of this House is overshadowed. Spin and self-aggrandisement are unacceptable. We owe it to the people of this country to consign spin and subterfuge to the past.' The PM paused and looked across at the opposition benches.

'It can be expected that members of competing parties will find themselves working together running the Ministries of State. Undoubtedly, there will be differences of opinion over some issues, but this should not stop efficient Cabinet Government. This House, its committees and the Upper Chamber will have the important role to scrutinise, improve and approve the proposals put before them. The Government has many difficult decisions to make in order to steer our country forward in an appropriate direction. What I am proposing is a move away from presidential-style politics to one where the Government is, as it was decades ago, fully accountable to Parliament. Our collective aim must be to get things back on to an even keel, to rejuvenate our economy and to rebuild our damaged international reputation. I commend these proposals to the House.'

With that the PM sat down to applause from all corners of the Chamber. He looked exhausted.

The Speaker called for the Leader of Her Majesty's Opposition. Silence returned to the Chamber as he stood up and raised aloft a pile of papers.

'I thought I'd been well-briefed by my team when I came to the House this afternoon.' Slowly and theatrically he lowered the pile of papers, turned and placed them where he'd been sitting. 'I won't need them.' He looked across at the Government benches. 'If my sources are correct, the Prime Minister has personally been working non-stop for the past three days as part of the effort to prevent the terrorists' attacks, for which I thank the Honourable Member. I shall be meeting with him later today and again tomorrow. Following these meetings, I shall report back to this House any concerns I might have. In the meantime there is much to digest and in the circumstances it would be churlish of me to find fault for the very sake of finding fault. The two Honourable Members opposite me have, with great openness, sought to provide leadership and the wherewithal to enable our country to extricate itself from the horrendous tragedy of Stratford.' He cast his eyes upwards towards the TV camera.

'I should like to pay my respects to all those who have lost and those who will lose their lives as a result of this nuclear catastrophe, and to thank all those in the emergency services, the armed forces and the intelligence services who have helped in our hour of need. I'd like to express my sympathy to all those who lost their homes or businesses in the "Isle of Stratford", and to thank all those people and companies who helped selflessly.'

With that, the leader of the official opposition party sat down. The eyes in the House, as if following a tennis ball at Wimbledon, moved along the front row and focused on the leader of the third political party. It was his turn. He had a reputation for holding strong environmental views and a nuclear disaster was something he had warned against over many years. Would he use the events of last Friday to put the knife in? So far, the Home Secretary, a couple of lower ranking ministers and a number of quango employees involved in the nuclear industry had resigned. Would he try to make this a resigning matter for the Prime Minister as well? He stood up and looked around the silent Chamber.

'It is on the record that my party places huge importance on environmental issues and has a profound distrust of matters nuclear.'

The House sensed that things were going to get interesting.

'The Stratford nuclear disaster will haunt us for generations to come and its occurrence is political dynamite. Its consequences will be felt by every individual in this country. A lesser Government might have tried to spin its way out of the quagmire. Instead, this Government has come here today with a rational, inclusive and cohesive plan, which I believe will provide the foundations for this country to prosper again and will bring environmental and sustainability issues to the centre of our culture.

'I look forward to meeting with the Prime Minister later today and again tomorrow morning. I shall come back to the House and report more fully on these discussions and will raise such questions that I believe require answering.' He paused and in a sombre tone added, 'I, too, wish to pay my respects to all those who have suffered and to convey my great thanks to all those who have helped in this time of need.' He looked around the House and sat down.

One of the colonel's team was beckoning Rafi to pick up the phone nearest to him.

It was Aidan. 'What do you think?' he enquired.

'That's unfair,' an ecstatic Rafi replied, 'you're the one with the screens in front of you.'

'The currency markets are seeing big support for Sterling. Several early punters bet on it going through the floor and have had their fingers burnt. The support since the Chancellor's statement has been unprecedented. And, Rafi, the fall in interest rates will leave the terrorists and their banks sitting on some mind-bogglingly large losses when the derivatives markets open tomorrow. Did the PM and the Chancellor perform some kind of miracle, or what?'

'Better than I could have prayed for,' Rafi replied.

'Basically, things are looking bloody marvellous. Must dash – see you around Rafi. Bye.'

Rafi called across to anyone within earshot, 'Aidan says that the markets loved the PM's and the Chancellor's speeches and that the terrorists and their bankers are financially being taken to the cleaners.'

Colonels Gray and Turner and their teams looked ready to drop. But they looked happy as they packed up their kit – the military operation was complete. The Wood Street Ops Room had served its purpose well.

Len Thunhurst and his team were jubilant. It was their turn now as the focus swung on to the arrest of those implicated with the terrorist activities.

A spreadsheet visible on the right-hand side video screen showed the tally of the arrests. The table of red, blue and black names – slowly at first, then more rapidly – turned yellow as the arrests continued.

Rafi looked at the TV screen. A well-known political commentator was attempting to sum up the activities of the afternoon. The words 'unprecedented', 'remarkable' and 'incomparable' were used frequently in his report. He finished by saying that it had been a great day for British democracy.

Rafi looked back across the room. The large screen showed 'Operation Dry Clean' to be progressing well. The number of arrests was rising swiftly.

Part 8

R afi had had enough.

Kate walked over and gave him a hug. 'Let's get some rest. I'm no longer needed.'

'Fine by me,' replied Rafi.

'I'm afraid it's time for normality to resume. No more chauffeur-driven cars. How about I get us a taxi?'

Rafi nodded. Fifteen minutes later they picked up an evening paper and got into the taxi waiting for them. The February evening was bleak and cold.

'Where to?'

'Clapham, please,' Kate answered.

'The traffic is awful – it could take a while.'

'No problem,' Kate replied and looked at Rafi. 'Is it OK if we pick up our stuff from the Savoy tomorrow? I hope you don't mind but I rang the hotel and told them that they can let someone else have our room.'

Rafi smiled at her. 'What else have you been up to?'

'Oh, there's one other bit of news,' she grinned. 'As of now, I'm sort of on holiday. I've been ordered to spend two weeks helping you convalesce.'

'That's the best news I've heard in ages,' Rafi replied.

'And it gets better. I thought you might like to get this back,' she said, passing him his wallet and personal effects from Paddington Green.

'Thank you. I can now pay for *Luigi's* and the hotel suite. And I can do some clothes shopping.'

Kate gave him a big hug. 'That sounds like fun – I hope I'm included! By the way, how did you get on with the hotel in Cornwall?' she enquired.

'They have found a small suite for us. I told them we'll be arriving tomorrow early afternoon and staying between ten days and a fort-night,' said Rafi.

Kate curled up against him.

'So much for me going out with a butch police officer,' he whispered into her ear.

'Don't be silly,' came the soft reply. 'They employ me for my brains and not my body, you wally!'

As the taxi approached Clapham, it turned into a tree-lined street off the Common and pulled up in front of a red brick terraced house.

'Home sweet home,' said Kate as she joined Rafi after paying the driver.

'Come on, let's get inside, it's freezing cold out here.' Kate unlocked the front door and they entered a small communal area, with two front doors. 'Mine is the upstairs flat.' There was a clunk as she unlocked her front door.

'Good lock,' Rafi commented.

'Yes; you never know who might come calling.'

Inside, on the mat, was a pile of mail – most looked like junk. Kate scooped it up and headed upstairs. Her flat comprised a sitting room, a small kitchen, a cosy bath-cum-shower room and a good-sized double bedroom at the back of the house. The place felt like a deep freeze.

'Is your central heating not working by any chance?'

'Sorry. I turn the thermostat down when I go out. Don't worry, it'll soon get warm.'

Kate scurried around – closed the curtains, lit the gas fire in the sitting room and headed off towards the kitchen.

Rafi joined her and they stood there waiting for the kettle to boil. 'Long-life milk, I'm afraid. Sugar?'

'No thanks.'

'Come on, follow me – let's get warm.' Instead of turning left towards the sitting room, Kate turned right and headed for her bedroom.

It was a friendly looking room; simply furnished. In the middle of the wall, facing the window, was a large double bed. Kate placed Rafi's mug of tea on one bedside table and hers on the other. He looked across at her, wondering what exactly she was going to do next. She'd slipped off her shoes, stripped off her coat and hopped fully clothed into bed.

'It's cold in here – I could do with your body heat to warm me up,' came the suggestive but gentle request.

Rafi sat on the side of the bed and took his coat and shoes off.

'Come on slowcoach, I'm freezing!'

He climbed under the duvet. Kate was right – the bed was freezing. Rafi moved over to her side and snuggled up. She wrapped her arms around him, with her gorgeous eyes inches away from his. He lay there staring into the sparkling deep brown colours, savouring the warmth of her body next to his. She moved forward and kissed him softly on the lips. He was in heaven.

'If it's alright with you, I thought we could have something from the freezer for supper and spend the evening in bed. How's the tea, by the way?' asked Kate.

Rafi reluctantly moved back to his cold side of the bed, took a couple of mouthfuls and returned to her warmth. He lay there thinking what a long time it had been since he had been in bed with a woman. He had known Kate scarcely a week! What were things coming to? Rafi felt happier than he could remember.

'Tell me about the hotel we're staying at,' asked Kate.

'It's just outside Newquay. It's got four stars and overlooks the Atlantic Ocean.

'Did you say the bedrooms were nice?' enquired Kate.

'Yep.'

'And?'

'They have big, cosy beds!'

'Just what the doctor ordered,' replied Kate, who snuggled closer to him.

The proximity of her body, which was now nestling on top of him, made it difficult to concentrate. He wondered what she was going to do next. She leant forward, gave him a lingering kiss on the lips and wriggled her body. The effect was electric. She kissed his cheek and, to his disappointment, rolled off him and slipped out of bed.

'Why don't I rustle up some supper?'

He watched her slim figure disappear out of the room and lay there enjoying the warmth of the bed and the anticipation of things to come. He stayed put. This was the first time in over a week that he had felt truly relaxed and comfortable.

Kate reappeared holding another cup of tea. 'I guessed you wanted to stay warm.' She left him to his tea and thoughts. Rafi sipped at it, savouring its warmth.

After a few minutes he thought it was time to get up, and went to see what Kate was doing. The temperature in the flat had returned to a comfortable level. He looked around him as he walked down the corridor to the kitchen and sitting room. The place was small, but homely. It was very different from his flat in Hampstead. On reflection, he came to the surprising conclusion that he preferred it here. This place had the essence of Kate and that made it special.

He walked into the kitchen.

'The pizza will be ready in fifteen minutes; sorry, the oven takes ages to get hot. In the meantime, I'm going to have a bath. I'd invite you to share it with me, but we would get stuck – it's rather small. The sitting room is nice and warm now. Perhaps the news might be worth listening to?'

Rafi turned and went into the sitting room. He picked up the remote controls and switched on the television. He eventually found the 24-hour news channels and flicked through them. On the first one he saw a photo of himself and heard the reporter saying that 'He had been instrumental in enabling the police to catch the terrorists . . .'

Rafi flicked to another channel. CNN was running a bulletin on the money markets and the American commentator was interviewing a foreign exchange trader who was describing the day's trading.

'Been quite a day! That British Finance Chancellor caught us on the hop. We thought Sterling was going to be a one-way bet down through the floor, but when we found out that our Fed, the ECB and the Central Banks of China and Japan – to name but a few – were piling in to support Sterling against speculators, we knew that they were beaten. As if that wasn't enough, the British Finance Minister then found a couple of hundred billion pounds without tapping the bond markets. The currency markets have given up the fight and settled down. The steam has literally gone out of trying to short Sterling. It's been one hell of a day; one I'll remember for a long time!'

The TV interviewer switched across to a stockbroker. 'Tell us, Irvine, about these new UK Government REITs.' Rafi listened to Irvine tell his American audience how it was the US who had created the Real Estate Investment Trust structure some decades ago. His view was that the UK Government had done something that some saw as brave, while many others looked at it thinking, 'Gee, why the hell haven't we done that?'

Before being cut off by the interviewer, the broker gave a single throwaway remark that made Rafi first smile, then chuckle, 'What has captivated us is this new UK not-for-profit corporation: like a public company but controlled by custodianholders – the people – and not shareholders. The change in accounting methods alone will bring huge efficiency gains. It's a great idea and will knock the stuffing out of our game theory junkies; hats off to the UK Chancellor.'

'What are the prospects for tomorrow?' asked the interviewer.

'It should be business as usual,' came the reply.

The cameras panned back to the interviewer in the CNN studio.

'Well, there it is. An extraordinary day on the money markets; the UK currency and its economy seem set to fight another day. Who would have thought it? It's a big surprise. Tomorrow the world's eyes will be on the reopening of the UK financial markets. The omens look good, but who knows? Will the London Stock Market hold its nerve or will it be a bloodbath?'

The timer in the kitchen started bleeping. Rafi switched off the TV. Kate was still in the bathroom.

'The bleeper's gone, what should I do?'

'Could you see if the pizza is cooked? If it is, could you put it in the top oven to keep it warm?'

'Will do,' he said as he went back into the kitchen. It was a fifth of the size of his. Small it might be, but nevertheless it worked well – like Kate, he thought to himself.

The pizza was cooked. He opened a tin of baked beans which he found on the side and poured them into a saucepan. How long had it been since he'd had baked beans? Ages. Probably university, he thought. With his larger than average salary his diet had gone upmarket. He gave the beans a stir.

Rafi's mind wandered and he found himself wondering what a young detective inspector might earn. Probably little more than a university research fellow, he guessed. It then dawned on him that, following the events of the last few days, he was effectively unemployed.

At that moment his thoughts took another turn. He smelt something sweet coming into the room. This was followed by a sexy hug from behind.

'A penny for your thoughts?'

'Oh, it's just dawned on me than I'm unemployed.'

'That's good news! Now you can do something worthwhile and not just because it pays handsomely. You know, when I saw your bank statements I could hardly believe what a fund manager was paid. On average, you were earning more in a month than I earn in a year. Though, I suppose that those of us protecting Queen and Country do it for the job satisfaction and to eat baked beans rather than caviar. How's supper coming along?'

'Pizza is cooked and the beans are hot.'

'Why are we standing around?' Kate had two trays quickly laid. 'Water or orange juice? No good offering you wine or a G&T, is it?'

357

'Orange juice would be great.'

'Do you mind if I have a glass of wine?'

'Not at all.'

In the sitting room, Kate put her tray on the floor in front of the gas fire and pulled across a small coffee table from alongside the sofa; she then lifted her tray on to the table and sat down cross-legged. He looked down at her; she was wrapped in a fluffy pink cotton dressing gown, with a nondescript towel wrapped around her head – but she looked gorgeous.

Rafi sat on the sofa and felt the warmth of the fire. He tucked into the food – it tasted good. He watched Kate open a bottle of wine, fill her glass and sip at its contents.

She caught him watching her. 'Have you ever drunk alcohol?'

'Not really. My parents, well my mother in particular, were strict Muslims and I grew up in a teetotal household. I suppose it was at university that I decided not to drink. I saw too many people getting smashed for no good reason, which really put me off.'

The conversation switched to their journey to Cornwall. Kate was amused to find that he didn't have a car. 'What about I drive and you pay for the petrol? Deal?' asked Kate.

'But remember I'm unemployed,' replied Rafi.

'Yes, but thankfully you have a bank balance which should tide you over for a year or three.' She yawned. 'Sorry, I have been surviving on catnaps for the past few days. If I stay up much longer, I won't be able to see straight driving down to Cornwall tomorrow.'

There was a lull in the conversation which was soon broken by Rafi. 'Would you mind if I went and showered?' he asked.

'Good idea. I'll clear up. Would you like a cup of coffee?'

'More orange juice would be nice, please.'

'I've put a spare towel on the chair in the bathroom. Sorry it looks yuk.'

He saw what she meant. The towel had definitely seen better days. He picked it up and was surprised to find that its shabbiness belied its softness. Definitely fit for purpose, he thought.

Rafi shed his clothes and looked at himself in the mirror. His wrist still looked puffy and badly bruised. It was an angry purple-blue colour. He'd got rid of the bandage as it had become the object of too much attention. From what he could see, his back boasted some seriously impressive bruises, but thankfully they all looked far worse than they now felt.

The shower cubicle was compact. At the third attempt he worked out how to get in and turn the water on without wetting the floor or getting dowsed in very hot or very cold water. He stood there, enjoying the warm water splashing over him. He looked around for some shampoo, washed his hair and picked up the bar of soap. It smelt of exotic eastern fragrances – very feminine. He gave himself a good scrub from head to foot, rinsed off the soap suds, turned off the shower and stepped out into a steam-filled room. He dried and walked out into a dark corridor.

He could see a small strip of light coming from under Kate's bedroom door and headed for it. Slowly, he opened the door. Kate was sitting in front of her dressing table looking into the mirror. She turned and looked at him. Her tired, freckled face was devoid of make-up – she still looked lovely.

He walked over to his side of the bed, shed his towel and climbed in.

'I'll be with you in a moment,' she said and with that the light on the dressing table went off. The room was now only lit by the small light on her bedside table. She walked over to the door, turned and unwrapped the towel from around her head, took off her soft pink dressing gown and hung them both on the back of the door.

Rafi lay in bed spellbound. The curves on her slim body were accentuated by the soft lighting. She turned her head and caught him ogling at her naked behind.

She slowly stepped backwards, then sideways. He felt his pulse race. She had a great body.

'Oooh! Do you like what you see?'

He didn't reply. He was captivated. 'Yes, you look stunning,' he eventually commented.

'Flattery will get you everywhere.'

Rafi watched as she climbed into bed. She turned off the light, disappeared under the duvet and came up for air with her head on his chest. The curtains were drawn but small shafts of dappled light came into the room around the curtains' edges from the lights outside.

Kate moved her body next to his and planted a soft kiss on his lips.

'You realise that we have known each other for eight days and have been going to bed with one another for four nights?'

'Yes,' he replied, 'it must be a record.' He couldn't wait to see where this was going.

'Well, the other nights we were both too tired to do anything . . . I was wondering, could we save our first time until we're in Cornwall?'

He felt he was going to burst. He was in an extreme state of arousal and was being asked to wait another twenty-four hours. He hesitated and, trying not to sound too disappointed, said, 'If you can survive until then, I can too.'

'I so hoped you'd be understanding. I know it may seem selfish, but to me you are the sort of person dreams are made of and I so want to cherish—'

Rafi gently kissed her mid-sentence and was rewarded with a huge hug and a smouldering kiss.

'Darling, I'm having enough trouble trying not to get any more excited,' he groaned.

'Sorry, I forget that it's more difficult for men to be restrained.'

They laughed, cuddled and swiftly fell asleep in one another's arms. The last week had been punishing for both of them.

Rafi awoke to the sound of light-hearted singing coming from the kitchen. Kate's dressing gown was no longer hanging from the back of the door. Perhaps a cup of tea would be on its way? He sat up and looked around her bedroom. He had worked hard all his life but it dawned on him that this was the first time he had felt really content and pleased with what he had done. Money had its uses, but couldn't buy happiness. There was a lesson there for him.

The door opened quietly. Kate slowly put her head around.

'Oh, good, you're awake. I wondered when you were going to come around. I have a cup of black coffee for you. Thought you could do with a pick-me-up. Did you sleep well?'

Rafi smiled and nodded as she came to sit next to him.

'I've finished packing. I didn't know what I'd need so I'm travelling light; a good excuse for some shopping. And I've rung the Savoy and they said all our belongings are packed up and ready for collection. I have some good news: MI5 have spoken to the hotel and asked for the bill to be sent to them. They left you a message: "Thank you and sorry we roughed you up."'

Rafi grinned and sipped at his hot coffee. Kate leant over and gave him a kiss.

'How long do you need to get ready?'

'Would fifteen minutes be OK?'

'Great. I thought that we could eat brunch on our way down to Cornwall.'

K ate's car was an old-looking, small Volvo. She drove through the London traffic quickly and confidently. They arrived at the Savoy in what seemed like record time and stopped near the front door.

Rafi walked behind Kate into the crowded hotel foyer.

At the main desk they were greeted by the manager, who seemed pleased to see them.

'I'm sorry you're leaving us. I hope you had a pleasant stay.'

'Every bit as good as I hoped,' Rafi replied.

'Your luggage is being collected as we speak and will be waiting for you at the front door. I hope you will come and visit us again soon; it was a pleasure having you both here. Sorry, I nearly forgot; I have some messages for you.'

There were messages from Kate's parents, Emma and Saara sending their best wishes and none needed an immediate reply. The last one, though, was from Jeremy. Kate read it and passed it to Rafi.

As he read the message, Rafi felt the colour drain out of his face. Their nightmare hadn't ended. The terrorist from Heysham had escaped from hospital – heaven only knew what he was capable of doing, even with a broken arm and collar bone.

'Doesn't look good, does it? We'll speak to Jeremy in the car. Let's go.'

They said their goodbyes to the manager and put the luggage, which seemed far more than Rafi could remember, into the Volvo's boot and across the back seat.

They turned into the traffic on the Strand and headed west towards the Hogath Roundabout and the M4.

As they drove along the raised section of the M4, Kate turned on her hands-free phone and called Jeremy. His phone went to voicemail so she left a message. 'Hi, Kate here. I'm on my mobile. Chat soon.'

The traffic on the motorway was surprisingly light and they made good progress out of London, past Heathrow and on towards Reading.

'How about brunch?' asked Kate.

'Great idea,' replied Rafi.

'There's a service station coming up shortly – is that alright with you?'

Rafi nodded. Baked beans and service station food, both in the space of twenty-four hours – how things were changing for him!

As Kate was filtering towards the service station exit, her phone rang.

'Hi, Kate,' said Jeremy, 'sorry to break in on your well-earned holiday, but something has come up. Aslan Popovskaya, the terrorist we captured at Heysham, has escaped from hospital. We haven't got a clue where he's heading, but given all that has been going on recently he's likely to be like a bear with a sore head. Where are you off to?'

Kate gave Jeremy the hotel details.

'I'll get a fax sent with his mugshot, just in case.'

Kate passed the service station, indicating to Rafi that they would stop at the next one.

There was a stony silence in the car.

'Why would he come after *us*?' Kate asked Jeremy.

'Well, I suspect it's Rafi he's after. Who's had their face plastered over the papers recently? Who, according to the news coverage, helped the police and messed up the terrorists' plans, robbing them of their multibillion payout?'

'OK, I get your line of thinking. But no one knows where we're going – or do they?'

'No, you're right, but better safe than sorry.'

'Do you have any leads on where Popovskaya might be?'

'We've one long shot which we're following up. Colonel Matlik and his Russian contacts have sent us details of all the other mercenaries that they have on their most wanted list. We've distributed the photos and names to all airports and ports, just in case one of them comes over to help Popovskaya. The new face recognition software at Heathrow airport has picked up a potential match. A brute of a man travelling on a Polish passport arrived there from Budapest an hour and a half ago. He has an uncanny resemblance to a former Chechen army officer, Radu Dranoff, and is on the list we've just received. We gave his and several other passengers' luggage a cursory search, and at the same time picked up his mobile phone number. I have a team tracking his mobile phone calls and his movements. At the moment he's on a coach heading for Oxford. Sorry, I must go. Do please keep in contact.'

'Will do and thanks for the call.' Kate flicked off her phone. They sat in silence until they arrived at the service station just after Swindon.

'Well, that's a hell of a way to spoil the start to our holiday,' said Rafi who looked across at Kate's strained face.

'You know what our problem is?'

'No,' he said.

'You and I have become too hot a story. One sniff of us being in Cornwall and the bloody paparazzi will be all over us like locusts. Hey presto, within less than twenty-four hours the terrorists will know where we are.'

'Well, at least Jeremy has a lead and the new Chechen arrival is probably only here to get Popovskaya safely out of the UK,' replied Rafi.

'I hope you are right. Do you know what I love about you, Rafi? It's your optimism.' Kate leant across and gave him a peck on the cheek. 'Come on, my tummy is rumbling. I need to keep my energy levels up for all the exercise we're going to take in Cornwall.'

They chose their food in the cafeteria. At the till Rafi pulled out his wallet and paid. Then he noticed that in amongst his other banknotes was a damaged £20 note which hadn't been there when he'd last looked. Attached to it was a Post-It with a scribbled message: 'You might like to frame this as a memento for when you need a boost!' It was signed by Jeremy. He smiled to himself.

Breakfast was far better than he'd imagined. The fresh coffee was good, as were the croissants. Kate enjoyed a full English breakfast. He looked across at her slender frame and wondered where she managed to put all that food. She scowled as she caught him staring at her.

'I wish I had your metabolism,' he chuckled

'Is that why you were staring? What a disappointment – I thought you were ogling!'

The journey from Bristol to Exeter was uneventful but then, thirty miles from Newquay, Jeremy phoned again.

'Hi guys!' He sounded upbeat. 'I've got some news for you. Our Chechen with the Polish passport received a phone call half an hour ago. It was from a mobile phone which we've traced to outside Lancaster, which is near where we had Popovskaya in a secure hospital unit. Putting two and two together we think that our two Chechen mercenaries are on their way to meet up. Thought you might like to know. I've sent a fax with their details to the hotel. I'll keep you posted. Goodbye.'

It had been a one-sided phone call as Kate hadn't been able to get a word in. Jeremy sounded upbeat, but they both felt it had been an act. Kate put her hand on Rafi's knee.

'Even if we jump to the conclusion that they are after you, at least we'll have one, maybe two, days before they'll know where we are. Jeremy and his team will look after us; don't worry,' said Kate.

He sat staring out of the window.

Kate looked subdued. 'Rafi, this is no way to start a relationship. We've known one another for just over a week and during that time you have endured more than most people have to suffer in a lifetime. Let's chill out for the next couple of days and I promise you Jeremy will keep an eye on our backs. If you want to start worrying, save it until after the paparazzi have found us. Then we will both be in the frame.'

Rafi looked into Kate's eyes and at her lovely face. 'I'd hoped to leave the nightmares behind. But at least I've got you with me. I agree: no worrying until our whereabouts are common knowledge.'

For the last half-hour of the journey they played a game: guessing what the hotel would be like. They knew it stood on its own headland and overlooked a long, sandy bay.

'You're a pessimist,' concluded Rafi.

'Yes, but with low expectations things must get better.'

'Is that why you decided on me as your new boyfriend?'

'Of course, how much worse could it have got? A man locked up as a suspect in a terrorism case, uncooperative and with a useless wrist to boot. Plus, smelly – no, *really* smelly – unkempt, and that's just for starters.'

They laughed and the mood in the car changed and became lighter.

Outside the weather remained foul.

They followed the signs to Fistral Beach, past a windswept golf club and into Headland Road. There, in front of them, was the Headland Hotel, an imposing Victorian-style red brick building overlooking the Atlantic Ocean and the surfers' paradise: Fistral Bay. Its long driveway was flanked by what looked like its own small golf course. The strength of the wind was pushing the rain horizontally. Kate drew her car up near the front door in an unoccupied parking space, where they sat for a while looking at the driving rain.

Kate looked at Rafi with a grin. 'Where did we put the overcoats?'

He smiled. 'In the boot, of course!'

'Will we get more soaked making a dash for it to the front door, or getting our coats out of the boot?'

'I have a better idea.' He picked up Kate's phone and dialled a number. When he got through he asked whoever was on the other end of the line, 'Would you by any chance have a spare umbrella or two? We're stuck ten metres away from your front door and we—'

A friendly voice interrupted him. 'It is rather nasty outside. I'll get the porter to come and help you in.'

Wielding a large umbrella in high winds and driving rain was a skill that Rafi hadn't considered until then. They were ferried one at a time into the hotel. Kate went first and Rafi followed, wet at the edges but not soaked.

He walked into the reception area. Kate was standing in front of a roaring open fire. She was beaming.

'This is just brilliant. I think I'm going to like it here.'

To his surprise she bounced over and flung her arms around his neck, giving him a kiss that was more appropriate to the privacy of one's own room. Kate finished her show of affection and drew back noticing that he'd started to blush.

'Sorry, I seem to get a bit carried away at times,' she said to no one in particular. The hotel was busy for off-season February. Rafi wondered if, like the Savoy, it had also taken more than its fair share of those left homeless.

At the reception desk they were greeted by an attentive receptionist who in no time at all had sorted out their booking and arranged for their luggage to be taken up to the room.

'We've filled up since last week. Please forgive us if the service is a bit slower than what you might have hoped for. We've managed to find you a comfortable bedroom, though.'

Rafi was disappointed. Oh well, he thought, if it's to be a double bedroom and not a suite, so be it – in the circumstances it was understandable.

He took the keys and, holding Kate's hand, followed the porter across to the small lift and up to the room, on the second floor. The corridor leading to the room was spacious and newly carpeted. Kate squeezed Rafi's hand in anticipation as they stood in front of the door. He opened it and they walked in. In front of them was a modest-sized sitting room with stunning views over the long sandy beach and the ocean. A large arrangement of flowers on the side-table added to the welcoming atmosphere.

'Where's the bed?' asked Kate, sounding like a young girl itching to explore. 'Let's try this door,' she said with a bounce in her step and disappeared into the next room. 'Rafi, look what I've found.'

He followed her and there in front of him was the wonderful sight of Kate lying on her back, spreadeagled across a large king-sized bed and bouncing up and down.

'This is great! I couldn't have chosen better if I'd tried,' said Kate. 'Nice, comfy bed – sorry, nice, big, comfy bed – great views and peace and quiet. Fantastic.'

Kate rolled off the bed, reached forward and gave him a lingering kiss. She stood on her toes and looked into his eyes.

'Promise me one thing,' she said. 'Let's forget the terrorists and enjoy the now. Tomorrow can look after itself. It usually does.'

He pulled her close to him and kissed her.

'Wooah boy!' exclaimed Kate as she came up for air. 'All in good time. Let's save that for later when there is no hurry and I can really enjoy you. But now there are things that need to be done first – I'd like to explore, find out what's on the menu for dinner and what the dress code is. I hope they do a proper clotted cream tea; sipping that in front of the open fire downstairs will do nicely for starters. Also, I suppose we should pick up the faxes.'

Kate had hardly drawn breath. Rafi looked at her; her eyes were full of sparkle and her face was radiant. He was going to enjoy his time here. She took his hand and led him to the door, where she stopped. 'You know, it's strange being in this style of building with its high ceilings and large open rooms. It brings back memories of living in a big house as a child. But this time I've someone I really want to share it with.'

Once downstairs, Kate collected Jeremy's fax which contained the mugshots of Radu Dranoff and Aslan Popovskaya. The three pages of information made for disconcerting reading. Popovskaya was made of stern stuff: he'd fractured his left collarbone, had had a pin put in his shoulder and broken his left wrist and arm in several places.

'Shame he's right-handed,' was Kate's comment.

It was getting dark outside, but the rain had stopped.

'How about a bit of fresh air to blow away the cobwebs?' suggested Kate.

They collected their coats from the car and headed off down the path to the beach. The wind had a bite to it. Rafi could smell the salt from the sea. The dark shadows around the buildings by the sandy beach brought back memories of his late night walk to Hampstead Heath to hide the USB stick; he shivered.

'You look cold,' said Kate. 'Let's go back and try their tea.'

It was as Kate had hoped: scones, clotted cream and strawberry jam in front of an open fire. They chatted ten to the dozen, sitting comfortably on a huge sofa while time sped by.

But their cosy little world was shattered when Kate answered a call from Jeremy.

She filled Rafi in. 'MI5 has intercepted a phone call; Popovskaya and Dranoff have met up, not ten miles from the hospital Popovskaya escaped from. Unfortunately, they have lost them and have no further information. Neil reckons that they'll lie low for a couple of days to let Popovskaya recover and then come after us. An SAS team is on its way to watch the hotel and to protect us. They should be here later this evening and we are advised to get another bedroom to sleep in – incognito.'

They dressed for dinner, then moved a selection of overnight things into the new bedroom the proprietor had found for them. Dinner was enjoyable; they ate hungrily and chatted, but somehow some of the vivacity had gone. The nightmare wasn't over yet.

Whilst they were having coffee in the sitting room, Jeremy phoned. 'An SAS team of three are keeping watch over the entrances to the hotel. They like the fact that the hotel is so exposed because it makes it difficult for Dranoff to creep up unnoticed. I hope to be with you in about twenty minutes.'

Sure enough, a short while later Jeremy appeared accompanied by a casually dressed individual.

'Please let me introduce you to your SAS bodyguard: Corporal Colin Johnstone. He'll be your shadow whilst Dranoff and Popovskaya remain at large. Have you eaten already?' enquired Jeremy.

'Well, yes,' replied Kate, 'but I can always find room for another pudding! Do come and have dinner so we can chat about things – you'll like the food.'

'Excellent,' said Jeremy.

'How about I find us a nice, quiet table in the dining room and see if I need to borrow a tie?' suggested Colin.

He reappeared a few minutes later. Jeremy and Kate were deep in conversation. 'Dranoff and Popovskaya have disappeared off the face of the earth. We tried to lock on to their phone signals, but their phones are turned off and they'd moved on by the time we went looking for them. They definitely know what they're doing.'

Jeremy and Colin tucked into a hearty dinner.

'Neil is sure that you're their target – payback time for those who got in the way,' said Jeremy. 'We have considered other possible targets, but we keep coming back to the fact that Popovskaya will be feeling pissed off, and *you*, Rafi, seem the perfect target on which to vent his anger. What worries us is who arranged for Dranoff to come to the UK to help Popovskaya. We thought we had all the main players under lock and key, and incommunicado. We know Miti is on the run in Africa, but we don't believe his influence goes this far. There has to be someone else out there – part of the terrorists' web – who's pulling the Chechen end of the strings. We're looking again at UKSOIL and the team run by Kaleem Shah to see if we missed someone, but haven't found anything yet.'

Jeremy paused. 'Neil doesn't think they know we are on to them. My colleagues are keeping an eye out for stolen guns or vehicles reported between here and their last known locations.'

'When do you think that they might come looking for us?' asked Kate.

'Unfortunately,' said Jeremy, 'as soon as the paparazzi are on to you, your location will become public knowledge. Realistically, you could expect company any time from tomorrow early afternoon. Neil would like you to stay put, so if they do come for you, the SAS can protect you. It would be preferable to you going into hiding and then wondering for how long they will be after you.'

The conversation moved on to the terrorists captured at Safi.

'They're due to arrive in Plymouth tomorrow. I shall be there to greet them; one of the perks of my job!' said Jeremy.

'How badly were the terrorists damaged by their investments in the markets?' asked Colin. 'Jeremy has been describing what they were aiming to do.'

'I spoke briefly to Aidan earlier today,' Rafi said. 'He says that the markets have been remarkably resilient. In the areas where the terrorists were playing the derivatives market, prices have moved sharply against them. They're sitting on some truly massive losses. With Maryam, Jameel and the sheikh unable to make contact with their dealers, their positions will be sold. Aidan reckons their collateral will be too little to cover their margin calls. This will cause real pain to the dodgy banks that acted as the intermediaries. Basically, they'll also be put through a financial shredding machine.'

Jeremy smiled. 'Good – serves them right.'

'Aidan is optimistic that several other shady people will be caught red-handed. He's been liaising with Neil, who's following up a significant list of very interesting leads. Maryam, it seems, is in bed with a number of European investors, many of whom are super wealthy, very well connected and of dubious character. Time will tell if they're just plain greedy or linked with shady operators,' added Rafi.

After dinner, Colin and Jeremy walked with Kate and Rafi to their room. Colin had been given a room on the other side of the corridor, near the top of the stairs, and proceeded to set up a selection of monitoring devices in their room and along the corridor.

They said their goodnights.

Rafi and Kate's new twin bedroom was comfortable and cosy. Rafi sat tentatively on the edge of his single bed.

'I'd been *really* looking forward to this evening,' said Kate. 'Now we're stuck with single beds and bugs. Sorry, but I'm not keen on sharing our fun with MI5 or the special services listening. And I haven't even had time to go shopping for a sexy nightie! Can we save the fun for tomorrow?'

Rafi looked at her and smiled weakly. 'Why not? If you can last, so can I!'

T he next morning was overcast and drizzly.
    Jeremy phoned. 'No sign of Dranoff or Popovskaya. Have you seen the morning papers?'

'Not yet,' replied Kate.

'Well, there's a picture in one of the tabloids of the two of you having dinner downstairs. If that's not a red rag to a bull, I don't know what is. The terrorists now know exactly where you are. Colin has asked for you to stay in your room. Sorry if it cramps your style, but—'

'That's alright,' butted in Kate. 'Rafi and I'll be fine.'

The rest of the morning passed slowly. Rafi read the papers and was in particular fascinated by an article in the *Independent* which gave details of the exclusion zone around Stratford and a summary of the building works that were in progress, and of those planned. It showed maps and explained how the transport and key utilities were being rerouted around the newly named 'Isle of Stratford'.

Kate meanwhile lazed around, read a magazine and wrote a postcard to her parents.

They opted for an early, light lunch in their room.

'Now what?' enquired Kate. 'I'm fed up with reading and writing cards!'

'I've an idea; how about spending the afternoon . . .' said Rafi as he turned on some music and pointed across to the bed – lest Colin was listening. He whispered into her ear, 'If we keep the volume down, no one will be the wiser.'

Kate moved across and sat on his lap. 'From time to time, you do have some good ideas,' she said softly, as she unbuttoned his shirt, her fingers lovingly teasing his hairy chest.

A couple of hours later, cradled in Rafi's arms, Kate was woken by the ring of her mobile. It was Jeremy.

'Hi there; just thought you might like to know that Jameel et al. are safely in custody on English soil. He and his colleagues look seriously disgruntled. All he wants to know about is what the long gilts index and interest rates are doing. We haven't broken the bad news to him, as yet. Oh, by the way, we've got Maryam under lock and key at a safe house. Neil is looking forward to playing her off against the other three. See you soon.'

'Thanks.' And with that Jeremy hung up. Kate picked up the bedside phone and rang down to reception.

'What time does the post go? OK, thanks.' She leant over and warmly kissed Rafi on the lips. 'I have to nip downstairs to buy a stamp; the post goes in a quarter of an hour. Sorry; sending cards to the family is one of the things we always did as children. I thought my parents would appreciate it.' Kate dressed quickly and left.

Rafi wrapped himself in a bathrobe and went to sit by the window. It was almost dark outside. The floodlights highlighted the driving rain. He sat there thinking of very little. Nearby, on the bedside table, was a Sig Sauer P226 revolver, which had been given to him by Colin.

'Its small size,' Colin explained, 'means you can carry it on you without showing the telltale bulge. All you need to know is that it has seven .38 calibre rounds, which will stop a man if you hit him anywhere in the torso. Remember, it has a safety catch on your thumb side for right-handers. Have you ever fired a gun before?'

'A .303 rifle at school when I was in the Combined Cadet Force.'

'Good. This little beauty only has a modest kick; aim a little low unless you've had time to cradle the gun properly.' Colin had shown him how to hold the gun. 'Be instinctive and please bear in mind that if you're aiming at a person ten metres away, your accuracy as an amateur will be in the order of two to three metres. Be careful of bystanders!'

Rafi recalled fervently hoping that he would never have to use the gun.

After having been given their respective weapons, Kate had put hers in her handbag and he'd left his on the table, as he didn't know what to do with it.

Rafi watched a pair of bright headlights arc down the windswept drive. They belonged to a silver Range Rover. It parked opposite the hotel and out stepped a well-built man wearing a flat hat, plus fours and a checked sports jacket; he also had a Barbour jacket slung over his left shoulder.

If it had been me in this rain, Rafi thought, I'd have had the Barbour on and not casually draped over my shoulder. Rafi watched as the man glanced around, turned and strolled towards the front door.

Something wasn't right. Rafi couldn't see his face, as it was obscured by the hat and his coat. He was walking straight towards the door. In front of him was a large puddle. He didn't walk around it but straight through it, and that's when Rafi noticed his shoes. They were heavy, black, scuffed leather boots – the sort one would associate with a navvy or a soldier. He was thickset and his gait wasn't that of a well-heeled City gent.

'Bloody hell!' Rafi gasped and jumped to his feet. He felt certain he had just been looking at Dranoff. He picked up his gun and bolted out of the room, running down the corridor barefooted, with his white bathrobe open and streaming out behind him. As he passed Colin's door, it opened and he shouted, 'Dranoff's downstairs and so is Kate!'

At the top of the stairs an elderly couple shrieked as he passed by them, baring all. Rafi grabbed the banister rail with his good left hand and swung round and down the wide stairs.

In a couple of bounds he reached the half landing. As he headed down the last flight of stairs, the man came into view, walking through the reception area. Rafi focused on what little he could see of his face. Yes, it was Dranoff.

Neither of the SAS men from outside was following him. Rafi saw Kate sitting across from the bottom of the stairs, sticking a stamp on her postcard. Dranoff was just on the other side of the glass divide between her seating area and the reception area.

Her eyes looked up and met Dranoff's just as he pushed through the glass swing door between them and out from under the Barbour came a sawn-off shotgun.

Bloody hell, no! It can't end like this, thought Rafi. He let out a blood-curdling scream, flicked the safety catch off and pointed the gun towards the terrorist. He couldn't shoot at him as there were too many people close by; with the gun in his bruised hand he could hit practically anyone within ten feet of what he was aiming at. But he *had* to shoot to distract Dranoff and to draw his fire. Still screaming, he let off a shot at the plate glass window which ran along the wall by the door Dranoff was using. There was a loud bang and a crash of broken glass.

Dranoff saw Rafi as a threat, swung his gun round and fired both barrels. The wooden banister rail at Rafi's side erupted into a swarm of flying splinters as he fell headlong down the stairs.

For Rafi everything went pitch black.

Slowly, Rafi opened his eyes. He could see nothing. He couldn't move; his head was in a vice. Where was he? To his left there was, he thought, a faint red glow and a dull bleeping noise. He tried moving again but nothing happened. His head ached, as did his stomach, right arm and thigh. He picked up the smell of disinfectant. It suddenly dawned on him; he was in hospital.

Rafi felt something warm in his left hand. He squeezed it wondering what it might be. It moved and squeezed him back. A grey shadow moved into his line of sight. His eyes began to focus. There, sitting by him, was Kate.

'He's coming round!' she called out in a croaky voice. Rafi's head was immobilised. He couldn't see who else was there. The door opened and light flooded in. He could see Kate's face out of the corner of his eye. She looked tired; her eyes were red and puffy.

'It's so good to have you back,' she whispered, holding his hand firmly, as if he might leave.

He saw a nurse bending over him. 'How do you feel?' she asked.

'Sore,' he replied.

'How's your head?'

'Sore.'

'Your leg?'

'Sore.'

'Your side?'

'Sore.'

'Your right arm?'

'Bloody painful, thank you.'

'It's to be expected, I'm afraid. What's the last thing you can remember?'

He hesitated, as his mind lurched back to the hotel reception area and the stairs.

'When Kate saw Dranoff . . . Just before I was shot,' he replied.

'Excellent; that's good news – no amnesia.'

Rafi felt his strength ebb away as he was asked a series of further questions. He fell silent.

'Nurse, how is he?' asked Kate.

'Considering everything, surprisingly well. I'll fetch the doctor to look him over.'

The nurse reappeared with a doctor in tow. The doctor carefully checked Rafi and his wounds, then turned to Kate.

'The bang to his head gave him severe concussion. Thankfully there doesn't seem to be any long-term damage. The antibiotics are fighting the infection to his wounds. I've never known someone add cat excrement to twelve bore cartridges.'

372

He paused. 'There may be some more splinters to be removed; it was difficult to pick them all up on the X-rays. The wounds to the right side of his stomach and chest are mending well. His wrist is badly sprained and his elbow has been relocated and should mend well too.'

He looked at Kate and Rafi. 'I've never seen such bruising. The initial X-rays appear to show that there are no broken bones, but I'd like to run a few more tests before we remove his neck brace.'

'Thank you,' said Kate. 'Can I chat to him?'

'Yes, but don't tire him. No more than a couple of minutes, then let him sleep.'

Rafi looked up and saw tears in Kate's eyes.

'I thought I'd lost you!' She slowly bent over and kissed him.

'How long have I been here?' he enquired.

'Nearly four days. I'm sorry we let you down.'

Rafi tried to smile, but his head and face remained immobile. 'That's OK. Silly question, but where am I?'

'Plymouth Hospital. You were making an awful mess of the hotel's carpets. There was a retired doctor on holiday in the hotel. He managed to stem the bleeding and insisted that you were taken to the nearest hospital with a major accident and emergency unit as quickly as humanly possible. He gave you an hour if you didn't get into a good A&E Department. Luckily, an SAS helicopter was waiting nearby. The retired doctor insisted on staying with you for the journey.'

'Just as well,' said the surgeon standing by his bed. 'You lost a large quantity of blood and needed a lot of patching up. Thankfully, underneath the mess you weren't as badly shot up as we had expected. You should thank Mr Welby for tipping us off about the shotgun cartridges smelling foul and the potential infection problems. You succumbed and ran a high fever for the first couple of days, but we were able to limit the complications. We've managed to help your natural defences fight the bacteria with strong antibiotics.'

Rafi looked at Kate. 'Have I missed anything while I've been out of action?'

'Not really. I've kept some newspapers for you to read, just in case.'

'Thank you . . .' Rafi mumbled and drifted back to sleep.

He remembered little of the next thirty-six hours. There were fleeting moments of consciousness followed by more sleep. Whenever he awoke, Kate was there beside him, holding his hand. Slowly, he returned to the land of the living.

One morning his neck brace was gone and he was no longer pinned into position flat on his back. The nurse showed Kate how the electric bed worked and how to adjust the mattress so Rafi could sit up.

The curtains were opened and daylight streamed in. As he was slowly brought up into a sitting position, Rafi looked down to see his right arm in plaster and his side, from his ribs to his knee, covered in bandages. He felt light-headed and his bottom felt burning hot. Kate smiled at him. Her face was tired but gone were the puffy red eyes.

'Thank you for saving my life,' she said. 'I shall always remember . . .' She couldn't continue as the horror of the gunfight flooded back.

'Was anyone else hurt?'

'There were a few minor cuts from flying glass, but otherwise you were the only casualty other than Dranoff, who was taken out by the SAS soldier following you down the stairs. Popovskaya has been captured and is safely locked away. It was all a bit of a cock-up,' Kate explained. 'The two SAS men watching the front entrance of the hotel missed Dranoff. What tipped you off?'

'Hunting and shooting types driving smart Range Rovers in smart shooting kit don't drape their Barbour coat over their shoulder in the pouring rain and don't wear scuffed, heavy, black boots. When I couldn't see his face, which he'd covered with his hat and his Barbour slung over his shoulder, I guessed it might be Dranoff. I picked up the gun and ran to warn you.'

Rafi stopped speaking for a moment. 'When he saw you and pulled out the sawn-off shotgun and swung it towards you, I thought I was going to lose you.' There were tears in his eyes. He couldn't see Kate's as she'd turned away.

Another person had entered the room – it was Colonel Turner. 'Good to see you in one piece. Sorry we let you down. Thanks to your quick thinking, a real disaster was averted. I hear you got peppered by the sawn-off shotgun. Your dive for cover and the ornate patterns of the heavy wrought iron banisters saved you. The wooden handrail was blown to smithereens. The SAS man behind you was very impressed by your reactions: shooting to attract the attention of the terrorist and diving at the same time. He wondered if you had military training.'

Rafi grinned. 'Serendipity. I missed my footing on the steps as I looked for the darn safety catch and for something to shoot at. I couldn't aim straight for the terrorist – there were too many people I could have hit. I tripped as I aimed at the big glass window.'

'Good work all the same. I'm pleased to see you on the mend. I'll drop by when you're up and about for a debriefing.' The surgeon appeared at the door. The colonel excused himself and left.

Rafi spent the next half an hour being brought up to speed on his various injuries. 'There's quite a list,' said the surgeon, running through them as if they were on a shopping list. 'A posterior dislocation of the elbow which has been successfully relocated, fourteen stitches in the head and two drill holes as a result of the emergency surgery to relieve the pressure, six pellets in the thigh and buttocks and several more in the flank which went into your intestines and lung – we've patched them up, but I had to remove a small part of you lung.' The surgeon paused and smiled. 'With a good convalescence, you'll soon be right as rain.'

'Thank you,' said Rafi weakly.

Time passed slowly, but Rafi started to feel stronger.

During a further inspection of his wounds, Rafi asked, 'Doctor, I have a question. How long am I going to be in here for?'

'If you can find somewhere quiet to convalesce and someone to care for you, you should be able to leave tomorrow.'

'Tomorrow would be great,' Rafi replied.

He spent much of the rest of the day chatting with Kate.

A kind physiotherapist arrived and went through a gentle exercise regime aimed in particular at his elbow. This was followed by a dietician who talked about what he should eat whilst his intestines and body mended. Late in the afternoon the surgeon and doctor reappeared. They were pleased with his progress. They chatted with Kate and to Rafi's surprise announced that if he wished he could be discharged immediately and return to the comfort of the hotel.

Rafi agreed, so Kate was given a series of contact names and numbers, plus a schedule of when he should attend the local surgery.

'Any ideas what we should do for clothes and headgear?' Kate asked the nurse. After a short discussion, Kate opted for the short journey to the town centre to buy Rafi what he needed. An hour later she reappeared carrying a couple of large bags.

'Sorry to have taken so long.'

Rafi dressed in comfortable, warm clothes. With Kate's help he stood up and for the first time in days he looked at himself in the mirror. He was horrified by what he saw. His eye sockets looked skeletal. Two thirds of his hair was missing. A jagged scar with stitches ran from just above his hairline to the top of his head. His scalp was a dark reddish purple because of the bruising.

His legs felt wobbly and he sat down on the bed more quickly than he'd intended – to the great discomfort of his unhealed wounds.

Kate spoke to the nurse about the practicalities of getting back to Newquay. They opted for the simplest solution and took a taxi. The journey seemed to go on forever. Rafi didn't know how to position himself. His body ached and his head throbbed. They drew up in front of the hotel at 8 o'clock.

The cold wind cut through his clothes. Kate helped him inside and across to the lift. The area at the bottom of the stairs looked very different. There were temporary carpets, boarding covered the plate glass window which separated the reception area from the seating area at the bottom of the stairs and also the stained glass window on the half landing. Builders' dust sheets were draped all over the banisters.

Kate had phoned ahead to check with the hotel that they were still welcome. The proprietor and his wife were there to greet them. It transpired that they felt their staff had let Rafi and Kate down, revealing their whereabouts to the tabloid press. The £500 bung that the chambermaid had received had been donated to a local charity. She'd kept her job on the basis that her apology was accepted. She was there waiting at reception with a bunch of flowers. She stepped across and passed them to Rafi. She took one look at him and crumpled, promptly bursting into tears.

'I'm sorry; I just didn't think. The journalist was very convincing,' she stuttered through her tears. Kate put an arm around her.

'It isn't your fault. He would have found us sooner or later. At least this way we're still in one piece. Your flowers look lovely. Thank you. Perhaps you could help us find a vase?'

Rafi was exhausted by the time he arrived at their room. He slowly shuffled into the bedroom and sat gingerly on the bed. His backside hurt like hell. He curled up on his left-hand side. Kate cradled his head in her lap.

For the next two days he remained holed up in the suite. His wounds were healing well and he started to get his energy back. Kate, it seemed, was enjoying her role as nurse.

On the second day the phone hardly stopped ringing. Saara, the major, Kate's parents, her brother and Emma all wanted to hear how he was and to pass on their love and best wishes. Jeremy phoned to apologise that he couldn't drop by to say sorry for the cock-up; he'd been given another assignment, which necessitated a bit of travelling, but he looked forward to seeing them soon.

In the middle of the afternoon, while Rafi was sound asleep, a call came in from the Prime Minister. Rafi was very groggy. The PM enquired after his health, conveyed his best wishes and hung up. A nice touch for someone so busy, Rafi thought.

Whilst he recuperated, Rafi went through the newspapers. Post-Stratford, things in the world were slowly returning to normality. In particular, there was one small article by Pete Lockyer that caught his attention: it showed a picture of Maryam in a smart suit sitting in a stately drawing room. Apparently she had not gone to prison, but was helping the police with their enquiries. Strange, he thought, and made a mental note to ask Jeremy what was going on.

In their little world, the hotel proprietor had been doing his best to protect them from any further unwanted press intrusion, but the situation was becoming untenable. Camped outside was a small village of TV crews and reporters. They needed to do something or they would get no peace and quiet for the rest of their holiday.

An idea came to Kate and she phoned Jeremy to get Pete Lockyer's number. She then phoned Pete to ask if he would do an interview. He jumped at the invitation and said he would be there first thing the next morning.

As dusk was falling, the hotel proprietor arranged for Kate and Rafi to be smuggled out in the back of a builder's van. The afternoon trip to the doctors was otherwise straightforward. The nurse looked at the notes from the hospital and set about changing Rafi's dressings and bandages. Fifteen minutes later he only had one dressing left on his side. All the others had been removed as she was pleased with how he had healed. Kate arranged a follow-up session for the last of his stitches to be removed and they returned surreptitiously to the hotel.

Psychologically Rafi was feeling much better. His headaches had gone and seeing the wounds on his body almost mended had been a real tonic. That evening they went downstairs for dinner. As he passed through the reception, Rafi observed that the repair work was almost complete.

In the dining room, they were met by the restaurant manager. 'Excuse me for saying, but everyone is curious to see how you are mending. They've seen the mess and, like me, find it incredible that you're still alive.'

He beckoned them forward. 'Your table is at the far end by a window overlooking the sea. It should be quiet, except you'll have to walk past everyone.'

'Not a problem,' said Rafi as he shuffled in. He became aware that the room had fallen silent and dozens of pairs of eyes were staring at them. As they approached the table, Rafi noticed that the two seats were facing the window and out to sea.

'Could you move our places so that we can look into the room? That way we won't look as if we're avoiding everyone.'

Moments later Rafi gingerly sat down. The restaurant manager reappeared with the menus.

Kate asked, 'Is the person I noticed as I came in the retired doctor who helped Rafi?'

'Yes, he's sitting over there with his wife.'

'Thank you.'

The menu was mouth-watering. Kate was in her element. Her healthy appetite had returned, helped by the long runs and swims she had enjoyed whilst Rafi was resting. She made her choice. Rafi was still hesitating and when the waiter returned, Kate passed him a sheet of paper.

'Sorry, darling, you're still on your limited solids diet; it shouldn't be long before your tummy is fully mended and you can have grown-up food again!'

'At least I won't have to cut it up!' he said, moving his right arm in its sling.

Her smile was radiant. 'I'm so pleased to be with you. I honestly thought you mightn't make it. The helicopter flight down to Plymouth felt like the longest journey of my life.'

She hesitated. 'Would you mind if I asked the doctor and his wife to join us for coffee? He was brilliant looking after you on your journey to the hospital.'

'That's a great idea.'

Kate got up and walked down to the doctor's table. They were surprised by the invitation, but like everyone else were keen to find out what had really been going on.

They joined Kate and Rafi in the sitting room for coffee. Rafi thanked him several times over.

'Just pleased to help,' replied the doctor, 'and the helicopter ride was a first.'

'I only found Rafi a few weeks ago – I couldn't bear to have lost him,' said Kate.

The conversation covered a wide range of topics. The doctor chatted about his time working in Manchester and the increase in gun and knife crime he had witnessed. 'I'm delighted that I had my arm twisted to attend a special training session on street war injuries – I'm pleased it came in useful.'

After half an hour of talking, tiredness overcame Rafi. He said his goodnights and retired upstairs, leaving Kate chatting to the doctor and his wife.

Back in the bedroom Rafi undressed with difficulty and surveyed his body. In many places, it was hard to see where one bruise ended and another started. His wounds were still sore, but the burning heat had gone out of them.

He curled up in bed. Next thing he knew it was morning and Kate was sitting at the bottom of the bed, in her running kit, eating breakfast.

He smelt the hot food. It made him hungry.

'Morning. I hope you don't mind me starting,' she said.

'Not at all. What's on the menu?'

'Scrambled eggs, croissants, fresh orange juice and coffee. By the way, we've got Pete Lockyer due here in about an hour.'

Pete was forty-five minutes early and caught Rafi in his dressing gown. Kate ordered breakfast for him and his cameraman, whilst Rafi slowly got washed and dressed. She explained the ground rules. 'Please treat Rafi as a close family member. We don't want anything published that he'll regret. We'll chat openly to you, on the understanding that you clear what you write with Jeremy's boss, Neil Gunton, at MI5.'

Judging by the size of his frown, Pete was none too happy with that suggestion and Kate picked up on his reluctance.

'It's quite simple. Much of what Rafi and I will tell you has been kept under wraps. There may be things we tell you that could jeopardise the investigations into this awful affair. Don't worry; there should be enough to keep you in stories for weeks!'

Pete gave his word. 'Having seen today's newspapers I appreciate your reticence,' he commented. 'The photos weren't very nice.'

Rafi caught the end of the conversation and glanced across to Kate.

'One of the guests took a series of photos of you at dinner last night and you looked quite awful in them. The proprietor was very upset. He'd asked all the guests to respect your privacy whilst you were convalescing. The culprit was the same reporter who passed the bung to the chambermaid. He got a guest to take the photos using a special hidden camera.'

'Quite how marketable is our story?' Rafi sighed.

'Red-hot,' replied Pete. He paused. 'Would you want paying?'

'What sort of sum would we be talking about?' asked Rafi, and Kate shot him a glowering glance.

'The full inside story, handled properly over a number of weeks or even months, would net you a six, maybe even a seven-figure sum for an exclusive. Basically, you could name your price. Is this going to be a very expensive trip for me?' enquired Pete.

Rafi looked across at Kate. She slowly shook her head.

'I think it would be churlish not to take the money,' said Rafi.

'But . . .' interjected Kate. She looked horrified.

'Seriously. Consider if the money was not for us, but for the hospices helping those with radiation poisoning. They must be overflowing. How about Pete's paper running an appeal to raise money for the hospices helping those suffering? The appeal could go alongside our story. It would be great publicity for the newspaper and be great for its image,' said Rafi.

As he paused to think, Rafi could see Kate visibly relax. 'If your paper were to start the ball rolling with, say, a £250,000 donation and top it up as more stories were rolled out, I reckon Kate and I would be very happy.'

Pete looked pensive. 'I reckon my editor would go with that if I got an exclusive.'

'Where else would we go?' said Kate with a huge smile.

They chatted for almost an hour and a half. For the photoshoot, the hotel proprietor arranged for them to be slipped out of the back of the hotel in a laundry van down to a nearby beach where the pictures could be taken in the morning sunshine. They returned using the same means of transport.

With the story and the photos in the bag, Pete made arrangements to meet with Neil, said his thanks and slipped off to London with his scoop.

At Kate's request, the proprietor briefed the journalists and TV crews camped outside that a press conference would be held the following morning, at 11 o'clock in the dining room.

Kate and Rafi spent the rest of the day chatting and discussing what he might do next and about her career ambitions in the police force. It was settled that he would move in with her for a couple of months before he made any decisions. It was a happy day. He had a future; one which filled him with great expectations.

They ate in their room that evening, turned in early and breakfasted early the next morning. Rafi tentatively tucked into a small English breakfast while reading the newspapers.

They couldn't miss Pete's article: it ran to twenty pages! On the front page were a smiling Kate and Rafi walking hand in hand, in the sun, on the golden sands by the sea. The trilby hat and the flowing scarf hid many of the scars and bruises, and all things considered he looked remarkably well. The headline under the photo was 'In good hands'. The article talked of Pete's breakthrough in tracking down the terrorists' getaway vessel, *Golden Sundance*, in Iceland and explained Kate's and Rafi's roles in unravelling the terrorists' plots. The article revealed the work that Kate's team at the City of London police and MI5 had done in finding the locations of the terrorist attacks. It also described the role of the Air Chief Marshal, the Prime Minister, the Defence Secretary and the head of MI5 during the thwarting of the terrorist attacks – and even mentioned Aidan's team working with the Chancellor of the Exchequer and the pulling of the financial rabbits out of the hat. There were photos of the hotel proprietor presenting the doctor and his wife with a large bouquet of flowers, as well as pictures of John, Emma, Giles and David.

The article included one new nugget of information. There was a mugshot of Miti Lakhani. Despite the best efforts of MI6 and the CIA, he had disappeared and the terrorist training camp run by him was deserted. Also, tucked away in the text, was a paragraph alluding to the fact that one of the terrorists had, at the end, tried to save their skin by doing a deal. Rafi smiled. It was another nice way of playing Maryam and the other terrorists off against each other.

The hotel's dining room was packed for the 11 o'clock press conference. Pete's story had whetted their appetite. Before the session Kate received a call from Neil, thanking her for getting Pete to talk to him before going to press. Basically, Neil told them that they could mention practically anything, except for the sleepers, but they should remember that the more they told, the more the journalists would want to know.

Kate and Rafi sat at a long table covered with a smart white tablecloth and flower arrangements at either end. Bright lights were trained on them.

The questions were like cannon fire. First they focused on the recent terrorist shooting and Rafi's wounds, then the questions backtracked to the lead-up to the Stratford disaster and, finally, they were asked their views on whether before the Stratford tragedy politicians had pushed the boundaries of spin too far.

'It takes two to tango,' Rafi replied. 'Irresponsible journalism goes hand in hand with spin. I applaud responsible investigative journalism which questions whether the full truth is being revealed by publicity-hungry politicians. More attention to the minutiae and not just to the big glossy picture would be welcomed.'

'What would you do about it?'

'Perhaps those journalists who cut corners and write things that are needlessly intrusive and damaging should be shunned by their colleagues. Yes, you have a press complaints body, but you know in your hearts what's acceptable and what's not acceptable. Persistent unacceptable behaviour should result in offending journalists being ostracised by their peer group. That would be a good start. Perhaps you should beef up your trade body and give it real teeth so it can determine what's ethical and proportionate, plus give it powers to discipline wrongdoers.' Rafi stood up, gingerly lifted up his shirt and showed the mass of scars on his flank.

'You don't want to see lower down! I've got these thanks to one man's desire to publish information about my whereabouts. He ignored requests that this information should be kept out of the press as it would endanger lives. The person in question brought to bear undue influence on an unsuspecting member of the hotel staff. Then he bribed a guest to take unauthorised photos of me, which you'll have seen in Sunday's papers.

'I applaud professional journalism: it's the lifeblood of a free society. I abhor journalism which is only interested in short-term gain and is a means of filling the coffers of the journalists involved and their bosses. You might like to ask the gentleman standing amongst you what his thoughts are.' The cameras turned on to a sheepish-looking individual. He stood silent and said nothing. No apology was forthcoming.

Kate stood up. 'As he has nothing to say, I propose we call it a day. Rafi and I came here for a holiday to recharge our batteries. It's not turned out as we had hoped. We've only four days left before we return to London and it would be much appreciated if we could have that time to ourselves.'

Against a barrage of further questions, they left through a side door, picked up their coats and headed for the fresh air and the solitude of the windswept beach.

The last four days of Rafi's convalescence went by far too fast. They chatted and laughed as if they didn't have a care in the world. It was a happy time. On Sunday, it was with sadness that they packed before their drive back to London. It felt like the end of the long holidays and the impending return to school.

Back in London, Monday morning felt strange. Kate set off for work early and Rafi was left in her flat alone. It was the first time for ages that he hadn't been with her. He missed her.

It was a sunny day; spring was in the air. On the spur of the moment he decided to look at Stratford and the new wall around the exclusion zone. He took the underground straight through to Old Street station and walked east towards Hackney Road. After about half a mile Rafi came upon a sign by the roadside. He was entering a restricted area. This was, he assumed, the beginning of a buffer zone. Not far ahead of him he could see a military roadblock in front of a fifty-metre strip of cleared derelict ground. Past this were a three-metre high, heavy-duty steel mesh barrier and the beginnings of a brick wall. Beyond that he could see piles of rubble, empty properties and, incongruously, a number of newly planted trees.

As he stood taking in the enormity of the dispossessed area, a soldier came across.

'This is a restricted area, sir. You should turn around and make your way back to the other side of the buffer zone.'

'Sorry,' Rafi said. 'I was only trying to fathom out the true size of the exclusion zone.'

'I understand that if you take the underground up to Hampstead or Belsize Park and walk to the top of Parliament Hill you can get a good overall view.'

'Thank you.'

Rafi returned to Old Street tube station and took the tube across to Hampstead. The journey brought back memories of the lead-up to his arrest; it all seemed eons away.

He was soon back on his old home ground. It felt strange; he was revisiting a chapter of his life that had been closed. He had left the keys to his flat at Kate's. As he walked down Well Walk, past his building and on towards the Heath, he wondered what his redecorated flat looked like. He shrugged his shoulders – that was for another day, he told himself.

Twenty minutes later he was standing on the top of Parliament Hill, 100 metres above the exclusion zone whose scale beggared belief. It was a miracle that the relocation and decontamination process had passed off without there being any major incidents.

Rafi strolled down to Belsize Park tube station, past the Royal Free Hospital. The sign to the oncology department sent a shiver down

Rafi's back as he fleetingly envisaged the many people contaminated by the nuclear waste and their sufferings.

An hour later he was back in Kate's flat. Physically exhausted, he settled down, read the papers and had something to eat. Whilst he missed Kate's company, he had always enjoyed having time to himself. Over the next couple of weeks he recharged his batteries and enjoyed the freedom of having nothing particular to do. His hair regrew sufficiently to cover the scar on his head and for him to stop wearing a hat in public. All his wounds had healed and he was beginning to wonder what he should do next. Of one thing he was certain: he would not be going back into fund management.

Yes, there had been several phone calls from prospective employers trying to entice him to work for them. The golden hellos on offer were mouth-wateringly large, but his heart was no longer in that line of work.

Rafi decided he was in no hurry and would give himself another month or two before starting to job hunt.

O ne evening, before Kate had returned from work, the phone rang. It was an ebullient Saara.

'Rafi, would you believe it? I've had a job offer I can't refuse.'

'Like what?'

'The Chancellor of the Exchequer invited me to Number 11 for a working lunch. It was just me, the Chancellor and four of his Treasury suits.'

'Sounds like fun,' replied Rafi.

'They want me to run a team which advises on the allocation of Research and Development grants spent at UK universities. Dealing with renewables, hydrogen fuel cells, energy efficiency, clean carbon technology, carbon sequestration, under sea storage and—'

Rafi interrupted her, as the list seemed endless. 'That sounds right up your street.'

'I know, isn't it great? I'd be involved with all the areas that could give the UK economy a competitive edge post-nuclear power.' Saara chuckled. 'I liked the sound of the job but I told them I had loyalties: my existing research work and Steve. And that I was very happy in Birmingham. You know what? The Chancellor started smiling. He said I made an excellent negotiator. He then floored me. He said that Steve's research had caught the eye of those at Imperial College and that they'd be asking him to work with them on secondment. Plus, he can bring his research team with him. The Chancellor has spoken to

384

my vice chancellor who thinks it's an excellent opportunity for us both! Basically, I was well and truly stitched up. But, Rafi, I wasn't pleased to find you were part of the fit up.'

'Pardon?' he replied.

'Well, they told me that Jeremy had spoken to you and confirmed that Steve and I were most welcome to use your flat on a long-term basis, as you were now living with Kate.'

'Of course you are, and it explains why Jeremy out of the blue asked me about you and my flat.'

'I've talked it through with Steve and the move is on. Isn't it fantastic?'

'I'm really happy for you. I'll send you a set of keys,' said Rafi.

'I'll be working at the Treasury and will have a workstation at Number 11. And they're practically tripling my salary. It's outrageous; I'm going to get paid shedloads to do something I love.'

'It's about time,' said Rafi.

'Rafi, are you sure it's alright for me to use your flat?'

'Of course!'

'Steve says he's looking forward to living somewhere without rising damp. By the way, how much rent should we pay?'

'How about what you were paying in Birmingham?'

'Surely that can't possibly be enough?' said Saara.

Rafi heard Kate unlocking the front door.

'Sis, don't worry. Enjoy the flat and let's chat again soon. I've got to go now – Kate has just got home.'

'Bye and thanks,' replied a very happy Saara.

Part 9

They'd been back in London for almost four weeks. Thursday had been a quiet day. Rafi had cooked supper, which was being kept warm in the oven, and he was sitting with his feet up reading the evening newspaper. He looked up at the clock. It was almost 9.30 p.m. Kate had rung to say that she would be a bit late, so he was not worried.

There was a clatter downstairs as Kate opened the front door, bounced up the stairs and greeted him with a hug and a lingering kiss.

'Sorry I'm so late. Supper smells good. Thank you for waiting.'

'I hope it's still edible.'

He noticed Kate's cheerful demeanour. 'Did you have a good day then?'

'Yep, it was quite something. It seems I've been promoted. You now see before you Detective Chief Inspector Kate Adams!'

Rafi listened to her story of how she'd been dumbstruck when she'd been called into a meeting with the commissioner. 'Emma is being promoted into my job. Jack, who did all the work on the terrorist sleepers, is taking on Emma's role and Peter Ashby is to become their sidekick. According to the commissioner, that left him with a bit of a problem as to what he should do with his newest detective chief inspector! I didn't follow what he was saying until he said, "Yes, Kate, the appointments board has approved your promotion. It puts you as the youngest DCI in the City of London. Congratulations." I was dumbfounded.'

Rafi leant across and kissed her.

'But that's not all. The commissioner carried on and added, "As to what we are able to offer you, we were wondering whether you and Rafi would care to join Ewan, the PM's permanent secretary and me for a meeting. Could we pencil in 3 o'clock tomorrow afternoon? If Rafi can't make it, let Beverly know and we'll rearrange it." I left feeling light-headed,' said Kate. 'I was only promoted to detective inspector last year. I seem to have missed a large number of rungs on the ladder.'

Rafi gave her another kiss. 'Fantastic! This calls for a celebration. It's what you deserve. I'd love to see your family's faces when you tell them the good news.'

He walked through to the fridge and from the back pulled out a bottle of sparkling white wine, scooped up two glasses and walked back into the sitting room. Kate had kicked off her shoes and was sitting on the sofa with her feet curled up under her.

'Look what I found in the fridge.' He passed the bottle to Kate. 'You can do the honours.' There was a loud pop as the cork flew up and made a small dent in the ceiling.

Rafi put a glass out to catch the effervescent wine as it bubbled out of the top.

Kate filled her glass. Rafi stretched his arm out and she poured an inch of the liquid into his glass.

He raised it. 'A toast: to you, the most talented policewoman in the City!'

Rafi looked into the eyes he loved so much and took a sip of the sparkling wine. It tasted different from what he'd expected. The little bubbles danced on his tongue.

Kate raised her glass and took a long swig. 'I've a confession to make: this isn't my first glass of champagne this evening,' she said with a chuckle in her voice.

Rafi smiled. 'You deserve being made a fuss of. What exactly does your promotion mean?'

'Heaven only knows! I suppose they want me to move somewhere, which is why they've asked for you to be there.'

They chatted over the well-cooked supper. Kate was buoyed up with the excitement of the news. As far as what the future held, all would be revealed tomorrow. They left the dirty plates where they were and retired to bed.

Kate was up and out of the flat early the next morning. Rafi tidied up and spent a leisurely couple of hours reading the papers. He was feeling rested. The terrors of the previous month were a thing of the past. He left in good time, dropped into a florist on the way and headed off for the meeting at Wood Street. He arrived almost fifteen minutes early and went up to the fourth floor office to look for Kate. To his surprise, he found Emma sitting at Kate's desk and opposite her was Jack.

'Hi there, I came to have a last look at where I was imprisoned and to convey my congratulations to the two of you.' From behind his back he produced a bouquet of spring flowers, which he handed to Emma. 'Congratulations and well done.'

Rafi turned to leave but Emma stopped him at the door. 'You can't get away that easily.' She placed her arms around his neck and gave him a peck on the cheek. 'You look after Kate, or else I'll come and sort you out. Got that? She's a very special girl.'

Rafi felt a firm tap on the shoulder. 'This is what you get up to when my back is turned: making out with my best friend! I should have guessed that the two of you had a soft spot for each other!'

Kate winked at Emma. 'Come on, Rafi, we're meant to be elsewhere – if you can tear yourself away from those sexy lips.'

Rafi looked into Emma's eyes and sensed a real fondness. He kissed her on the cheek and followed Kate down the corridor.

'Nice to see Emma again?' asked Kate.

'Yep,' Rafi replied. 'You've one hell of a good friend there. She left me in no doubt that I had to take good care of you, or else!'

Kate had a broad grin on her face as they entered Beverley's office. She waved them into her boss's meeting room.

It very looked neat and tidy. There, sitting at the table, was the commissioner, together with a dark-suited gentleman, who Rafi recalled as being the Prime Minister's permanent secretary, and Ewan from MI5. Kate and Rafi sat down opposite them.

The content of the meeting was a surprise. Rafi had gone along expecting Kate to be offered a posting far away from the south-east – somewhere like Manchester – and assumed he'd been invited along so he didn't feel left out of the process.

The meeting started with the PM's permanent secretary setting out his boss's stance. 'Following the recent terrorist attacks, the PM believes that the EU is missing a trick in the war on terror. Standards and ethics of what is acceptable and unacceptable, or what is legal or illegal, differ from country to country. Despite anti-money laundering legislation being enacted, there seems to be no let-up in the shady financial activities of terrorists and drug dealers. The PM believes there is an urgent need for transparency. More information needs to be in the public domain as to who controls which company or business.'

He adjusted his cufflinks and continued. 'The Stratford terrorists built up large business interests and concealed them right under our noses. The concern is that with a growing number of public companies going private and the enormous wealth of a relatively small but significant number of individuals, the authorities are losing sight of who is controlling what, *and* what exactly the money is being used to finance in the shadier recesses of our countries. At one level, profits are being channelled out of Europe into tax havens and at another, a growing number of private companies and individuals are operating as if they're beholden to no one. Giles, would you like to continue?'

'Yes, of course,' said Giles. 'Before Stratford, being an immensely wealthy person entitled one to low levels of scrutiny. Key questions weren't asked for fear of driving business away. The richer someone was, the more a blind eye was turned. There's a dichotomy: on the one hand we have the politicians who have power to smooth people's paths, but rarely have much personal wealth, and on the other hand there are those with immense personal wealth and insatiable desires, but who need favours to pursue their ambitions. Too many people view greasing a palm or two as a cost of doing business. There are, across Europe, growing levels of corruption and a lack of transparency as to what is going on. This trend concerns the PM.'

'DCI Adams and Mr Khan,' interjected the permanent secretary, 'the President of the European Commission is also very concerned that the lack of financial transparency and the dubious financial practices are encouraging criminal activities and resulting in billions of Euros of tax slipping away. He is creating a new task force, led by the former head of a German State police force. His team will comprise four senior detectives, four special advisers and a small team of technical specialists who have a detailed knowledge of criminal practices and money matters. It will be based in Luxembourg. The remit is to report to the EU President on the practicalities of making European-wide financial affairs more transparent. DCI Adams, you are requested to apply for one of the four senior detective posts.'

Kate's mouth fell open.

'Obviously, as this is a European Union appointment, there will be an interview process to go through; a shortlist has been drawn up and unless you tell the interview panel to take a hike, I would submit that the post is yours. You would be seconded from the City of London police force and be able to come back here at a future date. Salary and terms and conditions will, we believe, be acceptable. There would be a modest flat in Luxembourg included in the package. The post in the first instance will be for three years.'

Before Kate had the opportunity to reply, the permanent secretary turned to Rafi. 'Mr Khan, you have shown yourself to be very enterprising in unravelling the web that the Stratford terrorists had spun. The President of the EU Commission and our Prime Minister

390

have asked me to enquire whether you would be willing to have your name put forward to join the task force as a special adviser. You would suffer a significant reduction in remuneration, but it has been suggested to us that there may be other aspects of the job that would appeal to you, thereby making the salary less of an issue?'

There was a pause. Kate looked at Rafi and he at her. Kate had a smile on her face, which he took to be a 'yes'.

'Who would I be working for?' Rafi enquired.

'Well, that depends upon who you're talking to,' said Ewan. 'Officially, you'd be employed by the European Commission, but in practice you'd be on secondment from MI5. I have it on good authority that Neil and his team are very impressed by you. Intelligence will be an important feature of your work, hence your inclusion with our security services.'

'Are you interested?' asked the permanent secretary.

Rafi looked at Kate again and then back at the permanent secretary.

'Would it be alright for Kate and me to discuss this by ourselves for a few minutes?'

'Of course; do use the room next door,' said the commissioner.

Kate sat down with Rafi in the adjoining office.

'What do you think?' asked Rafi.

'I have a few concerns: first of all, could you bear to work *and* live with me? And how would you feel working *for* me? And also, do you like the idea of living in Luxembourg and travelling around Europe, working out how the system is being manipulated?' said Kate.

Rafi looked at her smiling face; there could only be one answer – 'yes'.

'Excellent. Shall we give it a go? If we enjoy it, great, but if we've been sold a pup we can always come back to the UK and find something else to do.'

'I don't think we should be seen to be too hasty. Why not ask them a few more questions before saying yes?' suggested Rafi.

They walked back into the meeting room and sat down.

'Your proposals are intriguing and interesting,' Kate started. 'How much autonomy would there be?'

'It will be a small team and it will have autonomy.'

'If I'm operating overseas, why is MI5 and not MI6 involved?' asked Rafi.

'Good point,' commented Ewan. 'MI6 know nothing about what's going on. We thought that, as you know us and we know you, it would be simpler if you were seconded from MI5.'

Rafi nodded.

'Will other national intelligence services be involved?' asked Kate.

'Undoubtedly. It's likely that each special adviser will have an intelligence background. You, Mr Khan, are the so-called ace up one's sleeve. Whilst the Kates of this world know their way around accounts and corrupt businesses, and intelligence service people have their skills, you have the real market experience and a sixth sense for the extraordinary.'

'Is there a pecking order in the team?' asked Kate.

'Yes. There's a boss, to whom you'll report, and, below you, you'll have a support team at your beck and call. As far as the four police officers and four special advisers are concerned, it's expected that you'll work as partners. The type of work you'll be doing doesn't go with structured hierarchies.'

Rafi looked across at Ewan. 'If I get the job, would it be possible to spend a few days with Neil's team to see what resources are at my disposal?'

'Of course!' said Ewan. 'If you accept this post you'll become one of us and will have access to the full scope of our resources. The PM himself places great importance on this specialist task force. There may only be a few of you, but what you might lack in numbers will more than be made up for by a combination of your individual skills and the resources behind you.'

'Why Luxembourg and not, say, Brussels?' enquired Kate.

'Luxembourg has become a major money and fund management centre. It's midway between the two European Parliaments – Brussels and Strasbourg – and it's within driving distance of Frankfurt, where the chief currently lives. Plus, it has a good little airport at Findel, five kilometres north-east of the city, which gives access to a large number of European cities. Also, there's a well-staffed British Embassy there. And I hear the standard of living is rather good,' came the helpful reply.

'Last couple of questions,' said Kate. 'Are the identities of the other people known at this point in time and, if so, when do we meet them? And what's their English like?'

'Yes, I believe they are, and English will not be a problem. If you have no more questions then I can tell you that your interviews have been arranged for next week. They'll be at the EU's offices in Storey's Gate, St James's.'

Rafi raised an eyebrow indicating that the address meant nothing.

'Bottom of Horse Guards Parade.'

'Got it – thank you.'

'Assuming you decide to take up the offer of the jobs, we've arranged for you to meet the team for dinner next Friday evening in Luxembourg, as guests of our Embassy there. That way you can see how you get on. On the languages front, I have to stress again that your would-be colleagues have an excellent command of English as well as each being fluent in a handful of other languages. Your support team will provide you with the necessary translators, should they be required,' added Ewan, helpfully.

Kate looked at Rafi. He winked back. She slowly turned and looked at the commissioner, at Ewan and then across to the permanent secretary.

'Who books the plane tickets and the hotel?'

'Funny you should mention that.' The commissioner turned over several pages of the notebook he was using, pulled out a sheet of paper and passed it to Kate.

'In case you said yes, here are the details of your e-tickets and the hotel you'll be staying at. We booked you on a flight from London City Airport on Friday; it takes off at 12.05 and lands at around 14.00. We've arranged for you to be met at the airport.'

Kate stood up, shook hands, said her thanks and goodbyes, and made for the door. Rafi stood up to leave after her.

'Mr Khan, would you stay with us a moment longer?'

Rafi sat back down. Ewan looked at him intently. 'Can you recall how you felt when you were at the Headland hotel and you knew that there was a person out there in the darkness who wanted to kill you and Kate?'

'Yes.' The thought sent a shudder through him.

'Please be under no illusion. We don't know what you and Kate may be getting into. There are powerful forces at work below the surface in Europe. These shadowy people have big vested interests and antiquated concepts of what are acceptable and unacceptable practices. Further-more, the enlargement of the Union has brought into our midst both hard-working people keen to improve their lot in life and, unfortunately, a quagmire of organised crime. These criminals, like terrorists, operate freely throughout the EU. To put it bluntly, you'll be entering a very murky world – the world of sophisticated, ruthless criminals. We at MI5 and those at MI6 will do our utmost to protect you as and when things get difficult; the Prime Minister has made it clear that you will have our full support. But it's your decision as to whether you're willing to leave the comfort of the City and cross over to our world and its dangers.'

Rafi thought for a few moments. The Bishopsgate bombing had claimed four lives, Stratford would claim innumerably more. If there had been better financial transparency the terrorists would not have been able to operate so freely. Perhaps they would have gone elsewhere or have been caught in good time. It was a no-brainer and if it was what Kate wanted, then he wanted to be with her.

'Thank you for your warnings. I'd like to attend the interview next week and – interview permitting – I look forward to becoming part of the team.'

'That is good news,' said the dark-suited civil servant. 'The PM will be very pleased.'

Rafi got up and went to find Kate. His life was changing fast. Only a few months ago he had been a well-respected and very highly paid equities fund manager. He was about to take a huge salary cut, work in Luxembourg and join MI5. Bloody hell, wasn't life fickle?

He found Kate talking with Emma in her old office.

'I'm being posted to Luxembourg,' he heard her say.

'Congratulations. I'll really miss you. Promise you'll keep in touch,' replied Emma.

Rafi turned to Kate. 'What do you have planned for the rest of the afternoon?'

'Well, I need to tidy my desk. Then I can start planning the next chapter of my life with my new partner,' she quipped with a mischievous look on her face.

She spotted a pile of messages on her desk. 'Would you believe it? I've had a call from Jeremy and he's in Luxembourg! He says he will be there to meet us at the airport on Friday and show us some sights, before he takes us to our hotel, which is near the Embassy.'

Rafi looked at Kate. 'What, pray, is Jeremy doing in Luxembourg?'

'Heaven only knows. But I hope he's been posted there; it would be great to have him as part of the team.' Kate hesitated. 'What time is it? I've just remembered a couple of things I need to finish off.'

Rafi looked at his watch. 'It's just gone 4.15 p.m.'

'Could we meet back here at 6 o'clock? Could you find something to keep you occupied for about two hours?'

'No problem.' Rafi flicked open his mobile and rang Aidan. He felt slightly guilty that he hadn't made more of an effort to keep in touch since that day they'd given the presentation at Number 10.

Aidan answered the phone straight away. He definitely wasn't at the office; from the background noise Rafi guessed he was enjoying a glass or two of champagne at a local hostelry.

'Hi Aidan, Rafi here.'

'How are you, you old sod? I thought you'd been avoiding me – great to hear from you. Where are you?'

'Wood Street.'

'It's POETS day. Do come and join us; we're in the Pavilion at Finsbury Circus Gardens. It's been a rather good week; we're a bit over the top, but do join us.'

'See you in ten minutes.'

The Pavilion was a short walk away; it was a likeable wine bar in the middle of Finsbury Circus, overlooking a bowling green. Rafi grabbed his coat, hurried downstairs and headed down Chiswell Street towards the wine bar. On arrival he was greeted by a joyous Aidan. He had taken a few clients out for lunch and they were still going strong. As an equities man, Rafi's path tended not to cross with the derivatives specialists. They tended to be high-octane people with a 'work hard, play hard' ethos.

'Let me introduce you to everybody, Rafi,' Aidan said, then paused. 'On second thoughts, there's no need as I reckon they all know you from your pictures in the papers!' To general amusement, those that Rafi hadn't met before introduced themselves. Aidan ordered him a freshly squeezed orange juice and Rafi sat down and listened to their stories. Aidan was on cracking form. He'd picked up a whole host of new clients after all the publicity he'd received for his work for the Treasury.

'Rafi,' he said, 'have you heard the one about the MD of a major international bank who one Monday morning turned up to the office to attend a video conference meeting with a major client, only to find that all the equipment had been taken away for servicing?'

There were howls of laughter around the table.

'And he thought that I had something to do with it! He saw that the market was closed and decided it was an omen to go off and have an extended lunch.' This was greeted by more laughs.

'You know, every time I meet the MD, he asks me how I'm getting on in the second-hand electricals market – some cheek!' said Aidan.

The conversation went from pillar to post and time flew by all too quickly. Rafi said his goodbyes and left the ever-merrier group to their next bottle of champagne. He arrived back at Wood Street in a taxi, picked up Kate and they headed for Clapham. It had been quite a day.

The Tuesday interview at Storey's Gate was just a formality. Rafi sat at one end of a long table with two grey-suited individuals sitting at the other end.

The first twenty minutes were spent completing a detailed CV about Rafi: schooling, degrees, employment, work skills and competencies, leisure activities, etc.

The first real question was: 'Do you think that your financial and analytical skills are appropriate for this position?'

'Yes,' Rafi answered, expecting a follow-up question.

'Thank you,' came the reply. 'We don't have any more questions. Do you want to ask us anything?'

Rafi shook his head.

'Good. On your way out, please pick up the envelope from the secretary next door. It contains your employment contract. Thank you for coming in.'

And that was it.

Kate had a similar interview. Back at the flat, they went through the contents of their envelopes. Kate was bowled over by the hike in her salary. There was an accommodation allowance, travelling to home allowance, even a clothing allowance. In her eyes the package was fantastic. Rafi's package was practically identical, other than his basic salary, which was a couple of thousand Euros less, but in the small print he saw that he would be getting a special allowance which brought him to a financial parity. He smiled. It was a nice touch.

Their flight out of London City airport on the Friday was un-eventful. Luxembourg from the air looked smaller than they'd expected. Jeremy was waiting for them and was on great form. He had been posted to the Embassy a couple of weeks earlier as a commercial attaché. He showed them the sights and at Rafi's request they visited the spot where Callum and the Mercedes had been found. Standing there, Rafi felt a pang of guilt. Next time he was in England he really should visit Callum's parents.

Kate and Rafi were eventually dropped at their hotel, with time to shower and dress for dinner.

'What do you think?' asked Kate. 'Do I look smart enough?'

The sleek, dark emerald, satin dress fitted her perfectly. Her matching high heel shoes lifted her almost to Rafi's height and accentuated her slim figure.

'Wow, you look stunning. Yep, you'll do very nicely!'

The dinner was held in a formal dining room. The Embassy had spared no expense. During the pre-dinner drinks Kate and Rafi were introduced to their prospective boss, Jörg Emcke. He was of average build and height, with receding hair – and introduced himself with great enthusiasm.

'I heard you wanted to know what my English was like. It's good, but I still find the English sense of humour impossible. Don't worry; I enjoy a good laugh, particularly when it's at the expense of those we catch.'

The individuals alongside whom they would be working looked genuinely unimpressive. They could have been having dinner with a team of auditors who were in the middle of a particularly dull company audit. However, Rafi soon found that appearances were very deceptive. The pairs were drawn from France, Italy and Poland.

The French police chief, Stephanie Doucet, looked businesslike. She was wearing a plain trouser suit and looked to be in her mid- to late forties. Rafi discovered that she had worked for the Parisian police force and then Europol and, like Kate, had specialised in criminal financial activities.

The Italian detective introduced himself as Celso Morassutti and his Polish counterpart was Ludomir Jablonkowski. Both, Rafi learned, had substantial experience of dealing with organised crime; the background of their sidekicks remained a mystery.

At dinner, Rafi's suspicions were confirmed. He had had a feeling that the group had met before and were sizing up the two newcomers. There was great interest in the jobs he had done. However, he sensed that they had been fully briefed and were only filling in the gaps. On the other side of the table, Kate was also being discreetly quizzed.

After the main course was cleared away, Jörg stood up. 'This won't be a long speech. A couple of hours should do!' He winked at Kate. 'Probably a lot less! As you know we've been tasked with advising the President of the European Commission on what should be done to improve financial transparency. He wants there to be a level playing field, so that when EU tax harmonisation comes in, it will be harder for EU companies and individuals not to pay their taxes. This unit's formal role is to be the data gatherers. The sums involved are immense, as is the political will. Tens, if not hundreds of billions of Euros per annum are involved. Technically we will be part of the European Court of Auditors, who conveniently have their offices around the corner from us in rue Alcide De Gasperi. We therefore will have excellent resources at our disposal.' He paused and then went on, 'That is the front under which you will be operating. Your real task is to understand how the criminal and terrorist fraternity use the current opaqueness of the financial markets to assist them in their activities. Whilst the ways of criminals and terrorists are not identical, the atrocity of Stratford shook us and made us realise that it was as if a small army had declared war. Our activities will remain covert. Our aim is not to go out there and arrest people or close down bent corporations; it is to gather evidence that others will use to thwart the criminals and terrorists. I trust we shall keep a low profile.'

Jörg studied Kate and then Rafi. 'Seven of us have met before on several occasions. Good progress is being made in setting up our office in Luxembourg. This evening we are joined by the last two members of our team. They perhaps look on the young side to us. However, their track record speaks for itself. They bring to the table cutting edge experience of the lengths to which terrorists and criminals will go in order to get their way. Their knowledge will complement our skills-base. You're a team of equals – if there's to be any pulling of rank that is my prerogative and my prerogative alone. Unless I hear any dissenting comments, I shall assume that you are all willing and happy to work together as a team.'

He looked around and then continued. 'On that basis, you will be expected to report for duty at our new offices a week on Monday. That, I trust, will give you sufficient time to sort out your affairs at home, to dust off your suitcases and to find suitable accommodation in Luxembourg.'

Jörg sat down, picked up a large cigar, chopped off the end, carefully lit it and started puffing as though he had no cares in the world – and smoking bans didn't exist.

After dinner things became more informal. They were ushered into a comfortable sitting room where they chatted and bounced ideas around. Rafi looked around the room: there was definitely an esprit de corps. The special task force was up and running.

At just after 1 a.m., Jörg said he was calling it a night and left with a simple parting remark: 'It has been a good evening. I look forward to seeing you all in our office on Monday week at 9 o'clock for a strategy meeting.'

It was almost 2 a.m. when Kate and Rafi walked back to the hotel, hand in hand.

The wind had a nip to it, but Rafi had a warm feeling inside him; it had been an exhilarating evening.

Back in the hotel room, Kate flipped off her shoes, sat suggestively on the corner of the bed and looked across at Rafi who had taken off his jacket and tie.

'What do you think of this situation we've got ourselves into?' She sounded very excited; it was as if she was on fire from within. 'I'm the luckiest girl in the world. My two wishes have come true: a fantastic job where I can do something worthwhile and a man at my side for whom I would do anything.'

'And what about my wish?' enquired Rafi.

She smiled and looked into his dark eyes. 'I wonder what that might be?' She turned her back to him and said, 'If you could help me with my zip . . .' but let her voice trail off.

Rafi sat next to her, ran his fingers provocatively down her back and felt a small shudder race through her.

Kate stood up and faced Rafi; her satin dress slipped silently to the floor, revealing her breasts enticingly covered by a lacy black bra, inches from Rafi's face.

Rafi sat still, taking in the sight before him. He was captivated. 'Do you like . . .'

Rafi kissed her. The sentence was left unfinished.

He felt his shirt being unbuttoned; as it went over his head, he stood up and moved closer to her. Her body was warm against his. Their lips met again – her tongue danced provocatively between his lips. He could taste a hint of Cointreau, which brought back memories of the orange-scented bath oils at the Savoy and the first time he'd seen her lovely body.

He felt her hands effortlessly undress him. Her fingertips tenderly caressed his naked body. Kate was enjoying the electric effect her teasing was having on Rafi's heightened senses.

Rafi reached over and switched off the light. He lifted the sheet and slid under the crisp cotton, closely followed by Kate.

'Spoilsport,' whispered Kate into his ear. 'I was enjoying exploring your body. Now where was I?' she asked playfully as she disappeared under the covers.

Rafi tingled all over as she slowly explored his aroused body. She worked her way back up to his lips and kissed him lovingly.

'I meant what I said: I'd do anything for you,' she said as she moved on top of him. 'At the Headland hotel when I saw Dranoff's eyes latch on to mine and the sawn-off shotgun come out from under his coat, I was petrified. I froze. Out of the corner of my eye I glimpsed you flying down the stairs screaming at him, trying to draw his attention away from me. It all happened so fast: me thinking I was about to die, you screaming, firing and Dranoff blasting both barrels at you. I saw the wooden banister rail disintegrate into splinters only centimetres away from your body and when you landed motionless in a gory mess at the bottom of the stairs . . .' Kate tenderly kissed his lips. 'In that split second, I realised how very much I loved you. You offered up your life to save mine. I was awestruck. It was as if my brain was rewired. I vowed there and then that if you lived I'd do absolutely anything for you; and that if I made you happy, then I'd be happy too.'

She snuggled closer. 'My fantasy is to make you blissfully happy,' she whispered into his ear.

The next morning, when Rafi woke, Kate was sleeping soundly in his arms. He lay there not wishing to disturb her, savouring the memories of the erotic night before – a night he would remember.

They had a late, lazy breakfast, showered together and were several minutes late for their meeting with Jeremy for a coffee in the hotel lobby.

'My, you're looking radiant this morning,' Jeremy said to Kate. 'I see that Luxembourg with a man in tow suits you.' He smiled at Rafi. 'Who's the lucky one?'

The question needed no answer.

'I hear that the dinner went well,' Jeremy continued. Rafi resisted asking whether they'd been bugged.

'Jeremy, how much do you know of what Rafi and I are up to?' asked Kate.

Jeremy smiled. 'Ewan has briefed me. I'm to be your liaison with MI5 and MI6. I'll be based at the Embassy and will have a desk next to yours in your offices.'

'That's great. Anything else I should know?'

'Don't tell Emma and Jack yet, but they'll be part of your London support team.'

'Fantastic!' Kate gave a gleaming smile. 'And is there anything more?'

'I understand last night you had lengthy conversations with the three police officers but found their partners less than forthcoming.'

'Yes. They were rather secretive.'

'Probably best if they bring you up to speed once you start working with them. Basically, Pierre Simmon works for the DGSE, La Direction Générale de la Sécurité Extérieure, which is France's equivalent to MI6. Luca Duilio gained an impressive track record with the Italian Anti-mafia Investigative Directorate; he'll tell you in due course what he's been up to for the past couple of years. By the way, Bernhard Michalak from Warsaw and he are good friends. Bernhard at one time worked for the Stasi in East Germany and then had a stint on

400

secondment to the FSB, the Russian Federal Security Service. He is a specialist on the whys and wherefores of organised crime in those former Russian states that are now part of the EU.'

Rafi looked carefully at Jeremy. 'They are a forbidding team, aren't they?'

'Yep, I'm glad that they are on our side. Heaven only knows what all of you will dig up.'

Their coffee was finished and they said their goodbyes. Kate and Rafi went off to explore the shops. After lunch, Jeremy had arranged for them to meet one of the Embassy staff who had been flat hunting on their behalf.

The afternoon was spent looking at apartments. The first looked nondescript from the outside, was comfortable and homely on the inside, but had poor views. The second flat was smaller. However, it was only a short stroll from the office, it overlooked a small square and was conveniently located for easy access to the airport. The main rooms were light and airy. The master bedroom was a good size and had an impressive en suite bathroom. In the basement there was secure parking for two cars.

Kate liked it and so did Rafi. It would make an ideal and comfortable home for a couple doing a fair amount of travel. They decided not to look any further.

'Is it within our budget?' Kate enquired.

'Money won't be a problem,' came the reply. 'When you've settled in, do let me know if you need any changes and I'll happily coordinate them for you.'

Four hours later, Kate and Rafi were back in Clapham, sitting on the floor in front of her gas fire. They were tired but elated by the prospects of their new lives.

Lying on the table amongst the post was a smart envelope with a crest on the back. It was addressed to both of them. Their company was requested at a reception and dinner at Windsor Castle, six weeks later.

The day of the dinner arrived. They had taken half a day off and arrived at Kate's flat in the early afternoon. Kate was dithering.

'It's alright for you; a dinner jacket is a dinner jacket, end of problem. What shall I wear?'

'I thought you'd already bought an evening dress?' replied Rafi.

'Well, that's the problem!'

'You've left it a bit bloody late!'

'No, it's just that I have a couple of options and then there's what shoes and jewellery to wear.'

'How's about you put all your choices on the bed and we go through them?'

'Would you be willing to sit through me changing in and out of things and faffing around?'

Rafi nodded, trying to look enthusiastic.

'Give me a moment and I'll get everything out.'

What seemed like ages later, Rafi heard a call from the bedroom.

He sauntered down the corridor, wondering what he'd let himself in for, and pushed open the door. There, standing in front of him was Kate with her hair up in a sophisticated style. Around her neck was a most exquisite gold necklace of blue gemstones with diamonds, pointing down to her lacy bra, panties, suspender belt and sheer silk stockings.

'Now watch this.' She walked into the evening sunshine. The blue gemstones in the necklace and the matching earrings turned a fiery amber colour, setting off her freckles perfectly. 'Magic, isn't it?'

'Stunning. What is it?'

'Blue amber. I've always wanted to wear it but never had the occasion before. It's been hidden away since my granny died a few years back.'

'Did she have the same colour hair as you?'

Kate nodded.

'I can see why she gave it to you. It's fabulous. I love how the amber changes colours so. You look ravishing.'

They walked back to the bed. Four long dresses were draped across the duvet cover.

Rafi picked up a pale gold dress which had an almost translucent quality and shimmered as it moved in the light. He wasn't certain about the colour, but Kate seemed to like it. He suggested she try it on.

'Do you think the colour is too much with my hair? A little shop in Milan made it and the matching shoes especially for me. I paid them a visit while I was working there a couple of weeks ago.'

Rafi watched as she slipped it on and noticed how it enhanced her subtle curves. He was amazed and very surprised. And there was something about the colour that accentuated the beauty of her skin and hair.

'It's perfect – you look ravishing. There's no need to look any further.'

'In which case we have a bit of time to kill,' said Kate suggestively, slipping off the silk dress. 'It's a bit cluttered in here. How's about we try the sitting room?'

The taxi arrived outside Kate's flat on time. The twenty-mile journey to Windsor Castle was good for the time of day.

Emma and Aidan had been surprised to receive official invitations from the Queen to celebrate the State visit by the President of the European Commission. Neither had expected the other to be there. The seating plan had them next to one another near the top table. Kate and Rafi sat opposite each other at the other end of the room with a European Council member, two immensely wealthy Continental European industrialists and a French newspaper editor, Jean-Michel Coeurs.

Kate and Rafi noticed a lot of famous faces as they mingled during the pre-dinner drinks. The Royal family, senior politicians and the movers and shakers of the British economy were out in force.

At dinner, Rafi's conversation with those sitting around him ebbed and flowed. It turned to international businesses and whether too many were exploiting accounting and taxation loopholes. Surprisingly, it suddenly got interesting.

The industrialist on Rafi's left explained, 'As the chairman of a listed company, I have analysts crawling over practically everything we do. I've got to play by the rules.'

'That's your prerogative,' countered the other industrialist. 'I find life so much easier running a private business. I have a flexibility that gives me a distinct competitive edge.'

'What about the Commission and its approach to matters financial?' Rafi asked.

This sparked off a lively debate.

'Remind me how many millions – or was it billions? – of the Commission's budgets were unaccounted for last year?' asked Jean-Michel, the journalist.

'I can't answer that question as the accounts aren't due out for several months,' countered the bureaucrat defensively.

'OK, what was the figure for the year before, approximately?' asked Jean-Michel.

'Roughly, in percentage terms, around . . . 1%'

This seemed to rankle Jean-Michel. 'That's over €1 billion. It would be bad enough if that was the correct figure, but I believe the true figure is far, far greater. Didn't the European Court of Auditors raise serious concerns about where the €80 billion spent on agricultural and structural projects actually went?'

'Yes, there are undoubtedly a number of grey areas,' replied the unembarrassed bureaucrat.

The topic of conversation continued until the speeches, but the disputed figure still hadn't been resolved.

Rafi mentally missed most of the speeches. His mind was on the recent conversation. Two things struck him: firstly, the lack of concern that the bureaucrat had about the Commission's unbalanced books and the system's opaqueness, and, secondly, the opportunities to which the private industrialist had alluded, which enabled him to play the system, make easy money and enjoy being accountable to no one. Then there was the journalist, Jean-Michel; he seemed to know his stuff. Rafi made a mental note that he was a man worth talking to.

After the dinner, whilst Kate and Rafi were waiting for their taxi home, Jean-Michel came over and said his goodbyes. He too was on his way back to Central London.

'Why don't you join us? We practically go past the front door of your hotel,' suggested Kate.

'Thank you,' he said.

During the forty-minute ride into London they chatted about various things. After a lull in the conversation he turned to Kate and said, 'I believe we have a mutual friend?'

'Who might that be?'

'Stephanie Doucet; she and I grew up together. I saw her for dinner a couple of nights ago. The conversation touched on the terrorist attacks in London and she mentioned that she had met you. I can see why she said that you reminded her of herself when she was younger. It seems you made quite an impression!'

The taxi came to a halt at the hotel and Jean-Michel climbed out. 'Perhaps we could have dinner with Stephanie sometime and continue this evening's conversation?' was his parting remark.

Kate playfully nudged Rafi in the ribs. 'Thinking about your dinner with Stephanie, are we?'

'No, I was thinking about our first night in Luxembourg and hoping you aren't feeling tired,' he said with a mischievous grin.

Early summer arrived; Kate and Rafi continued to travel around Europe. There had been a steep learning curve in understanding the intricacies of how the European Union, the Commission and big pan-European businesses operated.

Once every three or four weeks, they spent a weekend in London at Kate's flat. This Saturday, over a leisurely breakfast, Kate and Rafi were going through a pile of post. There were two smart envelopes; their backs bore the Royal Coat of Arms.

Kate opened her envelope and in it was a formal invitation to a Buckingham Palace Garden Party held in five weeks' time. In the envelope there was a second gilt-edged card which requested the pleasure of her company at an audience with the Queen an hour and a half earlier.

Rafi opened his envelope and he, too, had two invitations. He recalled how, on his return from Newquay, he had liaised with an enthusiastic SJ at Number 10 regarding the idea of a Garden Party. He had thought nothing more of the conversation.

'Wow, doesn't it look smart?' Kate exclaimed. 'What an excuse to buy a new dress!'

Rafi looked across at her beaming face.

'As luck would have it, I shall be in Milan again the week after next. You're lucky all you'll need is a smart suit.'

Charlie and Saara phoned during the weekend to say they, too, had received invitations to the Garden Party. They were very excited. After a flurry of phone calls, it was arranged that Kate and Rafi would see Saara and Steve for supper the night before the Garden Party and then meet up with family and friends the following morning.

The date of the Summer Garden Party was fast approaching. Kate and Rafi had become accustomed to their European travels. Over the past couple of weeks they had gone in opposite directions.

Jörg, their new boss, and their paymasters were giving them the freedom to research and delve where they wished. Jörg was first class at keeping people off their backs and keeping the politicians happy.

To the unsuspecting outsider, the team remained a nondescript data-crunching organisation. Progress was being made on a number of fronts. The team was gaining an increasingly useful understanding of how pan-European players operated and the areas into which organised criminals had been drawn. It had not initially been the aim of their investigations, but links between corruption, wealth and certain well-connected individuals were becoming apparent. Rafi wondered how long it would be before they knew how dangerous a can of worms they were opening.

Kate and Rafi's cosy flat in Luxembourg remained a tranquil haven.

In contrast, their office down the road was a different world. Kate and Rafi had slotted into the team remarkably easily. They worked well with the other members, though they suspected that in the eyes of some they were viewed as the junior partners. This had its benefits, though, as their colleagues seemed genuinely keen to help.

The week leading up to the Garden Party had been tiring. Rafi had been to Paris, Frankfurt and Amsterdam, whilst Kate had been to Prague and Milan.

They were looking forward to their supper with Steve and Saara on the Thursday evening before their outing to Buckingham Palace.

The hour's time difference meant they could catch the 6.00 p.m. flight to London City Airport and be in Hampstead by 8.00 p.m., London time.

They chatted for much of the flight, enjoying one another's company. They had learned at an early stage not to talk about work in public places.

During a lull in the conversation, Rafi browsed through an English newspaper where one story in particular caught his eye. It was a follow-up on some of the families made homeless by the Stratford nuclear catastrophe. It described how they had been relocated and rehoused, and the public support that they had received. The little girl whose teddy had become world-famous, and her family, had found a home in Norfolk. If the picture – which showed her with a broad smile clutching her teddy – was anything to go by, she was enjoying her new life. The article went on to report that she was one of the lucky ones; many of the dispossessed had still to find permanent new homes.

The journey from London City airport to Hampstead Heath was straightforward. The taxi pulled up in front of Rafi's old flat at 7.25 p.m. Rafi stood in the passageway by the front door to the flats. It was the first time he'd been back since that fateful February morning. It seemed light years away, but he was still uneasy standing there; too many vivid and painful memories flooded through his mind. Kate had thought that returning to the flat would have helped him to slay the ghosts of the past and stop his bad dreams. It certainly gave him the creeps.

Rafi pressed the bell. Saara answered. 'Do come in.'

The door buzzed opened and they entered. As they climbed the stairs, Rafi recalled his conversation with Kate on their return from Cornwall about where he might live. She had been surprised when he had asked if he could move in with her.

'But it's bound to be nothing like as nice as your flat. Jeremy tells me that they've done a good job in putting it back together again!' she had said.

'Your flat reminds me of you and nice memories – mine has too many ghosts,' had been his reply.

They arrived outside the front door to the flat. Rafi knocked. It sounded different, very solid. The door opened and there in front of him was his little sister, looking very grown-up.

'Come in, come in. Sorry about the chaos. We only just beat you here! Steve is dying to meet you, Kate.'

His beaming face appeared from the kitchen. 'Hi there, I'm Steve. Great to meet you at last, Kate. Can I get you a drink or a cup of tea?'

'Tea would be nice,' said Kate, as she and Rafi walked through to the sitting room-cum-dining room.

Rafi saw that his minimalist décor and furniture had been replaced by an eclectic mix of furniture and paintings. Saara and Steve's clutter was everywhere. Paperwork spread from the table, across the floor and on to the windowsill. It gave the place an untidy but homely feel.

Rafi looked at their faces. Their smiles said it all.

'We thought that, if it was fine by you, we would eat out at your favourite Chinese restaurant. Mr Cheung is looking forward to seeing you. He says his turnover has hit 'wock bottom' since you moved away!'

'Sounds good,' said Rafi.

'Let me show you around,' said Saara. 'The MI5 people arranged for the redecorating and the new steel front door. They said your old one had been sold for matchsticks.'

Rafi and Kate followed Saara into the spare bedroom. There were new curtains; the pictures on the walls he recognised from her bedroom in their parents' house and the duvet cover from her house in Birmingham. The bed and the furniture were new and very John Lewis.

'I hope your bedroom is OK,' said Saara. 'Kate, if you need anything when you get changed, please shout.'

'It reminds me of you and living with our parents. It's great,' said Rafi, who then looked into the bathroom. He recalled the conversation with a man from MI5, apologising about all his furniture and personal effects. He now saw what he had meant. *Everything* had been replaced.

'Come on – come and see what Steve and I have done to our bedroom.'

Kate and Rafi were ushered along the corridor and up the small staircase. 'Shambolic' would have been a good word to describe the look of their room. 'Cluttered' could have been an alternative.

'Isn't this great?' beamed Saara. 'So much floor space! Knocks our old house in Brum into a cocked hat!'

Rafi looked at Saara and noticed she looked a little apprehensive.

'It's been a hectic day. We prayed that your flight would be delayed, so we could have done a little tidying up.'

He walked over to Saara and gave her a big hug. 'It's great. I'm pleased you enjoy living here. You should see Kate's flat,' he added, at which point he received a sharp nudge in the ribs.

Saara looked at her watch. 'Mr Cheung is expecting us in thirty minutes. And Rafi, thank you – Steve and I love it here. I hope your bedroom is OK.'

Before leaving Saara's bedroom, Rafi walked over to the window and looked out. The Heath could be seen to the left and central London was in the distance. Rafi glanced down at the road. His heart missed a beat. There, in the evening shadows opposite, was the dark form of a large Mercedes car. Haunting memories rushed back. Kate, who was standing nearby, sensed his apprehension.

'Seen an old ghost?'

'Sort of,' he said.

'Come on lazy bones,' came a shout from downstairs. 'We don't want to keep the restaurant waiting, do we?'

Thirty minutes later, after a quick wash and change, they were standing in front of the restaurant. Saara was at Rafi's side.

'You first, big Bro.'

He opened the door. The sight that met his eyes stopped him in his tracks. There, standing in front of him, were John and Jeremy. To their left were Aidan, Emma and the doctor and his wife from Newquay. He looked around the room. It seemed that everyone was there. The commissioner was in deep conversation with Ewan at a corner table. The brigadier and Colonels Turner and Gray were talking to an elderly gentleman whose back was to Rafi. Suddenly it dawned on him; it was his grandfather's back. He looked across to the other side of the room and saw Kate's brother and partner. He glimpsed Kate's parents sitting down, looking very proper, with Air Chief Marshal Sir Nigel Hawser and the back of someone he couldn't quite place. Ah yes, it was Donald Hollingsworth, and next to him was Kate's former boss, David. He looked around again;

he'd missed many faces. So much had happened since Stratford; he had lots of catching up to do.

Rafi walked across the threshold and was greeted by a cheer. Mr Cheung, who ran this award-winning restaurant, appeared out of thin air.

'Mr Khan, so pleased to see you this evening. No takeaway tonight, I think?' he said with a chuckle.

Rafi looked around in amazement. 'I thought we were going out for a quiet supper,' he said to Saara. 'How on earth did you manage to arrange something so big and keep it a secret?'

Saara grinned. 'It wasn't easy!'

Jeremy stuck out his hand which Rafi shook energetically.

'Fancy meeting you again,' he said with a broad smile going almost from ear to ear. 'I had a devil of a problem travelling on the same plane as you without being spotted. Good training, eh? When Saara told me what she and her boss, the Chancellor, had planned for your party, I couldn't resist hopping on a plane. Oh, I forgot, the PM, the Defence Secretary and the Chancellor of the Exchequer send their apologies. They've got a meeting which is running late but they should be here in half an hour.'

'You're joking. They are not really coming, are they?' said Rafi.

''Fraid so. It seems the Chancellor reckons you deserved a proper thank you – it looks as if you're going to have yourself some party! Better be on your best behaviour,' said Jeremy with a grin.

'What can I get you?' asked John. 'Champagne?'

Rafi looked at Kate, who had started to shift into party mode. Her eyes sparkled and she looked fantastic in her summer dress.

'As this is a very special occasion, champagne would be great, please.'

As if by magic two glasses arrived.

Rafi gave Kate a peck on the cheek. 'Isn't this amazing? Did you know anything about this?'

'Honestly, no. But I should have guessed something was in the wind given the strange phone calls I've been getting from Saara and Emma over the past few weeks!'

'How's about we circulate? See you in a bit,' said Rafi.

The evening went by far too fast – so many people to talk to and lots of news to take on board. As Rafi worked his way around the large room, he came across a few faces he didn't recognise. The retired commander and his wife, their two 'daughters', the SBS 'boyfriends' and the two SAS soldiers were on good form recalling their escapade and their close call with the Moroccan Air Force.

Rafi was introduced to the crew of the first helicopter to carry concrete to the wrecked train, who by the end of the day had flown more sorties than any other crew. He then found himself talking to Arnold Owen, the data manager from Companies House, and Roger and Steve from the Immigration team. They seemed awestruck by their fellow guests and were standing quietly to one side – conversation with them was an uphill battle.

'Did you know,' Rafi began, 'that if it hadn't been for you three, we wouldn't have cracked what the terrorists were planning? I'm so pleased you could come. Whilst you are here, you might like to make the most of it – where else can you meet the head of MI5?' Rafi surreptitiously pointed out Ewan. 'Next to him is the Chief of the Defence Staff and shortly we'll be joined by the Prime Minister. We all owe you a big thank you. And, Roger, you might even pluck up the courage to tell the PM what you think of the system you work under!'

They visibly grew in stature and headed off to mix and chat with the other guests.

At that moment the PM and the Chancellor arrived with their entourage. Saara did the introductions, from which it became apparent she now had friends in high places.

The PM was apologetic. 'I hope you don't mind, but I've brought along a couple of gatecrashers. My last meeting overran and, as a penance for them talking too much, here they are.' He introduced the leaders of the two main opposition parties, who were now high-ranking cabinet ministers. They spoke briefly before the PM moved off to work the room as only a top class politician can.

The Chancellor was greeted by Steve and Saara. He was in ebullient form. The flak he had feared following the Stratford disaster had not materialised. His initiatives had worked their way through Parliament and were having a rejuvenating effect on public sentiment.

'I've been meaning to ask you a question, if you don't mind?' said Rafi. 'How close were we to joining the Euro?'

The Chancellor put his arm on Rafi's shoulder and ushered him to one side. 'Between you and me, it was close – very close! In the House, I was almost more worried when waiting to receive the message from the Bank of England which would tell me whether they'd done a deal with the Central Banks than the messages telling me if the terrorists had been captured. When I stood up we only had a couple of smaller Central Banks offering to support Sterling, but it was at an unacceptably low exchange rate and contingent on others getting involved. The Governor of the Bank of England did a fantastic job.' His voice went quieter. 'I am told it was a senior individual at the Hong Kong Monetary Authority who we should thank. He realised how inter-twined Sterling, the City of London and the international financial markets were. Anyway, within forty-five minutes he had three of the top twenty countries with the highest foreign exchange reserves agreeing to support Sterling. Then Japan, the US and India came on board and the rest is history.'

The Chancellor smiled, 'I was overjoyed when I read the message saying how much support Sterling had. I could scarcely believe my eyes. I must tell you how much I appreciate all you have done. Your foresight of what was going on in the financial markets and your and Aidan's team's proposals got me out of a very nasty hole. Thank you.'

Saara and Kate joined them. Rafi sensed that his conversation with the Chancellor had come to an end and he and Kate went off to mingle.

Food appeared. It was Mr Cheung at his best and Rafi told him so.

Plate in hand, Rafi was standing in the middle of the room, enjoying the atmosphere and taking in the scene around him, when he felt a soft squeeze around his waist from behind. 'When you started dating me you forgot to tell me that you were this well-connected. If I'd known perhaps I'd have taken you a bit more seriously,' said the seductive voice. 'Who would have guessed that so many of my friends are friends of yours . . .'

The sentence was interrupted by the restaurant door swinging open. There, filling a substantial portion of the frame, was a well-built man and behind him were a well-dressed man of indeterminate age and a stunning dark-haired young woman.

The deep voice rang out. 'Have I missed all the fun? Look who I met at the airport – a Dutch generaal! Someone should have told me Heathrow is further away than your City Airport; and whoever put in those bloody bus lanes should be told they screw up the traffic when you're in a hurry!' This was followed by a booming laugh. 'They tell me this is where we can find DCI Adams and an air chief marshal,' rang out the deep voice, 'and if I'm lucky, a Mr Khan might be hiding here, with some vodka – if he values his life!' The colonel paused. 'If not, I've brought some best Estonian Türi.'

Beaming, Rafi went over to meet Colonel Matlik and his two companions.

He stuck out his hand as Rafi approached. 'I hope you don't mind I've brought my daughter, Kristina, with me. She knows nothing of the

English ways. I thought if Emma and Kate were here to keep an eye on possible suitors, she might just be safe,' he said with a chuckle.

'And we have an invitation to see your Queen for tea tomorrow afternoon – such a nice surprise. Kristina has been impossible for weeks, fretting about what to wear. Now, where did you say the vodka was?' And off he strode as if he were a man on a mission.

Rafi looked across towards Saara. She was smiling. He sensed that the guest list was complete. Standing behind Rafi was the Air Chief Marshal, flanked by the Prime Minister.

'Prime Minister and Mr Khan,' said the Air Chief Marshal, 'it is my pleasure to introduce you to Generaal Wilm Van Dijk of the Royal Netherlands Air Force. Had Wilm not stuck his neck out for us and lent us almost all his fleet of helicopters and transport planes, we would have been in great trouble.' They shook hands and started talking.

Emma came over and introduced herself to Colonel Matlik's daughter, Kristina. The colonel reappeared with two glasses and passed one to his daughter. 'I told you they do things a bit differently here,' he said and he pointed out some of the more illustrious guests. 'Where else in Europe can one go to a local Chinese restaurant and meet the Prime Minister, the heads of the intelligence service and the armed forces, and two police chiefs – and find them all mingling with the public? There must be an election coming up soon!' he boomed.

David appeared at the colonel's shoulder and suggested he might like to meet Ewan. Emma took Kristina under her wing and they went off to find Aidan.

Rafi walked over to chat to his grandfather, but saw he was in deep conversation with Colonel Gray. He stopped and moved over to be with Kate, who was standing watching the party. Within moments he and Kate were joined by the two commissioners.

'We are most grateful to you for all you've done,' said Len. 'I always knew Giles had a good team at Wood Street.'

'I understand that we'll be meeting you again tomorrow,' said Giles.

'At the Garden Party?' replied Kate.

'No, before that,' said Giles.

Kate and Rafi looked puzzled.

'Has anyone told you why you're to see the Queen beforehand?'

'No.'

'Well, Kate, you're to be awarded the Queen's Police Medal and Rafi is to be given the Queen's Gallantry Medal. The police force is very proud of you, Kate,' said Giles.

They both looked at Giles in amazement and Rafi gave Kate a hug.

Ewan joined them. 'Thank you for the invite; Jeremy tells me that you're keeping him busy. Oh, by the way, did you see the photos of Maryam in the newspapers a couple of months ago?'

Rafi nodded. 'I recall reading an article which described her as helping the police with their enquiries and intimated that she had done a deal – is that true?' asked Rafi.

'You shouldn't believe everything you read,' said Ewan. 'In reality she's being totally uncooperative. The photo was a set-up. She'd thought she was about to be released on a technicality and was meeting a European human rights judge. The sheikh, Basel and Jameel, who are locked away in separate high security prisons, just happened to see the papers that day. They're furious! As the saying goes, "Divide and rule".' Ewan gave Rafi a friendly tap on the shoulder. 'Great party; if you'll excuse me there are a couple more people I should like to chat to. Do keep in touch.'

'Time to mix with family?' asked Kate.

'Good idea,' replied Rafi.

They walked over to speak to Kate's parents. They were sitting with their backs to the wall, taking in all that was going on in the room. Kate sat down next to her mother and gave her a hug, then got up and did the same to her father.

'I'm so pleased that you could come.'

'We almost didn't. But Rafi's sister sounded very charming on the phone and said how much it would mean to you,' said her father.

'We've been chumps haven't we?' said her mother. 'I'm sorry we didn't understand how important your job was to you and what you'd make of it. The commissioner tells us you're one of the – if not *the* – youngest chief inspector in Europe and are doing more good work in Luxembourg.'

'I think he's exaggerating a *bit*!' said Kate.

'He's not the only one who says that we should be very proud of you,' said her father. 'We are proud – very proud.' He paused then went on, 'With Marcus's help we have done up the attic studio in the main house. Do please use it as your home whenever you have time.'

Kate gave a beaming smile to her parents. 'That would be lovely, thank you.'

Out of the corner of his eye, Rafi noticed Saara talking with her grandfather. He smiled; they looked very happy together.

The conversation between Kate and her parents turned to small talk.

'Have I told you?' began Kate's mother, 'We've got your postcards stuck all round our kitchen cupboards. It was so nice of you to start up the family tradition again.'

Kate gave Rafi's hand a squeeze.

'You do seem to get around a bit these days,' continued her mother. 'Some weeks we seem to get a card every other day!'

Rafi sensed the wounds and hurts of previous years were forgotten.

The sound of a wine glass being tapped echoed across the room and was followed by the quietly raised voice of Rafi's little sister. She was standing at the side of the restaurant next to the Prime Minister, the Air Chief Marshal and Commissioner Giles Meynell. She had a champagne glass in her hand and was tapping it with a spoon. Silence fell over the room.

'Thank you,' she said. 'I am so pleased you could all make it to Rafi's surprise party. I should like to thank the Chancellor, my boss, whose idea it was to convene such a gathering and I would ask you to raise your glasses, please, in a toast to Rafi and determination!'

The Prime Minister moved to Saara's side. With a beaming face he looked around the room. 'For once I shall be brief.' He paused as he noticed a wry smile on many of the faces in front of him. 'If I were to pay my thanks to each of you here, who selflessly gave so much, it would take a very long time. I'm tempted . . . But not tonight!'

The PM reached for his glass. 'I would ask you all to lift your glasses and toast teamwork, and spare a thought for all those who lost their lives or their good health.'

The PM waited for his audience to finish sipping their champagne and for their attention to focus back on him. 'I would especially like to thank two people who have travelled a long distance to be with us this evening. Generaal Wilm Van Dijk and Colonel Hendrik Matlik: thank you for your help in our hour of need. I would ask you to raise your glasses and toast our distinguished foreign guests.'

The PM waited for silence to return. He raised his glass and looked around the room making eye contact with as many people as possible. 'To you all! You are a very special group of people and I praise you for all you have done.'

He moved to one side during the clapping. His place was taken by the Air Chief Marshal. 'I, too, will follow the precedent set by the Prime Minister and keep my speech brief. I should like to convey my personal thanks to the team I had with me on that fateful night. Their response and clear headedness was beyond anything I could have reasonably expected. I would ask you to raise your glasses to all those who risked their all in countering the recent terrorist attacks and to the Prime Minister, the Defence Secretary, Ewan Thorn, Brigadier Sparkman and Colonels Turner and Gray for their leadership.'

There was further clapping and a shuffling around, as glasses were sipped and recharged. The Air Chief Marshal's place was taken by Commissioner Giles Meynell. He looked across at Kate and John. 'During the investigation leading up to the snaring of the terrorists, we were truly fortunate to have the unerring resolve and meticulous help of a large number of people. I should like to pay my sincere thanks to all of you who made it possible for us to latch on to the terrorist plot. In particular, Arnold from Companies House, Steve and Roger from the Immigration team, Jeremy and Neil from MI5 and Rick and Phil from Manchester; they all deserve special mention.'

Giles paused and turned to David. 'Your team of Kate, John, Emma, Jack, Peter and our IT guru Greg did you proud. Thank you.' He paused and added, with a glint in his eye, 'But another time perhaps we shouldn't have to rely on someone locked up in a police cell and then get him to provide us with the services of his friends! Aidan, Bob, Alex, Donald, Matthew, Saara and, of course, Rafi – thank you. We owe you all a great debt of gratitude. I should like to ask you all to raise your glasses and toast tenacity and all those who helped in our time of need.'

Rafi caught sight of Kate's parents sitting holding hands with Marcus and Susannah beside them. He wished he could have captured their expressions and given the picture as a present to Kate. He looked round and saw Kate smiling at him; she too had spotted her family's proud faces.

Saara waited for the room to regain its stillness. 'That is the end of the formalities; I'm advised that there's no closing time and Mr Cheung assures me that he has more than enough food and drink to satisfy your appetites and quench your thirst. Thank you all for making this the most memorable of evenings.'

Saara seemed taken aback by the spontaneous applause and for the first time in ages looked a little self-conscious.

She came over and gave Rafi a hug. 'So how's the party boy?'

'Very contented, it's been a wonderful evening. Thank you for arranging everything.'

They were joined by Kate and made their way across to her parents, who looked extremely happy.

Her mother started the conversation. 'Kate, dear, this has been such fun, what an evening to remember! But now that we've had a chance to talk with you and have seen your friends perhaps we should be getting off; it's well past our bedtime.'

'Pardon?' interjected Kate's father. 'I thought we were having fun. Our hotel is not far, so why don't we stay for another drink or two and then head off?'

Kate's mother smiled. 'As you say, dear.'

'Rafi, might there be any decent Scotch on the premises?' asked Kate's father.

'I'll see what I can find,' replied Rafi. 'And then there's someone I'd like you to meet.'

The major raised his eyebrows as if to say, 'Who could be more important than the PM?'

Rafi found Mr Cheung and relayed the request for a bottle of his very best Scotch.

'Blended or single malt?'

'Would you bring both, please?'

Then Rafi went over and extracted his grandfather from the conversation he was having.

'Grandfather, do you like Scotch?'

He beamed. 'Is the Pope Catholic?'

'There are a couple of people I'd like you to meet.'

As they walked across to the table where Kate's parents were sitting, Rafi added Marcus, Susannah, Saara and Steve to his entourage.

Rafi approached the table. Kate's father was trying to decide which Scotch he preferred. He looked up and smiled.

'Major Sir Percy and Lady Yvonne,' Rafi said. 'It is my pleasure to introduce to you my long lost grandfather, Major Charlie Staveley, my little sister, Saara, and her partner Dr Steve Morris.'

Introductions complete, their conversation started slowly, then the two majors found that they had several interests in common.

Rafi noticed Kate standing hand in hand with her brother, who had his arm around his wife. They looked relaxed and content; after too many years of strife, calm had returned. He felt happy, very happy.

Kate's brother caught his eye and beckoned him over. 'Rafi, you're so elusive. I've been meaning to thank you; I've never seen Kate look this happy. You're a real tonic for her.'

Rafi smiled. 'I think it is I who should be thanking her. Without her I'd probably be languishing in some grubby cell, whilst the country had next to no electricity.'

Marcus looked carefully at Rafi. 'I'm glad you're looking after each other. Make the most of the time when happiness is in abundance. It's such a precious gift which few people ever get to appreciate. Please, for me, don't lose it.' The conversation changed as Saara, Steve and Marcus's wife, Susannah, came across to join them.

In a short time it was agreed that they'd all meet for a Sunday lunch at Leverthorne Hall and inspect Kate's new studio flat in the attic.

To Rafi, the next forty-five minutes flew past as lots of people came over to say their goodbyes.

Roger from the Immigration team made Rafi smile. 'I did as you said, bucked up courage, went over and talked to the Home Secretary. I apologised before I started telling him the system was run by data junkies. You know what? He's asked me to explain my concerns to one of his ministers next week!'

After saying goodbye to Roger, Rafi at last had a moment to himself. He took a step back to look around the room and see if he had missed someone that he should have talked to and literally bumped into a stunning blonde with long hair. Rafi smiled weakly at her. Then it hit him: he knew this woman. What a transformation!

'Sorry I was late. I hadn't realised that the PM's meeting was going to overrun,' she said.

It was the first time that Rafi had seen SJ outside her office environment. His senses picked up her evocative perfume.

She looked up at him from under her lashes and then casually said to Kristina, who was standing next to her, 'Have you been introduced to Rafi?'

'Yes, thank you.' Then, smiling at Rafi, she added, 'My daddy tells me you and your friends are very remarkable.'

At that moment the little group was joined by Kate.

'Hi, SJ,' said Kate. 'Hello again, Kristina. I've been talking to David and he tells me you're at university. Is that right?'

'Almost finished – I have my finals next month.'

'What are you reading?'

'Environmental sciences with biology.'

'Excellent – have you meet Rafi's sister, Saara?' enquired Kate. 'Her contacts are fantastic.'

Kristina shook her head.

'Let's find her. I will introduce you to her. We'll be back in a moment. Rafi you'll be OK with SJ, won't you?'

There was an embarrassing silence. 'I'm sorry,' stuttered Rafi, realising he'd been staring at her shapely body. He was starting to blush. 'You look so different with your hair down and in that amazing dress.'

'You approve?' SJ asked with her head tipped slightly to one side.

'I'm surprised that all the red-blooded men in the room aren't queuing up to get your phone number. I still can't get over the transformation.' Rafi cast his approving eyes from head to toe. 'You look stunning.'

SJ felt the hairs on her bare arms stand up. The visit to her friend who was a professional hairdresser and make-up artist had been worth the hassle.

She hesitated. 'Forgive me if it's private, but is it true that you turned down a six or seven figure sum from the newspapers and gave it to charity?'

'Sort of – yes,' Rafi replied. He sensed she was hoping for more. 'It seemed that the money would be better used helping those suffering from radiation exposure. Hospices survive thanks to donations and at the moment they desperately need money.'

'Have you ever visited a hospice?'

Rafi shook his head.

'If you and Kate have a spare moment sometime, perhaps you should visit one? I'm sure we could get you good press coverage, which would help boost their donations. I could even see if the PM had a spare slot in his diary so he could be there with you.'

'Sounds like a good idea,' said Rafi. 'Unfortunately Kate and I aren't in the UK very much these days.'

'No problem, I'm not going anywhere,' said SJ casually, hoping that this wasn't going to be the end of the conversation.

There was a pause. 'I'm sure I should know, but is Sandy Jane your Christian name or your full name?' enquired Rafi.

'Jane is my surname. I know, it sounds silly.'

'It's a nice name, better than Smith or Khan; there are hundreds of thousands of us,' said Rafi with a grin.

Kate returned to Rafi's side. 'Sorry, we had to wait a bit before I could introduce Kristina to Saara,' said Kate with a smile. 'What have you two been chatting about?'

'I was suggesting to Rafi that the PM might be able to help you in your efforts to raise money for the hospices.'

'That sounds like a great idea,' replied Kate. 'Rafi's sister works next door to you; she tends to know when we're over in London. If you come up with a plan perhaps you could liaise with Saara, so we can find a convenient time to meet up.'

SJ couldn't believe what she'd just heard. Surely Kate must have sensed that she was attracted her boyfriend? It wasn't fair that the man she thought was gorgeous just happened to have a charming, self-assured girlfriend – who she even *liked*.

'I'll speak with Saara and line something up. Nice chatting to you both,' said SJ. She turned and made eye contact with Kate. 'I've been meaning to ask . . . Wherever did you find your dress? You look absolutely gorgeous. Rafi is very lucky.' Before Kate could reply, SJ had left and was on her way to the bar.

'SJ seemed on particularly good form this evening,' commented Kate. Then she added, while smiling to herself, 'She's taken a fancy to you! She's stunning, isn't she?'

'Yes, but she isn't *you*!'

Kate lent forward and kissed him.

Over in a corner, Emma and Aidan were sitting together deep in conversation.

Kate squeezed Rafi's hand. He followed her look. 'They enjoy each other's company, don't they? From all Emma tells me, she's having a great time being wooed by Aidan.'

'I can't say I'm surprised. Emma would be a great catch for any man with a decent IQ,' Rafi replied.

Kate was about to comment, when the last of the politicians came by to say their 'thank yous' and 'goodnights'. It was almost 1.30 a.m. Only a few guests remained.

A beaming Pete Lockyer came over to thank Kate and Rafi for the great party. 'It's been an exceptional evening. The boys at the office will never believe who I've met tonight!'

Kate grimaced.

'Don't worry! I know this was a social; the evening is all off the record. Thanks again. You know where to find me if there's anything I can do to help.' And with that Pete left with a broad grin.

Kate left Rafi's side to chat to Emma, who was preparing to leave.

It had been the best party Rafi could remember. Standing thinking to himself, he felt the presence of someone behind him. A deep, quiet voice started talking to him from behind, so that no one else could hear. It was the unmistakable voice of Colonel Matlik. 'Rafi, my friend, thank you for this evening; Kristina and I very much enjoyed ourselves. By the way, I'm keeping track of all the work you, Kate and Jörg's unit are doing in Luxembourg. You have one hell of a team around you. I know your colleague Bernhard Michalak – he is a good Pole.'

The colonel's whisper became quieter. 'Some shadowy figures are coming out of the woodwork. My sources inform me that a number of racketeers and other undesirables from Russia and Central Europe were caught up in Maryam Vynckt's investments and suffered massive losses. Rafi, dear boy, a hornets' nest has been stirred up. Several of the large criminal organisations are seriously short of cash. They are furious and intent not only on replenishing their coffers but also on revenge. To complicate matters, their competitors have noticed this weakness. A new playing field is being created. Former allegiances have been shattered and a war of attrition has started.'

He paused. 'Desperate people do desperate things. The stakes have been raised and they may have to think big to survive. Be careful not to cross their paths – they are in a dangerous mood.'

Rafi felt the colonel place his large hand on his shoulder. 'Sorry, I have more bad news. Just before I left I was informed that the FSB have reopened their investigation into the death of Pinja Koit. They now think that the charred body in the plane crash was not his after all. Perhaps you could tell your people at MI5?'

The colonel's voice reverted to his normal deep growl. 'Great party, thank you, Rafi. Kristina has had a ball. She's very excited; it seems your sister has invited her over to shadow her for a couple of days' work experience; even offered to put her up. Say a big thank you to Saara for me. And, Rafi, remember: let me know if I can be of any help. You know where to find me.'

Rafi hesitated before replying; he was still taking in what the colonel had just said. Jörg Emcke's team were only in the preliminary stages of researching the financial grey areas and piecing together the web of cross-border crime syndicates. Colonel Matlik had given him another whole angle to consider.

Rafi turned around to ask him a question but he'd disappeared into thin air.

Kate was standing nearby.

'Have you seen Matlik?' he enquired.

'Yes, he left a moment ago, just after chatting to you,' replied Kate. 'You look as if you've seen another ghost.'

Rafi took a deep breath. A sense of foreboding came over him. If Matlik was right and the criminal classes were about to flex their muscles, Jörg's team had two groups to worry about. On the one hand there were those whose finances had been crippled by their losses in the derivatives markets – they needed to make money fast. On the other hand there were those champing at the bit to grab market share, intent on eliminating their weakened competitors.

A cold shiver ran down his back. And on top of this, Kate and he possibly had two rogue bulls to contend with: Pinja Koit with his Chechen contacts and Miti Lakhani, about whom they still knew practically nothing. They would have to watch their backs. Unwanted memories of the Headland Hotel crept back into his mind.

Kate squeezed his hand. 'Are you alright?'

Rafi pulled his overactive imagination back to the present.

'Sorry, I was just mulling over something Colonel Matlik said. Oh, by the way, Saara has offered Kristina a couple of days' work experience and invited her to stay after she has finished her university finals. Have you seen Jeremy?'

Kate pointed to the back of the restaurant.

'I won't be long; there's something I could do with asking him.'

Jeremy was sitting at a corner table talking quietly with Ewan.

'Am I disturbing you?' Rafi asked him. 'As it's work-related, would you prefer we chat when we're back in Luxembourg?'

'Not at all,' replied Jeremy. 'We were just catching up on a few matters relating to Maryam and her bank.'

Rafi sat down with his back to the room.

'We have managed to get into the bank accounts Maryam was using to fund the terrorist activities,' added Ewan. 'In some cases the payments go back over three years. She was using numbered accounts so at this stage we have not been able to put precise names to them. However, what has caught our attention is the series of large payments to an Estonian bank account, which stopped and then started again a week or so later but went into a bank account in Pakistan and another in Iran. We were speculating as to whether these accounts were linked to Pinja Koit.'

'Could I add something?' asked Rafi butting in. 'I have just been chatting to Colonel Matlik and he was telling me that the Russians – the FSB – have been looking into Pinja Koit's death. There seems to be considerable doubt as to whether he was on the plane that crashed.'

'When was that?' enquired Ewan.

'About fourteen months ago,' replied Jeremy. 'He makes a good addition to our team, doesn't he, sir?' said a beaming Jeremy. 'It seems Colonel Matlik trusts him more than you or I!'

Ewan nodded, deep in thought. 'Fourteen months ago . . . That ties in with the switch in the bank payments. So we can assume Mr Koit is still out there.'

'That makes sense,' added Jeremy. 'When Radu Dranoff arrived to help Aslan Popovskaya, I bet it was Pinja Koit who arranged it. He must have been involved behind the scenes coordinating all the dirty work. As I see it, he was so pissed off with you, Rafi, that he sent Dranoff to take you out. I don't see why he shouldn't still be seriously pissed off with you.'

Rafi looked shocked. He thought for a moment. 'How do you think UKSOIL, the suicide bombers and Kaleem Shah fitted in?'

'I am not sure,' said Ewan. 'The attack on the atomic weapons establishment at Aldermaston and the style of Kaleem Shah's operation have had me thinking. I am wondering whether it was the terrorists' insurance policy to get the Iranians on their side.'

'Pardon?' said Rafi.

'Well, let us assume for one moment that the terrorists' plans had been successful; Maryam, the sheikh, Jameel and Talal would have become pariahs in the Western world and would have needed somewhere to go to escape the reach of our laws.'

'Hence Iran?' asked Jeremy.

'That's my thinking,' said Ewan. 'Especially as they are prevented from having any nuclear capabilities. Iran doesn't like being excluded from the nuclear club and they can't have been happy with the UK's decision to upgrade Trident. One set of rules for us and another for them.'

'So do you reckon Pinja Koit is in Pakistan or Iran regrouping?' asked Rafi.

'Yes; probably Pakistan,' replied Ewan.

'But they have one serious problem,' interjected Rafi. 'They will have lost their source of funding!'

'Good point,' said Ewan, 'but we should not underestimate Koit's capabilities. I will bring MI6 up to speed and make tracking him down a priority.'

'In the meantime,' added Jeremy, 'if I was you, Rafi, I'd try and avoid dark alleyways – and that applies to Kate as well.'

'On the bright side, after Newquay, we at MI5 and the SAS owe you one, so we will do our best to keep an eye on you,' said Ewan.

Rafi was about to reply, when Saara ambled over. 'So this is where you have got to!' She was beaming. 'Now that's what I call a party. I hope you enjoyed it, big brother.'

'Fantastic. The best ever; thank you, Sis.'

'Steve is making a real party of it. I doubt whether I'll get him home for hours. I've given Kate my set of keys, in case you want to leave before us. Last I saw of her she was looking for you,' said Saara.

Jeremy smiled at Rafi. 'Let's chat some more back in the office.'

Rafi spotted Kate in the distance. He got up and shook hands with Ewan. 'Thank you for bringing me up to speed. If you will excuse me, I should go and see why Kate wanted me.'

'It has been a pleasure talking to you ... And Rafi, please, remember to keep Jeremy in the loop with all your thinking. I sense that these are still treacherous times,' added Ewan.

Rafi, with Saara beside him, went off to find Kate.

She greeted him with a hug and a lingering kiss, then jangled Saara's keys in front of his nose. 'How's about we say our remaining few goodbyes and then try out the new bed in your flat?' she said suggestively.

'Great idea,' Rafi replied. He felt alive. He had traded the comfy and highly paid world of the City for the adrenaline-filled world of counterterrorism, and to his surprise he wondered what he had ever seen in his previous existence. Then he saw in Kate's eyes the same fire that had burned that first night they were in Luxembourg and with a flutter of her eyelashes, his worries about the hazards that lay ahead vanished.

Appendix A

THE TERRORISTS' CORPORATE WEB

Prima Terra	**Fund Managers with large stakes in:**
ESSA plc	Executive Search & Selection Agency
Dewoodson plc	Property Services business
Renshaw Smithers plc	Niche financial intermediary – a deal maker focusing on public sector projects and out sourcing companies
Unicorn Sceptre Finance plc	Credit cards & student finance
Rainer Spencer & Mitchell	**Chartered Accountants which run:**
CGF Company Services Ltd	Company secretarial business run by Rainer Spencer & Mitchell
AGVC Ltd	**Acorn Growth Venture Capital which controls:**
AEIEA Ltd	African Estonian Import / Export Agency
AGVCFOF	Acorn Growth Venture Capital Fund of Funds
CCVH Ltd	Central City View Hotels
SJFR Ltd	Small Joe's Fish Restaurants
CDAFO Ltd	Commercial Development & Fit Out
HFFF Ltd	Hotel Frozen Fish Foods
PSSAF Ltd	Public Sector Services and Facilities
SPAD Ltd	Security Protection & Defence
UKSOIL Ltd	UK Students Overseas Initiative Live
PREH plc	**Prime Real Estate Holdings**
	A pooled property investment business which has Prima Terra and AGVC Ltd as major investors

Glossary

Annuities / REITs An annuity is used to provide pensioners with a regular income in return for a lump sum investment. For more details on the characteristics of REITs and their suitability as a substitute for annuities, and the beneficial funding implications. See *www.annuityreits.com*.

AWACS Airborne Warning and Control System. Undertakes surveillance, command and control, and battle management activities from specially equipped long range planes.

Basis Point One basis point is 0.01%. It is smallest measure for quoting a change in an interest rate or a yield. So a 50 basis points (bps) change is a % change.

Bear market / bearish A falling market / pessimistic.

Bull market / bullish A rising market / optimistic.

Call In the context of a derivative instrument – with an option contract it is the right and for a futures contract it is an obligation – to buy an underlying security / index / commodity / asset at a predetermined price on a specific future date. A speculator can make a profit if prices rise further than expected, as they can sell at a higher price in the market and at the same time buy at a lower price by exercising their future or options contract.

Capitalisation [market cap.] The value of a company.

Clearing house Acts as the intermediary between buyer and seller. Responsible for the settlement of deals done. Usually acts as a guarantor so that the buyer and seller get their money, even if one party defaults.

Close [to] To settle a position in the market – to sell a [financial] instrument.

CME Chicago Mercantile Exchange The leading US financial futures and options exchange.

Companies House The official UK government register containing information relating to UK registered companies. Based in Cardiff, Wales.

Company Secretarial Business An agent who is responsible for providing company secretarial services to a company. Its role includes keeping up to date: the company's information posted at Companies House, the company's share register – which shows who the owners of the company's shares are – and arranging shareholders' meetings.

Contract notes The paperwork that sets out the contract between a buyer and a seller of a financial instrument. It confirms the terms of a verbal (or computer generated) agreement to buy or sell. See *My word is my bond*.

Convertible Unsecured Loan Stock [CULS] A security / bond issued by a company to investors which can either be converted into new ordinary shares in the company at a predetermined price on specified date(s),or alternatively it can be redeemed on the expiry date.

Counterparty The party on the other side of a futures or options contract. Usually this responsibility is borne by the clearing house.

Credit Rating Agency Provides information to lenders or investors on the likelihood of the company or Government being able to pay back a debt. For example a company or a country with an AAA rating is expected to be able to meet all its financial obligations even in a severe economic downturn. The lower the credit rating the more expensive the cost of borrowings will be. Other credit rating companies provide information on individuals.

Debt service cover ratio [DSCR] Measures a property portfolio's ability to produce enough net rental income to cover its mortgage payments – interest and capital repayments. Lenders usually expect the DSCR to be in excess of 125%, i.e. the net rents are higher than the mortgage servicing costs.

Derivative Examples of derivative instruments are: futures, options and SWAPs. They are priced by the market with due regard to expected price movements in the future, i.e. their performance is linked to the performance of the underlying asset / index. Relatively small movements in the underlying asset / index price can translate into large profits or losses for those owning the derivative instruments. They are used by investors to hedge [protect] a position, and by speculators in the anticipation of making a profit, where they believe the market's expectations are wrong.

EGi Estates Gazette interactive. A leading provider of online news, research and information for the UK commercial property market.

Eurex [in Frankfurt] The leading Continental European financial futures and options exchange.

Euronext.liffe The leading UK financial futures and options exchange. It is also a clearing house.

FCP Fonds commun de placement. A collective investment fund popular in Luxembourg as it pays next to no tax. Broadly similar in concept to unit trusts in the UK.

Financial ratio Or accounting ratio. A ratio of selected values taken from a company's financial statements. Each ratio can then be compared with that of other companies and the industry average to see how the company in question is performing.

Focus A leading provider of online information on UK commercial property deals.

Futures A standardised contract, which places an *obligation* on both parties, for the delivery or receipt of a specific amount of a financial instrument – or commodity, etc. – at a set price, on a certain date in the future. With a financial futures contract one buys or sells a financial instrument – which for example may be linked to an index, an interest rate, an exchange rate, etc. The price of the future reflects the market's expectation of how the underlying index / interest rate / exchange rate, etc. will move. Financial futures are settled in money. Physical futures (e.g. gold, oil, corn) are settled by physical delivery. As there is an obligation to complete the transaction, the intermediary – a broker / bank – requires margin payments which protect them against any losses.

Where futures prices move against a speculator or investor additional "margin" payments will be required or the position will be closed (sold). Futures price movements can be very volatile when the underlying price of the financial asset to which the future is linked moves in an unexpected way. Speculators can put up a small percentage of the value of the contract (margin payment) and can then find themselves liable to make large additional payments if they get the market's movements wrong – alternatively if they get it right then large profits can be made. See also *Call*, *Derivatives*, *Options* and *Put*.

Gearing See *Leverage*.

Gilts Government borrowings (bonds) traded on the stock market. Investors are repaid at a predetermined date (redemption date). Interest is paid half yearly.

Hedge [to] To off-set the risk in another investment. See *Unhedged*.

HR Human resources.

Hypothecation In taxation it refers to an obligation to use tax revenues from a particular source in a particular way.

Income tax [1 penny increase] This raises the Government approximately £3 billion in additional tax revenues.

Indexhold A form of residential property ownership put forward to provide accommodation for key workers wishing to live close to their place of work in cities or major towns where house prices would otherwise be too expensive. See *www.indexhold.com*.

Inelastic In a market where supply is inelastic, small changes in demand dramatically affect the price by pushing it up (more demand) or pulling it down (less demand).

Instrument A financial product.

Interest rate contracts These financial instruments enable speculation on which way interest rates will move. They come in a variety of forms such as exchange traded futures and options contracts, SWAPs, and forward contracts.

Invisible [an] In the context of MI5 it describes a terrorist who is normally resident in the UK and who can therefore move around freely and unnoticed.

IPO Initial public offering or simply public offering, is when a company issues its shares to investors for the first time, usually via the stock market.

LCH.Clearnet Europe's main clearing house, a central counterparty that acts as a go-between when two parties trade. Once the trade is made, it acts as the guarantor for the trade. LCH.Clearnet undertakes the settlement for these futures and options markets.

LESLP London Emergency Services Liaison Panel. It normally includes representatives from the Metropolitan, City of London and the British transport police, the London fire brigade and ambulance service, local authorities, the port of London authority, the marine coastguard, the RAF, the army and the voluntary sector. Its remit is to provide a framework for the successful resolution of an incident.

Leverage [gearing] The term used to describe the use of debt or borrowings to finance the purchase of an investment or asset with the intention of increasing the investors returns – which happens when the performance of the investment or asset exceeds the cost of the debt. Where the returns are less, leverage destroys investor wealth.

Loan to value [LTV] ratio This represents the relationship between the amount of borrowings and the value of the property on which the money has been lent. Borrowings of £8.5m on property worth £10m would give a LTV ratio of 85%.

Long gilts / Long end of the gilts market Gilts that have over 15 years before they are repaid (i.e. to their maturity / redemption date). Their prices are very sensitive to interest rate changes. Rising interest rates result in falling gilt prices.

Margin The amount paid to the intermediary – broker / bank – who undertakes a futures transaction. This sum is to protect the intermediary from any losses that might accrue to their client. An initial margin is paid and this is followed by additional margin calls if the market has moved against their client's position. These margin payments are collected by the speculator's broker / bank, and passed to the clearing house, which calculates the size of the margin required. See *LCH Clearnet*.

Margin calls Where the speculator in a future finds the market is moving against them additional money or securities are required by broker / bank to maintain their safeguard. With financial futures contracts there is a contractual obligation to pay up for losses (or receive profit) at the expiry date. The margin payment is there to protect the broker / bank in case the investor cannot pay up.

Mortgage register A register held by Companies House, which lists for each company, the properties over which there is a legal charge in respect of secured borrowings thereon.

Multifactor models A financial model which incorporates many variables and seeks to identify how sensitive the performance of different investments are to different types of market-wide shocks, such as inflation, economic growth or interest rate changes.

My word is my bond In the City markets, the terms of a verbal agreement to do a deal are a legally binding contract.

Nominee name When purchasing financial securities, many buyers go through an intermediary, and the shares are registered in a nominee name. The users of nominee names are expected to file the appropriate disclosure forms, at which point the ultimate owner of the shares becomes apparent. The use of nominee names simplifies the process of transfers.

Nominee name management business An intermediary that acts as a custodian or agent for the buyer of shares and financial instruments and provides nominee name account management services.

Not for profit corporation A new type of structure put forward for publically funded bodies. See *www.custodianholder.com*.

Off balance sheet Usually refers to a liability which does not show up in the balance sheet of a set of accounts.

Options [traded] Similar to futures, but the buyer has the *right* and not the obligation to complete the deal. The investor or speculator pays an upfront sum to do a financial transaction at a specific future date and price. If the market or price has moved against them they can walk away from the transaction and their loss is limited to the initial sum paid. Traded options can be traded in the market right up to their expiry, and their prices to a large extent reflect the volatility of the underlying index / interest rate / exchange rate, etc.

Outsourcing The subcontracting of services or a process to a third party provider such that the day to day provision of the service becomes the responsibility of the third party.

Over the counter market Or OTC is a market which is not exchange traded, which means that the trading is outside the jurisdiction and rules of an exchange. Often a market made by a bank in one of their instruments, and where this is the case the investor / speculator relies on the reputation and financial robustness of the bank.

P45 The form that an employer passes a former employee when they are made redundant or sacked.

PFI Private finance initiative. Used to fund large public sector building projects. The contractors pay for the construction costs and then rent the finished project back to the public sector. Historically seen as a way of keeping the expenditure off the Government's balance sheet. PFI liabilities are now estimated to exceed £100 billion. See *PPP*.

Portfolio A collection of investments held by an investor / speculator.

Position The extent to which a speculator has invested and represents the extent of their financial obligation.

Position building The building up of a investment or speculative holding in a company or financial instrument over time through a series of purchases.

PPP Public-private partnerships. A collaboration between a public body and private company, in which the private body brings to the partnership management skills and financial acumen, and are paid for providing their services. See *PFI*.

Public Sector Net Cash Requirement [PSNCR] The size of the annual shortfall between Government revenues and expenditures – it is the fiscal deficit expressed in cash terms. The Government has three main ways of financing the PSNCR – selling of new gilts issues, issuing more notes and coins, and borrowing overseas. Of these, new gilts issues usually form the significant part of the funding of the PSNCR. Gilt prices are influenced by supply and demand. Excessive new gilts issues [or expectations thereof] push gilts prices down and gilts yields up.

Put In the context of a derivative instrument – with an option contract it is the right and for a futures contract it is an obligation to sell an underlying security – index / commodity / asset at a predetermined price on a specific future date. A speculator can make a profit if prices fall further than expected, as they can buy at a lower price in the market and sell on at the higher price by exercising their put contract.

REIT A Real Estate Investment Trust is a company that owns and operates income producing property – usually a portfolio of commercial property investments. In the UK REITs are quoted on a stock exchange which gives the investor liquidity – unlike investing in direct property. The investor in a the shares of a REIT receives dividends instead of rental income and the share price moves with due regard to the changes in value of the underlying value of the REIT's property assets and future performance expectations. REITs have a favourable tax position unlike the traditional listed property investment company which does not. The quality of both the property portfolio and the REIT's management team are seen as important ingredients.

Securities Financial instruments which may be shares in a company or debt obligations.

Sell-side promote The marketing of shares in a company by a stockbroker or a financial adviser to the company.

Sentiment The attitude of investors and speculators towards the market. It is said "Bullish views are driven by greed and bearish views by fear".

Settlement The whole process of closing a contract for buy or sell transactions, when in the financial markets money changes hands.

Short [to] To sell something in the expectation of buying it back at a lower price and thus making a profit. A common activity for speculators in a falling market. The opposite of to go long.

Short interest rates A rate of interest that is set today and usually refers to 3 month interest rates as found in the London interbank market – the market where banks lend to each other. This is also known as 3 month LIBOR – London Interbank Offer Rate.

Slush fund A colloquial term which describes a pool of money used for corrupt purposes.

Soft facilities management Or soft FM. The provision of services relating to the maintenance of a building such as cleaning, security, catering, reception, telephonists and the like. In contrast, hard FM is the provision of services that relate to the repairs and maintenance of a building's fabric, mechanical and electrical services, landscaping, energy procurement, IT and communications.

Speculator A person who bets against market expectations with the purpose of making a profit. Speculators are said to provide the market with extra liquidity and help smooth price movements.

Stake building The buying of shares in a listed company whereby the purchaser is intent on purchasing a sizeable number of shares.

TA Territorial Army – Britain's voluntary reserve land forces, which support the Regular Army.

Tight [price] Characteristics of an actively traded market where the buying (bid) and selling (ask) prices are close together (narrow).

Trade weighted exchange rate This is the measure of how a currency's exchange rate is moving in relation to all its trading partners rather than to any single one of them. The weighting reflects the volume of trade being done with each trading partner.

Unhedged Where a speculator is exposed to price fluctuations; i.e. they are unguarded against a loss. This loss in the futures market can be many times the initial outlay. This exposure may be further exaggerated if the speculator has financed their position with borrowed money. See *Hedged*.

Unfunded pension liabilities Public sector pension schemes are usually defined benefit pension schemes, which provide pensions linked to employees' final salaries, and are guaranteed by the employer. Whilst private pension schemes have strict solvency criteria to ensure that the appropriate pension payments can be met, public sector defined benefit pension schemes have less rigorous requirements. The shortfall between the total of the future expected pension payments less the assets held to meet these liabilities is the unfunded element – the public sector's unfunded pension liabilities are currently estimated by leading actuaries at over £1,000 billion. This is an off balance sheet Government liability.

Furthermore, state pensions are funded on a pay as you go basis using National Insurance (NI) contributions – so the NI contributions of those in work are used to pay the state pensions of those who are retired. As the percentage of people of working age declines relative to those who are retired, this shortfall will also grow significantly. See *Unit linked pensions.*

Unit linked pension A pension fund in which the benefits depend on the performance of the units in the investment fund into which the pension contributions have been put. Usually synonymous with defined contribution pension funds where contributions are paid into the fund and on retirement the size of the pension is determined by the performance of the fund and the amount of contributions made. Unlike defined benefit pension schemes, where the pension payouts – representing a percentage of the employee's final salary – are guaranteed by the employer, unit linked / defined contribution pensions are not guaranteed and are linked to the performance of the investment markets rather than final salary and the element of guarantee is minimal.

Un-provided for Where the cost of (or liability for) an item is not included in a set of accounts; it may also be said to be off-balance sheet.

Venture capital fund An investment fund which normally comprises the money of wealthy private investors. The fund invests in private companies with the aim being to enable the company to grow by using the venture capital moneys. The normal exit route is usually via an IPO of the private company. See *IPO.*

USB memory stick Or universal serial bus flash drive. A data storage device that uses the USB port of a computer. It has replaced the use of floppy disks. These USB drives are easy to use, removable and rewritable. Their small size, light weight and shape gives them their name.

Value at risk model Or VaR. A model which seeks to identify the exposure a financial institution or bank faces in terms of risk exposure to volatile movements in market prices.

Yield In the context of gilts, the yield represents the annual income return that the investor will receive. The total return (income plus capital gains / losses) also known as the gross redemption yield, is the return that would be received by holding the gilt to its redemption date.

Zero sum game Futures and options markets have a buyer on one side of a transaction and a seller on the other. One makes a profit the other a loss, such that when added together the total is zero.

Forthcoming Publications from
Galleons Green

'CHANGING THE PERCEIVED VIEW' SERIES

In a changing world, inertia can result in the perceived view becoming out of date. This new series from Galleons Green is written by experts who put forward alternative solutions to everyday issues.

In many areas, whether it be: business, health, science, art, or the environment, there are perceptions as to what the correct approaches or accepted methodologies are. This series is designed to widen the debate and to push forward the boundaries.

Each book has its own web site, to which readers comments can be submitted. These comments will be forwarded to the author, thereby providing the wherewithal for each book to evolve over time.

New Titles:
- Indexhold
- Annuities and Government REITs
- Custodianholders & Not-for-Profit Corporations

A new publication in the "Changing the Percieved View" Series

INDEXHOLD

Sustainable excellence: homes for key workers in top locations
ISBN-13: 978-1-906960-01-8

High land prices, a shortage of affordable housing, higher environmental standards, cyclical market conditions and a widening gap
between the haves and have-nots are putting relentless pressure on
the very people society needs: the key workers without whom public
services and the quality of life for the many would be greatly diminished.

This book puts forward a new land tenure – Indexhold – which builds
on the existing landlord and tenant framework to provide a new ownership structure for key workers seeking homes close to their place of
work in high cost areas, and for rural communities under threat from
second homeowners. The book also considers the role indexhold can
play in helping those home owners caught up in the sub-prime crisis.

For further details:

www.indexhold.com

A new publication in the "Changing the Percieved View" Series

ANNUITIES & GOVERNMENT REITs
Funding pensions and Government deficits
ISBN-13: 978-1-906960-02-5

Public sector funding deficits and pressures on private pensions have become a feature following the Government rescue of the banking sector.

This book considers the role Government REITs – Real Estate Investment Trusts – and mortgage REITS could can play in reducing: the public sector deficit, money supply and defined benefit pension shortfalls.

For further details:

www.annuityreits.com

A new publication in the "Changing the Percieved View" Series

CUSTODIANHOLDERS & NOT-FOR-PROFIT CORPORATIONS
Public sector business structure for the 21st century
ISBN-13: 978-1-1906960-03-2

How can public services be made more efficient, transparent and accountable to the service users?

This book sets out a new management structure: the Not-for-Profit Corporation, whose management is accountable to custodianholders.

For further details:

www.custodianholder.com